THE SCION CONSPIRACY

CRUCIBLE OF LEGACY, BOOK I

MIKE CAHOON

STAGHEART PRESS, LLC

To my brother Thomas, my first reader, who deserves more credit than I can give for his unwavering support.
To my Dad, the greatest storyteller I know, who first instilled a love of reading in me.
To my Mom, who taught me to fight for what I want and never settle.
To my daughters, who I love with all my heart and hope I always make proud.
And finally, to my wife Beth, who's constant love and support has made me the man I am today.
I could never have done this without all of you.

CONTENTS

PROLOGUE

A VOICE IN THE NIGHT

The night was still and thick with summer heat. Darkness hung heavy in the forest with only a sliver of a moon to shed its pale light. Shadows clung to the trees and even the nighttime sounds of bugs and small creatures seemed muffled. It was like a heavy, unseen blanket had been laid over the woodland. Sam was nervous. He had lived in these woods his entire life; played in the creeks and groves as a boy, stalked game trails and helped fell trees with his father once he was old enough. Yet, even still, this night made him uneasy. His pace was painstakingly slow, every step careful as he made his way down an embankment, trying to avoid making the slightest sound. Every crunch of leaves or broken twig under his foot seemed to echo in the stillness like the deafening crash of a falling branch.

Sam held his bow with an arrow nocked at the ready. His eyes darted back and forth, scanning for hidden figures in the shadows. Normally, he would have been thankful for even the smallest of moons, but this sliver of moonlight only seemed to give the landscape a ghostly quality, deepening the shadows that surrounded him and making them play oddly amongst the trees and underbrush. Every shift in the light birthed cloaked figures stalking through the dark, every whisper of wind was like the footsteps of a cutthroat sneaking up behind him. He wished he was back home before his smoldering fireplace, listening to it crackle and hiss as he sipped a summer ale in his high backed chair.

But somehow he had found himself compelled to enter the woods. He had tried to ignore it for days now, the call that only he could hear. It had come on slowly at first. The tickle on the back of his neck when there was no breeze in the air. A nagging in his mind like he had forgotten some indistinct task. Then, over time, it slowly took shape and became a whisper in a voice that seemed so familiar yet entirely foreign at the same time. It sounded like someone calling to him from so faraway he could not make out the words, only the tone; beckoning, full of a desperate yearning. The sound plagued him day and night, left him distracted and staring into the distance, straining to make out the words. Then one night, the sound became a voice, so soft he barely heard it. A woman's call, all kindness and temptation. It said only one phrase; *come to me.*

Somehow, he knew where it wanted him to go; into the woods. It pulled at him, and him alone, to leave the lights of his village and wander into the darkness. Something in that voice promised much. He heard a temptation, felt the desire of a woman who wanted him, who needed him to find her. But Sam was no fool. He had not yet reached his fifteenth year, but he knew voices in the night were strange and dangerous. He had grown up hearing all the stories of the dangerous creatures that inhabited the woods; witches and ghouls who made meals of men, fairies who stole lost children away, and spirits that lured wandering travelers into the marshes where they met their doom. After arguing with himself for a long while, he told his father and mother about the voice. They, of course, quickly took him to the local temple. The priest had told Sam it was an evil spirit, that it wanted him to abandon his family and his town. He had given him a symbol and told him to pray to the gods to relieve himself of this terrible curse.

Sam had tried. He really had. He had prayed every day, many times, with the fervor of a man on his deathbed. He grasped the symbol of the Mother until his palms were red and had a deep imprint of the matronly figure in each one. But the voice only came more often, becoming stronger and more insistent. He pretended it went away, seeing the worry in his own mother's eyes and hearing the whispers around town as people stole glances at him when they thought he was not looking.

But day after day he caught himself staring across the pastures to the wood line. At times he could almost see a woman standing there, beautiful, waiting for him. The voice wormed its way into every thought, pulled at his mind like a cat unraveling a ball of yarn, until he could no longer shut it out. It spoke to him lovingly, with the same quiet phrase over and over; *come to me.* He heard it even in his dreams, waking with a start, covered in cold sweat, only for that voice to still be echoing in his mind.

So it was that Sam found himself standing at the window of his bedroom in the middle of the night, staring across the dimly lit farms and fields beyond. The trees sat motionless on the summer night, stalwart sentinels guarding the secret siren that called to him even now. He cursed his weakness, tried in vain to have yet another talk with himself. To tell himself it was foolishness. He knew this was a trap, a honeypot meant to lure him in, only for some awful creature to devour him in the darkness. But even still, he found that his boots were on, then his cloak, then he was standing on the porch of his childhood home, the door still open behind him. In a moment of clarity he reached inside and grasped for his bow and quiver from where it hung from a peg by the door. If he was to die tonight, he reasoned, at least he would put up a fight. As he strode off across the fields, he never looked back.

N ow, in the dark, wooded landscape, he could still hear the voice. It seemed to grow louder now that he had entered its domain. *Come to me.* Over and over, echoing in his mind, dominating his thoughts. It pushed out his fear, his foreboding. It was like a white hot iron laid across his mind. It could not be ignored, it could not be looked away from. As he made his way, he became more bold. He stopped being careful with his stride, stopped watching for hidden enemies and ambushes laying in wait.

He hurried along, brushing aside tree limbs and bushes, crunching sticks and leaves underfoot. He splashed through a creek without a second thought and trotted along in his boots, making squelching noises with every step. His bow hung loosely from his hand, the arrow dropped without notice somewhere along the way. He was practically running now. He crashed through the underbrush, noise filling the night. He breathed heavily, anticipation building to a crescendo in his chest. He was almost there, he knew it was close. He knew *she* was close.

Suddenly there were lights ahead of him. An orange glow in the darkness. This was it. He knew it was what he had been looking for. He rushed towards it, unbothered by the branches that tugged on his clothes and tore little gashes in his exposed flesh. He was here, finally, after all this time. The nagging notion of dread that had been his constant companion and had begged him to turn back was deathly silent now. The enchanting voice was practically a scream as he burst through a bush and into the light.

He blinked. The voice had stopped so suddenly he was taken aback. Silence, except for the crackle and spitting of a campfire, filled his head for the first time in weeks. He was so unused to having his mind to himself, the quiet seemed more deafening than the voice had been. He stood in a clearing where a small band had made its modest campsite. There were several tents and three large wagons around a roaring campfire. The wagons were covered with canvas, nondescript, and their horses were tied up at the edge of the clearing, bridles and tack removed for the night. It was a caravan of some sort. Around the fire were several figures who appeared to be cooking. A spit was being turned by a large man with very dark skin crouching down beside it. On the opposite side sat two other figures, a woman with short red hair and patterned tattoos down her exposed arms and a man with one eye.

All three had turned to look when he had come crashing into their campsite. They did not say anything, but the woman stood up. Sam could see she was dressed in reinforced leathers, the kind of light armor that watchmen wore, rather than the heavy armor of the Legionnaires. She had a short, curved sword hanging from her belt and she moved with a grace that even Sam noticed immediately. It was inherently unsettling, like there was something predatory about it.

She stalked towards Sam and he took a step back. He silently cursed himself for being a weak minded fool when he realized he had dropped his bow in his mad rush to get here. She smiled. It was unpleasant, the curve of her lips seeming to mock him before she even spoke a single word.

"Are you lost, little boy?" She looked him up and down, even in the dim light he could see the way her eyes shone with a deep green hue.

"I-I was just...looking for someone..." He stammered. He was unsure of himself, trying desperately to get his bearings. He glanced towards the fire and saw the other two men were grinning and watching intently.

"Looking for someone?" She made a confused face, "Out here? In the dark?"

She was playing with him. He felt a bit of anger creep past the fear and uncertainty. He steadied himself. He let his hand drift around to the back of his belt where he always kept his hunting knife sheathed and tethered. It was still there, thank the gods. He grasped it. Feeling the worn leather gave him back some of his lost nerve. He stood a little straighter.

"Yes...I must've gotten turned around. I'll leave you all to it then." He started to back up, but never let his eyes off the woman.

She smiled, showing her teeth for the first time. They were pearly white and gleamed even in the dim light. "Oh no...no, no, no. You mustn't go so soon. We were just sitting down to eat."

She shifted her weight. Her hand rested on the hilt of her sword. Sam started to sweat. He knew these people were dangerous. Everything in him screamed at him to turn tail and run. But he knew deep down that these were the sort of people that would have no problem catching him, even in the dead of night. His only advantage was the knife he hoped they had not noticed him reach for, "No, thank you...I need to be going now."

Suddenly, the voice returned. Louder than it had been before. It hit him like a flood breaking through a dam. His knees nearly buckled, his vision blurring as he held his ears in desperation. But the sound was inside his head. *COME TO ME.* Over and over, he felt it tearing at his mind. It was still feminine, but now a roar rather than a beckoning whisper. A cold, unflinching command. Through his pain, he could see that the red haired woman seemed amused. She watched with curiosity, still grinning, "Something bothering you?"

He tried again to shake his head, but the voice persisted. He looked around, trying desperately to find the source. He needed to find it, felt as though he would die if he could not. Just as he thought his head would burst, a voice cut through the noise, "Go? But you're right where you need to be."

A new figure appeared from out of one of the carriages. It was a man with blonde hair and a slight build, with sharp features that cut harsh angles across his face. He was short, for a man, and draped himself in a fine cloak of rich red velvet. The strangest thing about his appearance, something Sam noticed almost immediately, was how *clean* he looked. Not a smear on his clothes or mark on his skin. No hair out of place, not a stitch of clothing unkempt. Like a nobleman or a scholar, completely out of place here in the deep woods. As he stepped out of the cart and into the dirt with the rest of the group, he seemed to glide in his soft looking shoes towards them. It took only the briefest of moments before Sam recognized him.

"You...were in the village..." he mumbled, still holding his head in his hands, "You're that magician...came through with the carnival...you read my fortune..."

Sam noticed the cloaked man held something which swung loosely from his left hand. It was hard to tell what it was at first. But once the man got closer, it looked, for all the world, like a small birdcage made of some kind of metal. Only, what it held was no bird. It seemed to be a solid ball of light. It floated in the cage, a sphere of pale gray-green suspended in the air. Once he saw it, he knew. The sound was coming *from* the light. He stared at it, unable to tear his eyes away from the soft glow. It called to him. He started to walk towards the light, even as the man was walking towards him. He never reached it.

The woman intercepted him. She dropped to one knee and swept his leg out from under him while he was mid stride. He slammed hard onto his back. Staring up into the starry sky he was disoriented for a moment, the voice still echoing in his head. As suddenly as it started, the voice was gone. He looked over and saw the man and the woman stood beside each other a few feet from him. The man had draped the cage with a cloth, the light entirely hidden under it. He shook his head, the silence again feeling so unusual. He groaned as he hauled himself into a seated position, staring at the two figures.

"What is that?" He muttered, staring at the cage.

The man in the cloak gave a small shrug, "That's not for you to worry about Sam. You have far bigger concerns now."

"You know my name?"

The man continued as if he hadn't heard Sam's question, "I brought you here, my boy, because you are special."

Sam was still trying to orient himself. His senses were reeling as if he had just torn free from the smothering depths of a relentless tide. The world crashed into focus, jarring, like he was a dreamer thrust awake after being lost in the depths of slumber.

He tried to make sense of it all, "What do you mean? Who are you?"

"All in due time." He turned, making a slight motion with one hand, "Kacey, if you please. We do have a schedule to keep."

The woman, Kacey, Sam had a moment to register, nodded and strode towards him. He had a second to react and remembered the knife. He reached back, grasped the handle and swung out in a wide arc.

The woman was fast. So fast Sam barely knew what happened. She reacted in a moment, stepping back while catching his arm mid swing. She turned his arm backwards, twisting so hard Sam yelped and dropped the knife. She kicked it and it went skittering away, disappearing in the dark. The woman grinned, her unsettling smile full of blazing white teeth, "You've got a lot of fight in ya, kid."

While still holding his arm, she hit him across the face with a gloved hand. Sam felt a burst of pain across his face and nearly passed out. He fell over into the dirt and tasted blood, thinking she may have broken his jaw with that one strike. He had been in scraps before, other kids in the village. But this was different, these people were trained, maybe even professionals. He tried to crawl away but he felt large, strong hands, which must have belonged to the two men he had seen before, grab his ankles.

They dragged him through the dirt, past the campfire. He tried to struggle, but he was barely holding onto consciousness at that point. He kicked his legs as hard as he could, trying to wriggle free. But a swift kick in the side sent a shock of pain through his entire body. He whimpered, tears of pain and fear forming in his eyes. But they did not let him go.

He was lifted roughly to his feet behind one of the carts. Inside, it was nearly pitch black, an open mouth which threatened to swallow him whole. He could vaguely make out a few box shapes near the rear of the wagon. The one-eyed man moved into his field of view and reached into the darkness. There was a metal clink and a door swung open. Sam was shoved forward, tripping over his own feet, pain still radiating across his entire body. As he crashed into the back of the cart it took a moment before his eyes adjusted and he saw what awaited him.

It was a cage. He was being forced into a cage. Panic swelled in his chest and overrode the pain and exhaustion. He swung wildly, desperate to get away. All he hit was empty air before another vicious strike landed, bludgeoning him low in the gut. It forced the air out of his lungs and he felt sick. Another blow to the stomach came right behind the first and this time he did empty his guts. The taste of bile mixed with blood filled his mouth as tears streamed from his eyes. Spots filled his vision. He was starting to black out from the pain.

Rough hands grabbed him on either side and threw him forward. He tumbled into the cage. Landing in a heap on the cage floor, gasping, trying and failing to catch his breath, Sam scrambled back towards the door. But it slammed shut in his face and he heard the metallic *clank* of a lock being bolted. He knew his one chance was lost. He collapsed on the floor and tried to rub the tears from his face, spitting blood and bile from his mouth. His hands were dirty from where he had landed in the dirt so he had to use his shirt, leaving stains all down the front. His head pounded. He hurt all over, waves of pain rolling over him and threatening to pull him under into the waiting embrace of darkness.

He fought it, tried to look around, get some idea of how bad his situation was. It was darker inside the cart than outside. He could barely see the crisscrossed metal bars of his cage. It was too small to stand up in, in fact it was barely large enough for him to sit up straight. This cage was designed to hold some sort of animal, not humans. He saw that he was surrounded by other cages to either side and behind. The ones beside him were empty, but after his eyes adjusted he was able to see that the one behind held a small bundle of cloth, huddled in the far corner. From within, two luminous eyes stared at him.

"Hello?" He whispered. His voice scratched in his throat, it hurt terribly to talk.

The shape stirred. Part of the cloth unfurled and a hooded head popped up. It was a girl. She was younger than him, maybe in her tenth or eleventh year. She had bright blue eyes and a mop of curls the color of good honey. She looked at him and he could see she had been crying. Her eyes were puffy and red and she had dirt streaking down both cheeks. She was frightened by his sudden appearance, eyes wide as she stared at him.

"Who...who are you?" She whispered.

"I'm Sam, who are you?"

"I'm...Evie."

"Evie, do you know who these people are? Or what they want?" He tried to keep his voice low but friendly. He did not want to scare her more than she obviously already was.

She shook her head, curls bouncing back and forth, "No! I've been here since last night and they haven't told me anything! I just want to go home!"

"Where are you from, Evie?"

"I'm from a village called Goodwynn. Do you know it?"

Sam blinked. That could not be right. Goodwynn was over three days travel East of his village, at least. Even if this caravan had been moving at top speed, it could not have been there last night. Unless, he had traveled further than he thought. But how? He had only been walking for...how long? He could not recall. The realization put a chill down his spine. How far had the voice made him wander?

Sam nodded slowly. He looked around at the other cages. He saw there were two beside Evie's cage, and he thought he could make out more behind her row. "Are there others? In here with us?"

Evie nodded back. She motioned behind her, Sam strained his eyes and thought he could see another form slouched in the cage beyond hers. She whispered, "That's Tomin, he told me yesterday. He's from Forkstown."

Another mystery. Forkstown was nearly two days South of Goodwynn. He shook his head. These kids must be confused about how long they had been captive. There was no way this caravan was moving so quickly. He tried to put it out of his head and press on.

"Have you heard anything about where we're going, what their plans are?"

She shook her head again. Tears started to well up in her big blue eyes, "They were talking about the coast...something about meeting up with a ship...but that was all I heard before the fancy man started singing."

"Singing...?" Sam was about to ask when he heard a voice. It was unmistakable. The man in the red cloak was singing. His voice was rhythmic and smooth and it sounded comforting. Sam thought he could have been one of the minstrels that came through town during the big festivals. It was hard to tell, but he thought he could hear the ringing of a small bell too. The song was simple, a lullaby, meant for children;

Come children, gather and listen close,
Try and remember how the rhyme goes,

See as the night's growing dark,
And feel the hearth getting cold,
Do not fear that shameful mark,
Come, leave behind lessons told,

Deep in the wood, the night calls,
Those sweetest sounds of summer,
Far beyond the tallest town walls,
Stir now from your restless slumber,

Walk down the winding wooded path,
Dancing in the pale moonlight,
Abandon your fear, leave your wrath,

Far from judgment, far out of sight,

The song rings true, the voice is clear,
Embrace children of the forest,
See there is no need for your fear,
Let your voices join the chorus.

Sam listened to it for a moment before turning to look back at Evie. She was passed out, head cradled in her arms. Suddenly Sam felt very tired. His mind felt like it had filled with fog and he could barely bring himself to focus on anything for more than a moment. The song was pushing everything else from his thoughts. He tried to shake clarity into his head but if anything, it only made him more tired. He grabbed the bars of his cage, strained to keep his eyes open. But it was in vain, and the tendrils of sleep worked their way into his mind and pulled him down into the warm embrace of sleep. He collapsed onto the floor of the wagon and the hard wood on his cheek was the last thing he felt before he was lost to the rhythmic sound of the man in red's voice.

ACT I

A Crime, A Criminal & A Question

STAGHEART PRESS, LLC

CHAPTER ONE

A WARRIOR & A LORD

A wild western wind blew through the peaks of the Horn as the morning sun was just cresting the horizon. Golden light burst through the darkness, driving back the mist which still clung defiantly to the cliffs and trees. The cold which had settled in overnight began to give way to a gentle warmth as the sun spread across the mountain range and spilled into the cracks and chasms of its peaks and canyons. Forest sounds filled the air as calling birds sang and small animals began scurrying through the underbrush.

High on a cliff above the woods, a group of climbers could be seen making their way upwards towards the crest of a high ridge. Six figures dressed in light armor of oiled leathers and metal studs, weighed down with various weapons and gear, connected with climbing ropes and rigging, scaled the cliff side at a slow, deliberate pace. The sounds of their grunts and muttered curses echoed over the cliffs, piercing the otherwise picturesque sunrise. They wore looks of grim determination on their red and worn faces, their clothes soaked in sweat and dirt as they pulled themselves upwards.

In the lead was a solidly built man with a short beard and close cropped, dark hair. He took a pause after nailing an iron spike into the mountainside and tying his rope to it. After wiping the sweat from his brow, he tugged on the rope a few times to test it, then leaned back and looked up toward the crest, judging the distance as he shaded his eyes against the rising sun. He turned to look over his shoulder at the men below him and cracked a brash grin.

"Come on, boys, almost to the top!" He pointed up, "Can't give up now!"

A seasoned man with hair and beard the color of untempered iron shouted back at him, "Shut your mouth, Cas, before I come up there and shut it for you!"

Prince Cassius Roth gave him a wide smile, then turned back towards the cliff side and grasped the rocks. He drove upward with his legs and reached for the next handhold, his broad shoulders straining against the leather and metal of his armor. The early morning light was finally giving him a better view of the mountainside and he quickened his climbing pace as he scrambled up the craggy cliffs, pushing faster now that he could see the summit was within his grasp. They reached the top within the hour, sore and filthy as they all collapsed in panting heaps around the ridge. The day had fully crested the horizon by the time they made their summit and the sun beat down as they passed a water skin around. The Prince was the only one who remained standing. He took a small sip before handing the skin off to another soldier, then began moving to examine their new surroundings.

The ridge was rocky but flat enough for some plant life, mostly scraggly trees and bushes. He could see where the mountain continued, a short distance away, the ridge sharply returning to a steep incline. Slowly, he stalked the ridge, eyes scanning the rocks and the sharp cuts of the mountainside. He was out of sight of the others, dozens of strides away, when he found what he was hunting. The dark mouth of a cave, stark against the brightly lit red stone and dirt, yawned in the cliff side. He crouched down behind a low thorny bush, and his hand rose to the hilt of the falchion strapped across his back, shaking it loose in the scabbard. Again, the wind blew through the mountain range, pulling at his hair and tugging on his sweat stained clothes beneath the tight buckles of his armor. With a slight cock of his head, he changed weight from his lead foot to the back foot, widening his stance.

Reaching down, he found a stone on the ground. After bouncing it in his hand a few times, he threw it at the cave mouth. The stone ricocheted off the cave wall and floor, echoing down the cavernous hole. Then there was a brief, pregnant silence. Suddenly, the sound of shuffling could be heard, softly at first, then louder. It was accompanied by heavy grunting and snorting and a sort of snarling growl that became louder and louder. Two creatures burst out onto the sun soaked ridge, clambering out of the cave in a rush to investigate the noise.

They were covered in dark, matted hair and taller than a man even when hunched and walking on their knuckles. The creatures had smashed, bear-like faces and sharp teeth which jutted out from their jaws at harsh angles. Even from ten paces he could smell the rank odor, wet fur and foul breath that made him swallow hard against the rising bile in his gut. They sniffed the air and turned over rocks, snarling and scratching at the dirt.

The Prince watched them intently, his hand still firm on the hilt of his sword. The closest creature turned towards the bush he was hiding behind and let out a long, low growl. Cassius grinned and stood from his hiding place as he drew his sword. The blade was single edged and sharpened fine as a razor, the flare clipped tip glinting in the morning light. He held it before him with both hands and stared at the creatures, each stalking out in opposite directions, attempting to flank him. He looked from one to the other, biding his time, waiting for his moment.

He glanced toward the creature on his right, then the other struck from his left. He heard its claws scrape the rocky ground as it launched itself towards him. He bellowed a loud, clear battle cry. His voice thundered off the mountains as he whirled and dropped to one knee in a single, fluid motion, bringing the blade up and pointing straight toward the beast. The impact rocked his whole body. The hairy creature screeched in pain. It had rammed itself into the sword, not expecting the Prince's quick reaction. The sword was impaled on the monstrous creature's shoulder nearly halfway up the blade. Cassius felt a spurt of warm blood soak his hands and smelled the stench of rotting meat on its breath. He barely had a moment to react before the other creature was upon him.

Cassius yanked at his sword, trying to rip it from the body of the beast to meet his second assailant. The impaled beast still thrashed and snarled at him, snapping and trying to swipe at him with its long, jagged claws. The blade caught on the creature's leathery hide.

"*Shit luck.*" The nobleman cursed silently under his breath before the second beast was on him. He shoved hard on the blade to push the first beast away and turned, raising his arms to defend his face, just as the second brought its claws down on him. He was rocked by the massive beast's bulk hitting him and he had to brace against it with all his strength. It grasped his arms with its clawed hands, finding purchase in his flesh. He snarled back at it, face only inches from its snapping jaws, the pain immense as blood oozed from under his armored bracers. He groaned with the effort it took to not let the thing drive him to the ground. Then, in one sudden motion, he pulled both his arms back. The creature had not expected it and fell forward as he dodged out of the way. Yanking a knife from his belt, Cassius drove it into the creature's flank.

It screamed in pain and took a wild sideways swing at him. Cassius let go of the knife, leaving it stuck in its hide, and fell backwards to avoid the blow. He caught sight of the first beast howling and coughing up thick, dark blood as it tried to rend the sword from its shoulder, clumsy, clawed hands unable to grasp the bloodied hilt. Fumbling in the dirt, he scrambled to his feet and rushed towards it. But then he felt something grasp his ankle and his leg was ripped out from under him mid stride. His face smashed into the dirt, and he gagged on the soil and rock as he tried to roll to face the creature. The second beast, blood soaking its fur around the knife still embedded in its side, stood over him with its jagged teeth bared as it let out a guttural growl. As it fell upon him, its maw spread wide revealing rows of jagged teeth, Cassius desperately thrust his left arm into the creature's mouth, grabbed its tongue and yanked.

The creature snorted and yelped in pain, snapping its mouth shut around his arm. He screamed and gritted his teeth. His bracer was only able to prevent some of the fangs from carving into his arm. Blood bloomed from under his clothes, painting his shirt and shoulder with red streaks. He raised his other hand and smashed it into the creature's nose, trying to get it to release its grip. Just then, another sound came from behind him and he chanced a glance to see the first creature, blood pouring from the wound in its shoulder where it had finally managed to pull the sword free, stomping towards them. Panic crept over Cassius and he began pummeling the second creature's nose, driving his fist into it over and over. It clamped down even harder, causing him to cry out in pain. The first beast was almost upon him, teeth bared as drool ran off its open mouth, its eyes fixed on the Prince's unguarded face.

A cry echoed across the mountains and the sound of men shouting came shortly behind it. Cassius saw something fly just over the creature he was grappling, before the beast behind him let out a howl of pain. He was unable to see what happened while under the hairy beast, but the creature suddenly jolted upright, releasing his arm and snarling in pain. Cassius hastily skittered to the side and saw that two of his soldiers, the gruff older veteran and a tall man with long black hair, were behind it with weapons out. The older man's sword had fresh blood dripping from where he had slashed across the creature's hindquarters. It whirled on him, making a wild slash with its claw, but the tall man brought his weapon, a curved ax he wielded with both hands, up in a rising arc. He timed the strike perfectly. The creature's arm was sliced open as a streak of blood burst through the air and painted the rocks and dirt crimson.

The creature bellowed, raising its head to the sky. But the noise was cut short as a bolt found purchase in its exposed throat. It gurgled, clawing at the arrow helplessly, before another bolt hit it from the opposite direction, this one burying itself into its upper chest. Cassius saw the last two members of his band were positioned strategically, flanking to either side about fifteen paces back from the fray. They both held crossbows and were already preparing their next shots. The creature thrashed violently but fell to its knees, blood pouring from all its wounds. The taller man strode forward and ended it's suffering with one final swing of his ax, severing its head from its shoulders.

Cassius whirled to face the last creature but saw it had already collapsed, breathing heavily with several bolts sticking out of its hide. The older man was across the battlefield in the space of a moment and likewise bisected the creature's head from its body. The Prince let his shoulders sag and breathed out a heavy sigh. The older man paused to wipe his blade down before bending to pick up Cassius' sword, still covered in the monster's ichor. The other men all made their way over, standing over the dead beasts.

"Your sword, Prince Roth." The older man said with an air of amusement, "Thought you'd have learned to hold onto this by now."

Cassius grinned as he took it. He wiped it down as he said, "I guess I'm just not the student you thought I was, Tanner. I might need some remedial work."

Tanner, the older man, snorted a laugh as he stroked his beard thoughtfully, "Perhaps. At the very least you'd think you'd know better than to try and take on the wylerbeasts alone."

"It wasn't intentional," Cassius made an attempt at lying as he put his sword away and gestured at the cliff side, "the wind changed and they caught my scent."

"You'd think someone who's spent their life hunting in these mountains would've thought of that before they wandered off." The tall man interjected. He was inspecting the corpses of the creature he had beheaded.

Cassius shrugged. He held up his bloodied arm, "Guess I've got a good reminder for next time, right Sergius?"

One of the two bowmen walked forward and pulled a pouch from his belt. He motioned for Cassius to sit and removed the bracer from his arm. Underneath was a gory mess. The bowman began applying a poultice and carefully wrapped the wounded arm with clean bandages. The men spoke about the creatures, but while his arm was being tended to Cassius looked back towards the cave, pensive as the wind ruffled his hair and tugged at his clothes. The others were caught up in examining the creatures and chatting amongst themselves, excited to have caught their prey.

But something bothered the Prince. Halfway through having his arm wrapped, a sound caught his attention. It was a scraping, scratching sort of sound and it was coming from above them. He looked up in time to see that a third wylerbeast had crawled down the mountainside. It used its long clawed hands and feet to hang from the rocks as it crept towards them, barely making a sound as it got within striking distance. He saw it just as it let go and pounced at his men.

"Move!" Cassius yelled, diving forward and shoving the big man out of the way. Sergius was thrown down and the creature landed on Cassius, knocking him face down into the dirt with its bulk, swinging its claws downward as it pounced. The claws dug into the armor on his shoulders, cutting through leather and cloth and into flesh. Cassius cried out in pain as the creature roared above him.

Amidst the shouts of surprise, there was the sound of bowstrings and the squelch of flesh being pierced. He recognized Sergius' voice screaming a battle cry and heard a sickening thud. Then the smell of blood filled his nostrils as he felt warmth ooze across his back. The creature let out a roar as he felt its weight come off of him. Cassius rolled to his side and watched as his men hacked the beast to bits.

He pushed himself slowly to his feet, cradling his partially bandaged arm, "Sergius, are you alright?"

The tall man looked at him with wide eyes. He was holding his ax, blade covered in gore and dripping, "I'll live, but if not for you..."

"It's nothing, good sir." He grinned through a grimace of pain. The other men joined them, the third monstrous beast dealt with, nothing left of it but a mess on the stones. They were all smiles and laughs now, wiping the blood from their own faces and hands.

"That'll be all of the beasts, aye?" Sergius asked no one in particular.

Tanner nodded, "Wylerbeasts hold to small groups. It's unlikely another would be off alone this time of day."

"Then we can get back to the village. Inform them they're safe from the scourge, then back home before Cas' father has all of our heads."

Cassius nodded. His arm and shoulder throbbed like they were on fire. But he grinned around at his men, "Now the real challenge, boys; how will you get this injured dullard down this mountainside?"

T hat evening, the fire burned brightly in the twilight as they enjoyed their victory. The grateful townspeople had cheered them on their arrival and insisted they throw an impromptu feast in their honor. Holwood was an unremarkable mountain hamlet occupied almost exclusively by herders, woodsmen, and miners, but they were eager to celebrate finally being rid of the scourge that had beset them since the start of the season. The villagers set out long tables in their little town square and burdened them with innumerable platters of braised venison and curried goats and chickens and let the ale run freely as they tapped barrel after barrel. An old man with gray teeth and a missing ear plucked out jaunty tunes on his lyre and pretty village girls ensured none of the men ever wanted for a dance. The tavern keeper, who acted as a sort of governor for the tiny town that was far too small to warrant any true official of the Barony, gave a speech through glassy eyes as he struggled heroically to speak without slurring his words.

"-and we...give thanks to our noble Lords..." The tavern keeper managed to call out, swaying on his feet, "our defenders, our heroes! The men who take on the Covenant! Who put *the people* first, before themselves...before their lands, their wealth, even their own lives!"

Despite his shortcomings, by the end everyone was cheering and clapping as though they had heard a dignified orator in one of the great public amphitheaters of the Capitol. Cassius leaned back in one of the chairs, taking a moment to rest his aching feet after entertaining dances with every girl in town, most of the women and one or two of the wizened old crones. He caught sight of Tanner on the opposite side of the table, his old face creased with the weight of the frown that was chiseled into it. He glared out over the celebration with a palpable air of disapproval.

Cassius called out to him over the table, "Oh what's the problem, you old goat?"

Tanner's frowns seemed to deepen as he gave Cassius a grim look, "We should be heading back. We're already gone far too long. Your father is going to have your hide for what you did, boy."

The Prince rolled his eyes, "Tell me, wise master, what did I do?"

"You were sent to be your sister's escort..." Tanner spoke deliberately, as though lecturing a child.

"Which she didn't need..." Cassius interjected.

"...yet you abandoned your duty to come to a village far from our route..."

"...to help *our citizens* in their time of need... "

"...and endangered your life, yet again, without your fathers approval."

Cassius gave him a look, losing some of the mocking note in his voice and leaned in closer, "These people were suffering, Tanner. Our people, what would you have had me do, ignore them to play escort to my sister and her entourage?"

"You're not just a warrior, Cas, you're a Prince of the Horn, of the Federation." Tanner's voice was dripping with frustration, "You have your duties."

Cassius stared at the older man. He studied the weather worn face with its deep set lines and web of faded scars. When he spoke, his voice was unwavering, "I know what I am. I may hold the title of Prince, but I hold another. One earned in my own blood, not granted by it. I am Dux Valorus, Cassius Roth. I took the oath, joined the Covenant, the same as you, Dux Valorus, Farris Tanner. I know you to be an honorable man. Tell me, would you follow a man who broke his Oath? Would you follow a Lord who cared more for the trappings of nobility than the lives of his subjects?"

Tanner grunted roughly, but he seemed to have trouble meeting the Prince's eye. He shook his head, "Boy, you think you know all the stones that make up the mountain, but there's more to this life than playing the hero."

Cassius grinned and drained his cup of ale. He wiped his hand on the back of his sleeve, soaking some of his bandages in the process, then stood and gave the old warrior a friendly pat on the arm, "That's what my father keeps telling me. Worry not, friend, if he couldn't beat that lesson into me by now, you were dealt a losing hand from the start of it. Try and get some rest, maybe even have a little fun for once. We'll leave at first light."

I t took them three days to traverse the rocky and wooded mountains as they made their way from the village of
Holwood to the Capital of the Barony. Finally, as their horses
crested the final ridge line, they caught sight of the massive city
sprawling out before them in the shallow river valley between
the mountains. Rothmount was a massive web of unorganized
streets and boroughs, winding around the natural rises and falls
of the valley like a forest of stone buildings. Most of the city was
constructed of heavy timber and red stone from the surrounding mountains, the squat utilitarian construction shunning ar-
chitectural flourishes. Two rings of thick parapet walls encircled
the city in concentric, uneven circles. Low towers interspersed
both walls at regular intervals flying banners with the Roth
family's ancient crest, a blood red bear on a white field.

At the opposite end of the valley, the High Road, a cobblestone snake wide enough for five wagons to ride side by side,
could be seen twisting down through the mountains from the
East Gate. The waters of the River Rhine rolled down the opposite mountainside and meandered lazily through the valley,
cutting wide arcs across the sprawling city. The River worked
its way around buildings and small farms, turning countless
waterwheels and feeding into several dozen stone aqueducts
that spread across the city. It exited the city walls on the western
end and tumbled down the mountains, following the gentle
slope towards the coast. Standing resolutely in the center of
the city, slightly higher than the surrounding maze of farms
and buildings and surrounded by its own wall, sat the ancient
fortress known as The Hold, the Roth's ancestral home and the
seat of the Baron of the Horn.

As the party approached the walls, passing farms and herds
of grazing sheep and goats, they could see armored figures pa-
trolling the walls, the tips of their spears and bows bobbing
above the parapets as they walked their routes. Large metal
gates covered in wicked spikes stood open to the people as they
pushed carts laden down with sacks and baskets or hunched

under their packs, hustling their way in and out of the city. A patrol of soldiers were stationed at the entrance, watching with vague disinterest as people went about their business. As Cassius and his men made their way to the city's outer wall, the watchmen took notice and snapped to attention. One of the guards called out, "My Lord, you've returned! The Unbroken City welcomes your homecoming!"

Cassius made a motion to set the men at ease and the guards nodded but still stood a bit straighter than before. As Cassius and his men made their way into the city, they rode amongst the bustle of people selling their goods and doing their business on the wide streets. Vendors cried out for people to buy all manner of food and goods, meat and vegetables sizzled on outdoor grills and steam rose from great clay ovens where bread and sweet cakes baked. Stray dogs, cats, and small children wandered amongst the crowds, scavenging what they could when they thought no one was looking. Several pens of animals were scattered throughout the streets with seemingly every creature from horses and goats to yaks and even a few camels available for purchase.

Children played and chased each other, screaming and yelling as they narrowly avoided the horses and carts. An army of decorators had already taken to the streets for the upcoming festival. Banners, streamers and signs in bright colors and unlit lanterns hanging from poles and strings which presided over all the major thoroughfares. Most of the folk nodded to the group or waved as they made their way. Some bowed deeply when they noticed the bear sigil on the Prince's armor. Cassius waved to them, shook hands and returned their greetings with a broad, earnest smile. The city thrummed and he breathed it in deeply, grateful to be home once again.

It took the party almost an hour to reach the center of the great city. Once they approached the final wall, the shadow of the great fortress fell over them like a menacing giant that blotted out the sun. Everything about The Hold was built to break any opposing force that dared try their hand against it. Every pace of the exterior walls were reinforced and thick, with murderholes running their length and spiked and double door iron gates at the entrances. The grounds between the exterior wall and the fortress itself were gouged with grate covered trenches which could be made to fall away and drop opposing forces into awaiting pits or be flooded from underground wells.

The Hold itself was an octagonal behemoth with soaring walls and two tiers of towers, a shorter exterior set of eight and a taller interior set of four, each with a large, menacing ballista at the top of it. They were designed so that if the exterior towers were taken, the interior ones could rain arrows and fire upon them. There were heavy iron gates which could be dropped separating the interior towers from the exterior at regular intervals on the fortress walls. Even inside The Hold itself, hallways were long, straight, and book-ended with large metal doors which could be used to section off opposing forces. The center of the fortress was raised above the level of entries and had gallery walkways which looked down over the halls that lead inside. It was a fortress unlike any other, and it had stood stalwart at the gateway to the South against innumerable assaults for the past fifteen hundred years.

To Cassius Roth, this was home. He made his way confidently across the grounds and strode into the fortress proper, leaving his men to tend to the horses. After questioning the guards to be sure of his destination, he strode through the hallways with confidence, passing grand tapestries and works of art, statues of his regal looking ancestors and artifacts encased in glass and gold. Finding his way towards the center of the fortress, he approached the doors to the Great Hall. The Hall was the center of the immense building, with a massive metal and glass dome above an octagonal room which rose the entirety of three stories, the tallest point of the fortress aside from the towers. The center of the room bore host to a great wooden table with dozens of chairs set around it.

This was where lords and kings and the greatest minds of the age had sat to make some of the most important treaties, alliances, and unions in history. Massive floor to ceiling tapestries depicting the history of the Horn and the Roth family hung on the walls, showing battles of old and dozens of lords leading their armies to victory. Some showed beasts and monsters not seen for an age after being driven from the land. One depicted the construction of The Hold, an incredible undertaking meant to forever secure the sovereignty of the Federation against invaders from the North and West. It was this tapestry that Cassius' father stood before, staring at it with his arms clasped behind his back.

Cassius' father, Lord Augustus Roth, Baron of the Horn, stood like the mountains he ruled over, resolute and proud. His long, dark hair and beard formed an orderly mane around his head, not quite covering the rough scars on his face and neck. He was not a particularly large man, but he carried himself with a confidence that seemed to dwarf others in the room. Despite wearing the traditional robes of his station, deep red and white with bronze trim and a heavy pendant of a bear to secure his cloak, he still carried the blade of a warrior at his waist, even here in his own halls. Cassius stopped a few feet behind him and called out, "Father, I see you're minding the royal tapestries again?"

The older man turned on his son. The fire in his eyes cut through the younger Roth's confidence as surely as any blade. Augustus' voice was low and measured, but there was no mistaking the harsh edge when he spoke, "This is no time for jokes, boy. You've disobeyed my orders, again. Worse, you've embarrassed this family."

"Father, I..." but the older man cut him off.

"You'll be silent now, son, or you'll wish those beasts would have done you in." His fathers growled threat cut his protests off in an instant, "When you first petitioned my council to take your men north, I told you those villagers were none of your concern. You knew we had already designated a cadre of soldiers to clear those beasts out; they had been working their way from village to village for half the cycle when you left for your fool's errand."

The Baron slowly began to stalk around the perimeter of the room, eyeing his son as he continued, "But you, in your pride, presumed to solve that problem all on your own, did you not?"

Augustus let the silence hang in the air, daring his son to respond. Cassius glowered at his father, chewing on his tongue to keep from speaking.

"The border villages are all suffering Cassius, not just Holwood. The creatures were pushed south en mass from the Highlands and the White Wood, since that plague overtook their herds in the winter, thinning the beasts' food supply. You've accomplished nothing by clearing out one den."

"I *accomplished* my duty, father!" Cassius could hold back no longer, "Holwood was the worst off and those soldiers would have taken another cycle to reach it. Those villagers would have been driven out before then. Lost everything! Our people will sleep in their own beds in peace tonight because of what we did!"

"Do not try to justify your childish glory seeking to me, boy!" Augustus roared like the great bear that his family crest had been modeled after, "Your duty was to escort your sister here safely, as I commanded you! Do you have any idea what would've happened if bandits or wylerbeasts or any other misfortune had befallen her or her entourage in our realm? Her marriage is the bond that holds our peace together. It would have been shaken to its foundations, maybe even broken! How many people would have suffered then? Did you forget that in addition to her husband, the Lord of the Highlands, she brought with her the rest of his family? Including your nephews? Not to mention her sister-in-law, the woman you are to marry?"

Cassius flinched as though he had been struck, but he somehow managed to erect a visage of defiance in the storm of his father's wrath. In a low voice he grumbled, "I never agreed to marry Allura Longstrider."

Augustus had made his way to stand before his son, seeming to tower over the younger Roth despite being of a similar height. He had regained some of his composure, sighing as he took on a lecturing tone, "Cassius, you are the firstborn son of the Horn. It is your duty to ensure the treaties of old are maintained as the age turns and your generation comes to power. It is far past time you come to accept that fact. You will marry that Northern girl, as your sister married her brother, and solidify the bond that will keep the peace for the next generations."

As his father laid his hands on his shoulders, Cassius felt like his father's gaze was burning a hole right through him, "Son, you are an excellent warrior, maybe my best. Your men love you. But it is time to put that aside, to rise to your station. I have tried to teach you what it means to be a Lord, to be the leader of your people. But to no avail. You're older than I was the day your sister was born, yet unmarried, wild as an unbroken stallion...and I've long run out of patience with your foolishness."

A look resembling pity crossed the older man's face and for a moment he seemed to hesitate before continuing. But only for a moment. He took a step back and addressed his son, voice taking on the cadence of a lord addressing his subject, "I have informed Lord Commander Viggo, you are to be stripped of your position as a Legate of the Legions of the Horn. You are to be banned from the Barracks and the men in your personal guard are to be integrated back into the general forces. I am also writing to the Tribunal of the Covenant to recommend that your title of Dux Valorus be revoked."

Cassius could not believe his own ears, "Father, this unheard of! I earned that title position in blood! I am a Lord of the Horn! You cannot-"

A cold steel had filled the voice of the older Roth, "I *can*, Cassius, and I will. You will be confined to The Hold until

I decree otherwise. You will remain here for this festival and
you will entertain our guests from the North. You *will* present
yourself to Lady Allura, and, come season's end, you will marry
that girl."

"I will not!" Cassius had lost all composure, as panic overtook
him. His mind raced and the judging faces of his ancestors all
around him suddenly made the giant hall seem far too small.

"You *will*, son; your sister and I have already arranged it and
the ministers all approve." Augustus glared at his son with a look
of unguarded disappointment, "I have failed to bring you to
heel, but perhaps this girl will succeed where I could not. Maybe
a wife can make you into a proper Lord. We shall see."

He called and two armored men entered. As Cassius tried to
protest, they grabbed him by the arms and escorted the Prince
out of the grand chamber. The last thing he saw of his father was
his back as he turned to examine the tapestry again, ignoring his
son's calls and curses as the doors were shut behind him.

Chapter Two

Son of a Sailor

As the *Cerulean Songbird*, a large merchant vessel with two masts and a broad bow, slid into dock in Redwater Port, the crew was set to their work on deck. They rushed around, throwing lines, drawing down sails and releasing the anchor, letting the great iron weight crash into the gray green waves below. The yells and general noise of the ship mixed with the sound of the water slamming against the hull. As it slowed to a stop just at the edge of the deep water docks, far enough out to accommodate such a great vessel, the ship shuddered as the heavy braided ropes went taut and held it in place.

Below the mad bustle on deck, Jayce Acosta sat on the floor of a large, lavishly decorated cabin with his hands outstretched in front of him. He was lean and dark skinned with brilliant blue eyes that were so clear you could almost see your reflection in them. His hair was close cropped with razor sharp edges and he wore well kept, fine clothes which were clearly tailored to fit him. Across from him on the floor sat his mother, Nadia Acosta. She bore the same striking blue eyes as her son which shone like crystals in her dark face. Her braided hair was up in a loose bun and she kept herself wrapped in a golden shawl. Her soft smile was kind and her voice was sweet and warm like summer rain when she spoke to her son.

Between them, an empty bucket sat on the floor. A few drops of water had formed in the air above the bucket, vibrating and churning in midair. Beads of sweat dotted the young man's forehead. He grimaced as he concentrated on the water, his fingers twitching.

"Relax, Jayce." Nadia said quietly, "Don't look for the water, feel it. Let your *soul* feel it."

"I'm trying," Jayce managed, barely breathing, "I can feel it there, but I can't take hold of it..."

"Don't try to hold it, my child, just let yourself be immersed. It's not a parchment you can hold in your hand. You must know the heart of it."

The air between them began to shimmer like a glass of water held to the light. It seemed to shift and fluctuate within itself. Then suddenly, more drops began to appear. They emerged from the floorboards and the sweat from his own forehead, drifting towards the space between them. They combined with what was already there until they formed a small undulating ball about the size of an orange.

Nadia clapped her hands excitedly, "Oh, my dearest, well done!"

Jayce smiled and watched as his creation spun lazily before them. Suddenly, the door slammed open. Jayce lost his concentration and the ball splashed into the bucket, sloshing over the edges and soaking the carpets. The captain of the *Songbird* stood there, his mouth set in a sharp frown. Jayce's father, Elon Acosta, was an imposing figure with his shaved and tattooed head, neatly trimmed beard and quick eyes that saw everything like a sea serpent searching for its prey. He strode across the room and leaned down, giving his wife his hand to help her up. The sheathed tip of the scimitar he kept on his belt beside an ornately crafted pistol gently scraped the ground when he bent over. Jayce scrambled to his feet as well, smoothing out his fine pants and shirt.

"How goes the trainin', my songbird?" Elon asked his wife, placing one hand on her cheek.

"Swimmingly, my dear Captain." Nadia gave him a lingering kiss. After they separated, she continued, "Few can connect to the soul of the sea the way your son can."

"Excellent! Let us have a toast then, before we depart for the festival." He waved absently towards the large cabinet on the far side of the room. As Jayce went and pulled out glasses and a bottle of dark liquid, his father continued in a brusque, businesslike tone, "We have quite the haul to bring to Rothmount this year. I'm sure Lord Augustus will be most appreciative of our contribution to the festivities."

"That's wonderful news, isn't it Jayce?" She had begun making a circular motion with her free hand while the other remained wrapped around her husband. Water was pulling itself out of the carpets and flowing back into the bucket.

Jayce had not said a word since his father entered. He nearly dropped the three glasses he held pinched between his fingers when his mother spoke his name, "Yes, of course, I'm glad you're doing so well, father."

Elon reached out and grabbed one of the glasses with one hand and the bottle with another, "*We* are doin' well son, we, not I. This Company is our family's legacy. It belongs to all of us, together."

"Of course father, I only meant you're the one who's done all the work. You make the agreements, it's your name people know us by." Jayce handed one of the glasses to his mother.

"Jayce, my boy, you're huntin' for sharks in the reeds." He pulled the cork out with his teeth and began pouring the drinks, "Your sisters each have their own boats that they captain *and* guide for. I may have started this business years ago, but your mother became my partner early on, it's as much hers as it is mine. And now your sisters are my partners as well."

He raised his glass. They all clinked their drinks as he toasted, "To the Summit! May this year be as profitable as ever!"

The dark liquor burned with a sweet sharpness all the way down his throat. Jayce had to get over a light bout of coughing before continuing, "I understand what you're saying father, I've no issues with our family business. I only meant that it's always going to be your business. No matter who you *partner* with, the Acosta Company is always going to be yours."

Elon and his wife looked at each other. Nadia tilted her head and gave her husband a look. Elon sighed, then motioned for them to hold their glasses out again.

"Jayce, your mother and I, we been thinkin'. We're old now, and we are only gettin' older. You must learn more about the business. Your gifts are a wonder and you'd be an asset on any ship. But you were meant for more than that. We need someone to take over this business one day, and we think it should be you."

Jayce took a breath. He turned away from his parents and looked out a circular porthole over the harbor and ocean. For a long time, he said nothing. When he finally spoke, he could hardly believe the words that were coming out of his mouth. But once he started there was no turning back.

"If you had asked me as a boy, if I would want to one day take your place, Captain the *Songbird*, I'd have said yes in a hairsbreadth." He smiled to himself, "I love this boat, I love the sea and I love being with my family...but I can't agree to be Captain. Not now, anyway."

"Jayce..." Nadia started to speak but he continued. The excitement was building and he could not help himself.

"My Gift has been growing, I can feel it. Since I was first able to reach out and feel the power of the wind, the depth of the ocean, I've wanted more. I want to learn more, to grow this power, to understand it." He looked at his mother with something akin to desperation in his voice, "I don't want to spend my life guiding ships and predicting the storms for fishermen and traders, I want to see what I'm really capable of. I...want to go to the Capital, to study at the University."

Nadia recoiled slightly, as if he had struck her. Jayce's smile faltered. He started to speak, but his father cut him off.

"So my boy, you want to be what, a sorcerer? A high mage? You want to sit at the feet of Lords and Ladies and peddle your influence at their tables?"

"No, father, I..." Jayce tried, but he spoke over him.

Anger had carved up the elder Acosta's face, he kept a level tone but he spoke faster and more harshly, spitting the words out, "You think yourself too good for the life of a merchant? Do you not appreciate the life your mother and I've given you here? Appreciate the *sacrifices* we've made?"

Nadia put her hand on his chest. He seemed to deflate, his tirade faltering for a moment. Elon turned away from his son as his wife stepped forward to continue the conversation in his stead. When she spoke, Nadia's voice was measured, "Jayce...I hear the desire in your heart. When I came into my power, I too felt the same. So did all three of your sisters. The call of the Gift is enticing, it is like the tide, it pulls you and calls you into deeper and deeper waters. Everyone who has been given the Gift feels the call to understand it, explore its depths, and yours is greater than most. Please understand, your father and I don't want to keep you from exploring your Gift, but there is so much about this you do not yet understand. You must hear your mother now, this power has perils you know nothing about yet."

The woman put her hand on the young man's cheek, gently cradling the side of his face. Her eyes searched his face, desperate to find some thread to grasp hold of, "You are so young yet, my son. You think the answers you seek are beyond the deck of our ship. Hidden away in some grand hall or held by some conjurer. But you haven't seen what the world is like. It is a dangerous place for people like us. There are those that would use you for their own ends, promise you all the skies and seas but give you nothing. When I was a child..."

Jayce took his mother's hand in his and tried to keep his voice even, but was unable to keep frustration from seeping through,

"Mother, I am no child. I know the world is dangerous. I know you faced your own terrors at the hands of malicious magicians. But I cannot learn the true extent of my powers within the hull of this ship!"

"Oh my child, what has wormed its way into your mind to make you believe that? I have been a Stormspeaker my entire life. I taught all your sisters, and they are amongst the finest guides that sail the seas. No spell monger or court sorcerer will teach you to speak to the sea and skies as I can."

In the earnest face of his mother, Jayce struggled to put words to his desire. His father spoke before he could gather his thoughts.

"Son, I've no touch of the Gift, but I think I know what this is about." He began, wheeling around, waving the bottle before him, "You want to be your own man, yes? To get out from under your mother's skirt tails and stand on your own two feet?"

Jayce looked from his father to his mother. He saw her searching his face as Elon rolled on.

"That's a desire I can indeed understand! When I was your age, I ran from home and was on the first ship that would take me before my parents knew I had abandoned our fishin' nets. That's the call that all young men feel! Here's what I'll do, when we return to the Breach at the end of the season, I will set you up to study under one of the magicians on a Republic Warship. The Commodore owes me quite a few favors after all." He chuckled to himself, "You'll get your adventure, get some time off this old boat of ours, and in time you'll come back and take over the business, just as we planned!"

Nadia pursed her lips, "A Warship, Elon do you think that's wise?"

"Oh, worry not, my songbird! The Republic has the greatest navy in the world! He'll be safer there than on any ship in our fleet."

"I suppose..." she looked from her husband to her son, "Jayce, is this what you want?"

Jayce knew his father. He knew when the man's mind was set on something. Resigned, he sighed and said, "Yes, father."

His father reached around his shoulder and pulled him in close with a one armed hug, "Then it is settled, let us have another drink to celebrate!"

A fter a few glasses more of the burning liquor, Jayce excused himself and returned to his cabin. Closing the door, he made sure to lock it behind him. His cabin was a simple affair when compared to his parents quarters, a small bed, a trunk, and a desk with a single window and cabinet for hanging clothes. A few decorations were hung from the wall and the place was littered with books. To Jayce, the simple room felt like a prison cell more than it ever had before.

He collapsed in his desk chair with a sigh. He slouched, disappointment worn like a cloak across his shoulders. After a moment, he leaned under the desk and pried up a loose floorboard with his fingertips. There was a small cache in the hidden space. A cloudy, white crystal, a knife with a bone handle, a handful of finger length metal sticks intricately carved with tiny runes. But what Jayce was after was a small book bound in worn black leather. It read, *Finding Fundamental Forces by Grande Mistress Marigold Tahhan* in spindly gold lettering across the cover.

Jayce placed it on the table with reverence. It had dozens of markers blooming out of its pages and as he flipped through he could see the scrawling notes he had made in almost every margin. The small print was interspersed with several torn and smudged pages, a result of the book's rough life at sea. It had cost Jayce nearly a year's savings to purchase from a shifty trader while on the Broken Coast who had seemed as eager to be rid of it as he was to stuff the coin in his purse. The book had been incredibly difficult to comprehend. Hidden away in the secrecy

of his cabin, he had spent many nights attempting the exercises
it outlined, to little success.

But despite his failings, he felt he had still learned more about
what his people called the Gift from this small tome than he had
from years of training with his mother. He sighed, shutting the
book. Then he stood and pulled a travel pack from a hook on
the wall. He began pulling clothes from the cabinet, carefully
wrapping the book in one of the shirts, and packed it in his bag
for the journey. It would not do for his mother or father to catch
a glimpse of it on the trip to Rothmount. He finished quickly,
throwing on his favorite traveling jacket and slinging his pack
over his shoulder before leaving the small, stifling room behind.

Jayce saw the crew were still unloading the ship once he had
made his way out into the mid morning sun. Large carts were
filled with barrels and boxes containing spices brought from the
Breach and beyond, their fragrant scents mixing with salty air.
His father was already there, shouting directions and berating
every misstep and indiscretion.

"Yari," the captain shouted, his booming voice carrying over
the noise on the din as he quickly paced the dock with his first
mate in tow, "I want this entire ship unloaded before nightfall.
No man goes ashore until it's done, aye? I will be personally
escorting the majority of the cargo up to the Capital and it needs
to be there by the time the festival begins, so we only have two
days' time. I'll be leavin' at first light, so the caravan must be
ready to go tonight."

"Aye, Capt'n." Yari was a tall broad man with long locks of
black braided hair and a hook where his left hand should be. He
appeared every bit the pirate of children's stories.

"You'll be mindin' the ship here and ensurin' the rest gets
gone off properly to where it's going in my stead. I'll be back
before the end of the cycle and we'll be off to the Empire. Keep
a sharp eye on 'em, hear? I don't want none of these fish-brained
water dogs gettin' into trouble durin' the festival and tyin' me
up, clear?"

"Aye, Capt'n."

Jayce managed to make a wide semicircle around his father, skirting the edge of the dock and blending into the crowd of sailors and laborers unloading crates and barrels. He made his way to land amongst the throngs of people disembarking, passing ships of all shapes and sizes. Some were merchant vessels where sailors were unloading cargo onto waiting carts, others were fishing boats which had massive nets and spears attached to ropes visible on their decks. There were also a number of warships with reinforced hulls and ballista leering out over the decks. There was even another Republic ship in port, flying the silver star and crossed swords of the Broadwater Breach emblazoned on a navy field. Large cannons lined the hull, black barrels gleaming in the sun. On the wharf, Legionnaires bearing the red bear sigil of the Barony of the Horn stood guard and closely watched the crowd, alert for any sign of trouble.

Jayce reached the shoreline, passing unnoticed under the watchful eyes of yet another set of guards who were stopping members of the disembarking crowd at random to question and search them. Once he was off the wharf, he stepped onto the cobblestone streets of Redwater Port. The age of the city could be felt in the weathered stonework buildings, resolute and timeless with carved archways and balconies which had stood for hundreds of years against storms and the sea. Redwater was one of the only safe places for ships to dock in the Bracing Bay and it had been a major hub for trade and travel between the Empire and the Southlands longer even than the Herronite Federation had existed.

As Jayce made his way across the streets past fishmongers and trader stalls, he noted how busy the old port city was. Every alleyway and intersection had a group of bystanders huddled around a Tale Teller, performer, or traveling merchant and their open cart. All the roving sailors and far traders had come to port for the Summit, hoping to empty their hulls to the large crowds and perhaps join in the festivities before undertaking their next journey. Working his way through the crowds and around the witchlights, poles with magical glowing glass balls meant for lighting the streets, he finally found his way to a small shop stuck in between a brasserie and a general store. As he ducked inside, he noted the store had a glass window emblazoned with silver lettering which read *Rory's Rarities and Reclamations* above a symbol of an open eye with a star in its pupil.

The store was dimly lit and smelled strongly of sweet incense, making the interior quite jarring compared to the brightly lit chaos in the streets outside. It was a deep, narrow building with darkly painted walls and an arched ceiling which bore host to multiple hanging glass bulbs of pale yellow witchlight. Heavy rugs ran the length of this room as did the rows of tall wooden shelves which lined both walls. The shelves were filled with every oddity and trinket one could imagine; jars filled with multicolored liquids and floating shapes Jayce could not quite make out, spindly golden tools of indiscernible purpose, the erect skeleton of an animal with six limbs and jagged spikes down its spine, to name a few were close at hand. There were also dozens of books scattered across the shelves, ranging in size and color, with some being very new and others appearing to be ancient. The far end of the chamber was blocked by a thick, black curtain, obfuscating the back of the store, but Jayce could make out movement as the lights flickered under the shade.

Just inside the doorway a fantastically fat man with a bald head and thick red beard sat at a large desk made of old, dark wood. The desktop was covered in ledgers, quills and loose paper, as well as a half eaten sandwich and flagon of ale as dark squid ink. He barely straightened in his seat when the young man entered, hardly deigning to glance up from a book he held in his short, pudgy fingers.

"Can I help you?" He asked in an uninterested tone. The man spoke with the same heavy, deliberate dialect everyone in the Southlands spoke. Up close, Jayce could see the flecks of food caught in his beard and teeth. He noted that under the man's large gut the wood and metal handle of a blunderbuss, a hand cannon far less fine than his father's, peaked out from where it was holstered in his belt.

Jayce spoke in Herron, giving the man a small wave as he began to dig through his bag, "Didn't mean to interrupt your lunch, I'm sure you're eager to return to it. But I'm just looking for the next book in a series..."

He pulled the black bound book out of his bag and handed it to the man. The fat man took the book with a glare and looked it over. He thumbed through the pages and gave Jayce a look, "Read it all the way through, aye, boy?"

Jayce nodded, glancing quickly around the room. The man handed the book back to him, a few greasy thumbprints still lingering on the cover. Attempting to subtly wipe it off as he rewrapped it in the shirt, Jayce placed it back in his bag. Snorting and grumbling in annoyance, the man had to grab at his sagging pants to keep them up as he lumbered to his feet. He motioned and Jayce followed him further into the narrow store, passing through the shelves of oddities.

Near the back, the fat man stopped in front of the last row of shelves before the curtained backdrop and started running his finger back and forth along rows of books there. He mumbled to himself while he searched, low voice punctuated by his heavy breathing. While he waited, Jayce strained to hear the low voices behind the curtain, at least two, having a nearly inaudible conversation in hushed voices. Despite his best efforts, all he could determine was that one voice seemed high pitched and squeaky, while the other was low and smooth like honey.

"Ah, here it is." The fat man pulled a small tome out from the second shelf from the bottom. It was bound in a deep red leather that was heavily worn, a casual inspection revealing torn pages and easily visible stains. The title, *Mastering Magic Models by Grande Mistress Marigold Tahhan,* blazed brightly in gold lettering on the cover and spine. Jayce reached out to grab it but the man snapped it out of his reach.

"Not so fast, boy," he gave a slimy grin, "you gotta pay first."

"How much?"

"Fifty silver pieces, Federal Marks, if you please."

Jayce blinked, "Fifty?! Outrageous! That's double what I paid for this one!"

The man shrugged, "It's a more rare book. Besides, it's the only one we've got."

"Unabashed piracy is what it is. What's wrong, afraid you'll starve if you don't swindle me?" He regretted the jab the moment he had said it, but his tongue had run away on him again, as it so often had a habit of doing.

The man narrowed his eyes and glowered at him, "Take it or leave it, boy."

Jayce checked in his coin purse. There were about two dozen coins inside of various nationalities and denominations. He sighed, wondering if he could have negotiated a better price had he not let his mouth get in his way, "Will you take a note?"

The fat man gave a heavy snort, "I doubt very much you have the seal to guarantee a note for that much coin."

Jayce reached into a side pocket in his coat and pulled out a small leather tool roll. Placing it on a table nearby, he carefully unraveled it. Inside, held in place with ties, were two small pens, a tiny vial of blue black ink, a roll of papers, a small knife with a black handle and a small seal. Jayce pulled the seal out of the bundle and held it out for the man to see. After only the briefest of glances at the symbol, a seabird with an ornate "A" on its breast holding a lightning bolt in one talon and an anchor in the other, the man changed his stance, eyes widening.

"I didn't realize *you* were with the Acosta Company, why didn't you say so from the start?" He didn't wait for the response before shoving the book into the young man's hand and turning back to wave at the shelf, "I would never have questioned your credit if I had known. Is that all you need? We have many other books on magic in stock, maybe *Terrestrial Telemetry*, or *Ferrous Theorem* has been a good seller this year, perhaps

the latest from Grandmaster Yoel? We have the printings from
several of his recent lectures at the Academy in Scivias."

Jayce grinned despite himself at the man's sudden turn of
temperament as he took the book, "That will be all, thank you,
good sir."

He deflated a bit, but he recovered quickly and showed Jayce
back to the front of the store where they filled out the credit
note. Once the note was filled out, Jayce took the slender knife
and pressed it to the tip of his thumb. He winced as blood welled
up and he smeared it on the Acosta Company seal. He then
pressed the seal in the corner of the note leaving an imprint
clearly visible in bright red, vivid against the white paper. He
was about to take his leave, when a voice called out from behind
him.

"Leaving so soon, young master?" A familiar, high pitched
voice called out.

Jayce turned from where he stood in the doorway. A rail thin
ghost of a man with a shaved head and thin mustache stood
there, clothed in green and tan silk with soft shoes about ten
feet behind him. He was holding a smoldering pipe that was
as thin as he was in one hand and Jayce could see his fingers
were adorned by several rings. He eyed Jayce with curiosity as
he looked him over with his dark, darting eyes.

"I have what I came for, sir."

"Yes, I heard, quite a good piece...for beginners." He seemed
to shift within his robes, giving Jayce the impression of a snake
coiled in on itself, "But if you're interested in more...*advanced*
literature, we certainly have such rarities in our private collection. Of course, a representative of the Acosta Company would
be welcome to peruse..."

Jayce hesitated. He suddenly felt like he was in the dark den
of some creature from one of the old stories; the kind that
lured sailors in with promises of wealth or pleasure. But those
were just stories, and all the sea monsters had been killed off

generations ago by explorers and the Legionnaires. He shook off his misgivings and turned around.

"Please, I would greatly appreciate seeing your stock."

The man gave him a wry grin and motioned for Jayce to follow. Jayce fell in half a step behind the man, asking, "I didn't catch your name, sir?"

"Why, I am Rory, the proprietor of this store."

Jayce could not shake the feeling he was missing something, but as the man led him through the black curtain, all misgivings were chased from his mind. The area behind the curtain could have been described as a sitting room; large leather armchairs with little end tables and personal lamps sat around a low oval table of dark wood. A great hearth occupied the back wall and low burning embers crackled and cast dim light on the picture of a ship in a stormy sea which sat above the mantle. What caught Jayce's eye though, were the shelves that lined both walls and were packed with dozens and dozens of books. The books were lined up neat and orderly, shelves unburdened by random accouterments like the front of the store, and arranged by author and title. Even in the dim light Jayce saw there were more books than he was able to count.

Jayce eagerly found his way to the closest shelves and began to read the titles; *Cursed by Uma Cromwell, Practicing Psychometry by James Jones, The Final Incantation by Geovani Hasani.* The titles went on and on, and Jayce wanted to read every single one of them. He noticed that Rory was still watching him intently, but was too engrossed to pay him much attention. It was not until another voice spoke, that he was startled out of his trance.

"If you would like to stay here a while and partake in some of our rare literature, we are happy to accommodate you. We always welcome young practitioners of the Art, especially those of such an *esteemed* background."

Jayce looked around the room, noticing for the first time there was a third person present. A well groomed man with long, dark hair and a pointed beard sat in the furthest armchair away from him, the shadows seeming to have hidden him during Jayce's initial impression of the room. The new man wore a fine gray court suit and a dark overcoat with silvered buttons which showed firelight dancing in their reflections. He stared intently at Jayce, a glass of dark liquid and small tome left to the side.

"My apologies, good sir, I did not see you there." He turned to the man and gave him a curt bow, "I am Jayce, it is a pleasure to meet your acquaintance."

The dark haired man waved off the apology as he stood. He was tall and lean, but not sickeningly slender, as the proprietor of the store appeared to be. When he spoke, it was with the same smooth voice Jayce had heard before. He noticed no hint of the Southern accent and struggled to place the man's origins, "No apologies needed, young master, we're all just scholars in search of knowledge here. It is a pleasure to meet you. My name is Lawrence."

Jayce took the man's outstretched hand reflexively. When he did, he felt the sudden, unmistakable spark of energy moving through his fingers and winding its way up his arm. He jerked his arm back, but Lawrence made a soothing motion, "Relax, my friend, it was nothing untoward. I was only getting to know you a bit."

Jayce attempted to recompose himself. He stood for a moment, letting the silence hang in the air, before finally speaking, "A bit forward if you ask me. Could've given me a bit of warning before."

"Just trying to get a feel of your disposition in the Art," the firelight threw strange shadows around the room and seemed to cling to the man as he spoke, "and it seems like you have quite the knack indeed. Now the question is, what's talent like yours doing with a simple shipping company? I certainly hope you're not acting as just another *weather witch*?"

Jayce flinched at the term. It did not escape the man's notice, "I meant no offense, young master. I simply want to illuminate the possibility that you may have other paths in front of you."

The man pulled a large silver coin out of his coat pocket and held it out. When Jayce took it, he saw there was a simple image of a blade wreathed in flame emblazoned on one side. On the other, the Herron symbol for the letter "B" was engraved twice.

"The Burning Blades...you're a mercenary?"

Lawrence wrinkled his nose at the word, "I am an agent of one of the most powerful independent companies in the world. As such I can tell you, there is a great need for men of your talents across the Sea."

"You mean Lorrailia?"

He nodded. His grin widened as he spread his arms, "The New World is still rich with possibilities for those willing to take it! Treasure, land, glory; it's all there just waiting for capable young people like you who can take the initiative! I can see that you're smart enough to grasp the truth; the future isn't here in these ancient, crumbling kingdoms, it's out there!"

Jayce caught himself grinning like a child at his fathers knee listening to stories. He forced his face back to what he hoped was an impassive expression and pocketed the coin, "Sounds like tall tales for small children..."

The smile slid from the man's face as he pivoted, his tone losing its grandeur somewhat, "Not at all, young master. I have seen many talented men like yourself make their fortunes across the Lancing Ocean. Besides, the Blades pay handsomely for good work. I guarantee we can beat the pennies the Acosta Company pays."

At that, Jayce straightened and squared his shoulders, "Sir, I appreciate the offer. But I am no mercenary, and I have no intention of dying on a battlefield in the New World anytime soon. If there is nothing else, I believe I will take my leave."

All the pomp seemed to have left the man as his shoulders slumped, "As you say, I would not presume your intentions."

Giving a small nod, Jayce tried to hand the coin back to him. But the man shook his head, swallowing his obvious disappointment as he forced a smile onto his face, "Keep it. You may find yourself looking for employment in the future. Consider it a calling card."

Jayce nodded again, tucked the coin into his pocket and strode past the gray suited man and the proprietor, who had stood by and silently observed the entire conversation. As Jayce made his exit, Lawrence called after him, "If you should change your mind, young master, we have men everywhere in the Federation! Ask for the Burning Blades and present that coin... tell them Lawrence sent you!"

Jayce left the store, passing the fat man who was back at his post behind the desk, and strode out onto the crowded, sweltering streets without looking back. When he returned to the docks, the sailors were still loading the wagons down with sacks and crates, sweating in the blazing sun. As he rejoined the Company caravan, passing by the oxen driven wagons, he double checked that his new red leather bound tome was securely wrapped in his pack. He carefully tucked the large silver coin in between the two books, hidden inside a shirt in the bottom of his pack, then hoisted the bag back over his shoulder.

He approached the lead wagon where his father was deep in discussion with the first mate, pointing a finger violently at something in a ledger. He passed them and heaved himself up onto the driver's seat of the cart where his mother was sitting. In the distance, they could see the cobblestone road stretching out away from the coastline and disappearing into the foothills, which then climbed up into the heavily wooded mountain range beyond. She glanced at him, a curious look on her face.

"I was looking for you, my son. Where did you get off to?"

"Not to worry mother, just outrunning an errand before the journey."

"Did you get everything you needed?"

Jayce grinned, "Oh yes, I believe I did."

CHAPTER THREE

THE SUN'S SUMMIT

E ven this early in the day, the Sun's Summit Festival was fully underway and Rothmount was thrumming with life and feverish energy. The longest day of the year was a time of celebration throughout the Everdene and the people of the Horn embraced it wholeheartedly. Yellow and white flags lined the streets of the city along with streamers and massive paper lanterns of varying shapes and sizes hung from every rafter and pole. There were banners hanging in every storefront with gaudy pictures of bright flowers or plump vegetables beckoning to the crowds. The cobblestone streets were littered with flower petals, brightly painted seeds, and confetti in a dazzling array of colors.

Traveling merchants had set up shop in every alley and square, selling candies, hot food and drinks, as well as garishly decorated clothing and hats, flags, ribbons, and toys. Jugglers, dancers and tumblers as well as illusionists and magicians wowed the crowds with fantastic displays. Shining, multicolored lights and images danced in the air above the crowds along with floating bubbles of various sizes that burst with musical sounds when touched. Musicians and Tale Tellers could be heard in every tavern, inn, and ale house, their noise adding to the ruckus in the streets and the building crescendo of the festival.

The people swarmed through the city like a sea of clashing color and sound. Men, women, and children of all ages, Southlanders and Northerners alike, along with a smattering of peoples from other nations, flooded the massive city. Women lined the streets placing flower wreaths on the festival goers as they flowed through the streets in their brightly colored clothes and painted faces and bodies. The paraders peppered the crowds of revelers with confetti and painted seeds as they passed and children ran about gathering what was left, hoarding it like it was precious treasure. The crowds all sang and shouted, fought and embraced, flowed between shops and vendors and taverns in an ever churning mass that swelled and pushed against the walls of the great metropolis.

The sun beat down on the crowds and intensified the smell of sweat mixed with cooking food and alcohol, filling the streets like a thick, invisible smog. Guards tried their best to manage the crowds but there was little they could do to pacify the unruly mob that had overrun their streets. Store owners and tavern keepers had extra security hired for the day, and there was a constant whirlwind as they tossed rowdy patrons back out onto the streets. The city was a chaotic mess which was only growing more wild by the hour. But none of the revelry compared to that of the spectacle found at the Red Amphitheater, who had gathered to watch the festival's greatest event, the Summer Tournament.

Every year, hundreds of soldiers, mercenaries, and fighting men from all over the continent found their way to the Summer Festival competitions in the great cities to win glory and riches, and to curry favor with noble houses. The crowd around the Amphitheater was packed tighter than anywhere else in the city. They stood shoulder to shoulder, with children hoisted above so they would not be crushed, struggling to see the action which took place in the circular dirt rings denoted with thick ropes. They screamed and cried out, clutching scraps of paper which showed their wagers.

As each combatant fell, there was a chorus of cheers and boos, wails and laughter. The dozens of minor exterior rings each hosted a different event, with some holding wrestling and barefisted bouts, while others had swordplay or staff matches. But in the middle of it all was the Amphitheater, a great circular arena with raised seating around its perimeter where crowds of screaming spectators watched as teams of armored combatants bludgeoned and beat each other in a grand melee.

Jayce sat with his parents in the raised seats, watching the tournament amongst the well dressed nobles and other wealthy elites. It had been a steep climb up the mountains, especially in this heat, and it had taken every bit of the previous two days for their caravan to reach Rothmount. They had arrived late and had not gotten the wagons unloaded until nearly midnight. Since the early hours of the morning, Jayce had spent his entire time being dragged along by his father from meeting to meeting, wading through the crowds of revelers.

They had collected coins and credit notes from a dozen businesses around the city and now his father was fixated on shamelessly glad handing the city's upper class here at the Tournament. Jayce stared at the fighters on the field as he half listened to his father's conversation with a reedy voiced lord of the Horn. They were discussing trade routes and the latest developments in the Republic. The conversation changed course to the current affairs of the Horn, catching Jayce's ear and pulling him from the melee.

"Yes," the nobleman said, casting a knowing glance at Elon, "it's quite the scandal. Apparently, the Baron has decreed his eldest son to be stripped of his privileges and confined to The Hold. No one is sure what the boy did exactly, but what I've *heard* is he abandoned his duties and led his men on an excursion to some small village up north. If *I* were to guess, I bet he has a mistress up there in the countryside, and probably with child, if the severity of our Liege Lord's decree is to be any indication."

Elon let out a laugh and playfully punched his son in the shoulder, "Hear that, boy? Sounds like your friend has got himself mired in a hell of a bog, aye?"

"Oh dear," Nadia muttered from the other side of her husband, "I do hope that fool boy hasn't gone and gotten himself in trouble. Such a kind heart, but such a reckless streak..."

Jayce blinked and turned toward the nobleman, "Are you sure about this? When did all this happen?"

Making a dramatic flair with his hands, the nobleman exclaimed, "This is just what I've heard around the court, sir, I make no claims of privileged knowledge, you understand. But I know our Prince is not in the Tournament today, and I've never known the Baron's bull of a son to miss a chance at violence."

Jayce turned away from the conversation as they continued onto other gossip. He turned the news over in his mind. It sounded unlike Cassius to abandon his duties, but a quick scan showed that the Roth's crest was not displayed anywhere amongst the competitors in the arena or on the sides in waiting. Worry rolled across his mind like thunderclouds, darkening his mood even further.

"Mother," Jayce leaned over and spoke quietly, "I need to know the truth of this matter."

The woman nodded and smiled, "Go find your friend, Jayce, we'll meet up with you tonight at the feast. You can accompany your father on his business dealings another time."

Jayce squeezed his mother's hand. Then he stood and pushed past the rows of seats and throngs of onlookers. He made his way into the crowds and started pushing his way through the mass as he made his way towards The Hold.

Even the ancient fortress was engrossed in the revelry, though admittedly it was a slightly more refined celebration than what was found in the city streets. Lords and Ladies

stood around the decorated grounds in their fine clothes, sweltering in the heat as they did their best to appear regal while
watching the entertainers perform. A Tale Teller spun an epic
story in one corner of the yard, while a minstrel performed her
tumbling for a group of children in another. A magician in a
white cloak threw multicolored fire into the air and several musicians wandered from group to group singing sanguine songs
and jaunty tunes. Servants in fine red coats patrolled the area
with trays of drinks and food and did their best to appear as
much a part of the scenery as the decor.

Jayce had just approached the gates when he heard a loud
booming sound and saw another mage had let loose an ethereal
dragon made of blue and red light which flickered and sparked
as it roared over the walls and circled above the grounds. It drew
polite claps and laughs from the crowd as it climbed high into
the sky before erupting in a shower of colored sparkles.

Guards stopped him briefly at the gate to verify who he was,
but he flashed his Acosta Company crest and was allowed to
enter the grounds. Of all the castles and strongholds he had
visited on his travels around Evardene, Jayce believed The Hold
had to be the ugliest. It was built to be a shield against which
armies of Oarenhiem and the North would shatter themselves,
and no amount of dressing up or festive coloring would hide
that fact. He passed among groups of the nobility and dodged
around the children, attempting to see if his friend was present.

He was so caught up in his search, that the handsomely
dressed young man who strode up was nearly upon him before
he noticed. His regal bearing was similar in appearance to Cassius, tan skin, dark hair and eyes, but he was younger and his lean
frame carried little of the muscle of his elder brother. He wore
his hair in a loose mop which hung around his head like a mane
and his summer outfit of white and amber trim was emblazoned
with the Roth family's red bear crest.

"Julius," Jayce said when he finally noticed the younger
Prince, extending his hand, "it's good to see you."

The young lord grasped his hand before making a motion around the courtyard, "Same to you, Jayce. You won't find my brother here, if I might assume that's who you're looking for."

Jayce nodded, "Makes sense, this isn't his typical affair."

Julius grinned his winning smile and shook his head, "No, it really isn't. But even still, he couldn't attend if he wanted to. Father confined him to his quarters."

"Truth be told, I'd heard some rumors..." Jayce leaned in close and lowered his voice, "Tell me the rumors are false, he's not sired a lowborn child, has he?"

Julius stared at him open mouthed before bursting into laughter, drawing the attention of a few neighboring party goers for a moment. He wiped a tear from his eye and composed himself, "I'm sorry, sorry...it's just that court rumors always seem to spread faster than horny hares. No, my friend, there's no new Roth bastard hiding in the Northlands, despite whatever the whisperings of nursemaids and servants might have you believe."

Jayce breathed a heavy sigh, "Well that's a relief. Pray tell, if it's not that, what could possibly possess your father to inflict such a punishment on him?"

The nobleman compulsively straightened his shirt, casting his own glance around the courtyard, "Ah, now there's a high hill to climb. My father, in all his wisdom, sent Cassius and his personal guard to escort Valeria, her husband, and their whole entourage South for the Festival. Well apparently, while on his way, Cas decided to help a village suffering from...some sort of incursion? I don't know, father says it was already being handled. But you know my brother, the big lout believes he's the greatest warrior to walk the earth since Amos the Brave, and maybe he is! But that's beside the point, of course. He decided to abandon my father's task to go off on some fool's errand."

"Well, that's not great news..." Jayce rubbed the back of his head.

"It only gets worse!" Julius threw his hands up, "My sister's party arrived here before he even had the decency to try and meet up with them, *and* they had Allura Longstrider with them! He left the girl he's meant to marry alone and without an escort all the way from the Highlands to Rothmount. Then he had the gall to show up here and expect praise for his actions."

"Cas has never been one for self reflection..."

"No, and now he's found himself in a predicament he can't fight his way out of." Julius took a drink off a passing servant's platter and downed it in a single gulp. He blew out a long breath and leveled his gaze at his friend, "Jayce, I don't believe I've ever seen my father so angry. Cas is going to need more than an apology and a smile to get himself out of this one."

Jayce nodded. He pondered things for a moment, but Julius spoke before he could, his face bereft of its previous joviality.

"I'm stuck here smiling at these suck ups and ladder climbers, but if you want to find Cas his quarters are still in the Western wing. He's in a bad way, Jayce, he could probably use a friendly face."

Jayce nodded again and they said their goodbyes. The Prince moved on to another group of party goers, his face and tone returning to their well practiced positions, and Jayce made his way into The Hold itself. As he passed a serving area, he subtly snatched a bottle of mulled wine and stashed it inside his coat before entering the building.

The halls of The Hold were far cooler and mercifully muffled the constant, tumultuous noise of the city. It took him a while to navigate the labyrinthine passages but he eventually made his way to the right place. Despite all he had heard, he was still surprised to see there were two guards posted outside his friend's quarters. They snapped to attention when he approached, hands falling to their swords. Jayce held his hands up, showing them his palms.

"Woah, good sirs, I am only here to speak with Prince Cassius."

One of the men sneered, "The Baron decreed no one is to be allowed in to see his son, until further notice."

Jayce nodded solemnly, "Of course, I understand. But, I'm sure you are missing the festival, stuck here all day..."

He let his hands dip and he slowly reached into his coat. They eyed him, but their gazes softened when he pulled the bottle out, "Maybe you would like some small taste of the festivities to enjoy while you're stuck here on this unfortunate duty?"

The men looked at each other. The closer one reached out and snatched the bottle out of Jayce's hand, examining it with greedy eyes, "You're just here to talk to him?"

He nodded, smiling.

"Fine, you can go in, but no funny business, you hear?"

"Of course."

The man grunted and rapped on the door. The banging of his gauntlet on the heavy wood echoed in the stone hall as they waited. The minutes stretched on, and the guard with the bottle shrugged, "Maybe he don't want to be disturbed."

Just then, the door swung open. Jayce was taken aback. His friend looked a terrible mess, dressed in wrinkled clothes with his hair and beard disheveled and unwashed. He had bags under his eyes and he had the sallow look of a man who had been heavy in the cups. Jayce noted his arm was wrapped in a bandage. He grunted, voice hoarse as he addressed the guard, "What do you want?"

"You've a visitor, my Lord."

Cassius looked past the guard and noticed Jayce standing there for the first time. It took a moment before his face lit up and he cracked a familiar grin, "Jayce Acosta, by the Gods, it's good to see you!"

He strode past the guards and grabbed the other man in a painfully tight bear hug. Jayce winced, as much at the sour smell as the pain. Once he let go, Cassius stepped back and grabbed him by the shoulders, "Come on, my friend, let's get you a drink!"

He led Jayce into his quarters, the guards closing the heavy wooden doors behind them. To Jayce, who had spent his entire life aboard ships in cramped cabins, Cassius' personal quarters seemed like a palace in their own right. Beyond the entryway, the first room was set up to be a large sitting area. Several chairs and two long couches on an ornate rug decorated in patterns of reds and oranges occupied the center of the room. A giant semicircular hearth sat cold and dark on one wall while a serving area with clay and glass bottles on heavy wooden shelves took up residence on the opposite side, bronze serving ware gleaming in the bright light which streamed in from large windows. The chambers were ordained with trophies and weapons and the menacing stuffed heads of great beasts.

Normally, Jayce knew the quarters would have been immaculately clean and tidy. But today, several bottles and cups were strewn around the room, many shattered, their sharp edges glinting dangerously, along with discarded plates and half eaten food which cluttered the surfaces. At the far side of the room, another set of doors sat partially open, revealing the disarray extended into the bedchambers beyond.

As soon as they entered, Cassius made straight for the bar. He grabbed one of the bottles, a clay jug painted in a ruddy yellow, and began searching for clean cups. He checked one before muttering something and carelessly tossing it to one to the side, the metal clanking as it skittered across the stone floor. Finally, he found two that he deemed worthy. He motioned to Jayce, who joined him at the bar, as he poured the cups full to the brim with a reddish liquid. Jayce examined his drink, noting red and green herbs floating in it, before clinking glasses with his friend and taking a good long draw. It was a strong, rooty sort of liquor and its bite was mellowed somewhat by a pleasant aftertaste. As he put it down, he saw Cas was still drinking. The nobleman did not put his cup down until the last drop was gone.

"So..." Jayce began, swirling the remainder of his drink in his cup, searching for the words, "I hear you had some misfortunes?"

Cassius nodded, the beads of liquor clinging to the edges of his beard. He wiped it away with the back of his hand before slamming his cup on the bar and pouring himself another.

"You could say that," he sounded bitter, nothing like the confident and kind nobleman Jayce knew, "my father's all but disowned me at this point. He stripped me of my command, instructed the Lord Commander to keep me from the barracks, even barred me from competing in the tournament this year. Worst of all, he's written to the Tribunal. He asked them to revoke my title of Dux Valorus."

Cassius put the bottle down after his cup was nearly overflowing and made a sound that was between a grunt and a growl. The fury flashed across his eyes at that moment was so sudden and intense it made Jayce recoil, his voice dropping to an angry hiss, "I *earned* that title, Jayce...paid for it with my own sweat and blood in the Highlands against the Northern raiders. I earned it when I defeated champions from across the Horn in the Tournament as a *child*, for our family's glory. I'm the one who took up the Covenant, spoke the words as I knelt before the Tribunal. It wasn't something I inherited from my blood. He didn't give it to me. It was *mine*, and mine alone...and he has no right to take it from me."

His knuckles were white as he grasped the cup, his face contorted in anger. He brought it to his mouth and drained it again, taking long, deep gulps. When he was done, he cast a forlorn glance at the bottle, smacked his lips and sighed.

"I apologize, my friend," he muttered, seeming suddenly embarrassed, "I'm rambling..."

"No, no need to apologize." Jayce clasped his friend on the shoulder, "That must've been hard, I can't imagine what you've been going through, cooped up here, with only your servants and maids for company in this drafty old castle."

Cassius managed a weak grin and cast his gaze around the room, "I suppose things could be worse."

Jayce rolled his eyes, "You nobles have it so hard, practically in living squalor in this hovel, aren't you?"

They both laughed at that. Cassius seemingly recovered from the worst of his bitter spirits, some of his usual swagger returning to him, "Enough of my troubles, what of you? How have your travels been? Tell me, is there any news from the Breach? What of Vinatieri? Tell me everything."

The two talked for hours, about everything and anything, the drink flowing freely. The sun had dipped low in the sky and the light coming through the windows had begun to take on an orange hew by the time Cassius was stoking a low fire in the hearth. The stones set in the walls at regular intervals around the room winked to life and began to emit a weak yellowish glow as their witchlight awakened. They sat on the couches before the hearth laughing and snorting as they passed the bottle back and forth. Cassius was loudly recalling another old story and they were both nearly in tears as they struggled to breath through their laughter.

"...and then you fell out of the cart, right in front of the old goat's table!" He managed through fits of laughter.

"Only because you wouldn't move your ape ass over and there was nowhere for me to sit." Jayce attempted to feign anger.

"Come off it, we were what, eight, nine?" Cassius waved his hands, "There was plenty of space on that food cart for two children! You just lost your grip!"

"Either way, I thought your father was going to murder the both of us!"

"I'm sure the thought crossed his mind to tan our hides raw." Cassius inclined his head, "Thanks be to all the Gods my uncle was there to laugh it all off. Those men from the Empire certainly were taken by surprise when they saw us fall out into the middle of their meeting."

"That they were, my friend." Jayce thought for a moment, "How is your uncle? I haven't seen him in an age."

"Lucian? He's good, last I saw him was when he was home for the Winter's Crest. He came for a visit with his wife and their daughter. Little Mariana has grown into a woman. I dare say they'll be marrying her off to some nobleman soon." A bit of the bitterness crept back into his voice.

Jayce barely registered it. The barest inkling of an idea began to form in his mind through the heavy haze of drinks, "Is he still in the Capital?"

Cassius cast a look at him, "Of course, he's still the Consul of the Horn. Why do you ask?"

"It's nothing. Just a bit of foolishness I can't get out of my mind." Jayce sighed, shaking his head.

The nobleman held out his arms in an open gesture, "You've been listening to me rant about my father half the night. The least I can do is help you work through some of your own demons."

"It's nothing serious, it's just...I've been thinking about going to the University..." He finally managed, his voice barely more than a whisper.

Cassius cocked an eyebrow, "Uthersanctorum?"

"It's just a fledgling's dream," he said quickly as he wrung his hands together, watching as the orange light casting shadows on his dark skin, "I've been working with my mother for some time now to understand my Gift. It only took me months to master what it took my sisters years to even grasp. My mother says I have more power than any of them, and deep down I can feel it, like an ocean churning inside me. But somehow, it always seems like I'm just grasping at the mist on the water, like I can delve so much deeper. I thought that maybe if I went to the University, if I studied with real masters, people who know what they're doing, that I could reach my full potential..."

He stared at the fire, his eyes searching in the dancing fire-light, "I love my family, but they just don't understand. My mother has had...bad experiences with people who practice the High Arts. Then there's my father. They both want me to stay with them, but I've no interest in being a merchant, nor a simple Stormspeaker. I don't want to spend my entire life guiding ships or haggling over pennies. I want to know what it's like to use *real* magic."

Cassius was quiet for a long time. When he spoke, his tone soft, words carefully measured, "Your family aren't your masters, Jayce. They can love you and care for you all they want, but they can't live your life."

Jayce gave him a look, "You're one to talk, how many times have you spoken to this girl you are to marry? Once, twice?"

Cassius flinched, "You've got me there, my friend. But I am a Lord, I'm honor bound to my role." He sighed deeply. But then the Prince stood, a smile spreading across his face, "But that doesn't mean I can't help you."

He strode over through the doors to his bedroom. Jayce craned his neck to watch. There was a brief period of shuffling and angry mutters as the Prince searched through the wreckage of his quarters. Finally, he came back into the room carrying a leather wrapped writing kit. He opened it on the table and pulled out one of the pens and ink. He scribbled quickly, his hand scrawling its sloppy way across the page. Jayce could see even in the dim light that his writing was atrocious. Eventually, he finished with a large, flowing signature towards the bottom. He cut his finger with a small blade and used a seal to place his family mark crest next to the signature. He looked it over, smiled to himself and handed it to his friend.

Jayce took the paper from him, careful not to smear the wet ink and blood, and read it over. He mouthed the words silently, before finally looking up and staring at his friend.

"This says your family is to sponsor me for entrance to the University. That you'll pay for it and you personally guarantee my success."

Cassius nodded, head bobbing up and down like an eager child, "At least one of us will get to live the life we choose."

Jayce shook his head, struggling to come to grips with what this sudden development, "Cas, you can't, I can't-"

"I can, and you will!" Cassius leaned in and grabbed him by the arms, "My father hasn't taken my name away yet and my uncle's always been partial to me. Present this to him and he'll do right by me. I'll get my valet to organize everything else. You'll take the first caravan South in the morning, to Stillbend. Then we'll find a rivership that will take you to Locklear, since crossing the great lake is the fastest way to get you to the Capital."

"But...what will I tell my parents?"

"Tell them it's your life!" Cassius growled, "Tell them this is what *you* want!"

"Cas, I don't know what to say..."

Cassius shook his head, "You don't have to say anything. If my father is determined that I'm going to be confined to these damned halls for the rest of my life, then the least I can do is use my position to help my friends."

Jayce stared at the paper. He looked up into the face of his oldest friend, the Prince he had met as a child wandering these very halls while waiting on his father to finish negotiating trade deals with the Baron. He wrapped his arms around the man's broad frame and embraced him, unable to find words for one of the few times in his life.

J ayce was still numb with shock when he left the chamber. A foppish attendant had come to make Cassius presentable for the evening feast, shooing the unexpected intruder out with a disapproving glare at the guards. Jayce made his way down the stone halls in a daze, still clutching the paper in his hand. When the thought of Cassius' uncle being in the Capital had planted a seed in his mind, he had hoped for something, perhaps an introduction. But this simple piece of parchment as good as ensured not only his entry into the University, but his livelihood as well. He could attend without approval or assistance from his family or anyone else.

The world seemed to move around him in a haze of confusing shapes and disjointed noises. The revelers and entertainers in the streets seemed a world away, their shouts and laughter muffled as he meandered through the crowds. Some part of him knew that he needed to prepare for the feast as well. But he could barely remember how to get to the lavish inn his family was staying at. He wandered in a daze for a long while before the familiar sight caught his eye; a woman sat astride a mountain goat with a wineglass in one hand, the sign for *The Mountain Maiden*.

Inside, the main floor was filled with singing, loudly clinking glasses and laughter as the patrons sloshed ale and wine onto the floors as they danced. There were serving girls rushing around with drinks and food and men struggling to carry new barrels of wine and ale through the crowd. He rushed through the common room and upstairs, heading down the hallway until he found their set of rooms. He knocked and was quickly confronted by the sight of his father in an ornate dinner jacket and fine silk white shirt halfway buttoned.

"Where have you been?" He exclaimed the moment, brow furrowed in fury, "We should've left for the Baron's Feast at sundown!"

Before Jayce could answer, the elder Acosta pushed something into his hand. Jayce looked down and saw it was a silver and sapphire brooch with his family's crest, the familiar seabird. His father pointed his finger in his chest, "Don't forget to wear it this time! Now get ready, we need to leave *now*!"

The door was slammed shut before Jayce had so much as said a single word. He looked down at the brooch in one hand and the paper still clutched in the other. After the feast, then, Jayce thought to himself, silent relief flooding over him, I'll tell them after.

CHAPTER FOUR

THE ARTIST

A ttending a feast in the reputedly Great Banquet Room of
The Hold was like taking a step backward in time. The
walls and floors were unpainted, leaving their ugly red stone
stark in the amber witchlight and the dancing fires of the great
hearth near the center of the room. Long tables of heavy timber,
like the kind one might find in a tavern rather than the halls of
a noble family, ran down the length of the room, laden down
under the weight of the large serving dishes. There were no
courses. Serving forks and ladles were passed back and forth
and shared between nobles and merchants and clergymen with
reckless abandon, all helping themselves at their own leisure, no
regard given for the progress of those around them.

It was chaos. Men and women skewered what they wanted
from the great heaps of food, unconcerned if they were reaching past their neighbor or over their food. There were massive
plates of multicolored potatoes and tubers flecked with herbs
and glistening with salt, dishes overflowing with every kind of
pepper and vegetable in the region and baskets of the strange
flatbreads the Southerners seemed to enjoy so much. Bowls of
thick, fragrant stews and curries which were so heavily spiced
they caused the eyes to water. Then, of course, there was the
meat.

Hunks of flesh hanging from bone and gleaming from being slow cooked in their own fats were unceremoniously served whole with large, cleaver like knives for one to cut their own pieces. Fowl sat suspended on roasting spits, dripping golden brown juices into pans of vegetables below. Almost to an item, everything seemed to be served as inelegantly as imaginable. The accompanying decor was not much better.

Great chandeliers made of wrought iron without filigree or ornamentation hung from the rafters, while long tapestries, unfashionable for well over two generations, were everywhere overcrowding the walls beside ancient weapons and armor and stuffed heads of monsters and beasts. The trophies and treasured artifacts were surely meant to inspire patriotic fervor, but for Juniper Faye the unsavory displays brought nothing to mind so much as the stories her mother had told her of foolish men and their bloody wars which had spanned for generations.

The woman observed the assembled crowd of nobles and high society hangers on with a deep frown cutting lines into her golden skin, her almond eyes narrowed as they glinted like shards of emerald, noting every detail with unchecked disapproval. Her perfectly styled hair wrapped her face in a dark frame under a stylish amethyst and gold hairpin, offsetting her chiffon dress of brilliant violet in a way which was eye catching, yet tasteful. Here in the halls of these near barbarians, she stuck out like a diamond amongst the dull stones. But more so than her outfit, her demeanor set her apart from the other guests. She daintily picked at her food, careful not to smear even the tiniest bit of her perfectly applied makeup. She ate with her chin lifted as she watched the rest of the mob, rigidly proper in a way that screamed of the highest pedigree.

Around her, the burly Northmen and the unkempt Southerners dug into their plates, uncouth as the dogs which wandered the chamber stealing scraps from the floor and gnawing on discarded bones. She delicately sipped at her goblet, the too sweet honey wine overpowering on her lips, as she counted down the seconds until she could flee back to her private quarters.

"How are you liking the wine?"

Slowly, Juniper put the glass down and glanced to her left. A Southern woman with dark brown hair and bright hazel eyes had slid into the seat next to her while she had been picking at her food. The newcomer wore a deep maroon dress with a golden lining and a brooch pinning it at her shoulder. The pin showed the profile of a stag with a large rack of antlers, its head raised as if in mid call. Her only other jewelry was a simple pendant engraved with the Roth's blood red bear. She stared at Juniper evenly, her gaze probing yet strangely approachable.

"It's a bit sweet for my liking, to be honest." Juniper ventured, trying to gauge the woman's intent. She was careful to chew through each word of Herron, as the language felt thicker than the fatty meat in her mouth.

The newcomer laughed, a musical sound which flowed from her easily. She held up her own glass, "Yes, well, we here in the South are not quite the vintners you in the Oarenhiem Empire are. But we do try our damnedest. Perhaps we can tap a barrel of your native spirits if you're in need of a taste of home?"

"No, no, that's quite alright." Juniper gave a thin smile, "I believe I can manage. Excuse my ignorance but, do I know you?"

"Oh forgive me, I forget myself. I am Valeria Roth, First Lady of the Longstrider Clan." She gave a perfunctory bob of the head to imitate the Imperial standard bow, then held out her hand with a twinkle in her eye.

Juniper took it and let the pieces fall into place, "You're the daughter of the Lord Baron?"

"And the wife of Damien Longstrider," she smiled knowingly, "but I want to know about you! You're the arcanist from Khanar?"

Juniper nodded. The revelation of who she was speaking to slowly began to lend itself to her observations. She was relaxed, leaning easily in the large chair with a wineglass held loosely in her hand, yet she had about her a sense of confidence. She did not display herself and turn heads the way some women might, yet she easily held the unspoken attention of everyone around her. The people nearby had moved out of her way, bunching together so as to not jostle her in her chosen seat. Juniper realized she was speaking to perhaps the most important woman in the room, daughter of one of the most powerful men in the Federation and wife to the man who controlled the entire Highlands region of the North.

She straightened up, turning from her food and fully facing the woman, as she put on her most pleasant and political pose, "I am. My name is Juniper Faye, my Lady."

Valeria shook her head and gave an offhand wave, "No need for formalities, us ladies should speak plainly with each other at least. We have so much to keep up with just managing the menfolk, wouldn't you agree?"

"If you say so, Valeria." Juniper struggled to make it sound natural as she tried to imitate the noblewoman's casual demeanor, "I heard you had just arrived some days ago?"

"Yes," she sighed and lifted her glass to her mouth for a long drink. She gave Juniper a look before continuing, "quite the journey, with this heat. Then there is this business with my damned brother. I should've just stayed in the North; there I would've had my comfy library, my own bed *and* there would've been a great deal less family drama to deal with."

Juniper glanced up to the head table. The Lord Baron was belting out a great belly laugh, an imposing figure with a mane of dark hair in a great furred cloak, looking for all purposes much like the beast that his sigil bore. To his left, his younger son, a well dressed sort who looked like he may have stepped out of a salon moments ago, was laughing as well. There was an old, heavily bearded man in gray who tittered politely one seat further down. To the Baron's right, the older son, powerfully built and looking uncomfortable in his fine evening wear, slouched in his seat as he sullenly stabbed at his food. A striking young woman with strawberry blond hair sat next to him, attempting to speak to the Prince in a sort of halting, awkward manner.

"I had heard rumors..." she ventured, testing the waters.

The Lady of the Longstrider Clan snorted in a way which was distinctly unbecoming of a woman of her station, "I'm sure you have. The whole city is buzzing about it like a hive of angry hornets. But my brother has dug his own pit and now he'll just have to lay in it. I just pray he's not stupid enough to fight this union I've worked so hard to set up with my dear, sweet sister-in-law."

Juniper blinked, "*You* set up the marriage?"

Valeria flashed a quick smirk, "Of course. My father, may the Gods love him, is a war hero and a leader of men and other such things, but he's got no mind for politics. My mother was the real brains of the Horn before she returned her bones to the earth, may the Grandfather have mercy on her soul."

The noblewoman made a quick double tap on her chest with her fingers and bowed her head. Juniper inclined her head as well, purely out of respect. The Faiths of these Southerners was worse than superstitions, but Juniper was not about to start a religious debate. Valeria continued, "When she passed on, I was the one who took up the reins of ensuring our future. I set up my own union with Damien, you know."

Juniper glanced over to the head table. Further down from the Baron's right, a tall, handsome man with blonde hair and a well kept beard was standing and waving his hands as he regaled those around him with some apparently highly entertaining story. His brilliant smile flashed in the amber light as he held out his arms wide to indicate the size of something, his muscles straining against the cloth of his shirt.

"Quite the sacrifice, I would say." Juniper ventured a sideways glance at her companion.

Valeria feigned a look of shock, then put on a regal veneer as she lifted her chin, "Any truly noble Lady thinks only of the good of her lands and her people."

Both women laughed at that. After a moment of recovery, Valeria continued, "I confess, I am very excited to see your performance tonight. I know my boys are as well." She again indicated the high table. Two small boys with mops of red hair and tan skin were seated at the end of the table fighting over a cake. "They have been talking about it for weeks. When the Emperor of Oarenhiem sends a personal envoy, everyone tends to take notice."

"I would be, if I were you." Juniper gave the other woman a subtle smile, hoping the light caught her eyes in that way that made them shimmer. Valeria raised one eyebrow. The Oaren woman shrugged, "I'm not called the Emerald of the Empire for no reason."

"Well," Valeria began, a small smile creeping across her face, "I suppose we are in for quite the show then."

The Banquet Room was darkened, witchlights dimmed for the performance, silent but for the crackling of the fire and the muffled sounds of distant celebration from outside. Juniper stood before the hearth, her narrow frame silhouetted against the orange glow from the low burning embers. Every eye in the room was upon her. She breathed deeply, blocking out the sounds of the hall, the smell of the food, pushing all thoughts out into the void. Going to the place in her mind she always did when she began a performance, she opened the white wooden door with a gold knocker the shape of a butterfly.

Inside, a child's room was laid out before her. There was a small bed painted white with pink sheets, a matching dresser with a mountain of woven animal dolls piled upon it and a window which seemed to show only an empty, endless white beyond. An ornate mural showing a field of flowers with an Oaren Skyship sailing above was painted against the far wall, a marvelous piece which was more suited to a palace's halls than a child's bedroom. She turned away from these things and approached the simple desk which stood in the corner. On shelves above the desk, paints and pens of every color sat corralled in cups along with brushes and chalks and thin razors alongside piles of paper and books. Juniper took a breath, sat at the desk and began to create.

A collective gasp rippled across the crowd as the first point of light appeared out of nowhere in the air, sparkling to life a few feet in front of the foreign woman. It flew out over them like a snake stretching into the air, all the way across the Banquet Room. Then it began to fan out and sprout thin tendrils which grew and expanded of their own accord. The light changed colors and shapes and seemed to solidify as it took forms; the trunk of a tree sprouted up in the center of the room, rising towards the ceiling and stretching out branches into every direction. Leaves unfurled and flowers of an innumerable variety sprouted from the branches. Their sweet scent filled the air and drew sounds of wonder as the crowd reached out and ran their hands through the roots and branches of the tree.

Suddenly, small forest creatures began to appear and scamper around the base of the tree and through its twisting canopy. Children squealed with laughter and tried to catch them as the apparitions darted around the hall, passing through their hands like smoke or mist of the water. Then the tree and creatures began to melt away, the light moving towards the ceiling. It changed hues and adopted new colors as it reformed into a great amalgamation of swirling light above them. Then it burst and it appeared as if there was no ceiling in the hall, only the open night sky. More gasps arose as millions of twinkling stars took shape and a great silver moon hung in the center of the chamber, the feeling of warm summer wind blowing on all the gaping faces.

Juniper was smiling now, her brow furrowed in concentration, her eyes still shut. She was weaving her hands before her in a showy pattern, but the real work was being done in her mind. She drew lines and patterns, traced shapes, splashed color across the pages only she could see. As the night sky faded, a warm rain pattered down over the party, many women screeching as they attempted to shield themselves from the phantom weather.

The rain stopped and grass bloomed on the ground, warmth washing over the chamber again as the sun rose in the distance. Then a shape appeared. It was indistinct at first, a blurry shape lost in the sun. But it grew rapidly, developing into a dread specter with a long body covered in scales, four bat like wings beating on the nonexistent wind, fangs and curved claws like great scythes that carved through the air with horrifying promise.

A woman screamed. Children whimpered and clutched their mothers, burying their faces in their dresses. A few men stood and put their hands to their weapons instinctively. Before anyone could do anything further, the terrible creature was upon them, passing through the crowd with an open jaw and a roar which shook the patrons to their bones. The great beast made a pass, moving over them to the far side of the chamber and began to shrink as it seemed to grow further away in the air at the end of the Banquet Room.

The lights coagulated in the center of the room, building into the vague shape of a figure. Then is coalesced into a regal looking Southern man with dark hair, dressed all in gleaming armor carrying a greatsword. A sigil spread across the cloak on his back, a golden eagle defiantly emblazoned on a scarlet field trimmed in white.

"It's Leon!" Some of the partygoers whispered, "It's Leon Asallar!"

Beside the man in armor, a second form took shape. Another man, a handsome Oaren with his hair pulled into a warrior's tail, dressed in dark leathers carrying a spear which ended in a long, thin blade, appeared beside the first.

More whispers rippled through the crowd. The name Seil was murmured around the room, some less than friendly. The scaled monstrosity had wheeled in the distance and was advancing rapidly on the two figures. They took up fighting positions, the Oaren holding the spear overhead. As the creature dived at the two men, eating up the distance between them as it passed through patrons and tables and platters of food, the golden skinned man let loose a cry and heaved his spear through the air. It flew true, finding purchase in the creature's wing joint. It roared in pain and crashed into the invisible ground, skidding towards the men almost as fast as it had been flying.

The armored Southerner deftly moved to the side as it slid through the middle of them, singing his sword in a low arch, removing a wing on the creature's other side in a single slice of his blade. The people in the chamber cheered as the two men advanced on the creature, which was struggling to stand from where it had finally crashed into a pile. It swiped out with a great claw but the Southerner caught it with his blade and the Oaren impaled the claw with a thin, single edged sword he had pulled from his belt. The golden skinned man took a moment to free his sword and advanced on the monster, raising his weapon dramatically before sinking it into the creature's scaled hide. Cheers erupted from the hall, shaking the rafters of the ancient fortress.

The creature gave a final roar before the light composing its body and the bodies of the two men dissipated into a dazzling display of multicolored bubbles which flew through the room in a wild careening flood. The lights spun rapidly around the mesmerized onlookers, weaving in and out of the crowd, under and over tables, around goblets and over plates of food, all soaring through the air until they swarmed into swirling clouds above the foreigner who stood before the fireplace. She held up her hand and they all descended into her outstretched palm, disappearing one by one until the last one blinked out of existence. When it was gone, the gentle amber of the witchlights began to grow brighter, bringing her crowd's faces back into focus. Juniper gave one last look around the room, her brow soaked in a sheen of sweat, her breath rapid and shallow, and gave a perfectly practiced bow to the crowd.

Juniper felt the familiar tingle of satisfaction as the crowd exploded into a near hysterical frenzy of applause and cheers. The adulation was unmatched by anything heard in that hall previously, even the introduction of the Baron himself had not brought such a frenzy to the crowd of the festival goers. Juniper raised her head, stood up with her chin raised, her face a picture of practiced poise, and flashed her perfect teeth as she let them shower her with well deserved praise.

"Well, that *was* something!" A familiar voice said behind her.

Juniper turned to see Valeria, still loosely cradling her cup in one hand, standing in the hallway. They were in an antechamber just outside the Banquet Room, the noise of the crowd only partially muffled as they were barely beginning to settle down from the performance. Juniper had stepped out to compose herself after allowing the assembled masses bathe her in their adulation for a lengthy series of applause and calls for encores, all of which she had firmly rejected.

She felt weak, light headed. The performance had taken everything she had, then perhaps a bit more. She leaned against an archway, a damp rag pressed against her forehead. The Lady of the Highlands approached her, a look of concern flashing across her face.

"Are you alright?" She asked, seeming genuine in her concern, "Can we get you something?"

Juniper shook her head, "No, it's only a bit of the spins. The performance is...taxing, you might say. I just need a moment to relax."

Valeria nodded. She held out her arm, "May I escort you to your quarters then? Perhaps you might lay down, rejoin the party when you're feeling up to it?"

Juniper nodded and took the noblewoman's arm. She was a good bit taller than her and Juniper felt it was almost like being pulled along by a man given her tight grasp and strong hands. They walked in silence through the red halls, past more of the regrettable decorations, simply listening to the sounds of revelry in the night. When Valeria spoke, it was in a soft, nurturing tone which seemed to suggest a certain familiarity despite the women only having met earlier this very evening.

"We don't get many visitors from the Empire here, you know," she began pleasantly, "mostly merchants and traders and mercenaries. I was very excited to speak with an official envoy, and a representative from the High Conservatory no less."

Juniper tried to sift through her pleasantries and understand why this powerful woman was so keen to speak with a glorified entertainer, "Yes, I was... honored to be trusted with the task."

Valeria gave her a look which was painfully skeptical, "What did we say about being honest, my friend? I know many in the Empire have a...less than favorable view of those of us in the Southlands. We are all mud farmers and horse humpers, I believe they say in your nation?"

Juniper nearly choked as she strove to suppress a yelp at the harsh language. She shook her head quickly and stumbled as she tried to respond, "Oh...of course not, my Lady...erm, Valeria...we don't think..."

The noblewoman gently cut her off, "It's alright, I'm not accusing *you* of anything, Juniper. Simply stating the facts. There has been a history of conflict and bad blood between our peoples for generations. I would venture to say since the First

Southlands War, although truth be told, our Federation *was* first birthed out of that conflict."

Juniper said nothing. She was still struggling to catch up, her mind moving too slowly, like she was underwater and trying to break through to the surface.

"But that is all in the past, at least, I'd like to think so. Progress means building bridges into the future, focusing on the positives, like your performance there. It was good to remind the crowd of one of the few times our two great nations worked together, even if there was some embellishment." She cast a sly look at the young woman on her arm, "Or perhaps I remember my history wrong and Prince Leon and Emperor Seil did not bring one hundred of their finest men *each* to bring down the dragon of Cutter's Isle?"

"There may have been some...creative liberties." Juniper shrugged.

Valeria laughed, her musical voice echoing in the halls and coming back to them like a distant ethereal song, "History is written by the victors, I suppose, and that beast isn't going to complain now is he?"

The two women began climbing a staircase, slowly moving around the corners at a relaxed pace. Juniper was beginning to feel better, but she was still feeling like she was missing something.

"You are, if I understand correctly, the daughter of one Oaren's noble families? One of the oldest, or so I've heard."

"My father is Chancellor Cristos Faye, he is the Head of the Emperor's Justice. My mother is Aria Faye, Dean of the College of Illuminators at the High Conservatory." She answered proudly, trying to straighten up a bit. The motion immediately seemed ridiculous to her, walking next to the woman who stood nearly a whole head taller than her.

Valeria seemed to take no notice of her indiscretion and smiled warmly at her, "That is quite a lineage. I often find the weight of such nobility can be a terrible burden. Do you find it difficult to carry such lineage?"

Juniper blinked and brushed the short hair back from her face over her ear. The question had never occurred to her before. She was unsure of how to respond.

Valeria seemed to read her mind, "You know, I was always trying to be like my mother when she was still with us. So calm, so collected. She held this family together. Now that she's gone, I find myself trying to fill her shoes, in a manner of speaking. I worry about the future, my father and, of course, about my brothers..."

The Lady trailed off. She paused, then gave Juniper a conspiratorial look, "You know, neither of my brothers has much of a mind for politics. Cassius is far too hot headed, too impulsive...and Julius, well, he's quite content to be left to his own devices."

Juniper was at a loss for words. The daughter of the Baron spoke to her as two childhood friends might, like girls giggling over boys at the festival ground. She was all smiles and sly looks and thoughtful questions. She inclined her head as if a thought had just occurred to her, "I am to make a trip to Oaren at summer's end. A political matter, boring as usual, I'll have my boys and my husband of course. But I have never been to the Empire. It would be nice to have a friendly face to call on in an unfamiliar place. After all, us women must stick together?"

Juniper was still unsure of how to respond as they approached the door to her room, a large suite in one of the towers not far from the Western wall. Valeria let go of Juniper's arm but then took her hands in her own the way a close friend might, eyes sparkling with excitement, "I have a grand idea! I'll invite you to the garden party with the Royal Family tomorrow. You'll be my guest of honor. You can meet my husband, children, and sister-in-law, and, of course, my brothers and father."

She gave Juniper's hands the slightest of squeezes and a big smile, "It's settled then, I'll see you tomorrow?"

The woman nodded her head in shock as she managed to mumble, "Of course, my Lady, erm, Valeria. It would be my honor."

"Wonderful!" With a last lingering look, she was gone in a swirl of red cloth before Juniper could process what had actually happened.

As she slid the door to her room shut behind her, Juniper shook herself and tried to collect her thoughts. The woman had been so disarming, so utterly straightforward. It was unlike anything she had ever experienced in the courts of Khanar. It was somehow unsettling, like the Lady of the Horn was able to see straight through her, to see the deepest secrets hidden away inside. Juniper decided she did not like the feeling. Besides, she had far more pressing matters she needed to focus on. The slender woman gave herself a last shake to try and bring herself back to the present. Then she took a deep breath, smoothed the front of her immaculate dress and locked the door to her chamber before striding across the large room.

She knelt down before a large traveling trunk of well oiled black leather with great golden buckles which sat near the foot of her bed. She undid the buckles and lifted the top, revealing a gold stained, wooden interior with an array of richly colored, fine clothing, several ornate jewelry pieces and a wealth of fancy shoes. She pulled a pile of clothes out and gently set them on the bed, careful not to wrinkle the perfectly folded fabric. Reaching her thin fingers down, she ran them along the inside edge of the case until she found the small bump then pressed it down. There was a soft click and a door opened up on the inside wall, revealing a hidden compartment. Inside was a large silver coin, a black bag, and a small, rolled up scroll tied off with a piece of string.

Juniper pulled the contents out and stood up, making her way over to the bed. She placed the scroll and the bag on the sheets, then turned the coin over in her hand. The coin was silver, emblazoned with a blade wreathed in fire on one side and a bold Herron symbol for the letter "B" inscribed twice on the other. She held it tight to her chest and focused on it, closing her eyes. When she opened them, a man in a fine gray suit with long dark hair and a pointed beard stood before her. He appeared faint, like a mist over the mountains in the early morning. The figure flickered slightly as Juniper took a deep breath and folded her arms.

"Are you ready to begin?" The figure asked, his voice warbly and indistinct, as though it was coming from the other side of a wall. His gaze was casual but there was an intensity behind his voice.

Juniper nodded. She glanced at the door as she said, "You're sure this will work?"

The figure sneered and waved a dismissive hand, "Of course. Don't worry, we don't make mistakes."

Juniper snorted, "Easy for you to say. I'm the one putting my hand over the fire."

"Better move quickly then," the figure gave an irritating smirk as it began to fade, "wouldn't want to get burned, after all."

With that, he was gone. Juniper huffed and shoved the coin into her dress. She turned back to the bed and snatched up the scroll, tearing the string off it. There was a series of spidery lines and symbols inked on the page, perfectly placed in an intricate interlocking design. She held the scroll in one hand while grasping the pouch in the other, frowning as she looked between the two. Finally, she sat on the ground cross legged and turned the pouch over, letting the contents spill out onto the floor. It was a fine, crystalline dust which shone in the witchlight like millions of tiny diamonds.

Once every last grain was out of the bag, Juniper tossed the bag away and held the paper in her lap. She took one last, long breath and closed her eyes. She began to block out the distant noises of the festival, still filtering through the window. She quieted the snapping and crackle of the fire in its hearth, letting every sense of the room fade away. Even the feeling of the hard stone floor on her rear end was muted as she let her consciousness float down towards the same deep place she went during her performance. In her childhood bedroom, she slowly began to draw.

Juniper could feel the magic begin to filter in from the space around her. The cold, solid energy stagnant for so long in the stones of the fortress, the force from the crowds which flowed through the city like waves off a tumultuous storm, the untethered energy which flowed through the very air itself. It all seeped from her surroundings and began to fill the well inside her. The well filled and began to run over as she tried to hold the flood in with her frail defenses. After a few minutes, she opened her eyes. The energy pulsed inside her like a second, far more powerful heartbeat, throbbing through every fiber of her body.

She felt the familiar warmth begin to build as she started to sweat, the pressure behind her eyes and in her ears building rapidly as she started to get the tingling sensation of a migraine. She looked down at the scroll in her lap, her vision already beginning to blur. She muttered and focused on the design, ensuring she kept the end goal in mind as she funneled the energy into the spell. There was suddenly a point of light before her, a swirling ball of brilliant white suspended in space above the pile of dust. She continued to mutter as she struggled to control it, the stored energy flowing out of her and into the ball of light like a torrent of water emptying from a punctured rain barrel. The ball grew and began pulling the dust in, grains floating upwards and disappearing into it.

Juniper could feel the last bits of reserved energy she had built up being pulled out of her and being consumed by the light. She felt cold as the extra heat was suddenly gone. Then with horror, she understood that it was not enough. The spell began to pull on her own energy, her life force. She shook as she struggled against it, a sheen of sweat covering her entire body. She threw out her tendrils of will in every direction, desperate

as she reached out to pull energy from anywhere she could tap
into it.

The stones beneath her cracked. The witchlights dimmed
and went out, leaving empty, darkened stones embedded in the
walls. The fire was extinguished and the logs dissolved in an
instant into a pile of ash. The air in the room became icy cold
and frost covered the walls and floors. Juniper gritted her teeth
as the last wisps of heat were pulled from her body. She noticed
her skin was blue tinted and the sweat had frozen, stuck to her
in little rivulets that broke off and shattered on the stone as she
fought for her life. She felt beyond tired, beyond exhausted. The
vitality was being siphoned from her very bones, like she was
being bled dry and left empty.

Then, as suddenly as it had started, it was over. The paper
before her and the pile of crystalline dust was gone. A slowly ro-
tating ball of smooth, gently pulsing white light remained. The
warmth began to return to the room as the witchlights flickered
back to life, dim bulbs winking back into existence. Without
having to look into a mirror, Juniper knew how she must have
looked, her cheeks hollow and eyes sunken like an invalid that
was overdue for death. She breathed in ragged breaths and felt
the air warm her freezing insides. She could not stop shaking as
she stared at the orb.

"*Bastard...*" She hissed between gritted teeth. She forced herself to take several more difficult breaths. Her fingers trembled
as she brushed the dark hair back over her ears. Then she pulled
the silver coin out of her dress and closed her fist around it. It
warmed in her palm, a slight comfort in her current state. She
held it up to her face and growled into it, "It's done."

With that, she dropped the coin from her weakened hand
and it rolled across the floor, coming to rest near the fireplace.
Then she fell back, collapsing in a heap on the floor, and let the
darkness overcome her.

CHAPTER FIVE

A WOLF AT THE DOOR

T he sun had finally set after blazing across the sky all day, but the heat remained as the day began to darken. Standing on the edge of a low ridge, sweat beading on his furrowed brow, a lone figure kept watch over the valley of Rothmount. He watched as lights blinked to life in the streets and buildings all across the massive city, the glow of fires dancing in the evening haze as witchlights emitted their steady glow. He thought about how much it reminded him of the reflection of stars in the dark water. Rubbing his hands through his long red hair, he sighed deeply. In this oppressive heat, it was not the first time he had entertained the idea of shaving off his unruly mess of auburn locks and scraggly beard. But he once again pushed the thought from his mind and resolved to instead find some of the loose fitting Southerner clothes to replace his heavy leathers and furs as soon as he was in any city for more than a few hours.

Under his distinctly Northern attire, a complicated web of tattoos showed flames stretching across his left arm and upper back, engulfing a wolf's skull interspersed with bold runes. A second image of a length of thorns and flowers encompassed a feminine hand stretching up his right side. Several scars crisscrossed his torso and back, mapping a history of violence that would be immediately apparent, even if one somehow failed to notice the various wicked looking blades and weapons tucked into his belt and strapped to his person. He dug into one of his belt pouches, pulling a large silver coin emblazoned with the symbol of a blade wreathed in fire.

He turned it over in his hand a few times before grasping it tightly and taking a deep breath. When he opened his eyes, he could see a figure suspended in the air in front of him. It was semi transparent, ethereal, as one imagined a spirit from the old stories might appear. The lean figure wore a fine gray suit and darkly colored overcoat with silvered buttons. When he spoke his voice was smooth like velvet, "Holton, are you ready?"

Despite Holton knowing the man was not actually there, that this was just a mage's trick, he carefully inspected the figure, eyeing his hands and watching for sudden movements, "We are, just make sure your people do their part."

The figure sneered, "Don't worry. My other agent has already completed her role. You do your part and everything will fall into place. Don't forget, you only have until midnight."

The figure faded and Holton tucked the coin back into his pocket. He turned away from the city and made his way back down the ridge. Below, a group of four more figures waited in the darkness beside their horses. Each was outfitted similarly to Holton, laden with weapons, tattoos, and scars. Two smoked short wood pipes, thin tendrils of blue smoke hanging in the air around them. As Holton made his way down the ridge, they emptied their pipes and began to ready their horses for travel.

"The wagon is stowed back off the road a bit, should be hidden enough. Are we all set to move on the city, Holt?" One of the figures, a woman with strawberry blonde hair and a ragged scar on her chin, asked as she handed him the reins to one of the two horses she held.

Holton nodded. He double checked that his saddle was positioned correctly and that his gear was secured before mounting. He patted his horse on its flank, whispering, "You ready to go, girl?"

The horse tossed its head and stomped and Holton felt the familiar tingle of eager acknowledgment in the back of his mind. He nodded and let it take the lead as he signaled to the group to follow him down the ridge into the darkness of the mountain forest.

I t was late when the group approached the gates to the massive city, the moon nearing its peak before it began its descent. People were scattered about in a haze of revelry, drinking and dancing in small groups around the city's entrance. The sounds of singing and shouting could be heard from inside the walls alongside music and intermittent pops and explosions. The occasional conjured images still streamed through the sky, a burst of color against the sea of stars. A group of guards stood by the gates laughing as they drank from large wooden mugs. They hardly noticed the group of newcomers until they were nearly on top of them.

"Woah, sir!" Called one of the guards, holding his hand up and hastily putting his cup down on a nearby barrel. He moved in front of the horses to stop them and wiped his mouth on the back of his sleeve, "State your business, if you please."

Holton dismounted from his horse, standing nearly a head taller than the guard. He put on a broad smile, "Good evening to you, sir. We are trappers working the Eastern Ridge who had intended to join in the festivities today. However, our work took longer than we thought and it seems we are running late. Hopefully, we haven't missed the whole celebration? I promised my men a good time for all their hard work."

The guard eyed the newcomer. He shot a glance at the other guards, continuing, "Trappers, aye? You said the Eastern Ridge...any luck over there?"

Holton reached back and untied a rope holding a large bundle on the back of his saddle. Underneath he revealed several

large sacks which dripped liquid. Each of the other men's horses
held a similar bundle. The red haired man gave the guard another broad grin, "Oh yes, we've taken four big ones just in the
past two days. We already offloaded the meat. Plan to sell these
hides and the horns in the morning...after we let the ale wear off
a bit, of course."

The guard nodded and grinned back, "I see the Son has indeed smiled upon you. Congratulations on your success. Go
then, enjoy your night."

"Much obliged." Holton gave the guard a nod and remount-
ed his horse. He motioned for the others to follow and they meandered their way into the city. Just before they were swallowed
up by the crowd, the guard called after them, "See to it your men
don't cause any trouble, understand?"

Holton gave a flippant salute over his shoulder and called
back, "We wouldn't dream of it, good sir."

T he group left their horses at a stable near the edge of
the city and began making their way through the outer
ring. They pushed through the throngs who caroused in the
streets. By this time of the night, many of the partier's painted
bodies were smeared from sweat and spilled drinks, their clothes
stained in a strange collage of colors. Young women laughed as
they dashed by in their thin summer dresses, boys chasing them
in their crowns of flowers.

Many people were passed out on street corners and in alleyways, with empty bottles and flagons scattered around them.
The remains of the painted seeds and streamers thrown during
the parades cluttered the gutters and streets and there were
discarded banners and signs lying abandoned all over. Several
empty barrels had been rolled out into the street and had fires
burning in them, casting them in dancing orange light which

complemented the witchlights. To Holton, it felt like he was wandering through the throes of some strange carnival.

The group made its way through the city's outer ring and passed a second set of gates and guards into the inner section. The streets were far less cluttered here and they traded herds of unconscious drunks and burning barrels for well manicured gardens and grand houses. They continued to trudge through the dwindling crowds until they reached the southern outskirts of The Hold. The guards here were more alert, real Legionnaires, not common watchmen. Nearly a dozen armored men standing at attention, swords and axes at the ready and not a drop of drink in sight. Holton directed his crew to duck into an alley where they were all relatively hidden from view.

"That trapper story won't work here, fellas." He began as he pulled his pack off and began rummaging through it, the others following suit, "We're going to need to sell this one."

He pulled out a gray cloak which was far finer than anything else he was wearing, along with a silk over shirt and a few pieces of fake jewelry. Two of the others, the woman and one of the men who sported a scraggly beard and shaved head, were pulling on similarly fine clothing. The last two of the group, one an Oaren with a thin mustache and short cropped hair, the other a Northerner with a long scar above his right eye who was younger than the rest, were keeping watch while they got dressed. Holton grinned at the woman as she grunted and yanked the flowing dress up over her shoulders.

"You look good in a real dress, Erin. First time for everything, eh?"

The woman shot him a ferocious glare, "How about I gut you like a fish, that'd be the first time you saw your entrails, aye, Holt?"

The men snickered and Holton held up his hands defensively. "Didn't mean nothin' by it."

Once the three were finished getting dressed they hurriedly cleaned themselves up, using rags to wipe away the road dust and grime from their faces and combing their hair. They looked each other over, then the group all gathered, squatting near the front of the alley. They had all tucked their tools and weapons discreetly into their clothing, covered their scars and tattoos in finery. For all the world, Holton thought they looked just like three stuck up nobles returning from a night of festivities.

"Alright," he began, shoving his gray cloak around his back and looking at the two large men, "once we're inside Jarryd and Barney will make for the East Gate. You two set everything up, but don't set off a damn thing until we give you the signal, you hear? Too early and it could be the end of all of us. You've got your supplies, Barney?"

The young man with the scar opened his pack and revealed two large bottles of dark liquid. He nodded and grinned. He snapped and a spark erupted from his fingers for the briefest, illuminating his harsh face for a moment, "I got everything I need, boss."

Holton turned to Erin and the man with the shaved head, each cutting a pretty picture in their finery and fake gold and jewels, "Erin, Taron, you two are good to go?"

Taron gave him a smirk, while Erin nodded. He gave each of the crew a quick last look and stood, striding out into the streets with a stiff walk and a look of self-importance plastered across his face. Barney and Jarryd broke away from their group and headed in the opposite direction, quickly melting into the crowded streets. Holton approached the Southern Gate, a massive double set of spiked iron doors, and the officer, a gruff older man whose rank was denoted with a golden brooch on his breastplate, held out his hand to stop them.

"Good evening sir, I must ask, who approaches The Hold at this late hour?" The officer asked in a gruff voice, looking the group of three up and down.

Holton put on a look of mock guilt and sheepishly told the soldier, "I am Chief Farrider's son, Danya Farrider, and these are my friends, Jameson Black Elk and Lillian Lightfoot. We're all guests of the Baron you see, we came down here with his daughter's company the day before last. To be honest, well, we snuck out to the city earlier, during the parades...I know it was a damned fool thing to do, but the party was so dull we were nearly falling asleep in the gardens up there. But we've got to get back now before we're missed."

The officer looked over them again, his suspicions seeming somewhat mollified. He motioned over his shoulder and one of the other guards brought him a scroll. He unrolled it and scanned the page, looking it over carefully.

"Farrider...Black Elk...Lightfoot, looks like you're all on the list." He rolled the scroll back up and handed it back to the man next to him. He thought for a moment and clicked his tongue, "Not very smart of you, running off alone like that. We've got a pretty safe city here, but even in the safest cities there's some unsavory characters. Foreign nobles like yourselves are good marks for bad men, you understand?"

Holton cast his gaze down before letting a small grin slip through, ""Yes, well, luckily it didn't come to that, right Sir?"

"I suppose not." The officer nodded. He motioned and the guards opened the gates, moving aside.

"Thank you, good sir, I'll be sure to mention your name to my father, Sir...?'

"Tanner." He made another motion. Three more of the guards stepped forward and approached them. Tanner gave Holton a crooked grin, "I'll have my men accompany you to your quarters, to ensure you don't lose your way again, my Lord."

Holton's smile faltered for a moment before he recovered and inclined his head, "Thank you, Sir Tanner. We appreciate your assistance, of course."

"Of course."

The group made their way down the hallways of The Hold, their footsteps echoing on the red stone. There were distant noises of the celebration still in full swing somewhere in the fortress, music could be heard interspersed with the muffled voices. While they occasionally passed a small group of stumbling and laughing nobles, for the most part the halls were empty. Holton and his companions followed two of the guards who took the lead while the third trailed behind. His gaze swept the halls, open rooms and darkened nooks, constantly searching, careful, thoughtful.

Both of his companions were shooting nervous glances at each other and stealing looks at the guards. The armored men were speaking in low voices, taking little notice of their charges as they took them to one of the wings of the fortress. They opened a large set of double doors and entered a common room which was decorated with tapestries and animal heads, large leather couches spread out over a furred rug in front of a massive hearth. Two figures hastily stood up from their entanglement on one of the couches, a young man and a woman, each in disarrayed fine evening clothing. The man took a step forward, smoothing the front of his shirt.

"Ah," he tried to put on an air of authority as he raised his chin, still holding his trousers with one hand, "excuse me sirs, what is the meaning of this?"

"Pardon me, my Lord," one of the soldiers began, indicating the group behind him, "we were just escorting these members of your party back to the quarters."

"Our party? I don't know..." The nobleman started, but Holton and his companions were already moving. He grabbed one of the guards from behind and bashed his armored head into the wall twice, sending stone dust and flecks of pebbles flying. Erin had pulled one of her knives out from under her dress and slit the throat of one of the soldiers from behind before he had time to react. Blood ran down the front of his armor as he crumpled to the ground.

Taron wheeled on the third guard, ducked down and threw his weight into the man's legs. They both fell to the ground with a resounding crash. They struggled for a moment as Taron clambered his way up, quickly wrapping his hands around the man's throat. The guard made a sputtering, gurgling noise as he twitched and spasmed on the floor before coming to a stop. The noblewoman screamed. Erin yanked the doors shut as Holton pulled a large, tapered knife from under his cloak and strode across the room towards the two stunned nobles.

"Wait, wait!" The nobleman yelled, putting his hand out to shield his face. He looked around the room wildly for something to defend himself, but Holton was on him in a matter of seconds. He grabbed the man's outstretched hand and dragged it around his back while kicking his knee out from under him. The man collapsed, letting out a yelp of pain and Holton put him on his belly. He held the knife to the man's cheek.

"Either of you two make another noise and I'll gut you like pigs, aye?" He growled.

The man nodded as much as he dared with the knife biting into his cheek. The woman was wide eyed and frozen, she had backed up into a corner and seemed to be trying to push herself through the wall. Erin made her way to the woman, tossing Holton a short length of rope as she passed, and roughly yanked her over to where he was. They proceeded to bind both of the noble's hands, blindfold and gag them, leaving them on their bellies.

"This changes things." She snarled in a low voice.

"It doesn't change anything," Holton replied, matching her tone as he stood and looked around the room. Taron had cracked open the door, and was checking the hallway. He turned and shot Holton a grin and a thumbs up. The red haired man nodded and motioned to his compatriots, "we just need to move quickly. Help me get this lot in that bedroom."

The nobles whimpered pitifully against their gags as they were dragged into the bedroom and closed in the darkness with the three dead guards. Taron locked the door with keys he had taken off one of the guards bodies, then broke the key off in the lock. He grinned as he held out the key stump for them to see.

Erin rolled her eyes, but Holton was already poking his head out and looking down the hallway. It was still empty.

It seemed luck was on their side this night. He whistled and motioned for the other two to follow him. They all took a quick moment, straightened their disguises and made sure to whip the blood from their hands before they all filed into the hall. Taron locked the door behind them and once again broke the key in the door, stuffing the ring of remaining keys in his pocket.

The halls of this giant fortress all looked the same to Holton, nothing but red stone and tapestries winding on forever. After walking for a few moments, he pulled out what looked like a simple bronze compass with a face which curved out like half a glass ball from where he carried it on a leather strap below his shirt. It fit easily in the palm of his hand and it felt warm as if it had been laid in the sun all day.

There were four hands of different colors and lengths which spun freely around the face in all directions. The points of the compass around the edges were simple hash marks with no letters to indicate direction. He waited a moment and all but one locked on a single direction, slightly downward, while the fourth continued to spin lazily. He motioned with his head and they all followed as he made his way along the path indicated by the strange compass, descending staircases and making their way deeper into the fortress.

The group followed the compass deeper and deeper underground, moving into the bowels of the fortress without incident. A few stumbles and loud laughs got them past the few guards they saw during their trek around the stronghold. Eventually they reached a point where they saw no one else. It was dark, dry and deathly silent under The Hold. The great fortress was an unsettling presence above, as though they could feel its malicious weight bearing down, threatening to crush them. Small witchlights were inlaid in the walls and cast dim, amber pools of light in the pitch black hallways.

They moved from pool to pool quickly, unseen terrors imagined down every hallway here in the depths of the earth. They passed large storerooms packed with neatly stacked barrels and boxes or old furniture and carpets. Some held artwork, decorated pots and marble statues, all packed in tightly and covered in a layer of dust. A few rooms looked like abandoned sleeping quarters, previously occupied for unknown reasons. There was occasionally the skittering of tiny nails on the stone, a rat dashing away before the group could get close to them, disappearing into the endless darkness.

"How far down do these tunnels go?" Taron asked, his voice low and gruff, seeming to boom in the silence.

"No one knows for certain." Holton replied, eyes fixed ahead scanning the tunnels, "This place is over a thousand years old, or so they say. They've been digging these tunnels since they built the damn place, so who knows how deep they go for sure?"

"I don't like it down here." Erin whispered, eyes darting around the dim corridor.

Holton nodded. The compass led them around a sharp turn and down yet another set of stairs. Erin whimpered a bit and Taron grumbled, but Holton ignored the growing pit in his stomach and pushed further into the darkness. At the bottom of the stairs they found a small antechamber and a giant reinforced set of metal double doors with hefty bolts which could be sunk into the floor and the walls. There was a small slit in the doorway and a rope which hung down from the top and was run through a hole to the other side. The compass leveled out and all four hands pointed at the metal doors.

Holton gave Erin a quick glance and she nodded. She pulled her evening gown off and jewelry and threw it in a pile on the floor. Underneath she wore her simple traveling clothes. She drew up her hair in a messy bun and tied it off with a length of cloth before rubbing her hands on her shoes and then running them down her cheeks and clothes, leaving her dirty and covered in a thin layer of grime. Taron and Holton took up spots on either side of the giant door and nodded to her.

Erin took a deep breath and reached up, yanking the rope sharply. The sound of a bell could be heard faintly on the other side of the door, clinking in the silence. A few moments passed. Then shuffling footsteps could be heard before the slit in the doorway opened. Dark, heavily lidded eyes peered out at Erin in the gloom.

"Aye?"

Erin cleared her throat and looked at the ground sheepishly as she spoke in a small voice, "I'm here to clean out the privies, good sir."

"It's a little late for that, ain't it girl?" The voice growled suspiciously.

She feigned distress as she bobbed her head, "Yes. Sir, my apologies but I've been so busy with the festival. They've been running me all day. I haven't even eaten yet and I'll surely be working until day break."

The man grunted sympathetically. He slid the peephole shut and the sound of metal sliding against metal could be heard several times. There was a loud thud and grunting as the man struggled with something very heavy. Then there were a few quick clicks and the door creaked open. The man stood there, a guard in an old and rusting set of armor with a graying beard and long greasy hair, with arm extended in a dramatic welcoming gesture.

Erin walked in while the other two held their positions, pressed against the walls trying not to make a noise. On the other side of the door a large circular room spread out in the dim light. A single table sat in the middle of the room with four chairs around it. Three other men in armor sat, a deck of cards, half eaten food and mugs with ale spread across the table between them. They all looked up for a moment when Erin walked into the room, but went back to their cards. There were other doors, four in total, spread out on the opposite side of the circular chamber, each metal and similarly outfitted as the one they had just come through. The greasy haired guard led Erin around the table and went to knock on one of the doors before she suddenly called, "Now!"

Holton and Taron were through the door, weapons bared as they sprinted across the room towards the men who were fumbling to stand and draw their weapons. Erin stabbed the greasy haired guard in the neck, his blood spraying across the wall and door as he crumpled. She wheeled around towards the rest of the guards. It was over in a matter of seconds. Between the three of them, the three remaining men were dispatched with savage efficiency, leaving a scene of carnage in the middle of the room.

Holton wiped blood from his face as he approached the first door. He examined it for a moment, the heavy iron of the bolts all slid firmly into place, three different locks all firmly shut. Taron had found the guard's keys and tossed them across the now bloodied table to him. Holton had the door unlocked quickly, the clinking of metal bolts sliding into place as he turned the three locks and slid the bolts out of their grooves in the walls. He grabbed the large handle of the door and heaved it open with some effort. The damn thing felt like it weighed more than one of the armored guards.

Inside was a tiny, simple call. Circular like the exterior chamber, lit by a single witchlight stone embedded in the ceiling under an iron grate, with a small bed pushed against the far wall, two buckets on one side and a desk with a chair on the other. The only occupant of this cell was standing as far from the door as she could possibly get, pressing herself against the wall at the foot of her bed.

The girl was in her mid teens, pretty with full lips, dark hair and brown skin which identified her as a native of the Horn. She wore a simple gray shirt and pants, no shoes and her hair and skin were remarkably dirty. To Holton, with her darting eyes and rapid breathing, she looked remarkably like many caged animals he had seen in his time. He had to fight the frown that thought brought on as he tried to look as friendly as possible. He stretched his hand out, "Don't be afraid, lass. We're here to rescue you."

She hesitated. Holton reached into his pocket and pulled out the metal coin with the blade emblazoned on it and showed it to her. Her eyes went even wider, which seemed to defy all the rules of nature. He held out his hand again.

"Can't..." she breathed in a small voice as she held out her hands.

Around her wrists were two iron bracelets. They were carved with a series of interlocking designs and seemed to sheen strangely in the magical light. She looked up and Holton followed her gaze. The same design was carved into the ceiling of the cell, around the perimeter and inlaid with iron. He brought his gaze back down and fixed her with the best smile he could manage.

"Oh, never fear, my dear; we have something for that." He rifled through his pockets until he found a leather pouch. From it, he pulled a rod of tarnished silver roughly the size of a key. It had a similar design to the ones on the bracelets and ceiling inlaid in its handle and wrapping down around it to the tip. He gave her a reassuring nod as he approached her, slowly reaching out for her hand with his. She glanced at the rod and put both her hands out.

Holton placed the key between her wrists and felt a slight buzzing twinge through his hand and up his arm. He felt the rod grow very warm, seeming to glow for the briefest of moments. He turned it, as one would turn a key, and the iron bracelets uncoupled themselves and fell to the floor with a loud clang.

The girl jerked her hands back, surprised. She stared at the irons on the floor for a moment, then rubbed her wrists, appearing to have a hard time believing they were gone. Holton started to examine the rough and red skin where they had been secured, but suddenly she was on him. A tight squeeze around his midsection. He almost pulled back before he recognized the hug for what it was. The girl was crying too, a gentle, soft whimper as her tears dampened the front of his nobleman's outfit. He pried her away and bent down so he was face to face with her.

"There's no time for any of that now, ya hear?" He said, gently but firmly, "If we're to get out of here we're going to need to move quickly. Quickly and quietly, understand?"

She nodded and wiped the tears and running snot from her face, leaving streaks through the grime. He led her out of the room and handed her off to Taron. The bearded man did his best to comfort the girl with an awkward pat on the back. Erin was working on the next door already and she beamed at Holton as he approached, "Look at you, big damn hero all of a sudden, aren't you?"

Holton rolled his eyes and started helping her. They repeated the whole process three more times, each time freeing yet another prisoner. The second prisoner was a young man with sandy hair and a birthmark on his cheek, the third was a middle aged Northern woman with raven black hair and a crooked smile, and the fourth was another young girl, this one clearly hailing from Oarenhiem, her golden skin and almond eyes similar to Jarryd. Each was in tears as Holton freed them from their shackles, having to be guided out into the main chamber. They all stared in silence at the dead guardsmen as Taron led them around the table and towards the front gate.

Erin checked the hallway and motioned for everyone to follow. The odd gaggle of children, hardened criminals and one woman made their way back through the dimly lit hallways, weaving around the narrow passages in the oppressive silence. Their footsteps echoed as they all tried their hardest not to make a noise, barely breathing, eyes straining in the dark. As they moved up the various stairs back towards the surface, the air seemed to get lighter with every sub floor they ascended. They gradually began to hear indistinct voices and faint music fluttering in through the walls and the vents. Once they reached the door which would put them back into the fortress proper, Holton held up his hand for them all to wait.

He cracked open the door, scanning the hallway and listening intently. He could not hear anyone close by and so they slithered into the hallway and he led the odd group through the fortress back the way they had come. Everyone was silent. The sounds of the festival were filtering about the halls all around them and in the maze-like fortress the noises made it seem like a guard was lurking around every corner. After what seemed like an eternity, they finally found their way to one of the exterior walls. They followed it back to the southern entrance, where two guards stood at attention, blocking their way out to the grounds. Holton held out his hand and everyone stopped.

He nodded to Taron who pulled a small, smooth black stone, polished mirror bright, with a runic design carved in it. He whispered into it, holding it so close it brushed against the whiskers of his beard. The runes shone for a moment, then the light went out and it was nothing more than a simple, shiny rock again. The group stood there, holding their breath. The children glanced around nervously, huddling together and the older woman put her hands on their shoulders in a motherly manner. No one dared to move a muscle.

Then they heard shouting. It was barely audible at first, blending almost seamlessly with the sounds of the crowds. But eventually it grew louder. The sounds of men screaming, not in celebration as they had before, but in panic as people rushed by the entrance. The two guards looked at each other and then began to move out of the doorway, curious as to what the commotion was. One of them turned to the other and yelled, "Fire! Fire at the Eastern gates!"

The soldiers darted out of the doorway and joined the throngs of people rushing across the grounds. Holton motioned for the others and they followed him to the exit. Outside, the grounds were a madhouse of people yelling and rushing about. The acrid smell of burning hung in the air. A plume of thick, black smoke rose above the eastern wall, churning angrily as it climbed into the night sky. Men and women cried out and soldiers shouted as they called for water and dirt and tried desperately to control the confusion.

Their ragtag group made it across the decorated grounds without attracting so much as an odd look from the distracted revelers and soldiers. They reached the exterior wall and the southern gate where they had first made their entrance. The massive gates were closed, but they were unattended and a small door to the guardhouse had been left ajar. The only guardian left was a massive, brindle hound tied there with a long chain. Its ears laid down flat against its head and it rumbled a long, low warning at the approaching group. Holton held up his hands for the rest of the group to wait and approached the dog. He knelt a hair's breadth from its snarling muzzle.

The creature strained against its chain, seeming almost to bend the metal with its ill intent. But then Holton caught its eye. The hound stared back, its growl rapidly dying in its chest. Its hackles lowered as it sat back and let its tongue loll out to hang out of the side of its mouth. The red haired thief scratched the dog's head, earning a rapid thump of its tail against the earth, and motioned for the rest to follow. The dog watched with curious eyes as Holton shepherded the rest of his group through the door, each pushing themselves as close against the doorway as possible as they passed within snapping distance of the furred guardian.

Holton took one last look at the massive plume of roaring fire and smoke and flashed a vicious grin. Then he followed the others through the guardhouse and out the other side into the city streets, now more chaotic than ever. The group melded into the mass of the festival patrons, blending in without so much as a curious glance.

CHAPTER SIX

CRUCIBLE

D ozens of sounds hit Cassius all at once. Women screaming, men yelling, children crying, a dog barking in the distance. A cacophony of collapsing walls, crashing as wood beams tore apart, the cracking of stone bursting from heat fissures. Over all of it, the roaring torrent of fire berated his ears and muffled everything with its unbridled fury. The smoke around the fortress' grounds was thick and the hot air stung their eyes and burned their lungs as he and several of the other guests from the feast rushed across the courtyard. The smog and dust blocked the eastern wall almost entirely from view, but the column of fire was still visible as it climbed into the sky and belched clouds of writhing black. Wind had carried flames to the banners atop the ramparts and they burned against the smoke darkened sky, quickly being consumed.

Rushing towards the fire, the group from the feast ran directly into an unruly mob of armored soldiers and painted, semi dressed revelers. People were pushing to move in every direction, some trying to move towards the fire, some away. Some carried buckets of water or dirt over their heads as they tried to reach the burning buildings, while others hefted partially burned furniture, clothes or trinkets as they tried to dart through the crowd with their pilfered treasures held tightly to their chests.

When the Prince finally arrived outside of the fortress, he was greeted by a sight that took his breath away. Three large buildings were on fire just outside the gates of The Hold. They had been the majestic homes of noble families earlier that night, multi-leveled with decks above and gardens surrounding. Now, all three glowed red and orange as fire twisted out of their windows and around the roof lines, spurting out of the eaves as it climbed the walls and erupted through the chimneys and upper windows.

The heat was intense. It pushed off the buildings in a steady wave which pricked at the skin like thousands of needles and stung the eyes. Even the trees and bushes which had artfully decorated the grounds around the homes had started to catch as fire seemed to be creeping out in every direction, seeking new places to take hold.

"By the Gods." Cassius cursed under his breath. He took a darting glance around him. Julius was to his left, Jayce to his right, and a small group of nobles and Legionnaires, including his brother-in-law, Damien, were behind him. All stared dumbfounded at the terrifying sight before them. Cassius steeled himself and took hold of Julius by the back of his collar.

"Julius!" He roared over the clamor, "Ring the bells, call the city guard back to The Hold! We need every hand! Water and dirt too, as much as you can get! *Go now!*"

Julius stared at him for a moment, glanced at the fire, then turned and ran back through the crowd, shoving soldiers and common folk out of the way. Cassius immediately wheeled around and grabbed his brother-in-law by both of his large arms, "Take half these men and go around the far side! We have to keep this from spreading! Do whatever you need to do, *don't let it get into any more buildings!*"

Damien nodded quickly, his blonde hair falling into his face as he shook it, "Yes, brother, I will see it done!"

The large Northerner began yelling and bodily grabbing at some of the closest men. He took off, bounding down the street with several members of the crowd following in his wake. The remaining men from the feast looked towards Cassius for some sort of guidance. He turned to Jayce, who was still staring open mouthed at the fire. He grabbed his friend and shook him back to reality.

"Jayce!" He bellowed, his voice already hoarse from sucking in smoke and hot air, "Can you call the rain?!"

Jayce was yanked from his stupor and looked up into the night. Aside from the churning black torrent there were no clouds in sight, just an endless expanse of darkened sky and stars. He shook his head, "I can't conjure clouds from nothing!"

The nobleman swore loudly and looked around. He spotted four men shouting and cursing as they tried to carry a barrel through the crowd towards the fire. He grabbed his friend by the shirt and dragged him through the crowd towards the men, calling for the rest of the crowd of party goers to follow. They reached the men with the barrel and he shouted, "Where'd you get the water?!"

The lead man, an older fellow with a scruffy, graying beard yelled back, "The river!"

"We'll get this to the fire, you take these men and get as much water here as you can!" He motioned to the small crowd around him. The scruffy man nodded without hesitation and waved his arm around his head. The others dropped the barrel and they began to work their way backwards out of the crowd. As the crowd of nobles started to follow, Cassius grabbed the closest Legionnaire by his collar and yelled into his ear, "Get a line going! We need a steady supply of water up here!"

"Yes, my Lord!" The soldier called back and took off after the group as they pushed through the crowd. Cassius turned back to his friend and indicated the barrel.

"Here's your water! Bring it with us!" He ripped the top off the barrel and began to shove his way back towards the fire, "Move! In the name of the Lord Baron, *move!*"

The crowd parted ever so slightly, just enough to let him push his way through. After taking a moment to collect himself, Jayce held out his hands towards the barrel. The signs of strain were obvious on his face as he concentrated, sweat beading up on his forehead as little veins popped out in his neck and besides his eyes. A steady stream of water flowed up into the air through the hole, accumulating into a floating mass in the air. Once the last few drops floated out, the merchant's son motioned and the amorphous cloud of swirling water floated along, following Cassius through the crowd.

As they approached the houses, the heat intensified. Cassius could feel it tearing at his clothes, singing the hairs on his arms and face. He held up an arm to shield his face as he examined the situation. A few men had been throwing buckets of water onto the fire, but it was hardly worth the effort they were putting into it. He turned to Jayce and pointed to the edge of the closest building.

"Can you get that water in there? As close to the side as possible? We need to keep it from spreading to the building next door!"

The young man nodded, sweat shining on the dark skin of his forehead. He moved his hands and the water streamed through the air, through a broken window, and flowed into the room on the far side of the house. There was a great, angry hissing and white steam rose up from the windows. But the fire was dying in that room. Jayce breathed heavily once the water was used up, as he bent over with his hands on his knees. Cassius clasped him on the shoulder and asked, "Are you alright, my friend? Can you keep this up?"

Jayce nodded and grinned up at him, "I'll do what I can."

Just then, the crowd parted and a group of men made their way to the fire as they struggled with another giant barrel of water. They heaved it down on the roadway with a series of groans and turned to run back towards the river. Jayce took a deep breath and stood up. He held out his hands and began focusing on the water again. Cassius nodded to his friend and began to yell to the crowd around him, calling for men to bring shovels and buckets. He grabbed a large spade from one of the gawking bystanders and began to throw loads of dirt through one of the open doorways. Members of the crowd began to come join him and they began the long work of fighting the roaring, spitting inferno.

The fires raged throughout the night and into the early morning. They were able to keep the majority of the flames contained to the three buildings until they collapsed in on themselves as the first streaks of daylight began to filter over the mountains and spill into the valley below. Dozens of men and women sat sprawled out on the ground, covered in ash and mud and dirt, breathing heavily, tools tossed to the side. Cassius sat on a pile of rubble, spade laid across his lap. It was covered in small nicks and the head was dented, the body singed and stained with soot. His hands throbbed with a constant ache and stung from where the skin had split from shoveling. Jayce laid on the burned grass a few feet from him, eyes closed. It was impossible to tell if he was asleep. Julius, his normally coiffed hair plastered to his head with sweat, leaned heavily against a wagon which had brought a dozen barrels of water, now empty, by the roadside.

Dozens more buckets also sat empty, scattered around the chaotic scene. Other men were lying about as well, sleeping or simply sitting in the rubble and staring at the destruction. There were still soldiers and civilians poking through the ruins of the buildings, using tools or spears to sift through the rubble, pouring buckets of water onto still smoldering ashes that had been hidden beneath. A group of women were moving amongst the crowd, handing out loaves of bread and water skins, some tending to those who sported burns or other wounds from the long night. Above the soot stained outer walls of The Hold, the singed and tattered remains of the Roth's standards whipped back and forth in the wind. What was left of the red bears of his family crest were now sat on fields of gray rather than white.

Off key singing came from down the road. A crowd of men covered in ash and dirt was striding up towards the gate, all belting out a loud tune which echoed through the morning air. Damien was in the lead, holding a shovel of his own over one shoulder and leading the chorus with a grin plastered across his dirty face.

"Cas, my brother!" The Northman bellowed, spreading his long arms out wide, "We are victorious!"

Cassius pushed himself to his feet with a great deal of effort. His legs were weaker than a baby foal's, his arms and his back screamed in protest as he made his way over to his brother-in-law. The bulky blonde bruiser beamed at him, "You all did a hell of a job over here, that fire was tamed far faster than any I've ever seen."

"You as well, Damien. But we had Jayce," Cassius jabbed his thumb at his friend on the ground, "and a few other Stormspeakers came to join us in the fight. They were able to get that water where we needed it."

Damien nodded enthusiastically. He looked around and motioned towards the ruined houses, "This is a hell of a thing, isn't it? Three great houses aflame, all at once? Seems a bit...strange."

"It is..." Cassius looked around, eyes narrowed, "I wonder what could've caused..."

Just then, the sounds of pounding feet and clinking metal on the cobblestone cut through the conversation. There were two Legionnaires approaching from the gate in a dreadful rush. They hustled across the street and moved through the loose crowd towards them. Cassius held up his hands.

"Woah there, men! Why such a haste?"

Both soldiers were breathing heavily. One took a few deep breaths and managed to gasp out, "The Lord Baron...he sent us to gather you all. He demands your presence in the Great Hall immediately."

Cassius looked to Damien, then over to Julius, "I suppose I must go. I trust you have this handled...."

"Sorry, no, my Lord," the soldier interrupted, "the Baron had called for all of you."

Damien blinked, "Me as well?"

The man nodded, "Yes, my lord. You, Lord Julius and Master Jayce as well."

Jayce sat up, apparently awake the entire time. Julius looked from the messengers to his brother. Both had puzzled looks on their faces. The Prince shrugged his shoulders.

"I suppose there's nothing for it. Let us see what my father has for us."

T he Great Hall of The Hold was strangely quiet for the size of the crowd gathered there. Every seat around the large table was taken except for the throne at its head, a monstrously large chair carved out of amber stained lumber and inscribed with intricate designs. Dozens of other people were standing or seated around the perimeter of the room. Almost every major lord and lady of the Horn was there, as well as the majority of other attendees from the night before. Jayce's parents sat in one of the corners along with several other notable merchants, all talking in hushed voices. Cassius noted Elon had left his sword behind, but the butt of a short barreled pistol still protruded from his belt. The entire cadre of Northerners Damien had brought with him took up a side of the room on their own, grumbling to each other and looking impatient. Near them, the visiting Imperial performer who had dazzled everyone stood leaning against a wall, nodding silently as Valeria whispered to her.

Damien strode over and put a hand on his sister's shoulder. She leaned into him, seeming to become very tired all of a sudden. He enveloped her in a tight embrace and gave her a kiss on the top of her head. As the morning sun was rising in the sky, light spilled in through the glass dome and began to heat the chamber, which still held the chill from the night before. Cassius looked around the room and noted that every entrance sported at least two grim looking Legionnaires and he glimpsed even more stationed outside the doors to every hallway. He leaned over to Julius and spoke in a low voice.

"Something's afoot," he said, indicating with a nod of his head, "there's far more men on guard than there should be."

Jayce cast a tired gaze around and frowned as he considered, "What would compel every merchant and trader from the Feast to be here as well? Most of them should be eager to move on now that the Festival is over."

The doors slammed open at the far side of the chamber. The whispers died in an instant and utter silence fell over the crowd as Baron Augustus Roth stalked in, still regaled in his dinner wear from the night before. But now his brow was furrowed and his face drawn, his eyes as hard as the rocks of very mountains he ruled over. Cassius immediately saw the rage boiling just below the surface. It reminded him of only a few days before, in this very room, when that same rage had been directed at himself. At the Baron's shoulder, an older, bald man with a matching gray beard and robe scurried along beside him.

As the ruler of the Horn brushed past the assembled nobility and guests he made a motion and the guards shut every door to the chamber, the loud thuds echoing in the silent room. He yanked the massive throne away, nearly sending it crashing over as it slid across the stone. He leaned over and placed his two fists upon the table, scarred knuckles digging into the hardwood as he glowered around the room. The gray bearded man stood a few feet behind him, rubbing his hands over one another as he cast worried looks at his lord. The Baron's dark eyes scanned every member of the crowd one by one, probing, hunting, as he spoke.

"It seems," he began, rumbling in a voice which dripped with undisguised menace, "that we have had a burglary."

Shocked whispers passed through the people, a few scattered gasps and wide eyes were cast about. The large man banged his fist onto the table and brought the room to silence again without a word. Every eye was upon him as he continued.

"Last night, during the feast, it seems someone was able to worm their way into the halls of our ancestral home, past our guards and our defenses. They presented themselves as wayward members of the Northlander party..."

Every set of eyes glanced over towards the group of Northerners that were standing apart on one side of the room. Valeria looked up at her husband, who made a comforting gesture with his hand. He moved to speak but Augustus continued.

"...under that guise, they were escorted to the Interior Eastern Tower, where Valeria's party was being accommodated. Once there, they murdered their escorts and proceeded to our catacombs. They gained access to one of our...lesser known holding cells, broke the prisoners free and were gone before we were aware of their presence. It would appear that the fire some of you spent the night fighting was intended as a veil to cover their escape. A ruse which has worked quite well, as we have not a single lead on where these thieves have disappeared to."

For a moment, no one spoke. Then, a few hushed voices begin to whisper to each other. The whispers gave way to angry muttering as accusations were thrown and people began to point at each other and gesture wildly. A few voices became a flood of angry calls and jeers. The noise grew and grew until the chamber was a storm of shouting and curses. People were on their feet, hands on the hilts of their weapons as Northerners yelled at Southlanders, nobles yelled at merchants, soldiers and retainers squabbled with bureaucrats and politicians. Through all this, the Baron stood, silently watching, his dark eyes piercing like flecks of iron ore glinting in the morning light. Julius leaned over to his brother.

"What is he doing? This isn't going to solve anything."

Cassius shook his head, "He isn't trying to solve anything. He's sweating them. A traitor would plan to be gone by now, but father hopes he's trapped him in here, with everyone else. If there's one amongst our guests, he's shaking in his britches right now."

It was Damien's booming voice that cut through the crowd, "My Lord Baron! We are missing two of our number, Jordaine Westwind and Roger Rhoads. Do you know what's become of them?"

The Baron cast his harsh gaze at his son-in-law, "Your vassals were found with the dead guards. They are being kept in our custody, until such time as we can be sure they were not involved in this crime."

It took a moment for that sink in, the proverbial wheels practically visible as they turned in the big Northerner's head. Cassius could see Valeria was far quicker. The red was rising in her cheeks and she cut her husband off just as he was beginning to raise a hand to object.

"Father," she growled, her gaze turning flinty in an instant, "surely you are not accusing your own daughter's family of conspiring against you?"

The imposing man held his daughter's gaze. Everyone in the room held their breath. But it was the Baron who spoke first.

"No, I am not accusing you. But do you believe it is impossible for any of yours to be turned against you? Are you so confident in your people?"

Valeria held his gaze but the intensity of her glare faltered. She tried to hide it as she plowed on, "We have *every* confidence in our number, none would betray us, or you. Tell me, what led you to suspect they might be involved?"

"They were the only survivors that met these intruders face to face." He replied, voice flat, turning his gaze slightly to face

Damien and the other Northerners, "Why would these ruthless thieves spare two nobles when they had no qualms about breaking into our stronghold and killing seven of our Legionnaires?"

Again, it took time for Damien to turn this information over in his mind. Several of his clan members grumbled around him, whispering into his ears and making urgent motions. He silenced them with a motion and spoke, choosing his words carefully, "My Lord...I do not pretend to know the ill intentions of villains such as these. Perhaps, they sought to lessen the punishment in case they were caught. Or, they may have hoped the confusion their mercy would sow would set us against each other. Whatever the cause, I see no reason to assume my people's guilt and I will personally vouch for their character."

The Lord of the Horn considered his son-in-law and daughter, still silently seething, but gave the barest of nods, "We will release them into your custody, *after* we are done questioning them. Besides, there is a greater issue at hand here. Namely the fact that these thieves knew of these cells' existence at all *and* knew enough about the prisoners they contained to free them is terribly concerning. Moreover, they were able to impersonate three of your people, move through this fortress, murder guards and escape without setting off any of our wards or guards. I was led to believe that was impossible, or am I mistaken, Breyer?"

The bearded man snapped to attention and hurried up to the large table. He quickly adjusted his robes and nervously combed his fingers through his beard, "Um, yes, my Lord, you are correct. It should be, erm, quite impossible."

"Enlighten us, if you please." The Baron swept his arm around the room.

He blinked, rubbing his wrinkled hands together, "Yes, of course, my Lord. You see, The Hold has many defenses both, erm, physical but also magical. Every layer of defenses, every wall, gate, and tower, is inlaid with ancient spellwork. A most, erm, formidable enchantment that permeates the very stones and mortar of this place. Yes indeed, it is warded against magical attacks of every kind; it will not allow one to pass through the thresholds while under any mystical guise, it protects those inside from having their mind entered against their will, as well as many other things. It's defenses extend to the catacombs and the cells. If any of those defenses were breached, The Hold will alert the Master Arcanist, that is to say, me and several others including yourself, Lord Baron, and Lord Commander Viggo. It would also have activated several quite comprehensive... countermeasures. A most masterful work of spellcraft, if I do say so, and a crowning achievement in the history of the University."

"And yet, someone was able to bypass all those defenses and slip in right under your nose?" Valeria asked. Cassius could hear the barely hidden venom behind each syllable as it was spit out of his sister's mouth.

"Well...not exactly..." The old man looked indignant as he rolled up his sleeve. On his wrist, he sported a bronze circlet which appeared as interlocking cords holding a large, clear stone. He held it up for her and the room to see, "This is the Keystone, it, erm, connects me to The Hold. If someone so much as conjures a flame within the walls of this fortress I am made aware of it. If one prods the defenses it pulls at me like, um...like the undercurrent of a great ocean. Why, during the Oaren woman's performance last night it was buzzing like a hive of angry hornets!"

He shook the artifact in the air for emphasis. But then, slowly, a look of bewilderment spread across his face. He touched it gingerly, frustration furrowing his brow, "Alas, somehow someone has found a way around our great defenses. The Keystone did not alert me to any intrusion last night, nor did it register the magic being wielded by Master Jayce or the other, erm, weather witches outside the Gates. That is how we first knew something was wrong."

Another collective wave of muttering swept the crowd. Cassius noted that Jayce took in a sharp breath at the words of the

Master Arcanist. Augustus gave the old man a withering glare, "What could have caused this, Master Breyer?"

"We cannot know for sure..." He looked around, eyes unfocused as he searched for the answer, "But I would guess, my Lord, that someone managed to dampen The Hold's defenses for a time. A most crafty saboteur, it would appear."

"How is that possible?" Cassius called out.

"A very complex and difficult spell I imagine, erm, my Lord." He scrunched up his nose as he thought, "You see, magic acts...much like water, it can exist in several forms. The Hold stores magic within its very walls to power its defenses and its reserves are quite massive. But this saboteur must've created a sort of...lock. That is why the Keystone was silent. Its magic was frozen in its state, unable to be used."

"Who could do something like that?"

"It would take a practitioner of extreme talent. Someone, erm, formally trained and exceptionally gifted." Several dozen eyes followed his gaze towards the yellow skinned woman leaning against the wall. She stood up straight and set her jaw as Augustus turned his steely gaze on his guest of honor.

"Lady Faye, it would seem that your intentions here are being called into question." The large man rumbled in a low voice.

She returned his gaze without flinching, speaking in near perfect Herron despite her harsh Oaren accent that was all splinters and broken glass on the ears, "I am an Illuminator, Lord Baron, here at the personal behest of the Emperor. I have no cause to sabotage you, your fortress, nor aid in the escape of your prisoners."

"Be that as it may, there is little doubt you are one of the few present who could have done so. Have her quarters been searched?" He called over his shoulder. One of the soldiers at his rear stepped forward.

"They have my Lord." The guard motioned and the doors to the rear of the chamber were opened. Two more Legionnaires entered carrying a large leather bound traveling chest between them. They hefted it onto the table and popped it open, revealing the contents to the chamber. Fine ladies clothing of soft fabrics and vibrant colors sat with a collection of expensive looking jewelry and a good number of shoes. The Baron motioned for the old man and he began to dig through the trunk, pulling out clothes in bundles and laying them out on the wood in wrinkled heaps. Cassius saw the Oaren woman bite her lip, silent rage storming just beneath the surface as she fought to keep her composure.

"If you're quite satisfied, *my Lord*," the phrase had all the reverence of someone cursing a snake, "I assure you, my wardrobe does not contain anything malicious."

He glanced at her without speaking and then went back to watching his ancient Arcanist. The old man had emptied the last of the trunk's contents and was sticking his head down into it, feeling around the inside of the box, running his hands over the fine leather. He poked and prodded for a few more moments before sighing, looking up and shaking his head. The Baron motioned for the guards and they began repacking the trunk, attempting to be gentle with the delicate garments but mostly failing in their armored, clumsy hands. After a few moments they closed the lid and hauled the luggage back out of the room the way they had come.

"I apologize for the intrusion, Lady Faye, but I am not yet convinced of the innocence of any party, just yet."

"Had it occurred to you, before raiding the contents of my closet, that perhaps these thieves brought their own sorceress to achieve their ends?" The woman's voice more than bordered on insulting. She spoke slowly, as though to a child.

"It had," the Baron ignored the biting tone, "but I must be diligent and search all the avenues by which we might've been betrayed. Rats this crafty are not so easily rooted from their holes."

The sun had well and truly risen now. The chamber was fully lit as the light streamed in through the glass dome ceiling, bringing with it the heat of the day. Cassius could feel the temperature of the room rising as the warmth of the day and the heat from the mass of bodies chased every last hint of night from the chamber. Several people had begun to fan themselves with hats or their hands while others shifted uncomfortably where they sat.

"Lord Baron," Elon Acosta called out in his clipped Vinatierian drawl, "no disrespect you understand, but it seems you have us fishin' for shadows in the dark waters here. Maybe if we knew somethin' about these prisoners, we might better get to the truth of this matter."

"Yes, father," Cassius spoke up, eyeing the Baron suspiciously, "it seems these scoundrels were informed, prepared and efficient. What sort of prisoners were you keeping that warranted such an organized raid?"

A few voices of agreement spoke up around the room. The large man cast a dark eye towards Valeria. The woman shrugged and something seemed to pass between them, yet Cassius could not say what. Augustus took a deep breath as he surveyed the room.

"Alright. The prisoners were being held for the use of malicious arcanums. Three young people, two girls and a boy, and a woman, the Witch of the White Wood. They were a cabal, a coven. They had been caught red handed by witch hunters and were being kept here, in secret, awaiting transport to Asaldon. They were to stand trial at Uthersanctorum University and be imprisoned at the Sovereign's discretion."

The room immediately exploded into a chorus of loud cries and angry questions. Some voices were on the verge of panic, others fury.

"A witch?!"

"The Woman of the White Wood! You had her here?!"

"How could you let her get away?!"

The voices stopped when the Baron pulled a large, devilish looking blade out his belt and drove it into the table with a resounding thud. Everyone stared at him. Cassius could hear the nervous breathing of those near him as they tried to draw as little attention to themselves as possible.

"My hospitality has been stretched thinner than any time in memory this day. If you presume to berate me within my own halls I would urge you all to *reconsider*." His dark eyes roamed the room, daring those around him for a challenge. None came.

With the doors closed, the chamber continued getting hotter. The air grew muggy, thick with hot breath and sweat as people began to dampen their shirts and robes. A few men had loosened their collars and the women were fanning ever more furiously. The musk that hung in the air was a pungent mix of the smells of bodies that were secreting an excess of alcohol from the night's celebration.

Finally, Cassius spoke up, cutting the silence that hung heavy in the thick air, "Father, uh, my Lord...have we no leads at all? Our witnesses can give no descriptions of their assailants? What about other guards? Surely someone can attest to what these scoundrels look like."

Augustus turned his gaze upon his oldest son, considering the man for a moment. Then he sighed, anger dissipating slightly. When he spoke, it was without the fire he had been breathing across the rest of the room all morning, "Unfortunately, what we have is bare bones. The gate guards and the Northern nobles agree there were three people, two men and a woman. One man was bald, while the woman and the other man had crowns of red hair..."

There was sudden movement amongst the Northerners, whispers and urgent talking. Valeria leaned over and said something in Damien's ear, giving him a look. The large man got a concerned look on his face as he spoke up, "Lord Baron, did any of the witnesses mention tattoos on the red haired man? Flames, on the right arm?"

"Yes, your people mention them." The Baron was frowning. He stared hard from his son-in-law to his daughter, "Do you two know this man?"

Damien nodded grimly, a dark look on his face, "He's an outlaw who has eluded the hangman's noose for years. His name is Holton Hart and he is notorious in the Highlands as well as the rest of the North. Our people call him the Red Wolf."

The words hung in the hot air between them. Valeria interjected, "But for all his cleverness, Hart has only ever been a particularly wily highwayman until recently. Reports indicate he was behind the robbery of the Coldwater Magician's College this past winter. Now this...he seems to be going far beyond anything he's dared before."

"So..." Breyer spoke up, speaking up again, "we can assume he has some sort of help. Someone who, erm, facilitated the bypassing of our defenses, gave them the tools needed to break in and most likely supplied them with the information about the witch and her coven."

"Then the question is," Cassius said to Julius in a low voice, "who would have the knowledge and resources to equip a common criminal to pull off a heist on the most heavily fortified fortress in the world?"

Julius was wide eyed, his voice barely more than a whisper, "More importantly, who would risk the wrath of not just the Horn, but the whole of the Federation?"

CHAPTER SEVEN

FORM & FUNCTION

B y the time the Baron let everyone out of the sweltering hall, Juniper felt like she had sweated out most of the water in her body. Her dress was damp and her skin glistened in the blazing summer sun. Still, she was not sure if the weakness in her legs was due to the loss of water or the nerves that she had barely been able to keep under control. That old relic and the brutish Baron had gotten close, so very close, to the truth. It had been pure luck that the Master Arcanist's ancient hands had missed the latch in her trunk which would have revealed the hidden compartment.

Considering he had deduced exactly how they had bypassed the fortress' security, the discovery of that scroll would have been all he needed to have her locked in irons in the bowels of The Hold. She held her chin up as she kept pace with the thinning crowd that was dispersing down the various hallways moving away from the Great Hall. Eventually, she found herself alone in a long hallway with picture windows looking down onto the lower levels of the fortress. It was lined with simple stone benches which looked anything but inviting, but she collapsed onto the first one like a sack of washing clothes set out to be retrieved by a serving girl.

Her mind was moving so fast she could hardly grasp the thoughts before they were swept away in the cascading current

of chaos. Her chest hurt from how fast her heart was beating. Breath caught in her throat. She struggled as the crushing
sensation grew steadily worse and worse. The walls around her
seemed to be folding in, her vision blurring in the corners. She
squeezed her eyes shut and buried her face in her hands.

In her mind, Juniper desperately sought for the sensation of
the familiar, the exercise she had employed for years to center herself. She remembered the feel of her imported silken
sheets, a ludicrously indulgent luxury, especially for a child. The
cool mountain air blowing over the peaks and roofs of Khanar and through her open windows. The smells of parchment,
fresh paints, pungent inks and dusty chalks filled her nose. She
breathed in through her nose, held it, and exhaled. The swirling
storm in her mind began to slow. She got her breathing under
control and her chest seemed to unclench. She felt the crushing
sensation begin to fade.

It was then that she felt the presence of someone watching
her. She opened her eyes and saw, with a start, that Breyer the
Master Arcanist was standing about ten feet from her, his hands
clasped firmly behind his back under his gray cloak. The grooves
of his craggy face were deepened with a frown that said volumes
as he stared at her. When he spoke, his voice seemed far more
confident than it had within the chamber, when the imposing
figure of the Baron had been bearing down on him.

"I must say, you kept your composure far better than I would
have expected back there. Our Lord Baron can be quite...daunt-
ing, yes?" The old man's gaze held something of amusement in
it, despite the frown on his face.

Juniper stood up, feeling a bit lightheaded at first. She steadied herself and crossed her arms over her chest, "He's a brute you
mean, like all you Southerners, from what I've gathered. Hardly
better than savages, the lot of you."

The arcanist inclined his head, "We might not be quite as,
erm, refined as you in the Empire, my Lady. However, you

might do well not to be dismissive of those who have thrice routed your ancestor's attempts at invasion."

Breyer unclasped his hands and brought them around in front of him laid out, palms up, for Juniper to see. There was nothing in them, but for a few calluses and scars. But then he turned his left hand over, closed it, and turned it back again. When he opened it, there was the scroll, bound in the piece of twine, just as she had repacked it in her trunk the night before. Juniper's breath caught in her throat once again as she stared at it. She forced her gaze to meet the old man's impassive eyes as she croaked, "What do you want?"

He snorted, "Don't be daft, child. I had you dead to rights back in the hall if that, erm, was what I wanted. I *want* you to tell Lawrence that sparing his amateur saboteur fetches me a heftier portion of the take."

The old man tossed the scroll to Juniper who caught in fumbling hands as she was staring at him slack jawed. She quickly stuffed it into her dress and smoothed it out, trying to hide the bulge with little success. The mage looked her up and down, a look that was remarkably close to empathy before it was quickly replaced by his studiously impassive expression.

"Perhaps you should reconsider this line of work, my Lady. You do have quite the gift for showmanship, after all, but *this*, well...it takes a strong stomach." With that, he turned on his heel and strode back down the hall, where a mousy young woman with a messy mop of copper curls waited for him. She flinched as he snapped something at her before falling in step behind him. They disappeared around the corner before Juniper could string a reply together. Just like that, she was alone in the long hallway again, still reeling as she tried to make sense of what had just happened.

The knocking at her door roused her from the uneasy embrace of a fretful slumber. She struggled to untangle herself from the unpleasantly thick sheets, more like something suited to a roadside inn than the bed of a noblewoman, and pushed herself to her feet. The knocking came again as she yanked on a robe and dragged a brush through her dark hair.

"One moment!" She snarled as she looked out the window and determined it was still somewhere in the early afternoon. The events of the morning had left her bewildered and exhausted and she had thought to sleep the rest of the day away. She was not scheduled to leave until the next morning and she had little interest in interacting with these people anymore than she absolutely had to. Once she had a moment to check herself in the mirror, she threw on a robe and strode across the room, yanking open the door without ceremony.

Valeria stood there. She was in a green robe with her hair pulled up in a workingwoman's bun, wearing only the pendant from the night before and no other finery. She gave Juniper a friendly smile, her face the picture of benevolence.

"May I come in, I thought you might need something to re-vitalize after the morning's...events?" She waved a hand behind her. A serving woman was waiting with a small cart which held two glasses and an array of covered platters.

Juniper nodded dumbly and the noblewoman entered, her servant in tow. They sat in the chairs before the fireplace, now cold with only ash piled in the hearth, and the servant laid out a few plates of simple snacks. Fruit, cut up and displayed artfully, dried meats and cheese and more of the flatbread with small jars of some sort of preserves along with two glasses of a nearly clear wine. When the servant had departed, leaving the bottle on a side table, Valeria took a glass and held it up to her, "Oaren Silver, from our special reserves."

Juniper, wrapped tightly in her robe, sipped the wine and felt the familiar crisp taste fill her mouth. She gave a small sigh and smiled, "A lovely vintage."

Valeria looked pleased with herself. She took another sip before plucking a small piece of bread and nibbling on the corner. Her voice was somewhat subdued when she spoke, lacking a bit of its usual confidence, "Juniper, I know this morning was...not ideal. My father is often...a difficult man to deal with. I hope you understand, we hold no ill will towards you."

Juniper blinked. The Lady of the Highlands, Princess of the Horn, was apologizing to her. It was absurd. In the Empire, no one of such a high station would ever dream of demeaning themselves in such a manner. Yet, here she was.

"My Lady, I mean, Valeria...I understand," Juniper was struggling to find her footing, "this is an unprecedented circumstance."

Valeria shook her head and fixed Juniper with a firm gaze, "No, no, that does not give us the right to be disrespectful of our guests, especially one as honored as you. For my father to empty out the contents of a ladies wardrobe in the middle of a crowded room...unacceptable. I'm sure they've been damaged as well, with those fool guards handling them. I insist, let me pay to replace them."

"It's alright, really, they've been laundered and returned to me already." In truth, several of her garments had been unrecoverable. The oil stains had already set by the time the clothes had been washed and were returned discolored. But for some reason Juniper found herself wanting to spare the Southern woman of her guilt, "Besides, I can afford more clothes."

"As I'm sure you can, yet the principle remains. Oh well, if you continue to be obstinate, at least accept my heartfelt apology and please, do not judge the Horn nor its people by this single indiscretion."

"Of course, you have been an exceedingly gracious host." Juniper nodded. She paused and chewed on some fruit thoughtfully. Finally, she found she could not help herself as she continued, "In fact, it did occur to me to ask, what has made you be so accommodating to a total stranger?"

"You do not believe we treat all our guests with such kindness?" She let her amusement show plainly on her face.

"Well, I doubt the daughter of the Baron personally spends so much time with *every* guest."

Valeria laughed at that, "No, I suppose not. To be honest I need you, Juniper."

"*Me*? For what?"

"I need...allies." For the first time, the easy smile and casual demeanor seemed entirely gone from the gregarious woman. She was leaning forward, cup left to the side. Juniper could not shake the distinct notion that she was suddenly speaking to a very different person than before, "There is...*something* happening. It's hard to explain, but something foul is spreading in secret. There's been strange movement across the North as well as here in the Southlands. Reports from soldiers encountering bands of heavily armed men moving throughout the backcountry with no explanation. Ships have also been spotted which are intentionally avoiding common ports, seeming to disappear into the open ocean when pursued. Not bandits, nor pirates, as few reports of conflict have been made. But mercenaries and freelance arcanists seem to have been hired en mass by an unknown employer. Someone is gathering a lot of power and trying to keep it a secret.

"What's more concerning, every time I try to look into this I seem to hit an iron wall. I asked a friend of mine in the Capital to look into some leads for me. A few days later she found her cat pinned to her wall with a note. It warned her to stop asking questions about the Burning Blades."

"The mercenaries?"

She nodded grimly, "It was even worse in the North. An agent of ours disappeared trying to look into the recent movements of the Houndstooth Company. His last message spoke of him trying to infiltrate a group working out of Port Wolfswood. But we've heard nothing for a month now, so our man is presumed dead."

Juniper blew out a long, low breath and rubbed her hands together, feigning nervousness. She glanced around the room, her emerald eyes darting across the windows and doors, "Do you think they have agents here?"

"I suspected before. But now, with this burglary, it is clear to me that my suspicions are well founded. We know someone is making moves, massing power, and we know this group is working across the continent. What I don't know, and what I aim to find out, is if they've got their hands in the Empire as well. So I need a good contact there...someone I can trust."

The wine tasted suddenly sour in Juniper's mouth and she had trouble meeting the woman's earnest gaze. She tried to fix her eyes on the incredibly unfashionable tapestries over the Princess's shoulder, but that did little to help ease her sense of anxious misgivings. She swallowed in an attempt to clear the lump in her throat as Valeria pushed on.

"This group is well connected and moving quickly. If they are a threat to the Northern Kingdoms and the Herronite Federation, then they may threaten the Oarenhiem Empire as well. Who knows how far this goes? As far south as the Broadwater Breach, perhaps Vinatieri? Hell, it could have spread across the sea as far as Lorrailia!"

"You think this conspiracy could stretch to the New World?"

Valeria gave her a meaningful look, "You know how the last great war went; mercenaries, privateers, and free companies across the world were the real winners. When our colonies declared themselves independent, they split up the New World amongst self proclaimed Lords and pumped up commoners pretending to be nobles. It was bad enough when the Broadwater Republic was the only independent power in the known world. Even guessing based on the loose estimates we have, whoever is pulling the strings has most likely already amassed enough power to pose a serious threat, no matter where their interests lie. All before anyone noticed."

Juniper blew out another long breath. Valeria's words rang in her ears. Her mind was moving at a breakneck pace, churning the information over. She started to speak up, but then she snapped her mouth shut and stared at the wine in her glass with hard eyes.

Valeria put a comforting hand on her arm. "I understand this is a lot. My cohorts and I have been working on this for months now, but we are hitting a dead end. We need help. But I also understand what I'm asking. I bear you no ill will if you feel these waters are too treacherous for you to tread."

"No!" She spoke far more quickly than she meant to. The Princess recoiled a bit, but recovered her easy poise quickly. Juniper kept her tone more even as she tried to gather her thoughts, "I mean to say, I will help you. If this...conspiracy is as dangerous as you believe, then it might threaten all of us. I should do what I can."

A smile lit up her face as the Princess grasped her hand in hers, "You are every bit the gem I believed you to be. I know between the two of us, we will be able to uncover whatever plot threatens our peoples."

"What would you have me do?" The Oaren woman folded her hands absentmindedly. Then she silently cursed at herself for the gesture, hoping the other woman would take that nervous tick as something benign.

"Nothing dangerous, of course." Valeria leaned back and took a long, slow sip of her wineglass. When she lowered the cup, a thin sheen hung on her lips as she cast a gaze across the trays, searching for her next morsel. It was distracting, and Juniper kept her eyes on the food so that she could focus on the conversation, "Just ask a few questions, speak to the right people at the right time. I need someone with...status, you understand. Spies and agents tend to be fine for gossip and general goings on, but *this* is something that requires a more precise approach."

Juniper blinked, "You have spies in the Empire?"

Valeria gave her a witheringly sympathetic look, "Everyone has spies everywhere my darling. We know of at least four of yours here in the Horn alone, plus another three in the Highlands. I just assumed that you, being the daughter of a Chancellor, would be more informed."

Juniper blushed, the rise of pink discoloring her normally pristine face. The Oaren noblewoman was left grasping at straws as she struggled for her next words, "Well, I'm not...he doesn't..."

Valeria's laugh cut through her chattering like a hot knife through fat, "I'm only teasing you, Juniper. Most court ladies don't dabble in the intrigue of court politics quite to the degree that I do."

The Princess let her tread water for a minute or so, casually snipping up a few odds and ends to make her next perfect bite. She had already popped the concoction into her mouth by the time Juniper found a reasonable response.

"What will you do, once you find out who is orchestrating this plot?"

"Well I suppose that depends." Valeria cocked her head, "On who they are and what their plans are."

The surprise must have been obvious on Juniper's face, as Valeria went on to explain, "If they intend harm towards any of us, we will obviously have to discourage them. But who knows, our interests might be aligned. I dare say we should keep ourselves open to all possibilities."

The comfortable feeling began to fade as Juniper felt a chill run up her spine. As she watched the Princess of the Horn casually spread preserves across another piece of bread, she wondered exactly what this woman might be capable of. Valeria gave her a knowing glance, "Who knows, perhaps we two can be the start of a renewed spirit of cooperation between our two great nations."

Juniper swallowed, "I had no idea you Southerners were so progressively minded."

"Burn enough bridges, you'll soon find yourself on an island. If you want to survive in this game, you must learn to work with what you have at hand."

As the caravan was loaded up with various bits of luggage Juniper sat stewing and staring at nothing, hiding from the unrelenting sun in a covered alcove of The Hold's courtyard. She watched the servants and porters heaving heavy trunks much like hers into the covered carts, struggling in their sweat soaked shirts. She turned a small, smooth stone over in her hand, black with a series of runic designs carved into it. A speaking stone, one which gave a direct line to the First Lady of the Highlands. It seemed, to her, to weigh more than all the gold and silver in her purse. She sighed and tucked it away into her dress.

The smell of singed stones and burned timber still hung in the air, even a full day past the fires being extinguished. She could see the people outside through the closed and barred gates, still sifting through the charred bits of structure. Men were loudly calling out orders as the remains of the ruined buildings were being removed by carts, piled high with black and gray refuse.

The previous day had been a testing one, that much she was sure of. From the first minute she had arrived in this ugly old city with its ancient fortress, she was never sure how far she was from being discovered. Any one of a million things could have gone wrong in this half baked plan, and clearly a few had. She had been incredibly lucky to have completed her part and gotten away cleanly. The business with that old arcanist still baffled her. She had examined it forwards and backwards and had yet to come up with an answer she could sit with comfortably.

Then there was the matter of the Princess. She was a creature of fog and shadows and misdirection, and Juniper felt a creeping suspicion that the woman would be keeping a very close eye on her for the foreseeable future. There was undoubtedly much she did not understand, much that was hidden from her. It was a precarious pit of vipers she found herself dangling over, one which threatened to consume her if she lost focus for even a moment. She hated the feeling.

When she turned back to the caravan, she was surprised to see someone had snuck up on her. He was a young man who appeared to be of the distant south, the Broadwater Breach, or perhaps Vinatieri, judging by his dark complexion. Juniper recognized him. He had been in the Baron's inquisition the day before, with the eldest Roth Prince. The young man was staring at her with his clear blue eyes, seemingly searching for something to say.

"I won't bite." She said, looking him up and down, "But you should know, I'm not really looking for a gentleman to come calling on me. I'm already spoken for in that department."

Her response took him by surprise, but he recovered quickly, "I mean no offense, my Lady, but if I were trying to court a noblewoman of the Empire, I would know better than to approach empty handed."

She cocked an eyebrow at him. He took a deep breath, opened and closed his mouth, then pointed to the caravan, "I'm...supposed to get on that caravan, same as you, and go back to Redwater today with my family."

"And?"

"I heard people say that you're a Master Arcanist, at the High Conservatory, yes?" The young man's words were coming faster now.

"They call us Professors in the Conservatory, but yes, essentially the same thing." Juniper tried to keep her voice pleasant, but felt her patience thinning.

"Ah, right, of course." The young man reached into his coat pocket.

Juniper felt herself tense immediately, the events of the previous days having set her nerves on edge, but then she saw it was only a small book bound in red leather that he had fished out. She recognized it immediately.

"It's just, I have an opportunity to go to the University, but I can't seem to work out any of this. I've read *Finding Fundamental Magic* and now this, but I just can't..."

Juniper held up her hand, cutting him off, "What is your name?"

He blinked, seeming to recognize his mistake, "Oh, my apologies. I am Jayce Acosta, of the Broadwater Republic."

"*Acosta*, as in the Acosta Company?"

He sighed heavily and nodded, "I am the son of Elon and Nadia Acosta."

"Such, *connected* parents. But your family hasn't gotten you any formal training in the Art?" She was observing him with a keen eye now, curiosity stoked as she ran over everything she knew about the wealthy merchant family in her mind.

"No, my mother has insisted on training me herself." He glanced over at the caravan, "But now, I have this chance to do something more. To learn the true Art."

Juniper snorted. The rude noise brought the man's attention sharply back to her, "What's so funny?"

She had not meant to make the noise, but now she could hardly hide behind niceties, "You should listen to your mother and stay on your ships, sailor. You won't like what you find at Uthersanctorum, or the Conservatory for that matter."

"What do you mean?" Any shreds of timidity were gone from his voice as he glared at her, "How could you possibly know that?"

"Because you've *settled*." She spoke as if to a slow child. She could see the confusion on his face and rolled her eyes. Trying to muster what little patience she had left, she tried to explain, "Your magic is set, like the clay of a pot or like iron once it's cooled. You are a Stormspeaker, yes?"

He nodded. The color had drained from his face a bit and his jaw was working as he chewed back the building anger.

"Then that is all you will ever be. Whatever ability you have is set in its form. No school of the arcane arts will be able to change that, now that you are, as you are."

"I...I don't understand."

"Damn *settled*, never know anything." She muttered to herself, then stood up smoothly and strode over to him. She snatched the book from his hands and flipped through it as she spoke, "These books are for children. Those whose magic is still unset, still malleable. It's no wonder they're no good to you."

She looked at him and saw the flood of confusion tinged with disappointment spreading over his face. He seemed to be collapsing in on himself as he stood there. Despite her annoyance, she found her voice had taken on a soft, comforting tone, "Jayce, wasn't it? I understand this is...distressing. But you must understand, children with the knack for the Art are brought to an arcane school to begin their training as soon as their talent manifests. Why, I started my training when I was only five! If just anyone with a spark could simply be trained to be a true master of the arcane arts, why would there be Stormspeakers? For that matter, why would there be Greenhands or Fireweavers? Don't tell me you've never wondered why anyone would *choose* to be a Skinsculpter or a Seer?"

Jayce was silent as he considered her words. Juniper shook her head and plowed on. It was better to break this boy's illusions now, rather than let him make a fool of himself in front of the University or, the Lord forbid, the Conservatory. They would eat him alive if he showed up there.

"You seem like a decent enough fellow, Jayce. But you need to understand, what you and your family do is one thing. But what I do, and what other people like me can do, that is...something else entirely. You can't just learn it, you have to be born with it. Only a small handful have the potential. And even if you *had* the potential, it has long since been lost. You are settled, and you always will be. Better you listen to your mother and continue your training. Stormspeakers are more valuable than ever now, with everyone rushing to explore the New World. You should be happy with what talents you do have."

She pressed the book back into his hands and gave him a sympathetic sliver of a smile, satisfied with her own tact. Straightforward and honest, yet not insensitive. Her mother would have approved. She had already moved to walk past him when he finally found his voice.

"You...you're wrong." His voice sounded strained, as though he were struggling just to get the words out.

"I'm afraid I am not."

"You are," he pushed through the hesitation creeping at the edges of his voice, "I can do it. I know I can."

She gave him another small, sad smile and held her hand up to show him a golden ring on her right middle finger. It held the sign of a Conservatory graduate, the ornate, seven pointed star, "Back when I was a student at the Conservatory, one of my Professors used to have a saying. He drilled it into us every day. He always told us, 'form and function are fine bedfellows'. My form has been laid out, as has yours, long before you or I were able to weigh in on the function, or the fairness, of them. There is an order, some of us are born to be arcanists, and some are born to...other things. If you try to fight the tide, you may find yourself stranded, far from a safe port."

He gave her a look that was equal parts confusion and annoyance. She indicated the caravan where the workers were tying down the final few bags and boxes, taking their positions in the drivers seats and calling for all passengers.

"It is time for me to be on my way, Jayce Acosta. I hope to see you on the road." With that, she strode across the yard, leaving the young man behind her as she finally took her leave of The Hold, the Horn and of the entire damned Southlands.

CHAPTER EIGHT

WINDS OF CHANGE

Heedless of the people moving around him in the busy halls of The Hold, Jayce sat on one of the astoundingly uncomfortable stone benches as he stared at his hands for a long while. It seemed like the Oaren woman's words were burrowing their way into his brain like sea snakes into the carcass of a whale. He wanted nothing more than to ignore what she had told him. To write it off, call her a liar, pretend he had never heard it. She had to have been overly harsh, trying to hurt him out of spite. Yet, something nagged at him. She had no reason to lie to him. Nothing to gain from it, no nets in this water.

Then there was what she said about his magic, about the books. He had never been able to get the techniques or the spells in the books to work for him. Not once, in months. Move water onto a flaming house by the barrel load? Sure. But create a ball of light the size of a marble or make a candle ignite? Not even a flicker. So what then, was that it? Was he just a Stormspeaker? Would he be a ship guide for the rest of his life? Maybe take over the family business like his father wanted?

The thought opened a bottomless ocean of depression in him. He saw the long years of haggling over the prices of spices and textiles stretch out before him like a bleak horizon. The smell of dried fish and hardtack seemed to fill his nose and caused him to shudder.

"Damn that stuck up illusionist," he muttered to himself, standing suddenly, "I'll be an arcanist if it kills me."

He turned to walk back down the hallway when a voice stopped him in his tracks.

"There you are boy, we been lookin' everywhere for you. It's time for this caravan to be gettin' some wind beneath its sails." His father, speaking in their native Vinatieri, said as he sauntered up the hallway, thumbs tucked casually into his belt. His wife was close at his side, soft features set with a look of concern.

Jayce turned to face them. He paused, shuffling through a dozen approaches to the conversation he knew he had to have in his mind. Each seemed more disastrous than the last. He might have saved himself the trouble, as his mother immediately identified the waves of panic on his face.

"What's the matter, child? Have you taken sick?"

Jayce took a deep breath and steadied himself. Then he blurted it out all at once, "I...I'm not coming back to Redwater."

His parents blinked at him for a minute, then looked at each other. He barreled on without waiting for them to object.

"I'm going to Asaldon to attend the University. I've already gotten a letter to help me get in the door, I know how I'm getting there. I can even finance it all. I...I'm going, no matter what. But I still just...I want your blessing."

There was a long silence that hung in the air heavier than the lingering smell of the fires. The red walls of The Hold seemed to be crowding in on them, seeming small and terribly claustrophobic. Jayce shifted from one foot to the other and clenched and unclenched his hands, trying to control his racing heart. His parents seemed frozen in time, neither speaking nor moving. He thought, for a moment, he had given them both a simultaneous case of heart seizure. When he was almost ready to reach out and shake them, his mother finally spoke up.

"Jayce," she said in a gentle voice, hand touching her husband soothingly on the arm to quiet him as he began to speak up, "I thought we talked about this..."

"You talked!" He said, a bit more harshly than he had intended, "You both talked, but you didn't hear a word *I* said. I'm not signing up with a Republic Warship. I'm not taking over the family business. I've tried to tell you this before, but neither of you wants to listen to what *I* have to say."

His mother recoiled a bit and Jayce felt the pang of guilt churn in his stomach. He started to say something, to try and ease the hurt clear on the woman's face, but his father cut him off.

"Big man all of a sudden, are ya?" His eyes flashed and Jayce could feel the fury flowing off of him, "You seen that yellow woman's show last night and got dreams of glory and riches in your head, aye?'

Jayce could feel the rising temperature inside him as he struggled not to scream in frustration. He tried to steady himself, took a ragged breath in through his nostrils. Nadia had put both hands on her husband's arm to try and quiet his rage but the man bore down on his son mercilessly. His father's voice pierced through his calm like a spear through the skin of a sea beast.

"You know what your problem is, boy? You got no *respect*! No respect for this family, no respect for the sacrifices we made for you! I clawed my way to this from nothin', but you, you've been given everything, never had to work a day in your life."

Jayce shut his eyes and clenched his fists. His father had taken a step forward and was now inches away from his son's face. His hot breath filled Jayce's nostrils. His ears rang with the harsh words. He tried to focus, to breathe like his mother had taught him.

"You know what? You should go to the University, you don't *deserve* the Company. You don't *deserve* to call yourself an Acosta."

It was like all the building wind had been let out of his sails all at once. The tension and anger flooded out of him and was replaced with a torrent of confusion and deep, black despair. He blinked and stared into the hard face of his father.

"Father..."

"Elon..." Nadia whispered in a shocked voice.

When the man spoke, his tone of resignation cut through Jayce more sharply than any blade, "Let's go, Nadia. Leave this magi to his studies."

Without another word, Elon Acosta sauntered past his son, shouldering him roughly to the side and not giving him so much as a second look. Jayce watched him go. He turned back to his mother, with a sense of building dread as he saw the look of disappointment on her face.

"Mother..."

She held up a hand to silence him, a jeweled ring with the Acosta Company symbol sparkling on her middle finger. When she spoke, it was slow, direct and measured.

"Jayce, my son, I know you're a gentle soul, you mean no harm in your actions. I know you thirst for knowledge. But you need to take a moment to ponder your actions. I have told you my story many times, but perhaps you have forgotten; that when the High Sorceress of Vess took me on as a child, I thought I was to be a great magi as well. But she was a cruel master. She used me and the other children like slaves, had us do petty magics all day and night for coin to line her pockets. Had I not escaped, had I not been found by your father...my life would have been one of unending misery."

Jayce sighed, "I know your story, mother..."

"Then you would do well to heed it." Her eyes were shards of blue ice, stark in her dark face, "These practitioners of the High Art that you are so desperate to join are not what you believe. They are sharks, ever circling, waiting for a hint of blood in the water."

"Your life is not the map by which the whole world charts its course, mother." He replied firmly.

She chewed at her bottom lip, staring hard at him, "Look deep into your soul, my child. Is forsaking your family what you truly desire?"

Jayce was quiet for a long time. He turned the words over in his mouth a dozen times, then a dozen times more. He finally met her eyes. The look he gave his mother was equal parts defiance and desperation, "If any of us is discarding their family, it is the man who just walked away from his only son. I want your blessing mother, but I will make my own decisions with or without it."

Nadia, returned his gaze with a sad look and shook her head. Then she put her hand on Jayce's shoulder for a brief moment, gave it a slight squeeze and followed her husband down the hall.

T he caravan had exited the city's outer wall and was winding its way down the cobblestone road beside the River Rhine towards the ocean. From this distance, it was barely visible, a thin snake of tiny shapes moving slowly across the rust colored landscape between pockets of greenery. Jayce stood leaning on the parapet wall of The Hold, watching it fade into the distance in the late afternoon sun. The pit in his stomach had grown deeper and deeper as the caravan had grown further away. He could feel the swarming storm of self doubt rolling over his thoughts and urging him to return to the familiar comfort of his parents, who were rapidly fading into the distance. Yet he remained rooted to the stonewall like a statue. There was a cool breeze flowing across the mountains and into the valley. Jayce took a deep breath and let it calm his unruly mind.

"Finally gone, huh?"

Jayce opened his eyes and saw Cassius standing a few strides down the wall. The nobleman wore casual robes, yet still had his sword lashed at his side, ready as ever. He strode towards his friend, a casual grin on his face. The bandage had been removed from his left arm, leaving a jagged pink scar bright against his tan skin. Jayce nodded towards it.

"Another souvenir?"

"For the collection." The Prince rubbed at his arm, "Itches like crazy though."

"I would imagine." Jayce shook his head, "It's a good thing you're tough, my friend. I know very few men who could take the beatings you have and still reach for your sword with a smile."

Cassius grunted in agreement. They stood there for a long moment, quietly looking out at the horizon. The gentle rise of the mountains caught the afternoon light on their cliffs and rock faces, evoking a richly painted mosaic of reds, oranges, and yellows. A few clouds drifted gently towards the west, crawling along on the swells of the summer heat. When Cassius finally spoke, he was gazing out over the landscape with a wistful look, "I've always loved the view from up here. Such a beautiful country, don't you think?"

In truth, Jayce had always found the Horn terribly monotonous and unremarkable. He grinned at his friend, "I supposed, if you like big old rocks and overly self important hills. Then again, I hear you Southlanders are a bit too friendly with your horses, so we might have different standards..."

The Prince swiped a good natured blow at his friend, who ducked out of the way. Jayce turned and pointed back in the opposite direction. The city stretched out across the valley, filling the two concentric walls to the brim. Beyond, towards the east, the wide cobblestone road led away into the mountains.

"Guess I'll be headed that way tomorrow." He said, unable to fully banish the Oaren woman and her words from his mind, "No reason to delay now."

"You sound unhappy about the prospect. Did your parents take the news as poorly as you predicted?"

"Worse. But that's only half of it. That damned Illuminator, from the party, I can't get her out of my head. I spoke to her about attending the University..."

"And..?"

Jayce shook his head, "She told me I could never be an arcanist, that I was *settled*, whatever that means. She told me I would only ever be a Stormspeaker..."

A heavy hand on his shoulder brought Jayce's spiraling ramble to a stop. Cassius was giving him a steady look, dark eyes focused on him, "Jayce, you might be the cleverest man I've ever met, and, from what I saw at the fires the other night, you're a damn fine weaver of magic. I don't know much about the arcane arts, but I know anyone would be a fool to reject you."

Perhaps it was the dry air up here in the mountains, or it might have been the sun shining into his eyes. It definitely was not the pit in his stomach finally lightening for the first time since his mother had walked away from him this morning. Whatever it was, Jayce found himself rubbing a spot of wet from one eye as he nodded. His voice felt caught up in his throat all of a sudden and all of his usual wit seemed to elude him.

The Prince dropped his hand and graciously gave him a moment, ignoring the emotion that had overcome his friend as he looked back out over the parapet. Jayce took a few deep breaths and pushed everything back down, calming himself. When he turned back to his friend, the grin was back on his face and he was thinking about the future with excitement for the first time since he had gotten the letter from Cassius.

"So that's my plan. What will you do now, your Lordship?" Jayce indicated the road beyond the wall, "Will you bring the bandits who broke into The Hold to justice?"

Cassius shook his head, a bitter frown biting at his face, "No, I have no command any longer. My father has not lifted his decree, in spite of recent events. So I am still bound here, within the walls of this fortress, until I am made a *proper* lord."

Jayce frowned and puffed out his cheeks. The Prince looked miserable, staring listlessly across the city. He leaned heavily on the stone of the parapets, head resting on one upturned hand. Jayce stared down at his hands, pondering them for a long moment. Finally, he mused out loud, "Why do you think anyone would want to free the Witch of the White Woods?"

The Prince shook his head and made an irreverent grunting noise, "Who knows? Seems mad to me."

"I would suppose," He began, rubbing the short stubble that had grown at his jawline and mentally noting his need for a shave, "someone wanted her for her magic...but that's far too simple an answer. There are plenty of freelance magicians in the world. It would have to be someone who was willing to make an enemy of the Federation and the Northern Kingdoms, at least those that border your Barony. Maybe even the Empire as well, seeing as they implicated the Oaren performer. Unless of course it was the Empire that perpetrated the whole thing."

Cassius frowned, lines set deep into his brow as he pondered the issue. "That would be troubling...but assuming it's not them, the Republic then? Or one of the Vinatierian nations then? We've heard rumors the Scivian Dynasty is unsettled."

Jayce shook his head. "No, my father would likely have heard of it if it was someone in the Republic, and the nations of Vinatieri have their own sorcerers, outlaws and otherwise. There's just not enough incentive for one of them to organize a heist of this difficulty to break one witch and her coven out of The Hold."

He scratched at the battlement, breaking a pebble loose. He flicked it into the street below and held up his fingers. He began counting down on them as he listed the points, "This was someone independent. Whoever it is, they are well connected, well informed, well financed..."

"It could be a group." The Prince ventured.

"Most likely," Jayce agreed as he rubbed his hands together, "very few individuals in the whole of Arieha would have the knowledge and ability to pull something like this off alone. I think the real question is, what could a group with that type of power, connection, and influence already possibly want with the Witch?"

Cassius shrugged, looking more puzzled than ever. Jayce sighed and leaned back on the parapet. He glanced over the wall and was surprised at what he saw. Julius was there, properly primped hair and outfit impeccable as ever. He was standing just below them in the courtyard. He called out, waving one hand above his head. Jayce looked over and Cassius shrugged at him, the two made their way down the stairs and met up with the youngest of the Roth children.

"Hail Julius, what tears you out from your wine and books on this fine evening?" Cassius said haughtily.

Julius gave him a smirk and motioned towards The Hold, "There's no peace for anyone in there. Father is still raging like a bear with a thorn in his paw. Valeria is trying to help him come up with a measured course of action, but I don't need to tell you how hard it is to deal with our father's temper..."

A grim look overtook the elder Prince once again as he glowered at his brother. Julius only continued smirking, defiant in the face of his brother's menace. He moved on smoothly, not missing a step, "In fact, that is the reason I'm here. Valeria requested I find you for some sort of family meeting."

Cassius made a face, "Our father wants me present for an important meeting? Aren't you more suited to that sort of thing?"

Once again, the younger brother sidestepped his sibling's jeers, "Valeria wants you. I hardly think our father is giving you much thought at the present moment."

The frown deepened in the elder Prince's face and Jayce had to stifle a snort of laughter at his friend's pain. Cassius shot a look towards him, then heaved out a heavy sigh. He motioned across the yard, "I suppose we better get on with it then."

Julius cleared his throat, "You should come too, Jayce."

"Me?" Jayce blinked, "But why?"

"Valeria asked for your presence. I don't know why. Perhaps she wants a witness in case father murders us all before the day is done."

Night had fallen on The Hold by the time the three men had made their way through the winding halls and stairs of the fortress. The witchlights had sparked to life and their amber glow was beginning to wash out over the stone, giving the walls and floors a hue like fire dancing in the dark. As the three reached the Library, they could hear the Baron's voice before they even opened the heavy wooden doors.

"You are playing games of chance with both our realms, Valeria!" The Baron's voice boomed as they entered.

The Library was a large, long hall much like the Banquet Room, with vaulted ceilings and long windows along one side. However, unlike the rest of the fortress, the windows here were stained glass which colored the moonlight streaming in through depictions of various nature scenes. There were rows of lightly stained shelving which lined every wall, climbing like trellises up towards the tall ceiling. The rows of shelves also ran down the center of the room, all carved with the designs of delicate vines and flowers, an intricate wonder of craftsmanship. They held books of every size and color imaginable, filling the room with the smell of old paper and leather. Jayce silently gaped at the room as they crossed the threshold, thinking to himself that it was like stepping into a totally different world from the rest of The Hold.

In front of a giant hearth which held position in the center of the room, a sitting area waited invitingly with large easy chairs and long couches before it. Valeria sat in a reclined position, seemingly at ease as her husband loomed behind her chair like a great shadow. The Baron stood before the hearth, frame illuminated by the glow of the crackling fire behind him. The dark look on his face was similar to the one he had worn in the Great Hall during his inquisition of the party guests.

"...you cannot assume," the Baron continued the conversation that had been taking place before they entered, face contorted into a mask of anger, "that you know what these people are going to do! You don't know anything about that Oaren woman!"

Valeria held his gaze with the same rigorous intensity, "I assume nothing, father. I know enough to know what she is going to do."

Cassius, Jayce and Julius made their way over to the sitting area. Julius threw himself down into a chair unceremoniously, while Cassius stood opposite his father. Jayce placed himself awkwardly off to the side, still not sure what he was doing here. The Baron seemed to barely notice him as his dark eyes fixed on his eldest son.

"Finally managed to get yourself here?" He rumbled, hardly bothering to contain the bite in his voice.

"I *just* asked Julius to bring them." Valeria cut in, motioning vaguely. She indicated one of the open seats, "You really should all sit down. This isn't a duel."

"Not yet..." Cassius growled as he stared at his father. The older man returned the look without flinching.

Valeria rolled her eyes and spoke as if she was a mother scolding misbehaving children, "I swear, you two are worse than my own bickering boys. Did you both forget we have greater matters to deal with than your petty squabbling?"

The two men held their stare for a moment longer, before the Baron gave a grunt and looked to his daughter, "How could I forget my own daughter undercutting me like a sapper felling a castle wall?"

"What in the world are you two about?" Julius asked hurriedly, before his sister had time to respond, waving a hand around at the assembled crowd, "What's the big secret that you have brought us all here to reveal, Valeria?"

The eldest Roth sibling cast an appraising glance around the room, "I know who is to blame for the heist."

A moment of silence passed as all the eyes in the room came to rest on the Valeria. She let the words hang in the air, a pregnant pause before finally letting the rest of her family in on the secret, "I believe it was a group of mercenaries called the Burning Blades."

Jayce blinked. The memory of the man in the fine suit stood out in his mind. He blurted out, "I met a man from the Blades in Redwater!"

Every face turned to look at him. He felt as though the room had suddenly grown much hotter in an instant, "He...tried to recruit me. He gave me a coin..."

Valeria's eyes widened and she shot her husband a glance. The rest of the Roth family seemed to chew this information over in their private thoughts. Julius's voice cut through the awkward silence, "Val, how could you possibly know that?"

"We've been looking into the Blades, as well as other mercenary groups, for months now." Damien spoke up, broad face lighting up as he motioned down to his wife unnecessarily.

Valeria patted his hand and continued, "It seemed prudent, considering some of the strange goings on lately. I've made several efforts to infiltrate their ranks. One of my more successful agents has found evidence that the group was planning something. Men and money moved around, gathering information here and in the Highlands, the sort of things you need for a big, important operation..."

She gave them all a meaningful look, her honey brown eyes as hard as veins of amber in the flickering light, "But more importantly, our agent has recently given us evidence that someone has been speaking to the Blades about The Hold. Now that we know the results of those conversations, it's clear someone has betrayed us."

Cassius unfolded his arms. Julius cast a worried look up at his father. The Baron's face was lined with a deep frown as he glowered by the hearth. Jayce did his best not to attract any attention to himself trying in vain to be invisible in his chair. Valeria pulled out a piece of paper, hidden in the folds of her dress, unfolded it carefully and held it up for them to see.

"This was taken from one of the company's officers in the Capital. It speaks of a dragon slumbering in the mountains and emphasizes the importance of not waking it. It also speaks of the treasures it holds in its cave...below the ground." Valeria rolled her eyes, "Obviously, whoever wrote this was no genius at ciphers. But they *were* knowledgeable enough to understand how our defenses worked, and they were willing to give that knowledge away, probably for a price."

"You had this letter before the break in?" Cassius demanded, "You didn't think to warn us?"

"I warned our father..." Valeria cast a glare at the imposing figure by the mantle, "what was it you told me? Oh yes, you had the situation well in hand...'no army's breached our walls in over a thousand years, and they're damned well not about to start now' or something like that?"

Jayce wasn't sure if it was possible for the large man's frown to get any deeper, but the lines seemed to be doing their best to carve their way down to the bone.

"You told me you had information that someone was talking to the Burning Blades about our defenses. I was expecting an assault, not a burglary. Perhaps if you were more concerned with protecting our home than playing your game of shadows we'd have been ready when the wolves came baying at our doors!"

Jayce felt the man was deflecting poorly, yet he was not about to willingly wade into the drama unfolding before him.

"Perhaps," Julius's voice cut in, redirecting the tension once again, "we should let sleeping hounds lie."

Father and daughter held their lingering glare for a moment longer. Finally, Cassius cut in with a harsh voice, "You're both playing games with the lives of our people. You both knew someone was targeting us. Either of you could have called for the festival to be canceled, or for The Hold to be locked down at the very least. But neither of you did, and now a score of our people are dead, either in those fires or murdered here in our own halls."

Julius gave his older brother a look that was overflowing with frustration. But Cassius pointedly ignored him and pushed on, his tone seeming to be ever digging towards a nerve as he focused his attention on his sister, "I'm guessing you haven't wasted a moment on that, eh? Already planned out your next move?"

Damien started to speak but his wife again put her hand on his, calming the big man. Valeria took the obvious jab in stride as she moved past his words with her usual grace, "I have. *We* have, as a matter of fact, father and I. Seeing as we don't know who the snake in our garden is or where they are at the moment, our next steps must be exceedingly careful. Our turncoat could be here in The Hold, and we will be thorough in our search, of course. But, the traitor could also have been on the other end.

"Father was holding those prisoners in secret until representatives from the University could collect them. So, it is safe to assume there were people there who knew of our guests and enough about our abilities to be valuable to the Blades. Therefore, it is vitally important that we figure out if they have a source inside the University. So, what we need is a man on the inside."

As Valeria's eyes came to rest on the sole non-familial relation in the room, Jayce felt his blood run cold. The deep pit that had finally seemed to disappear reformed itself in his stomach as his mind raced, desperately trying to keep up.

Cassius looked from his sister to his childhood friend, a look of understanding slowly creeping over his face, "No, Valeria, absolutely not. Are you mad? You want *Jayce* to be your spy?"

Valeria did not break her gaze for even a moment, "Of course I do. A new student, the perfect person to ask questions and try to learn the ropes, you might say. Besides, we're already paying for his tuition, or was I misinformed when our treasury master told me you had given your friend here a writ for unlimited funds from our personal stores?"

Cassius gritted his teeth, but managed to growl, "I have just as much right to our coffers as you do, Valeria. You don't get to set terms."

"No, but he does."

The Baron had taken a few steps forward and now his silhouette hung uncomfortably over Jayce. From this close, he could see the strands of gray in the big man's dark hair and beard. When he spoke, the strong scent of whiskey and smoke rolled off of him in a noxious cloud that made Jayce almost as nauseous as the nerves that were sending constant signals to flee from this room as fast as possible.

"Listen, lad," the big man rumbled, seeming to strive for a tone approaching kindness, "I know my son has made certain promises to you, ones which you've already based important decisions on. I've no intention of leaving you unhorsed in the wilderness. Your parents have been friends to me and my Barony over the years. But you must understand, what we are facing is a potential danger to the stability of our nation. If we don't root out this threat, it could lead to ruin for the entire continent. We *all* need to do our part."

Jayce did not have to sift too deeply through the man's words to understand their meaning. He shrugged his shoulders, giving Cassius a helpless glance, "How could I say no?"

"There's a good man." Augustus clapped a heavy hand on his shoulder, squeezing a slight wince from him. He turned his gaze to his son, "You could learn something about service from your friend."

Cassius narrowed his eyes and opened his mouth to start another argument, but Julius interjected again, cutting him off. "So Jayce will be our man in the Capital. But that doesn't solve all our problems. We still don't know if we have a leak here at home, *and* we still have no idea who hired the Blades in the first place."

Valeria gave her father a look before continuing, "We're working on that. Father is continuing his investigation here, as will I in the North. As far as who hired the Blades, it could still be anyone. So all we can do at this point is to pull up the weeds until we find the source of the rot."

Cassius shook his head and made a noise somewhere between a snort and an exasperated sigh, "Gods...this is all a fine plan you've concocted, sister, but if we know the Blades organized the heist, why not just take your evidence, go directly to Asaldon and demand justice from the Sovereign himself?"

"Of course your first impulse is to tip our hand." Valeria rolled her eyes, "The moment we go public, the Blades will know we're on to them, they'll make moves to cover their tracks. We'll lose any chance to figure out who's been financing their operation..."

"...Or we'll have the jump on them and wreck their plans before they have a chance to kill any more of our people!" Cassius interrupted, "I'll go. Me and Jayce can travel to the Capital together, then I'll meet up with Lucian. Together, we can go before the Sovereign..."

"No, Cassius." Augustus declared, "You are to stay here. With all this uncertainty, our family needs to secure our position in case someone is making a play for the Horn."

"Meaning...?"

"We need a clear line of succession to the Barony. I need a suitable, *stable* heir, preferably with heirs of their own. So you are going to expedite your marriage. You and Allura are to be married by the end of the cycle."

At this, the room broke out into an uproar of angry voices. As the family meeting descended into a raucous squall of petty arguments, Jayce leaned back in his chair. He let his mind turn over the events of the last hour or so, finally coming to grasps with his position. He closed his eyes and felt the beginnings of a migraine forming, already regretting the part he had agreed to play in this scheme.

CHAPTER NINE

FUGITIVES & CRIMINALS

H olton had led his odd group of traveling companions west from Rothmount, following the River Rhine as it wound down the mountains towards the sea. There was a steady stream of bodies moving en masse on the road to Redwater Port, caravans of merchants and tradesmen, groups of sailors headed back to their ships, farmers and herders back to their homesteads. The stench of sweating men and horses filled the air as the summer heat beat down on the travelers like an unrelenting master spurning a beast of burden.

It was easy for the group to blend into the crowd, once they had donned their disguises. The five thieves and their four fugitive charges were dressed in gaudy outfits, brightly colored with large collars and frills and eye-catching adornments. They rode in a loose cluster, four of the thieves on horseback surrounding a covered wagon driven by Taron with the witch and her coven riding in the back. On the side of the cart, a sign was scrawled with swirling letters which read, *Petyr Periwinkle's Prancing Players*.

The red haired brigand rode at the head of his small procession, wearing a green cap with a long purple feather stuck in it at a jaunty angle. Erin trotted along on her horse beside him, reddish blonde hair done up in a braided bun, tugging at the high collar of her bright gold and blue outfit.

"I still don't understand why you insist on us wearing this shit, Holt." She grumbled, glaring at him, "You couldn't have disguised us as another group of fur traders or merchants?"

Holton flashed her a wicked smile, "What's the matter? I think you make a fetching trouper."

If looks could cause wounds, Holton would have suffered a fatal injury from the glare she shot him. She growled, "I look like a damned clown."

"Exactly!" Holton made a sweeping motion to the crowds around them, "Everyone we've passed has looked at us, yet none have given us a second thought. Besides, what sort of trappers would have three children with them?"

Up ahead, a group of Legionnaires was watching the crowd as it flowed past them, upturned spears and half helms gleaming in the afternoon light. Their grim faces scanned the crowd for conspicuous travelers. The soldiers already had one of the larger groups pulled to the side of the road ahead of them. They were in the process of rifling through the carts, an ever growing pile of boxes and chests amassing on the roadside as forlorn looking men and women watched, sweating unprotected under the oppressive sun.

A red faced, portly merchant with a bushy beard, clearly the leader of the group, was screaming at a disinterested looking officer who presided over the men as they hauled yet another chest out of the cart. The merchant's complaining was loud enough for every passerby to hear as clearly as if they were the ones enduring his wrath.

"...I've been traveling this road to the Capital every season for ten years!" The man's veins were popping out across his neck, "I was personally invited to the Baron's feast! Yet you treat us like...like, *commoners*?!"

The officer looked unperturbed, sweat beading down his face from under his helmet, as he answered in a practiced monotone, "We are searching *every* traveler on this highway that meets our criteria. The Lord Baron has decreed we cannot risk the fugitives from Rothmount escaping through Redwater Port."

The red faced man rolled his eyes in a move so exaggerated they could see it from horseback fifty paces away. He threw his hands in the air and his voice took on a tone that was soaked in venom, "So you think your fugitives are hiding in the back of my carts? You're wasting everyone's time here. If they're headed for Redwater, they'll be cutting their way through the backcountry, not out here on the High Road for everyone to see!"

The officer finally turned to face the man, his face still holding that practiced, blank expression, but there was an unmistakable hardness in his eyes, "We have other men combing the backcountry, good sir. If you have a concern with our methods, we would be happy to escort you back to The Hold so you may bring them up to the Baron personally."

At that, the merchant deflated like the sails of a ship that had lost the wind. He sputtered something unintelligible and avoided looking the officer directly in the eye. The soldier seemed satisfied and went back to observing the work of his men. As Holton and his group came within close proximity of the soldiers, the officer looked up at them.

Holton looked back and nodded to his group. They took the cue immediately. Barney began to pick at a lute and Jarryd beat on a hand drum, both abysmally off beat, yet playing with lively enthusiasm. Taron, from his spot in the driver's seat of the wagon, began to bellow out a bawdy song in a rich baritone. Erin pulled her horse next to him and added her voice to the mix, harmonizing with Taron's performance with ease. Holton wheeled his horse in a few quick circles, kicking up small clouds of dust from the cobblestone road. He leaned down and placed a hand on the horse's flank, speaking to it under his breath. The horse bucked and began to walk backwards, moving down the road at an easy trot. Passersby began to stop their journeys and crowd around the group, clapping and laughing as they watched the impromptu show.

The road quickly became clogged with gawking travelers and the flow of traffic started to jam up. The Legionnaires tried to move people along, pushing and yelling to no avail. Holton spoke to his horse again and it reared up on its hind legs, walking forward with its front hooves up in the air as he hung on to its neck to avoid sliding off. This drew even more cheers, and more guards were now rushing over to try and disperse the crowd. Eventually, the guards succeeded in moving some of the onlookers on their way, enough that the officer was able to stride right up to Holton.

"That's enough!" He yelled over the music and the noise of the crowd, "We need you to cease immediately and move along!"

"But these good people are loving it!" Holton called back, willing his horse into a high step which nearly caught the officer in the chest with a stray hoof.

"Move along, sir! Or we'll be forced to detain you for interfering with our investigation!"

Holton looked sullen and brought his horseback to an easy saunter, "If you insist, good sir."

"Yes, please, move along!" The officer pointed down the road in a huff.

Holton gave him a slight tip of the cap and motioned for the others to stop. The music died out and the crowd they had formed slowly rejoined the traffic on the roadway. As they moved down the road, they passed close enough to the red faced merchant and his carts to see his ugly glare as they left him and his caravan behind, waylaid with their gear and goods strewn across the ground.

Night had fallen and Holton's group had set up camp off the main road, just outside of a small town. A low fire crackled, pushing back the darkness. They all sat in the dirt around it, nibbling on crusty bread and hard cheese, staring into the flames. Barney picked at his lute as he reclined against a fallen tree and Erin sat beside him softly singing along. The three children sat clustered together and slightly apart from the rest, whispering amongst themselves.

He had learned their names were Alice, Louis, and Madeline at some point along the trip, and that they called the witch Mother Mary. She sat on a log close behind them, seeming to hover over her flock like a great, dark bird, wary eye watching for any sign of trouble. Holton was picking at his nails with a knife, clearing away the road grime, when Alice, the dark haired girl he had rescued first, spoke up.

"Sir?" She called out to Holton, ignoring the hand of the other girl who grabbed her arm, "Can...may I ask you a question?"

"You just did." Taron called out, drawing a few chuckles from the other thieves.

The girl ignored him and pressed on, "I just...you still haven't told us anything. You said you would explain everything, back before we left Rothmount, only..."

As she trailed off, Holton pushed himself up to a more upright position. He stared at the girl for a moment and she withdrew a bit, but then he gave her a broad smile, showing his teeth, "So I did. What do you want to know?"

She glanced at the other two, uncertainty clouding her face. But she took a breath and spoke up, "For starters, who are you and why did you help us escape the dungeons? You have that coin but none of us have ever seen any of you before."

Holton glanced at the woman behind them for a moment, but she only stared back at him, dark eyes gleaming in the firelight. He eyed the children, "I have several names, but most call me Holton Hart."

The boy, Louis, took a sharp breath in. His voice was barely a whisper, "I know you..."

"Aye? What do you know?"

"You...you're the *Red Wolf*, you're the most notorious outlaw in all the North." His voice quivered with something between fear and awe, "You stole the Lord of the Low Pines prized jewels from his own stronghold. You robbed the great banking house of Blackwater Bay and nearly ran them out of business."

Holton said nothing, only stared at the boy, eyes fixed on him with amused interest.

"They say...you broke into the Coldwater Magician's College...murdered the Keeper and stole some of their greatest secrets."

He held up a finger to make his point, "It's not murder if it's in self defense."

The children stared at him for a moment saying nothing. The dark haired girl spoke again, a quizzical look overriding her apprehension, "But...how did you manage to get the better of a mage? Surely he had spells and wards?"

Holton considered this for a moment, "You're Alice, right?"

"Alice Carroll."

"And you're a witch, Alice Carroll?"

She nodded, a smug look on her face.

"Cast a spell on me."

"What?"

"Go on...anything you want, as quick as you can."

She scrunched her nose, but brought her hands up. There was a dull thud before anyone had a chance to register that the thief had thrown his knife. It was embedded in the log the witch was sitting on, barely half a pace from Alice's head. She stared at it, arms still hanging in the air. When she turned to look at Holton, horror in her eyes, he was grinning again.

"I've dealt with magic men of every kind, girlie, the North is crawling with 'em. You know what I've learned about magic? It's *slow*."

He leaned back against the wagon wheel behind him, folding his hands behind his head. The other members of the crew were watching, grins wolfish in the firelight. Alice was still frozen until the witch reached over and gathered her up in an embrace, holding her tightly. She gave the outlaw a fierce glare.

"I see the Blades spared no expense when they chose which agent to send." Mary spat at him sarcastically, "Did we spend all that time trapped darkness only for you to torture us with your little games?"

Holton met her gaze evenly, "I intended no ill will towards your ward. That's a lesson all mages need to learn. Perhaps if those men in Coldwater had known it they might still have their lives."

She said nothing as she let the girl go. Alice's eyes were bleary but she still met his gaze. He nodded to her and she pursed her lips, forcing herself to nod back. After a moment had passed, the older woman collected her thoughts with a great sigh and fixed him with a stern look.

"Why did they send you, Master Hart?" She began, anger still lingering at the edges of her voice as she eyed him, "You don't know us. Are you even a member of the Blades?"

"No, no..." Holton shrugged, "I am...an independent party. They sent me because I'm the best there is at what I do. Clearly, your freedom was worth it to someone. They have paid our little band here a great deal to see you safely delivered."

She nodded, considering him. Holton went on, "Now, I have a question for you. The mercenaries have spent a pretty penny on you. I wonder why that might be? What arrangement do you have with them?"

"You took the job without knowing anything about our purpose?" The witch raised an eyebrow.

Holton shrugged, "The coin was good. But now that you're here...perhaps you'd care to enlighten us?"

"Lawrence was the one who hired you?" Holton nodded and Mary gave him a wicked smirk, "Then you'll need to speak with him if you want those answers."

The thief worked his jaw, unable to keep the annoyance from his face, but he let the topic drop.

Mary took advantage of the lapse in conversation and pressed him, "Can you tell us where we are bound?"

"The coast. We're headed to Redwater, where we are to meet up with our mutual benefactor."

The witch made a face. She glanced around at the group of thieves lounging in the rapidly deepening darkness, then over at the lights of the town. She furrowed her brow.

"And, what if we don't want to come with you?" She asked, an unmistakable edge to her tone.

Holton slowly sat upright. He kept his eyes on her, the question hanging in the air as the fire danced between them. There was a heaviness to the summer night. The heat bore down like an oppressive, unseen weight that threatened to smother them. He spoke in a falsely bewildered tone, "You know, I hadn't even *considered* that..."

He looked around at the other members in his party. Their smiles had slid away. A grim readiness had replaced it, their hard eyes fixed on their leader. Hands slid to the handles of their waiting weapons. He gave the witch a meaningful look, holding her gaze while he spoke in a matter-of-fact manner.

"There are guards combing the countryside and monitoring every road in the Horn for your coven, as you've seen. You can bet that they'll be searching the towns and watching the ports closely. You might choose to take your chances against the arrows and spears of your pursuers, but you've been taken by hunters once already. If it were me in your place, I would wager on us. For my own sake, and for that of the children."

The witch looked down at the three young people seated before her. They looked up at her, eyes luminescent as they seemed to hold a silent congress with their caretaker. She sighed and nodded.

"Good." He clapped his hands and motioned to the brigand with the mustache, "Jarryd, you're on first watch. Barney will take second, then Taron, Erin, and I'll take the early shift. I suggest you all get some rest, tomorrow will be another long day in the saddle."

B y mid afternoon the next day, the group had made its way down the mountain without further incident. They had passed many groups of guards but as Holton had assured them, none gave them more than a passing glance. The witch and her charges had been mostly quiet since the conversation the previous night, keeping to hushed tones and giving the gang of thieves a wide berth. The sun hung at its peak in the sky, once again beating down on them with its unrelenting heat. But now, on the down slope that led out of the mountains, a steady wind blew cool air off the ocean helping to abate the sun's assault somewhat.

The wagon wheels whined and squealed as they descended the switchback road which carved its way down the steep hills towards the coast. The land here was too rocky and steep for most farming, but herds of goats watched the steady stream of travelers flow past with impassive expressions as they munched on scrub grass and hardy bushes. Holton had fallen in next to the cart, his horse stepping in time with the ones that pulled the heavy load. He was chatting with Taron when Alice clambered out from the covered area, squeezing in next to the bearded man. She gave her rescuers a pointed look, bringing their conversation to an abrupt end.

"Something on your mind, girl?" Taron asked, tone amused.

She nodded and looked at Holton, "How did you know that disguising us as a group of players would work? Why aren't the guards taking a closer look at us?"

Holton glanced at Taron, but he only shrugged. Holton looked around, motioning for the girl to see, "Do you see all these people? A crowd is a better cover than any cloak or hiding place. The soldiers are too busy looking for someone trying to sneak past them to be concerned about us."

Alice thought about this a moment, running her hands through her long dark hair in a compulsive manner. She considered this, "Is that how you were able to get into The Hold?"

Holton nodded and smiled, "I've been in this line of work for a long time. The most important thing I've learned is that no matter how good the defenses you build up are, people are just people. You can build walls and gates and use magic to guard a place, but if someone opens the door for you, none of that matters, does it?"

The girl smiled at that. She was perhaps approaching her fifteenth year, if Holton had to guess. He noted a certain boldness in her eyes as she spoke. The events of the previous night did not seem to have discouraged her curiosity.

"That's your secret, then?" She pressed on, "That's what makes you such a grand outlaw?"

Holton and Taron both laughed at that. The girl pushed out her lip a bit, pouting at their reaction, but the red haired man held up his hand to soothe her, "The only thing that makes an outlaw grand is living to see the next day. The size of the job doesn't matter if you're not alive to enjoy the haul."

Alice considered that a moment. Then she went on, "But breaking into The Hold, that must've been a hell of a risk."

"We had a good plan, resources, and the information to make it work. Still, it was no mere caravan robbery."

"So the Blades picked you because you're the best?" She cast a skeptical eye at the group, "Because they couldn't do it themselves?"

Holton grinned, "Damn right. Taron here can break any lock made by man. Erin knows her way around a good disguise and would have been part of a true traveling show in another life. Jarryd is a former Imperial soldier, absolute hell with a blade, and Barney's the most dangerous Fireweaver in the North."

She shot a surprised glance at the young Northman who grinned devilishly and wiggled his fingers at her. Sparks flared between his fingers and before he closed his fist and extinguished them.

Holton snorted, "How do you think we got those houses in Rothmount to go up so quickly?"

Alice considered this. Then she cast a quizzical eye down at his horse, "And you're a Wildwhisperer, right?"

Holton cast a look over at her, "Don't miss much, do you girl?"

She shrugged. He smiled at her and held a finger up to his lips, "Best keep that secret to yourself, girlie. I've worked hard to ensure the Law never catches wind of it."

The group had reached the bottom of the mountain and began making their way across a stretch of flatter land before reaching the large iron gates of Redwater Port. There was a crowd of people awaiting entry, groups of Legionnaires checking the travelers before they were allowed to enter the city. They had several caravans pulled off to the side, searching them and questioning the occupants. Holton called out to his group and they gathered into a close knot around the cart. He spoke in a low voice, just loud enough to be heard over the clopping of horses and the ever-present hum of the traffic on the road.

"Alright, this'll be the toughest track yet." He pointed to the soldiers up ahead, "They're likely to stop us and ask their questions. We all know the story, right?"

The group of thieves and their fugitives gave him a series of quick nods. He met all their gazes in turn, "If something goes wrong, we scatter and meet up at the *Last Look* on the Southern Wharf. No more than three to a group."

They all nodded again, their expressions running the gambit from grim determination to barely contained terror. Holton gave a reassuring nod and another broad grin. They approached the rear of the crowd at the gates as the guards to make it to their party. When the armored men finally reached them, Holton put on his best smile, leaping down from his horse and sweeping off his cap in an elaborate flourish.

"Gentlemen!" He began, "We are so happy to make your acquaintances! I am Petyr..."

"Where're you bound?" One of the soldiers cut him off roughly, holding up a gloved hand, "Papers of transit?"

"Of course." Holton recovered quickly and whipped out a bundle of neatly folded parchment from an inner pocket, "We are to leave on the 'morrow for Oarenhiem, aboard the *Tidewater*..."

"This says eight in your party." The soldier interrupted again, "Are the others in the cart?"

"Aye, good sir." Holton motioned to the cart, "My wife, our daughter, and son, and one of my men's daughters all ride in the back. We cannot afford to keep horses for the lot of us, you see. Only the ones we need for the show. Tell me, have you heard of our company..."

"Tell them to come out." The soldier strode over to the cart impatiently, still clutching the papers in one hand.

Holton followed with the other Legionnaires following closely behind in a loose cluster. Holton wrapped a knuckle on the side of the cart and called out, "Dear, please join us out here, there are some men here who want to speak with you."

The witch came out from the covered wagon, pushing the canvas flap aside as she stepped down onto the cobblestone. She was dressed in similarly flashy garments as the others, dark hair held up with ribbons of bright yellow and red which matched her dress. She came to stand beside Holton.

"And the children." The soldier demanded, crossing his arms.

Holton called out and Alice and the other two stepped out, standing awkwardly at the back of the caravan. The soldier looked them up and down, inspecting their colorful outfits with a discerning eye. He gave Holton a hard look and turned to the children.

"Which of you are their children?" The man asked, nodding his head towards Holton and the witch woman. Louis and Alice stepped forward, the dark haired girl meeting the man's hard gaze while the boy stared at his feet. Erin had hidden the boy's birthmark with an application of the cream used by courtesans to hide bruises and scars from prospective clients and stained his sandy hair dark to match Alice's. The two could have passed for brother and sister at a glance. Unfortunately, they could do nothing to hide their ages. The guard scanned them, glancing back at Holton and the witch, the children's alleged parents, then to Jarryd and Madeline, comparing the sets.

"Tell me, where have you been?" He asked the two, glancing briefly at the paper in his hand.

"Rothmount, for the festival." Alice answered immediately, "Our family performed at the Hall of Heritage."

The soldier consulted the paper. Then he asked, "Where are you headed?"

"Oarenhiem...the capital city, Khanar, to perform for Lord Ghant. It's his name day celebration two days from now and he's called for players from across the continent."

Holton grinned behind a hand as he pretended to scratch at his beard. The witch at his side spoke up, tone impatient, "If that's all sir, the children really do need their rest if they are to perform..."

The soldier silenced her with a hand, not taking his eyes off the two children. He consulted the paper again. "What ship are you taking to Oarenhiem?"

Alice started speaking again but he held up a finger to silence her and focused his attention on the boy. He was frozen in fear.

"Well?" The man demanded, "Do you have no idea what ship you are bound on, boy? Did your father not mention..."

"The *Tidewater*!" Louis blurted out, finally finding his voice, "We sail on the *Tidewater* tomorrow at daybreak, with Captain Tobias Sybil. He's taking us to Cape Lissandra where we will take the White Road to the Capital..."

The soldier frowned as the boy trailed off. He stared at the paper, furrowing his brow as his eyes scanned the writing. Holton cleared his throat.

"Sir? I understand you are a busy man, I assure you my family and our troupe are nothing if not well intentioned. You can search the cart if you wish, you'll find naught but our gear and our instruments. We are nothing but honest players, trying to make our way in this world. We have naught in this world but our wagon and our love." As he said this, he pulled the witch in close with an arm around the waist. He leaned in and planted a kiss on her lips, as if to emphasize his point. She tensed for a moment, then relented. They lingered for a moment, and when he let her go, the soldier was holding the papers out to them. He looked uncomfortable at the display.

"Get on your way then, and be quick about it. We have lots of people to check here."

Holton grabbed the papers and stuffed them back in his inside pocket, giving the guard another tip of his hat. The group gathered themselves and rejoined the rest of the crowd as it shuffled its way through the gates and into the city.

They made their way through the crowded streets, constantly jostled by the flow of bodies and goods moving to and from the ports. Redwater's narrow streets were designed in ages past and were never meant to hold crowds of the size leaving from the Festival. It took them nearly an hour to make their way to the Southern Wharf, and by the time they had all the travelers were glad to get a rest. The *Last Look* was an ancient seaside alehouse, in need of repair but built solidly of stone and heavy timber to withstand the storms.

As they entered the cool, dimly lit interior of the common room, they all breathed in a sigh of relief to finally be out of the heat. It was a standard affair, with simple furniture built to withstand steady use and a great hearth in one corner of the room which sat cold. Erin ushered the group to a table near the back of the room while Holton strode up to the bar, pulling his cap off and stuffing it in an inside pocket. The barkeeper looked him up and down, raising an eyebrow.

"Fancy dress, friend." The man remarked as he rinsed out a metal goblet and shined it with a rag that looked too dirty to clean much of anything.

"Indeed. If you like it, you should see the outfit my horse has. Puts these rags to shame."

The barkeeper chuckled at that. He motioned to the rest of the group that was settling in near the back of the room, "Drinks?"

Holton nodded and the man snapped at a waif of a servant girl who had been leaning against the counter at the far end. She stood up, in no hurry, and wandered over to the table. The barkeep shook his head, "Damn girl's lazier than a house cat in a high castle."

Holton shook his head sympathetically, "So hard to find good help these days. I do appreciate your efforts though. If I might trouble you for something else, I'm expecting to meet a man here..." The barkeep leaned closer, expectantly, "...a tall, dark fellow, dresses like a Lord in dire need of a meeting with a bandit in a back alley. Have any such men come through here recently?"

The barkeeper stroked his chin, then reached below the counter. He pulled out a small, sealed envelope and slid it across the pitted and scarred bar top to Holton conspiratorially.

"Your man came through in the wee hours this morning. Flashed a lot of shiny coins around and gave me a few marks to pass this on to you."

Holton thanked the fellow and joined the rest of his group at the table. They were already in their cups as he ripped the letter open and scanned it. He read it twice, carefully committing the details to memory. Then he held it out to Barney who put a

single finger and touched it. The letter caught fire instantly with
a bright flash, drawing curious glances from the waitress and
barkeeper. He held it until the fire was singing his fingers. Then
he dropped what remained into an almost empty flagon and
watched it sizzle in the remnants of an ale.

Erin leaned over to him, glancing at the smoldering remains
of the letter, and asked in a low voice, "Is everything alright?"

Holton stared into the rapidly dying flames as he rubbed his
fingers together, feeling the slight burn which had left his skin a
bright pink hue, "There has been a change of plans."

Chapter Ten

Sundered

Cassius sat on the edge of one of the large easy chairs, staring at the smoldering hearth of The Hold's library, waiting with his hands clasped before him. Harsh lines etched into his brow and cheeks, the dark circles under his eyes only accentuating his grim visage. Obviously, he had hardly slept, his mind still churning like a pit of vipers from the night before. He turned the arguments over and over again in his mind, trying to reexamine them from every angle, but only succeeding in making himself more frustrated. The sun was still in the east, having just crested the mountains as it climbed its way into the sky.

Mid morning light spilled in through the stained glass, coloring the books and shelves in a dazzling array of colors and blurry images. The sweet sounds of birds could be heard, calling the city to wake and go about their days. Normally, the morning was a time he looked forward to. He would exercise in the courtyard or the Legion Barracks, running the yard or sparring with one of the men in the practice arena. He enjoyed getting out in the crispness of the mountain air in the mornings, working up a good sweat and getting the blood moving. But that was the furthest thing from his mind today. A dark cloud harried him, shunning the light and pushing all pleasant thoughts from his mind, leaving only grim pondering.

The door hinges cried out in protest as they were opened and a servant led his sister in. Valeria wore a simple night robe, her hair wrapped up in a messy bun. Though she was still disheveled from the night, when she looked at him her eyes became as sharp as well hewn razor blades. His sister took a seat and stared at him without so much as a greeting, waiting to speak until the servant brought the door screeching closed behind her as she fled the palpable tension.

"What possessed you to drag me from my chambers at such an ungodly hour, Cas?" His sister demanded, ice hanging on every syllable. All the pretense of agreeableness which usually graced her voice was gone.

"You're making the wrong decision." Cassius did not hesitate, his tone direct and his demeanor blunt, "I know you've convinced father already. You're the smart one, the one who pulls all the strings...but you're wrong about this."

"Really?" Her voice was incredulous. She burrowed into him with her eyes, beads of cold fire which were relentless in their intensity.

"Yes. This conspiracy you're chasing, this cabal, whoever they might be...they're already here. This isn't some game to win, not anymore. They've attacked our home, Valeria, found a weakness and exploited it to get at us. We have at least one traitor, that's a certainty...the time for tricks and subterfuge is over."

Valeria considered him from behind her glare, but said nothing, so Cassius pushed on.

"Jayce told us he met a man from the Blades in Redwater last night. You and father said you'd send word to search for the man he saw, brushed it off, but I know you better than that. It worries you that you didn't know the Blades were operating there. I saw it plain as day on your face. You cannot pretend you and father have this situation under control, not anymore..."

"So what would you have us do, then?" Valeria cut in, voice harsh. She was angry enough, there was no mistaking that, but there was something deeper there. He thought he knew what it was.

He tried to bring the rage in his heart to heel. He cast his gaze to the side and thought about the long days he and his siblings had spent in this room, managing to calm the tone of his voice somewhat, "Call for aid, Val. We need to tell the Sovereign about what's happening, about your suspicions about this conspiracy. I know you're afraid..."

"Afraid?!" Valeria sneered at her brother, "I'm not afraid, Cas, I'm just not a fool. You would have us risk exposing our weakness to our enemies, risk losing what advantage we have over them, for what? To hope the Sovereign believes you, firstly. Then what? Send the Dawn Plains Legions to the Horn to root out the villains?"

"To ensure he can take steps against this plot, whatever it is, in the Capital." Cassius insisted, feeling the frustration creeping back into his voice, "If this is as widespread as you say it is, you have to know we won't be the only targets. For all we know the Senate..."

"For all we *know*, the members of the Senate are involved."

"Come on, Valeria. You don't truly believe..."

"You have no idea what I think, and you have no idea what you're talking about. Don't worry though dear brother, I have everything well handled." Valeria held a note of finality in her tone.

Cassius shook his head and gritted his teeth so hard he felt his jaw ache. He shoved himself to his feet and began to pace in front of the hearth. He could not help the notes of desperation which snuck into every syllable, "If you won't tell the Sovereign...then convince father to let me go to Redwater. You know if anyone can find the thieves before they make their escape, I can. If these men were crafty enough to get past our home's soldiers, surely they'll make it past the soldiers at the port."

Valeria shook her head, a sliver of a grin sliding across her lips, "You're needed here brother, we need to ensure our family's grasp on the seat of the Barony remains solid."

"What use am I to anyone here?" He threw up his hands and stared at the ceiling, "Gods, if I have to hear about marrying your sister-in-law *again*..."

"You're still seeing things so simply, brother. You think this is one of the old stories you love so much, but those are for children. As father keeps telling you time and time again, you're not a child anymore. Your desire for glory and honor is nothing but selfish."

"*Selfish*?!" Cassius glared at her, rage building up in his voice, "Everything I've done is for this family, for this Barony! Every battle I've fought has been for us, to bring us glory and defend our lands and our name! I've spilt my own sweat and blood for our people! What have you done, hmm? What have you sacrificed..."

Valeria stood so suddenly, it took her brother by surprise. He had to stop himself from stepping back as his sister, a full foot shorter than him, locked her fierce gaze upon him, "Don't you dare talk to me about sacrifice! I've been sacrificing for this family since I was a *child*. While you were out playing soldier, I spent every day helping our mother, the one who actually ran this Barony. We made all the decisions while you and our father fought your battles and tournaments and had your duels. Even when the sickness took her, I sat right here in this very room until the end, helping her sign the documents because her hands were too weak from the Withering eating her from the inside out."

Tears had sprouted in his sister's eyes. She brushed them aside with the back of her hand as she glared at her brother. Her voice trembled as she hissed the words through gritted teeth, "Where were you, Cas? Where were you and father while our mother was dying? Fighting *pirates*?"

Cassius stood still as a stone. He had little to say, even if he had been able to find a way to form words.Valeria gave him no time to respond, pushing on, "When she died, who took over? Our father? The Ministers? It certainly wasn't you or Julius. No, it was *me*, handling everything. All me, all alone, just like she was."

She held his gaze a moment longer, shaking slightly, before becoming overwhelmed. She backed off and turned away from him, wrapping her arms around herself as she stared at one of the stained glass windows. Her voice seemed faraway when she finally spoke. He wondered if she were thinking about the same long gone times they had spent in this room, "Did you know he built this library for her?"

It took the Prince a moment to speak, the words catching in his throat, "Yeah, after they got married...it was a wedding present, right?"

Valeria snorted, "More like an apology. They were married in a hurry because he *had* to go to the New World to fight in the war. There needed to be an heir, preferably with an heir of their own, in case our grandfather died and father was the oldest. So they sent our mother up here from the Broken Coast, there was a wedding, then he left her here, all alone. They were married under a new moon and he left before the start of the next cycle."

"But he came back...to see her..."

"Twice. I was two years old the first time I met our father, four the second time. When he finally came home for good I was nearly five." She looked wistfully around the room, now fully lit as the sun had well and truly risen into the sky, "He had this built while he was gone, imported the stained glass from the Coast so it would feel more like home for her. It was to give her some small comfort while he was away...I suppose. She loved this place so much..."

Cassius watched his sister for a moment, the last traces of his fury far gone. She seemed slight at that moment, not the confident woman he knew her to be, but the girl who had spent her days curled up with a pile of books in the hidden nooks of this fortress. The one who had clung to her mother's skirts and hidden behind her as she moved through these halls. He put an arm around her shoulder, as gentle as he could manage. She flinched, but let it rest there. Eventually she leaned her head against his shoulder.

"I miss her too, Val." They stood there for a long time. Watching the sun play across the colored glass and paint the room with its menagerie of shades and forms.

Eventually, she sighed and stepped back from him. She still hugged herself, but she met his gaze with unflinching eyes, "I know you think every problem can be handled with a sword, Cas, but this is the real world. You are the eldest Prince of the Horn, and we need you to do your duty, just as I've done. The Legionnaires will find the prisoners, father and I will handle this conspiracy. We need you here, safe, to secure our family's future."

Cassius shook his head and clenched his jaw. He sighed, meeting his sister's gaze. He implored her with his eyes, desperate to get her to understand, "Then leave Jayce out of this, if you won't give me anything else, grant me this one favor. He's no spy, Val, you know that. I never meant to involve him in...all of this."

Valeria hesitated. She frowned for a moment, but then shook herself and her steely eyed mask was repainted on her face, "No. I know he's your friend, but we need him. This is bigger than him, or me, or you. He's the best chance we have of finding corruption in the University. If we don't find the rot now, we're risking the entire forest in the future."

Cassius swore under his breath and Valeria set her jaw. She began to stride past him towards the exit, but he caught her arm.

"If he gets hurt..." He growled in a low voice.

"It'll be in service to the nation." Valeria cut in coolly. She let her expression soften by a fraction and added, "For what it's worth, I wish there were another way. I've always liked him."

With that, she shook her arm loose and left Cassius alone in the library, staring after her as he stood bathed in the multicolored light.

I t was well past noon when the Prince made his way across the courtyard, stepping quickly and hefting a bag over one shoulder while carrying his sword strapped over the other. He wore his lightest armor, sturdy leathers which only covered his most vital areas, over traveling clothes. The sun hung high in the sky and the entire city baked under its heat. He entered the stables, thankful for the partial relief of the shade. The smell of hay and horses filled his nose. He set his bag down and began searching the stalls until he found his brown charger.

A massive beast he had named Rearden after one of the famous warriors of Herronite legends. The horse had been his companion for nearly five years now, raised by his own hand since it was a foal. It whinnied and pawed at the dirt when he approached, eager to be on the move, but he soothed it with a few quick words and pats on the flank. Careful not to attract too much attention, he saddled the beast and led it toward the gates, scooping his pack on the way.

He walked the beast across the courtyard, squinting against the sun, towards the West Gate. He carefully avoided direct eye contact with any of the dozen or so guards, servants and laborers he passed in their comings and goings around the fortress grounds. The majority of the decorations which had adorned the yard for the Summer's Summit were already gone, with only a few workers still removing hanging lanterns and streamers from the highest points. If not for the heist, it would have been business as usual in the city by now.

But as he approached the gate, the presence of a full crew of soldiers betrayed the heightened security. He approached them with a wave, coming to a stop as a tall man in armor stepped out from the others to address him. Sergius, who had been part of his personal guard for nearly three years, grasped him by the forearm, placing a friendly hand on his shoulder.

"Cas," he began, casting an eye across the nobleman's freshly saddled horse, lingering a moment on the pack strapped to its back, "how are you my friend? How is the arm?"

Cassius grinned at him and patted the side of his horse's neck, "I'm good, my friend, and recovered, for the most part. I was thinking of taking Rearden for a ride outside the city. He needs to stretch his legs, you know confinement doesn't suit him well."

Sergius eyed him, misgivings plain on his broad face, "The Lord Baron's decree still stands, Cas, you are not to leave the grounds."

The Prince stood there, unmoving. He gave his friend a long look, "Sergius, you're the soldier I should aspire to be. But more than that, you're my friend. I would not ask you to betray your Liege Lord..."

The tall soldier searched his face for a long moment, "You...chose an *opportune* time to take an afternoon ride, my Prince."

"I did, my friend."

The two stood facing each other for a moment. The sun was relentless as it beat down on the men. Both were sweating in their armor, Sergius in ornate Legionnaire's plate and Cassius in his oiled leathers. The soldiers behind the tall man glanced at each other nervously, shuffling from one foot to the other. The air was heavy with unspoken anticipation of what was to come.

"I suppose..." Sergius began, but stopped and looked past the Prince as he saw another figure coming across the yard.

Julius, well groomed and all in finery as per usual, rode up on his own horse. The sprinter was lighter than Cassius' great beast and its golden coloring made it an anomaly in the region. As the younger Prince brought his horse up next to his brother, it gave a whine and stamped its foot, clearly displeased it was not being allowed to run across the open yard. Julius gave them all his usual winning smile and looked at his brother.

"There you are Cas, I thought I told you to wait for me."

Cassius looked from Sergius to his brother, trying not to let the surprise show on his face, "My apologies, Julius..."

"No matter," he waved a careless hand and turned his gaze on Sergius, "my brother and I are to go riding out in the countryside today. Don't worry about my father's decree, I'll keep my eye on him."

Sergius stared at them both for a moment. Eventually, he relented, inclining his head and motioning to the other soldiers to move aside. Cassius gave him a quick nod, clapping his friend on the shoulder. Then he mounted his horse and the two noblemen rode out of the Western Gate, horses clopping down the cobblestone streets of the city.

They rode in silence for a long while. People waved and called out to them as they made their way through the city. Many they passed reached up for a greeting and offered tokens of appreciation, but they only waved back politely. Cassius was staring at his brother, who kept his gaze pointedly on the road ahead of them. Finally, the elder Prince could bear the silence no longer.

"What are you doing here, Jules?" Cassius demanded.

"Helping you escape, obviously." The younger Prince replied simply, blowing a kiss to a young girl who leaned out of an upper window in one of the homes, trying to get a good glimpse of them as they passed by. The girl squealed and turned a shade of red Cassius associated with apples at the peak of their flavor.

"But, how did you know where I was?"

"You're not hard to predict, Cas. After last night, I knew you would do something... *dramatic*. I gave the serving girl for your quarters a handful of marks and asked her to let me know if you seemed like you were getting ready to leave." He cast a sidelong glance at his pack and leather armor, "Not exactly being subtle, were you?"

Cassius gave him a hard look. Julius only grinned, "Let me guess, you're going to Redwater, right? To catch the thieves?"

The older Prince started to argue, but then reconsidered it and nodded. Julius gave a slight nod, seeming pleased with himself. He considered something for a moment, "Did you tell Val?"

Cassius thought back to the morning's conversation and flinched, "We...discussed it."

The younger man sighed as he guided his horse through the gates of the inner wall. The guards there watched them go, but made no move to stop them, only placed a closed fist over their chests in a sign of respect. Cassius returned the gesture, while his brother only waved lazily at them before continuing. He bit his lip, "Sounds like it was a productive conversation."

"She thinks I'm most useful stuck up in The Hold, bound to her sister."

"She might not be wrong."

Cassius gave him another look, "Then why are you helping me?"

Julius sighed again. He met his brother's gaze for the first time, surprising him with the earnestness in them, "Because you're right, Cas."

He cast a look over the city, carefully choosing his words, "Father and Val, they want to keep playing this game. They care about *winning*. But you're not like them, and neither am I. I know if I let you go after them, if you start...well, being *you*, you'll wreck their plans and they might withdraw, go into hiding. We might not learn who told them about the prisoners. We may never find that out. But...that's not what's important."

Cassius said nothing. He watched his brother, seeing the conflict cutting contours into his expression that looked painful even at a distance.

"We have to think about these people...they're what's important. We have a chance to stop this now, before it becomes a conflict, before it spreads across the land. Yet, they're too scared, of what? Showing our hand? Losing our advantage? *Lineage?*" The young man shook his head, hair swishing around his head. He brushed it back with his hand and gave Cassius a look. He was smiling.

"I know you, Cas. I know you only want what's best for people. *Dux Valorus* and all that. I know you'll do everything you can to stop these conspirators before they do something horrible." He paused thoughtfully, "And if you can't, you'll make sure the word gets to the Sovereign, won't you?"

Cassius could not help the swell of pride that filled his chest as he sat up a bit straighter in his saddle. "I will, Julius. You have my word, I swear it."

Julius laughed at that, "I'm not sure what the word of a *former* Dux Valorus is worth these days...but I'll take the word of my brother."

The elder Prince flinched a little at the jab, but he recovered and gave his brother a good natured grin. The two rode in silence for a moment.

"Father's going to be furious." Cassius stated plainly.

"So will Val," Julius grinned, "and I'll be there to take the brunt of it."

"Will you be alright?"

Julius nodded, placing a hand on his chest dramatically, "I'll find a way to manage somehow."

Cassius rolled his eyes and suppressed a chuckle under his breath. But as they continued down the cobblestone streets, making their way closer and closer to the outer wall, Julius's look got more serious again.

"Cas...do you think they're right? Do you think this is the beginning of something catastrophic?" Julius had a strange look on his face, distant yet somehow overtly aware. He seemed to be trying to take everything in at once and managing none of it.

Cassius rubbed his beard, recently trimmed so it bristled under the leather of his gauntlets, "Perhaps, if this cabal is as large and well connected as Val seems to think it is, it could be the start of someone making a major play for power. I don't know what other reason someone might have to hire all the mercenary companies from across all of Evardene."

"If it does...if this really is the start of a war, I won't be much help." Cassius looked over and for the first time, his brother did not meet his gaze. His eyes were held firmly by the stitch work of his saddle.

Cassius let the statement hang in the air for a moment. He saw the shadows of doubt hidden behind the swaggering confidence. He reached out and grasped the reins of his brother's horse suddenly. He brought both beasts to a stop within a stones throw of the outer wall gates.

"Julius, why would you say such a thing?"

It was Julius's turn to roll his eyes even as he tried not to meet his brother's gaze, "It's nothing, you should go. Father will have heard you left by now."

But Cassius would not be dissuaded as he held firm on the younger man's horse, "I'm not concerned about father right now. Why do you speak like this?"

The younger Prince struggled to form the words as he still kept his gaze on anything but his brother's eyes, "I...I've done nothing, Cas. I'm not a fighter. I haven't fought in any wars like our father, nor defended our people, like you. I'm not a soldier, and I'm not even a leader. I've not earned the Dux title. You, father, Val...all of you have been of service to the nation, to our Barony, but all I've ever been is the son of a nobleman. I worry...that I have neither the courage nor the strength of character to be more."

His shoulders were slumped and his face crestfallen at the sudden admission. Cassius grasped him tightly by the shoulder with his free hand, causing the young man to flinch away. But he held him firm, forcing him to look him in the eyes.

"Do you know what I thought the first time I accompanied our father on a campaign into the backcountry? When we were hunting Old Jack and his band of cutthroats?"

Julius shook his head, dumbfounded.

"I thought I was going to die. I was scared and shaking and I couldn't shit right the whole week. I could barely eat and I sat up every night wishing I could be home, safe in The Hold." Cassius's intense look was only deepened by the grim smile which worked its way across his face at the memory, "I was barely in my thirteenth year and had never swung a sword against a man in combat before, but father left me to guard the rear of the caves alone, to watch for stragglers. The boy I killed that day was maybe two years older than I was, and I got lucky. He was sloppy as he came at me, didn't watch his footing, tripped, and I ran him through before he could recover."

His brother stared at him speechless, eyes wide.

"After, I sat in the dirt, covered in his blood, and cried until Tanner found me and cleaned me up. He told father how I had bested that boy in combat and all the men celebrated that night, toasted me and told me how I was going to be a great warrior one day."

"What, why are you telling me...?"

"You can't ever be *ready*, Jules, no one is, not me, nor father, and everyone is afraid, no matter what they tell you. Dealing in death is an ugly, dirty, dark business, but you can't run from it, can't hide from it either. When it comes for you, you have to face it head on, with both feet under you and your weapon in your hands." He gave his brother's shoulder a hard squeeze, "Life is much the same. Those men, they had been raiding farmers, killing whole families. If we hadn't done what we did, they would have kept at it. Who knows how many more innocent people would have suffered?"

Julius was silent as he pondered this for a moment. Cassius handed him his reins, which the younger Prince held limply. He stared at his brother as Cassius collected himself. Then he gave his younger brother a long, steady look and smiled at him, "You're stronger than you think, Jules, you've shown that today. You'll make the right calls when you need to, don't worry."

The younger Prince bit his lip. He shook his head, "But I'm not a fighter, Cas. You know...you've seen me in the sparring ring. I'm awful."

"Well, not everyone is meant to be a warrior. The old philosophers say the nation needs thinking men as much as it needs men who can swing a sword. Good men who put the people first, who protect the nation. Too many are like our sister, too eager to fill their coffers, to serve their own ends. But you can be different. You can be a true Dux Servitas."

Julius considered this for a moment. He finally spoke up, "Do you think about him often? The boy you killed?"

The elder Prince looked off the way they came, back towards the ancient fortress on its hilltop. It had taken them over an hour to walk their horses across the vast, sprawling city and now the red stone was painted in the afternoon sunlight. He thought of the many times he had seen that vast structure with it's imposing towers and tall walls and thought of it as beautiful, in a way. But as the fading light deepened the hue of the stone, it gave the structure some hint of life. At this angle, looking up at it from the city's lower streets, the light made the stone look like the gently rippling flesh of a great creature. The Hold seemed to be waiting, hungrily sat upon its hill for the next people to cross its threshold as it glared down at the valley below like a great dragon in the old stories.

He sighed, shook the thoughts from his head and nodded, "Every day, Jules."

His brother gave him a look, before reaching an arm out to him. Cassius grasped it and they held each other by the forearm for a moment.

"Safe travels, brother." Julius said, giving him his winning smile.

"Thank you, for everything." Cassius grinned back at him, "You're a better man than you think you are. Our people owe you a great debt."

"Perhaps. I'll wait to collect until after I see what wrath I face from our dear sister."

They both grinned at that and finally parted ways. Julius sat on his mount and watched his brother direct his horse through the outer gate of Rothmount, past the thick, double walls and towering turrets of the city, and make his way down the road towards Redwater. He did not turn back for home until Cassius was long out of sight.

ACT II
Unwelcome Inquisitions

STAGHEART PRESS, LLC

CHAPTER ELEVEN

DISAGREEMENTS

The skies over the Oaren Peninsula were darkened by dour clouds, casting shadows across the land. Heavy winds whipped a summer storm off the sea and through the gray mountains. Rain soaked the city of Khanar, capital of the Oarenhiem Empire, painting the stone of the spindly towers and intricately decorated walls with a dark sheen. The breathtaking behemoth of a city was carved into the side of a mountain in two dozen terraces, the tiled roofs of thousands of buildings cutting across the levels in orderly rows.

Slashes of green crisscrossed the expanse of stone, delicate elevated gardens and well manicured parks of flowers and topiary intertwining with the streets and buildings. Many of the larger estates held private gardens, often displayed out on upper sundecks and patios, the houses lording their collections above the rest of the city. Along with gardens and green spaces, aqueducts interspersed the city, descending from the mountain's peak, carrying water throughout the streets into innumerable smaller systems and feeding fountains decorated with majestic figures of the Empire's history. Even in the rain, the city was a breathtaking fusion of engineering and art. It displayed itself proudly, like a beacon on the mountain, a testament to the strength and power of the Empire.

An enormous, sprawling estate with its own high walls and opulent grounds presided over one of the city's highest terraces; the Great Conservatory of Khanar. Inside the grounds, the main building extended out from the mountainside in a massive semicircle with a domed central roof and a dozen smaller domes at regular intervals along its perimeter. Another dozen circular outbuildings dotted the grounds with walking paths which gently ambled through the lush gardens, winding around statues and fountains to connect them to each building to the others.

Each dome was made of opaque glass with a wound circle of intricate gold designs inlaid into it. Despite the gray day, the domes glinted and shined like giant gems on the mountainside. If looked at from the top, the compound looked like nothing so much as half an enormous compass that burst forth from the mountainside and pointed out over the city.

To Juniper, stalking through the rain across the opulent grounds of one of the Oarenhiem Empire's most exalted institutions, it all seemed as routine and common as fields of cotton might to a farmer. As she burst into the antechamber of one of the outbuildings, she soaked the decorated entryway in water and mud, dirtying the inlaid filigree without a second thought. She yanked her violet cloak off and tossed it carelessly over the silently roaring maw of the gold and jewel encrusted dragon statue which sat facing the door. Her short hair was plastered to her head from the weather, framing her eyes which flashed like green fire in the witchlight. An ancient man with severely thinning hair sat at attendance behind a small desk, popping up from a poorly concealed nap when she entered. He tried to call out to her, but she was already striding through the atrium past him, leaving a trail of wet and muddy footprints in her wake across the pristine floors.

Her fierce expression warded off any who might have thought to approach her, earning her a wide berth as she stalked up the stairs and down the hallways adorned with fresco paintings and detailed busts. The jeweled bracelets and necklaces jangled on her golden skin, sounding like the warning rattle of a snake preparing to strike its next victim. Finally, upon reaching the end of a long hallway, she blew through a set of fantastically ornate doors without so much as an attempt at formal announcement. Inside was perhaps the most lavish interpretation of what could be called a workspace imaginable.

A massive table of heavy timber, designed with delicate carvings of geometric shapes in intricate patterns which stretched up the legs and flowed across the edges took up the center of the room. Across its surface were neatly organized tools and instruments made of gold and copper, along with several small stacks of books, papers as well as fancy pens and small glass containers of various materials with labels scrawled across them in a swirling hand. Around the table matching chairs were interspersed with silk cushions of deep crimson, and a similarly colored carpet covered the stone floor. The walls were lined with mahogany shelves of books, small boxes and expensive looking knickknacks all neatly organized and presented with an impeccable sense of taste. A large hearth of stones which pulsed red without any visible fire filled the space with a comfortable warmth, a noticeable change from the hallway where Juniper had just entered from.

In front of a large window which stretched to the vaulted ceiling, a thin man stood watching the rain fall with hands clasped behind his back. He had a shaved head and the red light of the false fire glinted off his gold skin. But it died in his eyes which were a cold gray, joyless as a blade. When Juniper crashed in through the door, he turned to face her, an amused expression on his face.

"Ah, Professor Faye, so good of you to join me. Would you care for..."

"I've no patience for your nonsense today, Lysler!" The woman hissed in her native tongue. Even in her anger she noted how it felt good to form the flowing syllables of Oara after so many days speaking the clumsy language of the Southerners. However, she had little time to enjoy the sensation as she blustered into the room in a flurry of wet clothes and whipping hair and stalked around the table. She was in his face in scarcely a moment, teeth gritted as she spat her words, *"Five days!"*

He showed no sign of concern, his grin never faltering, "Why Professor, whatever are you talking about?"

"Don't play games with me, old man!" His smug demeanor only served to stoke the flames of her fury further, "I left Rothmount five days ago, barely making it out with my life, and you have the *nerve* to act like you don't know what I'm angry about?"

"I can assure you..."

"Not one message, not a single word from you! I was supposed to meet Lawrence in Redwater three days ago but he's up and vanished on me. I reached out to both of you in every way I could think of and got *nothing*." She was glaring at him from under her mat of wet hair, "Then, I finally got back to the Empire, on my own I might add, and you *refused* to see me?!"

"Don't be so dramatic." Lylser told her motioning towards one of the chairs, "Won't you sit? You can dry off, maybe have some tea...take a moment and let that temper die down a bit so we may continue in a more, *civilized* manner."

She bit her cheek to keep from screaming at him. But despite the fury that was desperately clawing to get out from inside her, she knew on some level this was not going to get her anywhere. She forced herself to draw in a ragged breath and slowly blow it out through her nostrils. Then she took another, and a third, remembering the breathing exercises she had learned as a child in this very school. Deep breaths slowly brought her pulse down and the rage subsided, replaced by a white hot ingot of burning focus inside her. She approached the table stiffly but did not sit. She glared at him across the menagerie of instruments and tools and neat stacks of parchment.

The bald man sighed, sliding into the seat closest to the window. His movements were too smooth, almost serpentine in their unsettling grace. He stared at her with those unfeeling eyes as he spoke, making Juniper's insides feel cold despite the anger that still swelled there.

"You have done well in your task, Professor Faye." He began, his sickly smile still clinging to the edges of his mouth, not touching the rest of his visage, "The Hold was breached, our agents were successful in their mission. But there was a... *complication*. Somehow, word of our associates presence in Redwater reached the Baron. Lawrence was forced to flee from The Horn before he could meet with you or collect our prizes. The risk was too high..."

"You couldn't have told me? Warned me that our plans had been compromised? What about *my risk*?"

"Communicating with you directly was not an option. It would have been bad enough if you got caught, but if it got out that the Conservatory was involved in any way, that would have been disastrous." Lysler began absentmindedly fingering a golden instrument on his table. It looked like a tiny scale which rocked back and forth over the point of a triangle. He pushed down on one side then let go, setting it off its steady beat.

"So you...you were going to *abandon* me, if they discovered my part in the heist?"

"Come now, Juniper, you're a true Professor of the Conservatory now, albeit a very new one, not some child playing with dolls in your mother's office. I should not think to coddle you."

Juniper bristled at the comment. But she managed to get her flaring emotions under control once again as he continued.

"Besides, it would not have changed a thing. You would still have had to make your way back here, in your own time, and we would still be sitting here having our meeting. Only on more *agreeable* terms, perhaps."

Juniper closed her eyes and let the words wash over her. She was still furious, but something within her heard the truth in his statement. Maybe it was the years of brutal instruction at the hands of self satisfied old men like this, or perhaps the ingrained societal standards of her highborn station, but either way, she felt the familiar sensation of being forced to swallow her more inflammatory inclinations. She felt it like sour bile in her guts, churning within her as she forced a thin smile onto her face.

"Perhaps." She hissed at him through her teeth, "Whatever the case, it is done now. Will we be moving forward now, or will we need more recruits first?"

The door opened behind her and a small, elderly woman in a white frock came in, wheeling a cart which glided along the marble floors noiselessly. She poured steaming tea into two delicate porcelain glasses and placed one before each of them on the table. She left the kettle between them on a woven pad to protect the table and bowed deeply, first to the bald man, then to Juniper. Lysler waved her away with an unconcerned flick of the wrist and she wheeled her cart back out, shutting the door.

As the older professor began to sip his tea, Juniper watched, impatient as she waited for him to be finished. He was in no hurry, seeming to relish drawing the moment out as he watched her over the rim of the glass. Finally, he smacked his lips in approval, placed the cup back on the table, and turned his attention back to her.

"Have you done your clearing exercises? You seem quite on edge this morning. Perhaps the residual is giving you some trouble?"

Juniper blinked and stuttered. She finally blurted out, "Yes, of course I've done my exercises! And I don't appreciate your insinuations..."

He held up his hands, his unsettling smile returning as he looked her up and down, "I only ask out of concern for your well-being. We wouldn't want you *settling* now, would we?"

She stared at him squarely, "I can handle my own affairs."

He shrugged and took another maddeningly slow sip from his cup. Juniper rolled her eyes and let out a huff, "I didn't come here to watch you drink tea, Lysler."

"Oh, no? Then what did you come here for, Professor? What would you like from your Dean of Alchemy?"

"I *want* to be kept in the loop." Juniper was gritting her teeth so much during this meeting her jaw was hurting, "I want to be updated. Are we moving forward, or not?"

Lysler's grin was still plastered to his face as he spoke, slowly enunciating his words, as if to a child, "We will move forward when the time is right. You will be told once the operation is ready, just like everyone else."

She stared at him. She clenched and unclenched her hands as she imagined wrapping them around the man's thin neck. She did not even attempt to make an attempt at propriety, letting her distaste for this man carve her face as she scowled at him.

"If you have an issue, perhaps you should speak to your dear mother. She is our fearless leader after all." If anything, her displeasure made his sickly smile widen even further, "If that is all, I'm sure you have work to catch up on after your trip. Good day, Professor."

He indicated the door with another lazy flick of his hand. She stood for a moment, trying to work out another retort. But then she realized every moment she stood in this spot, unspeaking, clenching her jaw with violent daydreams playing through her mind, she made herself look all the more foolish. So she spun on her heels and strode out the door with her shoulders back, not deigning to cast a parting glance in his direction. She left the cup of tea sitting untouched, still steaming on the table.

I t was the earliest part of what could be called evening when a knock came at her office door. What little light there was on this gloomy day was just starting to dwindle, rain still slamming into the windows and beating on the roof. She removed a set of thin framed reading spectacles and stood from her pristinely organized desk, then moving through the narrow, cramped office of an Associate, which she still occupied despite her recent rise in station, she made her way towards the door. Opening it, she was not surprised to see her mother standing there in the hallway..

Aria Faye looked like she could have been her daughter, if she were about three decades older and with long, lustrous hair instead of Juniper's short style. She wore a violet cloak, an exact match of her daughters, but for a gold brooch emblazoned with the simple symbol of a sun, marking her as the Dean of their department. She entered the small office without a greeting and strode over to one of the chairs, sitting without waiting for invitation. She indicated the other chair and Juniper sighed deeply before joining her mother. The older woman looked her daughter up and down.

"It's so cold in here," she began, rubbing her hands together, "would you be a dear and stoke the firestone?"

Juniper reached over and touched a small stone, which already glowed with a faint red light as it sat on a shelf in its own stone bowl. It lit up suddenly and both women could feel waves of heat that flowed off it and warmed the room immediately. The elder Faye sighed in relief and made a motion casually around the office.

"We really need to get you out of this Associate's office and into a true Professors suite, now that it's been made official. One with a good hearth, of course." She smiled at her daughter, "Youngest in our College's history, quite the achievement."

Juniper nodded absentmindedly, staring at the now steadily pulsating red stone. The short strands of her hair fell into her face and her mother reached over, brushing them back over her ear. "You know, I wish you would consider growing it back out, dear. You have such lovely hair after all, and this *new style* your generation favors is so..."

Juniper pulled away and gave her mother a reproachful look, "We've discussed this mother, I like it this way."

Her mother sighed, clasping both hands in her lap in a demure gesture, "Well, I just thought that perhaps some nice young man might like it better..."

"*Mother...*" She gave the older woman a hard look earned her the smallest of smiles and a gesture of submission.

The older woman paused for a bit before continuing, "So tell me, how was the trip?"

"It was...fine," Juniper stated plainly, "the performance was a great success."

Her mother nodded, "...and the people? Did you enjoy experiencing the culture of our Southern neighbors?"

She made a face and squinted at the memory, "It was like stepping back in time. The decorations, the clothes, it all seemed so...base. I thought I was going to perform for a noble family, but it seemed more like an alehouse by the docks."

Aria nodded again. She clucked her tongue, "The peoples of the Southlands have always been a bit less refined than we are here in the Empire. I heard there was some trouble...afterward?"

"The Baron was furious when he learned someone had broken into his fortress."

"Did he hurt you?"

"No, I'll need to replace some of my clothes, but for the most part he just blustered and glowered at me." Juniper snorted, "I did get lucky though. Did you know their Court Arcanist was working with the Blades?"

Her mother looked at her thoughtfully for a moment, pondering the question, "No, but I suppose it makes sense. They never told me who their contact in The Hold was. He would have had knowledge of the Baron's prisoners, known enough about the defenses to guide the thieves through them, plus he would have easily had enough knowledge about the feast and the guests invited to provide information for their cover stories."

"But why did they need me then?" Juniper asked, holding up a hand in a puzzled gesture, "If the Court Arcanist was a traitor, why not just cast the magic dampening spell himself?"

"Well," her mother began, choosing her words thoughtfully, "perhaps he didn't want to risk being caught. Selling information and actually assisting in a betrayal against your own nation are two very different levels of danger. He may not have had the capability to perform the spell either. It was a complex and dangerous task you undertook, Juniper..."

"Believe me, I am aware..." Juniper muttered, but her mother was still speaking.

"...also, and I believe this is the most likely scenario, an enchantment of the type which protects that fortress is incredibly sophisticated. It would be full of fail safes and contingencies. I wouldn't be surprised if the same amulet that gives him control over its defenses prevents him from acting against it. It might even have killed him if he had tried."

Juniper thought about this for a long moment. The sound of rain filled the quiet as they sat in the small space and each privately considered recent events. Juniper was still staring into empty space when her mother clapped her hands suddenly and brought her back to reality.

"I heard you had a meeting with Dean Lysler. How did that go?"

"Poorly. The man is an ass."

Her mother winced and placed a gentle hand on her daughter's knee, "That is not an appropriate way for you to refer to a fellow member of this staff, especially a senior one. What happened?"

"He refused to apologize for stranding me in Redwater and ignoring my attempts to reach out to him, then stonewalled me when I asked about the...project." Juniper ran her fingers through her hair, sighing in frustration, "I swear that man just enjoys provoking me."

"My sweet blossom," the older woman shook her head, "Lee has always been a vain man with a cruel streak like a viper. Age and the loss of his daughter has only distilled his spite. It causes him to strike at everyone in his path, believe me, you are no special case."

"I don't understand how a man like that becomes a Dean in the greatest arcane school in the world."

"Parentage, mostly." Her mother stated matter-of-factly, "That, and a heavy dose of his own machinations. But it must be said that for all his flaws, Lee is the very best at what he does. If not for him, we wouldn't be undertaking this great project in the first place. It was he and I, along with Dean Ghibli, who started this undertaking. We founded the Ceaseless Scions."

Juniper pouted and glared at her own hands, refusing to acknowledge her mother's redeeming words for her hated colleague. Aria had a small, wistful smile as she looked at her daughter, "Despite all your achievements, you are young still. You will learn; we don't always get what we want in this world. You will resent the people you have to work with at times, you might even hate the work that you do. You will find it hard to continue, but one day, you will find your purpose. That thing that eclipses all else in this world and makes the problems you face now seem so trivial."

Juniper looked up at her, meeting the older woman's soft gaze. Her eyes were green like her own, but less bright now, faded, less full of life. They didn't flash like emeralds but were deep like pools of mountain water.

"There's something else..." Juniper said suddenly, breaking the unspoken spell as they both shook themselves free of the moment.

"What is it dear?"

"The Princess, Valeria, she...approached me during the feast, and after. She wanted to be friends..."

"Friends are always..."

"But it wasn't just that," Juniper cut her mother off, "she told me about suspicions she had. Of a conspiracy, about a threat to the safety of the whole continent. Spoke about mercenaries and hidden plots and asked me to make some inquiries here, in the Empire."

The frown on the older woman's face became deeper and deeper until she finally placed a hand over her mouth, chewing on her fingernail delicately. It was a gesture she had worked hard to eliminate from her subconscious, one Juniper recognized immediately. Her mother was deeply worried, more so than she had been before her only daughter had left to undertake the dangerous mission to assist in robbing a leader of a foreign nation.

"She...asked you to *spy* for her?"

"I...she never said *spy*, just asked me to do some digging, help her look into the possibility of the cabal being here in the Empire." Juniper protested but her mothers concern pricked her nerves. She leaned forward on her knees, "What's wrong? Is there something I'm missing?

"Did you agree? To help her, I mean."

"I...I thought I should. It would have been suspicious not to, right? I mean, she said it was a threat to the entire continent. That the Empire could be in danger...who would say no to that?"

Aria shook her head slowly and her long hair cascaded over her shoulders. She leaned back in the chair and a strange smile came across her face, one that belied the sudden fierceness in her eyes, "What a clever little *snake*..."

Juniper cocked her head at her mother.

"She's trapped you. If you were not involved in this conspiracy, you would go to the Emperor immediately with this request, anyone of sound mind would do so for fear of being labeled a traitor. Whether *he* was involved or not, he would send word to the Roth's immediately denying any knowledge of it, most likely pledging his support to root out this cabal if it had reached the Empire. But, since we know he is not involved, we can be sure he will immediately begin an inquiry as soon as he hears of this. He will want to ensure his hands are clean of this plot and avoid an international incident, which I'm sure Valeria Roth knew he would do too."

"So why not just *not* tell him?" Juniper asked and immediately regretted it when she saw the scornful look on her mothers face.

"If she doesn't receive word from the Emperor, she is going to reach out to him directly. If you don't tell him, you might as well be admitting that you're involved, and by extension, so is the Conservatory. Only someone involved in the heist would hesitate to tell the Emperor. In fact, the longer you wait, the more suspicious it is. Plus, I'm sure she knows there's no way we can fake an Imperial communication. It has to be genuine."

Juniper put a hand over her eyes and thought back over the conversations she had with Valeria Roth, Lady of the Longstrider Clan and Princess of the Horn. It had been so quick, and she was so kind and warm, and her fear seemed so genuine. Juniper had not even hesitated, even for a moment. Now she saw it for what it was, a trap, one so subtle she had almost fallen into it. She reached into one of her pouches and pulled out the speaking stone the princess had given her, staring at it in amazement.

"She did say she was coming here at the end of the season, for some sort of diplomatic meeting. That would be the perfect opportunity to speak to the Emperor." Juniper said slowly, turning the stone over in her hand, "So now, we have to begin an Imperial Inquisition...into ourselves."

Her mother nodded sympathetically. She sighed and patted her daughter on the knee again, suddenly standing.

"There's nothing for it now. I will make an appointment with the Emperor tomorrow. We will just have to tread...very carefully from now on. We cannot afford for this endeavor to be thrown off course. The Emperor must make his trip as scheduled to visit New Oarenhiem for the Winter's Crest."

She turned and walked back across the room towards the door. Juniper followed her, quickly trotting along in her mother's footsteps. The older woman turned quickly, and Juniper found herself staring directly into her mother's eyes all at once.

"You should spend some time with your Father. He misses you fiercely. I don't think he's been out of his study since you left to go on your trip."

"I will," Juniper promised, "soon."

"Good." She gave her daughter a quick hug and opened the door. She made her way into the brightly lit hallway before giving the younger woman one last look, "Besides, it will give me a chance to *finally* introduce you to the family that has moved in next door to us, the one with that nice young man who works in the Court of Concessions."

Juniper started to protest but her mother had already swept her cloak over one shoulder and was halfway down the hall, walking with her head held high as she moved through the halls of the Conservatory with unassailable conviction. Juniper shut the door with a deep sigh and wandered over to the window. She pulled out a small, golden locket and stared at it. The rain still fell against the window in sheets and the sky was darkening quickly. Juniper could just barely make out the far off smoke from the Burning Isles, the ever smoking volcanic islands that resided far out in the western sea. She leaned her head on her hand and watched the storm barrage her city, letting her mind wander as she tried not to dwell on the day's events.

CHAPTER TWELVE

THE DAWN CITY

W hen Jayce disembarked from his ship, gray skies hung heavy over the streets of Asaldon, capital city of the Dawn Plains and the Seat of the Herronite Federation's Sovereign. A western wind was blowing a strong storm off the Lancing Ocean but the Horn had borne most of the beating, leaving the rest of the mainland with only a smattering of summer showers and a darkened horizon. The heat made the wet air humid and thick and it clung to the earth like an invisible blanket. However, the weather did nothing to dampen the largest city in the nation, as the streets were pulsing with the constant flow of movement and overflowing with sound.

The massive, sprawling metropolis started in a roughly built grid system but quickly lost any sense of overt design as it spilled out from the shores of Lake Locklear, a body of water so large one could easily have mistaken it for an ocean. The city swelled across the flatlands outward from the shore in a chaotic web of white, tan and reddish brown buildings, losing shape as it formed boroughs and neighborhoods on the city outskirts, making confusing patterns and disorienting tracks that led in circles. There was a tall stonewall which marked the outlines of the original city, but the growth had long since spilled past its old boundaries and it stretched uncontained in all directions.

Inside the city, the cobblestone streets were lit with witch-light lanterns, glowing with low light due to the darkened skies despite it being midday. There was a steady flow of traffic, pedestrians, mule drawn carts and horse and oxen drawn wagons moving through the streets endlessly at all hours. As Jayce made his way through the crowded streets, he thought this might be the busiest city on earth. As he was buffeted this way and that, he felt like he was a pitifully small ship cast to sea in an endless storm. It had taken him all of four days to reach Asaldon, leaving from Rothmount on the High Road and heading east until he had boarded a riverboat in Stillbend.

They had followed the tumbling waters down from the Horn until they reached the western edge of the Great Lake. He had switched vessels in Belhaven, continuing his journey on a flat bottom trading barge which had cut across the lake and taken him right to the Federation's capital city. It had been mostly uneventful but for the sailors and fishermen who had seen his fine clothes and all but demanded he join in their games of dice and cards. He had had to make excuse after excuse and listen to their grumbling the entire trip, as he had not a single mark to his name. He refused to use the promissory notes since the confrontation with his parents, keeping the book of receipts and recognizable crest stashed away in his bag.

As he finally turned off the wide, crowded main street onto one of the less busy side roads, he noted the change in architecture. The tall, cramped buildings of the city gave way to large manor houses with their own small, fenced grounds. Both sides of the street held several of these miniature estates, each flying their own flag at the entrance. As Jayce made his way down the street, he noted the various nations and kingdoms represented. First came the houses of the various foreign emissaries; there were the green and yellow and white flags of the Northern Kingdoms, displaying their various animals or trees or weapons proudly. Beyond them, the black flag of Oarenhiem was prominently displayed with its wide jawed yellow serpent menacing passers. Then, there came the familiar blue backed silver star and crossed swords of the Broadwater Republic, which sent a pang of homesickness through him, followed by the flags of the nations from the distant southern continent of Vinatieri. There was the purple cross of the Scivian Empire and the stylized red drake of Karigon.

At the end of the row, the Consuls of the Baronies flew their own flags under that of the Federation, a golden horse parading over a red field trimmed in gold filigree. Jayce passed the white tower of the Broken Coast, brilliant on its blue and yellow field, as well as the orange horse's head of the Fiery Expanse and the yellow hawk of the Dawn Plains. Beyond the grand houses the street opened up to the Basilica, home to the High Senate, a massive building which was lined with archways and columns and had several bronze domes along its length.

When he finally found the roaring red bear of the Horn, he tried not to notice how it seemed to stare down at him with contempt, laden with wet and dripping from the morning weather. A single guard was stationed, leaning against the wall and tightly wrapped in a cloak, as he tried to force himself to fit under a small outcropping. He only noticed Jayce when the young man was all but on top of him, suddenly springing to attention with his hand grasped around the hilt of his sword.

"Woah, there, son, what business have you here?"

Jayce held up his hands and put on his best smile. He indicated the large building beyond the gate, "I'm here to see Lord Lucian Roth."

The guard looked him up and down and grunted, "What's your business?"

Jayce hunted in his coat until he produced a sealed envelope. The original letter Cassius had written for him was in there. But there were other letters now, from the Baron and his daughter, with other instructions which would direct his future here in the capital and most likely, the rest of his life. The guard looked the envelope over without opening it, noting the seal and then gave him a small nod before leading him through the gate.

Inside the manor, Jayce was led to a sitting room with a crackling hearth, where the guard told him to wait, closing and locking a heavy wooden door behind him as he left. Jayce idly examined the room, in particular noting the masterfully illustrated painting of a massive snarling bear doing battle with a Legionnaire on horseback which towered above the fireplace. It struck him how much the warrior depicted bore a likeness with Cassius, or perhaps the Baron. It was undoubtedly intended to be one of their ancestors.

He was still staring at it when he heard the clink of the lock and the guard reentered, leading a couple that practically reeked of regality. The man was tall and lean, with coiffed dark hair and a short beard, looking for all the world like an older version of Julius. The woman was a beautiful northerner, her bright skin and red hair rather striking, even to Jayce who had spent so much of his life traveling. They both had a rosy glow to them, and the woman carried a half empty glass of deep red wine in one hand. When the man saw him, an immediate, broad smile broke out across his face.

"Is that Jayce Acosta? What a pleasure to see you, my boy!" Lucian Roth declared, throwing his hands out wide in a show of a greeting. He grasped the young man in a hug and lifted him off the ground a few inches. Jayce thought he felt his ribs go a little from the pressure, but he managed a weak smile.

"Mari, this is Jayce Acosta, a dear friend of my nephews, and indeed of our whole family. This is my wife, Lady Marigold Walden."

"It is a pleasure." Jayce took the woman's outstretched hand and gave it a firm squeeze.

"Acosta?" Marigold cocked an eyebrow, "As in, the Acosta Trading Company, of the Republic?"

"The only one I know of, my lady." Somehow he managed to keep his gracious smile.

The woman looked him up and down with an appraising eye, "Interesting..."

Jayce braced for further questions but none came. Lucian smiled and motioned for him to sit. Lucian took the chair opposite and his wife sat with him. Jayce noticed she was still staring at him. He tried awkwardly to break the silence.

"Is your daughter about? I haven't seen her for quite a few years."

"Mariana?" Lucian grinned, "Oh, she should be at her studies, but I'm sure she's out with her gaggle of girls somewhere. She's become quite the socialite here in the capital."

"Well I'll have to catch up with her some other time." He trailed off, unsure how to breach the mounting silence. Luckily, the seasoned politician did it for him.

"So, my young friend, I received word from my brother that you were sent here to study at the University?"

"Among other things." Jayce fished the letters from the inside coat of his pocket and handed them to the Lord.

Lucian flicked the letters open and casually began skimming the pages. As he moved on to the second, then the third, his demeanor became more serious. By the time he reached the end of the third letter, the one with the signature of the Baron himself emblazoned at the bottom, he was leaning forward in his seat and reading with his brow furrowed. Several moments passed with only the crackling fire punctuating the pregnant silence. The Lady Marigold had shifted her focus to her husband by this point and when he was done reading he held the letters out towards her. As she took them, Lucian stared at Jayce with a face that belonged to a different man than the one who had entered only moments before.

"You know what these letters say?"

Jayce managed a thin smile, "That I am to enter shark riddled waters with no lifeline."

Lucian blinked, then exchanged his concerned look with the broad grin he had worn moments before as easily as if he was changing hats. He leaned forward in his chair and gave Jayce an earnest smile as he placed a hand on his shoulder, "At least you'll have your sense of humor to help keep you afloat."

The University of Uthersanctorum was located on the Western side of the city, easily identified by a series of tall towers visible from almost anywhere in the sprawling maze of buildings. There were five towers, each adorned with metal inlay in intricately woven patterns and designs. Four towers sat at equal points around the outside of the building. The first was wrapped with a pure black metal which climbed the spire like vines, while the second was adorned with reddish copper weaving thin as threads, the third bore brilliant silver lattice work and the fourth held deep bronze rivulets embedded up its body all the way to the dome. The fifth tower was in the central part of the goliath building, dwarfing the rest with its size and grandeur. The stone of the main tower was also inlaid with complex designs, similar to the towers, but in a pure, gleaming white metal. The roof of the central tower was entirely covered in the white metal and shone so brilliantly in the bit of morning sun that managed to break through the clouds that Jayce believed it would be blinding in full daylight. The entire structure encompassed the space of multiple city blocks, erupting from the sea of the city like a proud ship cresting the waves of the lesser structures that surrounded it.

As they approached the gates of the University, Jayce stared and struggled to gain control of his slack jawed expression. It was like a palace from a children's fairy tale, unmatched by anything he had seen in his travels across most of the known world. As he followed Lucian through the large gates and into the grounds he was met by an equally spectacular sight. The interior was immaculate, with ornate fountains and manicured lawns laid out in whimsical and inviting designs. Exotic birds and animals, some he recognized as native to Vinatieri and some he did not know at all, roamed about amongst trees and bushes that were grown into the shapes of animals and men.

Paths of white stone wound through it all, leisurely strolling about the grounds. There were small groups of what he assumed to be students lounging in various corners of the gardens. They wore matching suits of simple gray and white, with only various colored armbands or broaches to differentiate them. Most had small stacks of books or rolls of parchment, hands stained with ink and eyes tired from focusing on their studies. They watched the two men as they approached the main building, whispering to each other and casting curious glances after them without any attempt at subtlety. As Jayce and Lucian stood outside the ornate golden inlaid doors to the main building, the older man gave him a sly grin.

"So, are you going to knock or just stand there looking like a fish?"

Jayce gave him a look, snapped his mouth shut, and cracked his knuckles, hesitating. Then he took a deep breath, extended his hand and rapped twice on the door. For a moment, nothing happened. The bustling of the city was a constant low murmur in the distance but no answer came from within. They glanced at each other and Lucian shrugged. Jayce lifted his hand again, but just as he was about to make contact with the door it swung open.

A slender woman with long, perfectly straight hair streaked with silver stood staring at them down her upturned nose. She wore a smart gray dress and her thin face was framed in spidery spectacles. She barely seemed to tolerate speaking to them, her voice reedy and riddled with impatience, "Who calls on the University of Uthersanctorum?"

"I am Lucian Roth, Consul of the Horn." The older man stepped forward. Today, he wore a double breasted coat with several metallic cords on the chest and had his ceremonial sword hanging loosely at his side, to complete the outfit. Jayce guessed it was the same uniform he wore while serving in his role on the High Senate, "I am submitting a prospective student to be enrolled in the University on behalf of the Baron."

The woman gave Jayce a long, probing stare before answering, "This one? But he is so...old."

Jayce flinched. It was not the answer he had been expecting. However, the statesman rolled on in spite of her protest.

"Regardless, it is the wish of the Baron that he be given the trials and enrolled. We have made arrangements to pay his tuition in full."

The woman cocked an eyebrow and inclined her head. She opened the door the rest of the way and motioned for them to follow her inside. As they entered, it took Jayce a moment to adjust to his new surroundings. They had stepped into a sort of antechamber, a small room with a few chairs, a desk set to one corner and a small circular fireplace in the center of the room with glowing red rocks inside. A set of large doors was set to either side and another was placed directly ahead. The only decoration in the room was a massive oil painting of a severe looking man with iron gray hair and a long beard wearing black robes and holding a staff in one hand. The woman indicated the two to sit and took the chair on the opposite side of the desk. She peered over the tops of her glasses and held out her hand, "Papers?"

Lucian handed her a folded letter which she quickly skimmed. She then refolded it and placed it carefully to the side. She steepled her fingers and seemed to do some unknowable calculation in her mind as she stared at the two of them for an eternity. Finally, she looked to Jayce and spoke, breaking the oppressive silence.

"You are aware," she began, each word deliberately enunciated, as though speaking to them was an indignity she could hardly bring herself to suffer, "that our students normally start at a younger age?"

"No, I mean, I was not aware of that."

"Quite younger, in fact. We normally admit our students between their eighth and twelfth years, with some outliers of course. You are, what, in your twenty second year?"

"Twenty third." Jayce managed to croak out. His mind raced beneath what he hoped was a calm exterior.

She seemed barely registered that he had spoken before continuing, "We find that students in your...*situation* are incapable of making the necessary adjustments needed to properly adapt to the brand of instruction we provide here. Furthermore, this letter says you have some skill with magic already?"

Jayce nodded his head eagerly. He held out his hand and focused. He reached out and felt the tendrils of energy floating through the air around them, willing them into motion. The stillness of the room was suddenly upset. The air began to move and shift and a wind suddenly blew around them. The woman casually put a hand on the letter to keep it from blowing away as Jayce pulled the air into his hand and formed a tiny cyclone of dust and dirt in his palm. He held it for a moment and then let it go. The wind dissipated. He smiled and looked up, only to see the woman frowning at him.

"Ah, I see, you're just a *Stormspeaker*." Her tone was dismissive and Jayce immediately bristled. She seemed not to notice but continued undeterred, "We find that those with prior...instruction in the arcane outside our walls suffer the most when they attempt to undertake our curriculum. You know, Stormspeakers, Greenhands, Wildwhisperers...*those sorts*."

Jayce blinked at her. He glanced at Lucian, but the man was only staring thoughtfully back at him, a frown set on his face. He took a deep breath and tried to remain calm.

"Are you saying you won't let me train to become a sorcerer..."

"Please," the woman wrinkled her nose, "sorcerer, wizard...those terms are as antiquated as witch or warlock. We try not to perpetuate such outdated ways of thinking here. We use the term *arcanist* to refer to practitioners of the Art."

"Alright..." Jayce tried hard to control his tongue, "are you telling me you won't let me train as an *arcanist* then?"

The woman gave him what might have been the single most condescending smile he had ever been dealt in his entire life. There was a knowing look in it that was infuriating, "Oh no, the Roth's have pledged to pay your tuition in full, in perpetuity. I have never known the University to turn away a *paying* student. I simply wanted to give you some...fair warning. To set your expectations, let's say. I'm only looking out for your best interests."

Before the biting retort was able to worm its way free of his mouth, Lucian cut in, "Thank you, for your concern miss...?"

"Andrea Whistler...Master Arcanist, third class, Headmistress of Apprentices."

"Yes...very nice to meet your acquaintance Andy..."

"Andrea..." she corrected, but it was Lucian's turn to ignore her comments.

"...and while we appreciate your assessment, we will be making our own judgments on our investments concerning young master Acosta's progress, if you'd please."

The woman briefly looked like the Lord had reached across the table and slapped her. However, she was quick to recover and was speaking before the moment had enough time to define the interaction, working to recover ground, "Yes, well, you are of course welcome to spend your considerable resources wherever you may please..."

"Glad I have your permission."

The woman gritted her teeth so hard Jayce thought she might break her bony jaw. She forced her words out without an ounce of the patronizing tone she had held just a moment ago, "I did not mean offense...*My Lord*."

"Intent has very little to do with outcome." The man's tone chilled the room and made Jayce do a double take. The man that was reclining in the chair beside him had reverted without warning to that other version of himself. This man, the Consul of the Horn, was very different from the affable uncle of his childhood friend he thought he had known, "If that is all, please show my young friend here to his enrollment, before your intentions become muddled again."

The woman managed a stiff nod before stiffly rising to her feet and beckoning them to rise as well, "Please follow me and don't stray. These halls can be very confusing. I wouldn't want to lose you."

She led them through the door to the left and down a long hallway lined with windows on one side and oil portraits on the other. As they passed the figures, Jayce noted they were all of men and women in robes, most elderly, who he assumed were notable graduates of the University. The Mistress led them up a set of stairs and down two more hallways, passed doors and rooms and stairs up and down, moving away from the outer walls towards the center of the massive building. Eventually, they reached a triple wide hallway lined with doors on either side. Andrea snapped at an elderly woman in a simple frock, a servant from the look of her.

"You there!" She demanded in her grating tone, "Fetch Edwin, tell him we have a new student, then go prepare one of the empty apprentices' rooms."

The woman nodded curtly and shuffled off in a hurry, gathering her skirts to keep them from tripping her up. Andrea turned to face the pair of men behind her.

"This is the apprentices' quarters," she began with a flippant wave of her hand, "it's the same on the next three floors as it is on this one. You will be on one of the upper floors considering your age. Washrooms are at the end of the hall, we serve three meals a day in the Great Hall, someone will show you how to get there, and we have strict schedules for those in training. You *will* adhere to them, and all the rules of this University, or you will be removed, no matter who your patrons might be."

She threw Lucian a piercing glance but his attention was consumed by the grime under his nails. She looked momentarily vexed but was again quick to recover, "You will be placed in remedial classes to learn the basics, considering you are starting from scratch. We will make no special accommodations for you, do you understand? It will be up to you to catch yourself up to speed."

Jayce met her gaze with a cold sort of defiance that had begun to build in his insides and clarified his thinking in a way that made him resolute, "Don't worry about me, Mistress. If there's one thing us Stormspeakers are good at, it's finding our way in hostile waters."

She snorted, "We shall see."

A middle aged man that had a face like a basset hound had approached and stood looking to her for further instruction. She snapped that Jayce would be moving in and to prepare an upper level room for their new student. Then she turned on her heel and stalked away from the group. The man looked around at them, clearly dumbfounded. Jayce glanced over and Lucian winked at him, a broad grin on his face once again. They followed Whistler out of the apprentices' quarters and deeper into the University.

As Jayce sat on a sundeck on one of the upper floors of the University, he looked out over the city. The rain had let up briefly, a spot of clear skies in the middle of the dreary day. He could pick out notable landmarks, the shining domes of the Basilica, of course, as well as the great Amphitheater on the Northern end of the City and Sovereign's Palace near the City Center. Further out from the city proper, beyond the walls, the buildings became more spread out, slowly transforming into a suburban hybrid where each home had larger and larger estates, often with walled grounds of their own. Even from this distance, he could tell any of these were grand buildings which could be considered palaces to most men.

There were also miniature town centers outside the walls, with small areas of shops and stores that were only meant to service their own neighborhoods, creating the sense of dozens of towns all crushed together to make one massive behemoth. Eventually, these miniature towns gave way to sprawling farms with fields of crops and animals with wide fields that stretched away and out of view. Through all of this, the Hale River cut a wide and gently winding path, ambling south from the great lake, though the city proper, past the estates and manor houses and into the farmlands beyond. The river hosted innumerable docks, high bridges, factories, and granaries with their waterwheels and an armada of small boats, making it as busy as any of the city's crowded streets.

Behind him, muffled voices could be heard through the wall of full height glass windows. Lucian was speaking with the Lord Archmage of the University, a hooknosed, stork of a man named Octavius, who was so tall and thin Jayce worried he might have been blown over when the door to the balcony had been opened and he had been promptly escorted out here so the the others could speak in private. He leaned over the railing and watched the gray clouds roll lazily across the sky, the scent of the storm filling his lungs.

It reminded him of the sea, the smell of salt and rain over the open ocean. He wondered where his parents were at that moment. Already in the Oarenhiem Empire without doubt, probably on their second or even third port by now. He sighed deeply and imagined the rocking of the ship beneath his feet, wondering if he would ever really get used to the alien stillness of dry land. The door behind him clicked open and Lucian strode out onto the balcony. He was wearing his customary grin and clapped Jayce on the shoulder as he walked over to stand next to him.

"Everything's set," he told the young man with a cheery tone, "they'll ensure you have everything you need. Also, I've made a special mention of the little interaction we had on our arrival, so you shouldn't worry about any more of that nonsense."

Jayce winced a bit. Not even here a full day and already making enemies. He tried to muster a grin of his own, "Thank you, Lucian, for everything."

The statesman leaned on the railing beside him so he could look him in the eye and lowered his voice to a conspiratorial tone, "It is *I* who should be thanking you. If there is some type of corruption in these walls, it's a threat to the very security of our entire Federation. You are performing a patriotic duty here, my boy."

"Can it still be patriotic if I'm not a citizen of the Federation?"

"Semantics!" He waved a hand, "What's good for the Federation is good for all of the continent. What do you think happens if this nation falls? The Republic won't be far behind. Don't forget your little alliance was once a part of the Herronite Federation, before you pirates and cutthroats split off and made your own little nation."

Even when insulting his people, it was hard to be angry at the man. Jayce had to admit, he was good at his job. Jayce grinned, "We just got tired of paying taxes so fat cats like you could live it up here in the Capital."

Lucian threw his head back and laughed, "Perhaps you have a point there, my friend."

The two stood there for a moment and looked out over the sprawl of buildings and streets that seemed to go on forever. Jayce wondered if this city or the Grand Channel was larger and could not decide. He was about to ask Lucian his thoughts when the older man suddenly spoke up.

"I meant to ask you last night, but the wine and old age has made me a bit forgetful...did you speak with Cassius before you left to come here?"

Jayce blinked, "I...I told him goodbye the night before I left, after Valeria and the Baron told me about their plans for me here

at the University. I didn't see him in the morning, I left on a
caravan before daybreak."

Lucian chewed at the inside of his cheek a bit, seeming to turn
the information over in his mind.

"Has something happened?"

"He...has taken his leave of the Hold, unannounced and unbidden by his father. The same day you did, in fact. I received
word from my brother, he wondered if you could share any
information on the subject."

Jayce shook his head, not finding it hard to believe the news.
He believed immediately that Cassius would run away from
The Hold, despite everything. He sighed, "Cassius was...very
upset. When the Baron took away his Command and threatened his Dux title..."

Lucian made a snorting sound that was decidedly not lordly,
"He was upset about losing his Dux title?"

"Well, yes..."

Lucian shook his head, "Do you know where the title of Dux
came from? After Adrien Asallar, glorious grandfather of the
Federation, united all the horse tribes of the Southlands and
won the war against the Oarens eighteen hundred years ago, he
had dozens and dozens of debts to fulfill. He had promised so
many men land and titles and riches to create his alliance, he
couldn't possibly satisfy them all. He was building his palace
and establishing this very city, trying to sort out the baronies
and satisfy a hundred feuding lords...then, *bam*! Just like that,
he died in a raid from the Northern clans."

Lucian slammed his hand down on the banister to make his
point. Luckily, he either did not notice Jayce jump or chose to
ignore it.

"When Adrien's son, Petyr, inherited the throne, he still had
all those debts. So he and the Barons created a title for warriors
who had distinguished themselves in battle. It came with no
riches, but it let you have the *potential* to own land and to
sit on their newly created Senate. It was all promise, but as

much substance as a fart in the wind. All it really meant is you got to sit at your Baron's table during feasts and act like you were a somebody in the war. All the business of protecting the Federation and of serving its people was an afterthought. That's when they expanded the title to include *Servitas* and *Regas*. But because anyone can be a part of the Dux Covenant, noblemen or commoners, even women, it's been the carrot that the Federation has been dangling in front of people since its inception." Lucian held out an imaginary carrot and dangled it in front of Jayce, "Be the hero, fight the wars, enforce the Sovereign's will. Never mind the title gives you nothing of substance. It's a fool's idea of glory."

Jayce stared at the man for a long while. He had never heard anyone speak about the illustrious title that way. He was, for once, at a loss for words.

Lucian gave him a look. His eyes seemed very far away suddenly, unfocused yet following a ghostly scene that played out in some other world, "When my brother and I went across the sea and fought in the New World, I saw men throw themselves at the enemy trying to prove themselves worthy of that title. Lords who never stepped foot in the mud would make promises to living young men, only to grant the title to their corpses later the same day. All those bodies buried in that strange soil..."

"I...I guess I've never thought of it that way."

The older man seemed to regain his cheerful demeanor and managed a shadow of his former grin, "Well, that's just life isn't it? Hopefully, Cas isn't off chasing a fantasy somewhere, and if he is, maybe he'll figure it out before it's too late. Come on, let's get this finished so we can get a bite to eat together before I have to go. I should probably show my face at some point in the Senate today."

Jayce took one last look out towards the great city before he followed Lucian back into the Archmage's office.

Chapter Thirteen

Flower From Stone

Hot summer air, heavy with moisture from all the recent rainfall, crowded the city streets as the sun sank low over the horizon bringing a humid night with it. A breeze blew off the Lake over the docks, barely a disturbance to the thick blanket of heat that hung over the city. It wound its way up the cobblestone streets, moving through the alleys and markets. The wind carried the rhythmic lapping of waves blended with the chattering crowds and musical tones from the taverns and bars which lined the waterfront and floated on the breeze. The sound chased away any hope of a peaceful night.

There were sailors and merchants coming and going and the street vendors calling out, the city still raucous late into the night, a noisy backdrop to the oncoming evening. Through the crowds, a slender, hooded figure in a dark coat made its way, easily weaving through the swathes of people and working its way eastward. Dodging around a man as round as the barrel he was carrying, the figure dipped into an alleyway. Striding up the narrow path she descended an unmarked set of narrow stairs leading towards a small side door. The figure raised a slender, pale hand and knocked twice, waited, and knocked again. The door cracked open and a balding man with a sallow face peeked out.

"Do you have a delivery?"

The cloaked figure pulled back her hood, revealing a cascade of golden hair which framed her angular face. Her eyes were piercing globes in the dim light that scanned back and forth constantly, like an alley cat hunting for its next meal.

Her face held no humor as she replied, "I have a shipment of fresh flowers for the Butcher, if he'll have it."

The bald man grinned as he opened the door the rest of the way. She strode inside and it shut behind her with a heavy thud, then a metallic clang as it was locked with irons. Inside was cool and dark, a basement below the waterline. The young woman had entered a small room which held a number of boxes and sacks piled against both walls on either side of her, lit from above by a single glowing stone. There was a stool and wicked looking hammer resting in the corner where the guard had been posted. He motioned for her to follow as he unlocked another door, opposite the first.

This second chamber was much larger than the first, long and narrow, with a low ceiling, stone walls and floors. It was even cooler than the first, with metal rods affixed to the walls and ceiling running down the far side of the room. These were used to hold heavy iron hooks, from which hung a variety of dead and butchered animals, their fluids dripping into troughs which were inlaid into the floor and ran towards large drain holes covered in grates. To the left were more stacked up barrels and sacks, as well as shelves packed with jars and boxes. To the right there was the sole set of stairs which led up out of the basement.

In the center of the room was a colossal table made of heavy timber, wider than a man and almost as long as the room itself. An iron rack was suspended above the table, from which a variety of knives and various tools were hung. Standing at the table were several men, all wearing leather aprons and working intently on various carcasses, breaking them down for sale. They joked and cursed loudly as they worked, grunting and sweating despite the coolness of the room.

This room, like the previous, was lit by the glowing stones in the ceiling. However, it was filled with smoke from a half dozen pipes and rolled tobacco which were clenched in the teeth of the workers. The scent of flesh, sweat, and smoke was nauseating in the tight space, assaulting her nose like a high tide wave breaking against the pier. If she had not been so familiar with the onslaught of foul smells she might have gagged.

The balding guard walked around the table and grabbed the attention of a large figure who had been closely inspecting the hanging carcasses. He turned around and a grin broke out across his broad face, revealing jagged rows of yellowing teeth. The man was so tall his head nearly scraped the ceiling, and his large form filled the tight space as his belly and muscles strained against his smock and leather apron. His shaved head stood in stark contrast to his wiry beard and the hair which was thick on his arms and the exposed part of his chest.

When he got close, the golden eyes that peered out from under his heavy brow were like fierce spotlights in the gloom. He peeled off a thick pair of gore covered gloves and put his giant hands gently on the shoulders of the lady. He loomed over her, his colossal bulk dwarfing her slight frame.

"Lyra, you've been gone far too long," he put his hand under her chin and turned her head back and forth, casting a keen eye over her, "and you look like you haven't eaten a bite since you last left."

Lyra stood before him without flinching as she gave him a thin smile, "It's good to see you too, Hector. Don't worry, I see you've been eating enough meals for both of us."

He gave a barking laugh which caused many of the men to turn around quickly, bloody tools still in hand. He patted her on the shoulder and nodded approvingly, "Still got your thorns I see, my little flower."

Lyra failed to contain a flinch but kept her confident face as she stared back at him, "I have news...opportunities may have presented themselves to us."

Hector gave a nod towards the stairs as he finally dropped his hands from her shoulders. Some of the tension went out of her as the big man turned to move to head upstairs and she strode after him. They made their way out of the basement and through another heavy wooden door. They entered a warehouse of sorts, which was far larger than the room below, at least four times the size with high ceilings and thick support beams which spanned the space above them.

On their side of the building were more stacks of boxes organized into rows and more piles of bags lining the walls. At the far end of the room there was a carriage bay with three large doors which sat open to the warm night air. Two empty carts sat there with the horses unbridled and stowed in stalls off to the side. A third cart was being unloaded by more men, pulling off heavy canvas sacks and piling them to the side with lots of grunting and cursing to punctuate their labor.

The bearded man turned away from them towards the back of the building. Another door led into a smaller chamber which was separated from the warehouse. This room was set up to be a storefront and office of sorts. A large, standing height counter was set up with high seating on each side. Scales, various measuring tools and stacks of paper with bottles of ink and quills were laid out in an orderly fashion. Behind the counter, next to the door they had come through, was an open cabinet with rows of books, handwritten ledgers, trinkets and various bobbles. The walls of this space were adorned with several maps of the city and surrounding countryside and had been annotated with pins and scribbled notes. Double doors led out to the main road, closed and locked now, and a glass storefront window was ordained with block lettering which read simply, *GARNER'S* with the words *IMPORTS & EXPORTS* printed slightly smaller below.

Hector grabbed a bottle of brown liquor and glasses from a cabinet by the counter and sat in one of the chairs. He pulled the cork and poured two generous glasses. Lyra could feel him watching as she slowly walked around the room and examined the various maps.

"Are you having much luck with the Southern farms?"

The large man put the bottle down with a heavy thud and clicked his tongue, "Not as much as I'd like. Those stubborn herdsmen are resistant to the modern way of the world. But give it a few more well timed visits from our men and they'll get the message."

"If they don't?"

"Well now, we need to lockdown that supply, otherwise Boone and his boys will make their move. So, one way or another, those beasties will be coming through *this* storehouse." His grin belied a cold calculation in his gaze. Lyra nodded and made her way to the table where she picked up the glass.

"To fates paid..." she began holding out her glass.

"... and fortunes made." He ended, clinking her glass. He turned up the cup and finished it in a single gulp. She took a sip and felt the foul rotgut work its way down her throat and burn in her chest. She swirled the glass as he poured another for himself and leaned back in the chair. The big man absently thumbed through a few of the papers left out on the desk, numbers and notes scribbled from the day's business, as he asked, "So, what news have you brought me on this fine evening?"

She took the seat opposite him and took another sip of her drink, pursing her lips at the taste, "Well, you know I've got my contacts at the docks?"

"Aye, girlie. You have a great deal of friends."

"One of them told me about an unusual visitor. A young man coming as a passenger on a freight ship from the Horn. He was well dressed, asking for directions to the Consul's manor."

Hector's attention was drawn away from the ledgers, his eyes turned upward as he leaned in with sudden interest, "You thinking this boy might be a courier?"

She shook her head, "I thought so at first, but I asked after the crew he came in with. A few drinks earned me some interesting rumors. The sailors mentioned he was bound for the University."

The big man rubbed his chin, staring at her. He took another sip of his whiskey and inclined his head for her to go on.

Lyra bared her teeth at him and leaned forward, "...they mentioned the name, *Acosta.*"

Hector sat back and stared at her, eyes widening, "*Acosta*...as in, the Acosta Trading Company?"

"It would appear that way, yes."

Hector crossed his arms. He furrowed his brow as he sat, deep in thought for a long moment. When he spoke, he stared hard at her, "What would you have me do with this knowledge, my flower? Snatch him off the street?"

She shook her head, staring at the table, working through the problem in her head, "No, at least not yet. Even alone, he's likely no easy target. We've no idea what he's capable of. The Company has many weather witches and capable mercenaries, and if he fights and we kill him, he's worthless to us. Then, even if we subdue him, the minute a ransom note reaches them they'll pay a damned mage to find us. We know they keep their contracts in blood, like we do. We'd have the Legion in our midst in a day, unless we paid a mage of our own to veil him. But that would cost."

Hector nodded. His shoulders relaxed a little as he rubbed his chin, "You're thinking through the problem. This opportunity must be handled with a gentle hand. Why would a member of the Acosta Company come to the Capital without circumstance and be interested in seeing the Consul of the Horn, much less the University?"

Lyra held her hands up. She considered the question carefully, trying to see the angles like the beast of a man before her had tried to teach her for all these years, "The crew said he was in a hurry. Perhaps he does have a message from the Horn? Something private that can't be sent by a normal courier. Something involving the University?"

"Most likely. The trappings of politics are tricksy business. Mayhaps there is a secret alliance in the works. The Acosta Company has grown large and influential, and we already know the Republic has big ambitions..."

"So then what is he hoping to find here? Allies?"

"Aye, girl, *friends* would be my bet."

The woman stood and stalked away from the table, before stopping and turning to stare at the large man, "You'd have me be this merchant's *friend*, then?"

He stared back at her, unflinching under her icy glare.

"Hector, this is a powerful merchant with ties to the nobility. He's not going to spill secrets of state to me."

Hector stood, glass in hand as he walked around the counter, "Your wits haven't gone from you a bit since that day I found you. You were a starving child, stealing to survive. You were like a flower growing out of the stones of the street, a beauty even then. But you've always had your thorns. You tried to stick me with a rusty knife when I caught you trying to cut my purse, do you remember?"

He had worked his way to stand directly in front of her. She looked up at him with defiance, but softened somewhat. Her expression had lost the chill. He placed his mitten-like hand over her shoulder once again, then moved it to cradle the side of her face, "You were always special, even from the start."

"What of the other wayward children you've taken in?" She nodded towards the door, where the men labored outside, "Your boys, your soldiers. Are they not so special?"

He sighed and smiled, "They are, of course, but they lack your eyes, girlie. They can't see the angles like you can, read the truth behind the truth. But I know you, you can do anything you set your mind to. You've worked the high born merchants and nobles before. You'll figure this boy out."

She managed a half smile and he moved to embrace her. She stood stock still and let herself be enveloped, eyes closed, not lifting her arms to return the hug. He seemed not to notice.

When he let her go, she took a deep breath and turned towards the front doors. She took a step, then half turned.

"Have you heard anything more about the missing children?"

"From Wetrun? Not much more than before." Hector had already turned back to stand at his table and was thumbing through the papers again, "Two of them were spotted over on the west side of town before they up and vanished, but that's all that's come across my table."

Lyra frowned, "What's the number up to now?"

"Seven, eight...? I dunno..." he waved an unconcerned hand, "None from the docks, nor the Lower End. Besides, Wetrun is Mother Moore's territory, and I'm sure she can handle her own...and if she can't, let the Legion sort it out, that's what we pay all these taxes for, isn't it?"

"And what about the tax they pay to you?" Lyra muttered under her breath as she unlocked the door and shoved it open.

"Hmm?" The big man called over his shoulder without looking up. But Lyra was already back out in the evening air, disappearing into the crowd.

I n truth, the land outside the walls on the eastern side of Asaldon should have been a marshy floodplain, uninhabited by all but the snakes and rats. But because the city had grown so large and unwieldy, the poorest of the population had been pushed into this area where the river overflowed. Because of this, the streets of the eastern slums were eternally a mess of mud and wet, leading to the nickname, Wetrun. The houses sat on low stilts, tightly packed together shacks of wood and thatch.

In the muddy alleyways grim looking people sat idly playing with dice or bones on upturned barrels and boxes, while children made do with mud pies or wrestled in the dirt. There was no sign of the hustle and bustle of the main city here. People moved slowly, trudging as if every step was a titanic effort. Small tendrils of smoke snaked up from dozens of chimneys as Lyra reached the edge and she smelled the particularly pungent scent of many slowly simmering stews being prepared in the innumerable hovels.

She had her coat wrapped tightly around her, her hood once again casting shadows over her face. The rain had not favored this part of town and it was earning its namesake tonight. Her soft leather boots made slight squelching sounds in the muck as she strode along, moving through the sparse streets. Few she passed on her way looked up or paid her any mind. It was the sort of place where people kept to their own business. As she turned a corner, she eyed one of the houses. It was much like the others, simple, stick built and barely held together, topped with a patchwork roof of thatch. Two men sat on the porch, both large, dangerous looking boys with knives openly worn on their belts and clubs at their sides. When she approached, they nodded to her and one opened the door, letting her in without a word.

Inside was dark and musty, decorated with heavy wall hangings of canvas and animal skins to keep out the weather. Herbs and various plants hung around the room, drying along every cross beam and rafter. It was stiflingly warm inside the hovel and the pungent, floral scents were amplified in the humidity. An ancient woman sat over a great cauldron bubbling in the corner, wrapped with a shawl despite the oppressive heat. She was stirring the liquid with one hand and pouring a handful of spices into the pot with the other when Lyra entered.

The woman took little notice of her, seemingly enthralled by the swirling liquid. The younger woman moved to stand beside her, watching her turn the ladle in slow, continuous circles with her wrinkled hand. The crone's eyes were milky and unfocused and she shook slightly, tremors of age moving through her with ill intent. For a long time, they stood in silence. When the witch finally spoke, her voice was that of a much younger woman, smooth and rich like wild honey and untainted by the age that had wracked every other part of her.

"You are distressed..." Mother Moore stated plainly.

Lyra wrinkled her nose. She did not like the woman's way of knowing her mind without speaking, "No, just tired. I've been across the whole of the city tonight, and I have further yet to go."

"You should rest, child. Your youth can only take you so far."

Lyra almost protested, but caught her tongue. She had not thought of herself as a child in her living memory. But to the aged woman, everyone might as well be a child.

"Hector didn't have any useful information about the missing, only that two of the children were seen on the West side of the city before disappearing."

Mother Moore nodded her head slowly, gray hair bobbing up and down. The steam from the cauldron wove around her face, making fleeting patterns in the dim light, "The Butcher is always busy with his own business..."

Sweat was already beading on Lyra's forehead. She was ready to be done with this place, back out in the fresh air. She crossed her arms and stared at the old woman.

"Have your people found anything else out?"

"Nothing of substance..." She replied vaguely, "different children from different families, nothing tying them together, except they were all from the poorest districts of the city. Each child was here one day, gone the next, like smoke in the wind..."

Lyra pursed her lips, "Do you know, are there any missing from the wealthy districts?"

Mother Moore shook her head and gave a tight smile, "No one shares their secrets with us, my child. The river doesn't flow backwards. The only thing we know is that our own are disappearing. That is why I sent word to you, asking for your help."

The young woman narrowed her eyes and glared. There was no recognition of the challenge from the old crone, who went on stirring without hesitation. Silence overtook the small shack once again. Mother Moore stirred her pot and only the sound of the embers crackling and popping punctuated the quiet. Finally, Lyra uncrossed her arms. She rubbed her sweaty palms on her pants and motioned towards the door.

"Well...I have a lot to do tonight. I should be on my way."

Mother Moore said nothing. Lyra turned and moved to leave, but then the old woman spoke up, "One thing, dear...if you're going to be near the University, you'll want to keep your wits about you. I hear the whispers, closer now than before."

Lyra blinked. She tried to keep the shiver from her spine but it worked its way through her bones despite her best efforts. She knew there was something off about the old woman, a power that was real, not like the charlatans that ran their scams on people down by the docks. But it was always unsettling when you knew for certain the hag had been rummaging around in your head. She swallowed hard and turned back.

"I could never hide anything from you, Mother, not since I was a child myself."

Mother Moore made no motion to indicate she heard her. She continued speaking without acknowledging the accusation, "You might also keep an eye out for any signs of our younglings. We know at least three of the missing were touched by the Old Mother. Now, apparently, two were seen near the University before disappearing."

There was a moment where neither woman spoke. Lyra worked her jaw as she turned the information over in her mind.

"You...didn't tell me some of the children had the Gift."

"Many children have a touch of the Gift in their blood. It seemed like happenstance before...but now? One is not so sure."

The young woman considered this a moment longer. She shook off the surprise before continuing, "Mother, do you know anyone who might get me into the University? Considering your own...*skills*?"

Lyra jumped when the ancient woman let out a sharp, short laugh. The harsh sound could have easily been mistaken for the ugly cry of a crow. She turned to face Lyra for the first time, her clouded eyes seeming to glow as they focused on her in the haze and dim light.

"The mages of the University wouldn't *dare* associate with my kind, even if my kind were allowed to walk in the light of day." The old woman grinned, showing rows of rotting teeth and inflamed gums, "I'm not a good guest for polite company."

The temperature seemed to have risen by several degrees. Lyra felt light headed and fought to keep her stomach from churning inside her. When Mother Moore spoke again, it seemed from further away, through a haze.

"But if you're asking for my help...I might know someone who can get you inside, for a price."

She managed to keep from sprinting out the door for a breath of fresh air, turning back towards the woman and her bubbling pot. She tried desperately to focus as the old woman gave her her instructions. Outside, the dark came on quickly, chasing the last traces of daylight over the horizon as the night filled the city.

I t was deep into the dead of night by the time Lyra approached the University. The monstrosity sprawled across the space of at least four city blocks, shoving aside the boroughs and neighborhoods around it. The great white walls appeared unguarded, but she had dealt with enough wealthy aristocrats and merchants to know protecting what they had was always their top priority. She circled the entire compound twice, noting that all three gates that sat shut against the streets of Asaldon at this late hour with no guard to ask for assistance.

Satisfied, she turned down a side alleyway and moved through the narrow passages between shops and businesses. She sidestepped a form wrapped in a ragged cloth leaning against a barrel and around a pile of broken furniture until as she approached a door in the rear of one of the shops. The red paint was old and peeling and the door had a simple sketch of a flower on it, with no other indications as to the building's use.

Lyra reached up and gave a quick knock. A click could be heard almost immediately and odd, purplish light filtered out into the alley as the door creaked open. An incredibly slender man with dark hair loomed in the doorway, staring impassively at her.

"May I help you?"

"Yes...Mother Moore sent me."

The man blinked a bit too slowly at her. His dead eyed gaze was unnerving, the thin skin and visible scars on his cheeks and neck not helping matters much. Lyra had some difficulty not recoiling when she felt him look her up and down.

"Come in."

The man moved aside and she entered. She heard the lock click back into place as the man closed the door behind her and she examined her new surroundings. The room was long and narrow, lit by very dim witchlights that were a violet color rather than the typical amber. Every wall was lined with heavy shelves and hooks, all loaded with pots and planters. The strangest assortment of vegetation and fungus were growing out of every container, spilling out onto the shelves or climbing the walls.

There were multicolored mushrooms, dark flowers, mosses that had colonized large sections of the shelves they sat on and leafy ferns in shades of blue, black, and purple. Various copper instruments were lined up with meticulous care on a small desk in one corner of the room, gleaming in the low, ethereal gloom. The lean man moved to lean against a table, his slight hunch giving him an especially ghoulish appearance given the surroundings.

"So...Mother Moore sent you, did she? What is it that she needs from Elias?"

Lyra drew herself up as she stood in the center of the room, trying not to get too close to any of the shelves. She was no expert in plants, but these had a distinctly nefarious look to them.

"It's me that needs something. I have to make contact with someone in the University," she began, standing with her shoulders squared and returning the strange man's gaze, "can you get me inside?"

Elias licked his lips. Again, Lyra had to stifle an involuntary shutter. "This is...possible. But it will require no small effort on my part, and some risk. What are you offering in return?"

"Do you know the Butcher?"

The thin man curled his lip, "By reputation..."

"I am one of his lieutenants. Do this, and I'll owe you a favor."

Elias turned and examined one of his potted ferns. It had purple leaves with strange, vibrant pink streaks through them. He ran one hand over the closest leaf as he considered the offer.

"The Butcher handles a good deal of shipments in and out of the city, yes?"

Lyra gave a curt nod.

"Can he ensure some shipments get to the Expanse for me? Dorria, specifically?"

The young woman shifted her weight from one foot to the other as she considered the proposition, "We don't send much that far south...there are other parties that lay claim in that area. But we might be able to make it work, how much weight are we talking about? And what kind of risk?"

"Oh, just a few small bags of seeds...nothing so sinister the Legion would be worried about." The man's stomach curdling sneer of a smile plainly suggested it was indeed something sinister he intended. But the University was a well guarded chest of treasures and Lyra had few options if she wanted to make contact with this merchant.

She shrugged, "It shouldn't be a problem."

"Excellent..." Elias's smile widened and he turned back to face her, "Then let us begin working on getting you into that school."

CHAPTER FOURTEEN

INTO RED WATER

A storm had been lashing the coastline of The Horn for days by the time Cassius found his way to *Rory's Rarities and Reclamations*. It had taken him two days to reach the city of Redwater, then sneaking past the soldiers had been no mean feat. The city watch and the Legionnaires who had been sent to look for the missing fugitives were swarming across the city like a wave of angry ants. Luckily, he knew Redwater well and could be inconspicuous when needed. He had stashed his leathers, along with almost all his royal effects, in the hills before coming down to the coast and left his beloved horse, Rearden, stabled near the gate. The only indulgence he had allowed himself was the sword he wore at his belt, reasoning a merchant or laborer was as likely as a nobleman to carry one for his own defense.

The rain soaked his traveler's cloak and the simple clothes he wore as he approached the shopfront, pausing only briefly to look at the emblazoned eye with a star in its pupil before pushing through the door. As the bell jingled, Cassius pushed his hood back and gazed around the strange store. It was narrow and deep, with the only visible entrance and windows being at the front. The entire place was too dark and the rear was blocked by a curtain, only deepening the gloom. He found himself on edge, wondering at the possibility of men hiding just on the other side of that veil.

A fat man with a red beard sat behind a desk to his left. When Cassius entered, the man put down a pastry mid-bite and eyed the newcomer suspiciously. The noble noted the man's hand drift down to his waist in a manner he probably thought was inconspicuous.

"Yes, what'll it be then?" The man grumbled, beard full of crumbs.

Cassius shook off his cloak leaving a pool of water at his feet on the floor. He put on his friendliest grin, the one he plastered on while making mandatory appearances in the royal court, and approached the table.

"Hail, good sir. I hope you can help me. I've come seeking a man..."

Cassius was suddenly looking down a barrel of dull gray steel. The big man had moved quicker than he might have expected, pulling the blunderbuss out from under his expansive gut and leveling it at the Prince. His chubby fingers gripped the wood of the handle so tightly his knuckles were white.

"Are you with the soldiers?"

Cassius knew how these blasting powder weapons worked, even though they were uncommon here in the Federation. Mostly he had seen them wielded by pirates from the South, raiding their way up the western coast of Evardene until they had reached the Oaren Strait. But even from the little he had seen, he knew they were dreadful in combat.

"No!" He said quickly, holding up his hands, "You've got the wrong idea. I'm here from the Blades. I was told to come here to find Lawrence."

The man's red beard twitched as he squinted at him, "I've never seen you before. What's your name? Where's your coin?"

Cassius slowly lowered one hand as though reaching for his belt pocket, "My name's Jon, and I'm new...and if you'll hold a moment, my coin is right in...*here!*"

He pivoted to the right and threw his hand across to shove the barrel of the weapon in the opposite direction. Thunder erupted. The sound rattled the windows and shook the foundations of the building, drawing clouds of dust from the rafters. Fire and sparks belched out of the barrel and a large, smoking hole appeared in the door, cracking the windowpane into a glass spiderweb. A spray of splinters burst into the air, showering them both in sawdust and wood chips.

Cassius felt his ears ringing and knew he had only seconds. He forced himself to recover, ignoring the sharp smell of burning that suddenly assaulted his senses and stung his eyes so badly they watered. The fat man was fumbling with the weapon. He looked like he had broken it in half and was trying to stuff a metal oval into it.

The Prince reached across the table and grabbed the fat man by his shirt with both hands. He let out a yelp like a frightened dog as Cassius dragged him over the table, scattering papers and pens and the half eaten pastry across the floor. The Prince slammed the big man onto the ground and put one knee in his considerable gut, pinning him there.

The man moaned in agony but Cassius paid him no mind. He yanked the hand cannon out of his grasp and stuffed it into his belt. Then he grabbed the man by the jowls and held him steady as he stared down on him, teeth bared like the wolfman from the child's fable. He practically growled his words, hoping for the full effect.

"That was *uncalled* for."

The man whimpered and groaned, spittle escaping his mouth and wetting his beard as he struggled to breath with the full weight of a grown man digging into his guts. Cassius cast a quick glance through the hole in the door. Noises of panic were coming from outside. People were calling for the guard.

"*Shit.*" He glanced toward the back of the shop, "Is there a way out back there?"

The fat man took in a sharp, shallow breath and grimaced. Cassius pushed off his back foot and pressed his knee into the man's gut even harder.

"Yes!" He breathed, barely able to speak, nodding furiously with what little energy he had left in him.

"Show me."

He stood and hauled the big man up before he had taken in the first ragged breath without Cassius' knee in his guts. The Prince shoved his prisoner towards the back of the shop, casting a quick look back to make sure no one was entering the store behind him. They pushed through the curtain and into a dimly lit sitting room. The shadows sat heavy around the shelves of books and trinkets, a cold hearth nestled on the other side of a collection of large chairs.

The witchlight lanterns were barely burning this early in the day, so it took a long moment for their eyes to adjust to the gloom. Cassius pushed the big man along and they both moved towards the back wall. A heavy door of dark wood sat nearly invisible in the right corner of the room, hidden behind the edge of the last bookshelf. The shopkeeper pulled out a set of keys and shoved one into the lock, clicking it open.

As soon as he had opened the door, Cassius pushed him inside and shut the door behind them. They were in a storage room of sorts; small, cramped, lined with shelves and stacked boxes. Another door, presumably leading outside, sat opposite the first. Cassius dragged a heavy box up against the door behind them as the fat man fumbled with the keys to open the back door.

Once it was open, the shopkeeper started to exit, but the Prince grabbed him from behind and forced him down onto a stool in the corner. He took a moment to compose himself as he stared at his captive, watching the man's beady eyes dart around, staring longingly at the door which sat cracked open.

"I need information," Cassius began in a voice that made dark promises, "and you're going to give them to me."

"Rot in the Hells!" The fat man spat at his feet. He seemed to have gathered his courage again, "I ain't tellin' you nothin."

Cassius sighed deeply. He reached behind his back and pulled out the long hunting knife from its sheath. The defiance in the fat man's eyes immediately withered away and was replaced with panic.

"Wait, wait! I just...I don't know anything..."

The Prince of The Horn turned the knife over in his hand and moved to stand directly in front of the big man. He crouched down so he was at eye level with him, so close he could smell the fresh butter from his pastry mixed with the faint sickly sweet of rotting teeth. It was an odd blend of scents that made Cassius a bit sick to his stomach.

"Look..." he cocked an eyebrow to ask his question.

"F-Ferron." The man managed to sputter out, eyes not leaving the glinting knife blade.

"Ferron...I *need* information, and I don't have much time to get it. Those people will have the City Watch here in minutes, probably soldiers too. But what you know could save hundreds of lives, maybe even thousands. So I have to get you to talk, no matter what." Cassius looked meaningfully into the big man's small eyes and tried to give him a reassuring smile, "Just tell me what I need to know and I'll be on my way."

"I...I don't know anything...like I told the guards when they were here before..."

Cassius looked down at the ground. He took a deep breath. When he exhaled, he looked up at the big man, clapped the free hand on his shoulder and gave him a small, sad smile, "Okay...you don't know anything."

His red beard twitched again as his face relaxed a bit. Then the Prince grabbed the man's shirt and pinned him up against the wall with one arm across his throat. Halfway sliding off the stool, Ferron sputtered and gasped as the pressure slowly built on his throat as he struggled to hold himself in that awkward position. Cassius pressed the dagger against the man's cheek, drawing the tiniest bloom of red. It swelled into a ball and streaked down the knife's edge, collecting on the hilt and seeping down into droplets that stained the man's already grease smeared shirt. Behind them, he could hear that people had entered the shop and were looking for the source of the explosion.

"I'm out of time, Ferron. I need an answer, right now..."

The big man was turning red as he grasped at the Prince's arm, scratching at his shirtsleeves with filthy nails and leaving grease stains. His eyes watered and he let out a gasp, "Okay...just...let me go!"

Cassius pulled his arm away suddenly and the shopkeeper collapsed backwards against the wall. A stream of spittle ran from his mouth as he coughed, struggling to catch his breath. It mixed with the tears, matting his beard in uneven clumps. He glared up at the Prince with hate in his eyes from where he sprawled out on the stone floor.

"*Bastard...*" he muttered under his breath, wiping what he could from the mess on his face and flicking it onto the floor. When Cassius moved to grab him again he quickly threw up his arms, "Okay! Okay, just, hold on...the Blades have a deal with the owner of this shop, Master Rory. He's been letting them operate out of here, store their goods in the cellar, that sort of thing..."

"How long?" Cassius could hear the voices growing louder behind the barred door.

"Several cycle's guess? Since the start of last season at least, it's hard to remember."

"What are they doing here? What are they after?"

"I don't know, honest, I'm just security." Ferron cast a forlorn glance at the blunderbuss stuffed in Cassius's belt, "Probably not anymore now though."

"You can get another job." Cassius grimaced. Someone began knocking behind them, calling out and trying the lock. Ferron shot a hopeful glance at the door but the Prince showed him the point of his blade and the big man's eyes were fixed on him again.

"Are you gonna kill me?"

"Depends," Cassius leaned forward and stared hard at him, "can you tell me where Lawrence is?"

"I have no idea." When he saw the grim expression the Prince gave him he held both hands up, "I swear, on my mother's soul, they don't tell me nothin'! But you could ask Master Rory, he's thick as thieves with them!"

Someone was putting their shoulder into the door now. It whined and creaked as it bowed in its frame.

"Where?" Cassius demanded, menacing him with the knife.

"The *Captain's Clutch*, it's a social club, north side of town, he's always there!"

A loud crack announced the door splitting from the jam and an angry voice called out as someone tried to shove their way into the room. But Cassius was out the back door and into the alley before they could get inside, throwing up his hood and rejoining the crowd in the streets of Redwater before anyone could stop him. He walked for ten minutes through the wind and the rain, taking several turns and changing directions multiple times before finally coming to a stop on a less busy side street.

He leaned up against the cracked wall of a bakery, closing his eyes for a moment. The smell of fresh bread and hot ovens filled his nose as he steadied himself. When he finally opened his eyes, he looked down at his hands. They were rock steady, as always. But his heart pounded in his throat and he felt bile fill his mouth. He swallowed hard and tried to push the hate filled eyes of the shopkeeper from his mind as he began trekking north through the storm.

C assius stood in an underpass with his hood still raised against the weather, dripping water from his cloak as he stared through the evening mist. The *Captain's Clutch* was just across an open square, soft, multicolored lights spilling out into the streets from every window as the sound of music and laughter upset the quiet of the evening. The storms had let up a bit and the soft patter of rain on the cobblestones and tiles was only punctuated by the ever-present lapping of waves against the seawall.

The club was a three story sentinel of stone and salt brined lumber situated at the end of a long wharf, most likely an old trading station, whose windows looked out at the sea on two sides. As he stared at the building, he found himself wishing for his armor for what felt like the one hundredth time that day. He took a deep breath, checked to make sure the knife and sword were still secure in their sheaths, and started across the square with a deliberate stride.

A miserable looking man hunched in the overhang in front of the main door, half sitting on a bar height stool with a wicked looking crossbow resting on his lap, sharp eyes watching his approach. He waited until Cassius was at the bottom of the short set of steps that led up into the building and held out his hand.

"Woah, there big fella," he readjusted the bow so that it was facing slightly forward, not at Cassius directly, but close, "where do you think you're off to with that sword at your side? This here is a private club, and I don't believe I've seen you around before."

Cassius stopped and pushed back his hood. He put on his friendly grin again and put his hands on his hips, "I'm told this is the place to be if you're looking to drink in good company."

"Aye, but that doesn't change the fact that you're not a member."

"What does it take to be a member?"

The man gave an evil little grin, "Trust me kid, if you *could* be a member, you wouldn't need to ask me how to be one."

Cassius shrugged and dug into his pocket, pulling out a small sack of coins. He jangled the purse in his hand, making sure the guard could hear the coins clinking against each other, "I guess I'll just need to take my purse and go then..."

"Hold on a second..." the guard's eyes lit up as he leaned forward a bit, "How much you got in there, fella?"

"Depends," he shrugged and gave the man an evil grin of his own, "how much does it take to get in the door?"

Cassius was able to negotiate his entry for only five silver marks, but the guard made him leave his sword at the door. He chewed his tongue thoughtfully but relented, reasoning this was the best way to get inside. As the guard let him into the dimly lit building, he had to take a moment to let his eyes adjust. He was in a large tavern-like room, a long bar of dark, shiny wood occupying the wall to his right with velvet lined stools. A raised stage sat opposite the bar where a slender woman was singing a vibrant melody to the accompaniment of a seated man playing a large lyre.

Her voice filled the room as she danced and winked at the patrons in the low light beyond the stage. They hollered as they clinked their drinks and clapped, slapping their knees and the tables a bit too hard. Each table held small brass braziers burning in the center, a shallow dish with a plate suspended over it. The guests took turns placing small pinches of brown and yellow powder on the plates and plumes of different colored smoke rose in thick, lazy clouds that hung in the air. The guests breathed the smoke in deeply as they closed their eyes, sighing and grinning broadly in appreciation.

Cassius moved through the dim witchlight of deep red and purple hues, trying not to breathe too deeply. He could feel his head already beginning to spin as he approached the bar. He worked his way around wobbling, richly dressed patrons and scantily dressed servers, barely avoiding the tables and chairs which seemed too tightly packed in the space. A heavyset woman with an ornate flower arrangement tattooed across her shapely chest stood eyeing him from behind the bar.

"What can I get you, sir? Are you here for yagie or the silver dust? Or are you looking for some...companionship?" She made a vague motion to her head, "We have all kinds here."

"No, just an ale, Rock Brown, if you have it." He shook his head and blinked. He tried to refocus on the woman as she handed him a foaming mug of deep brown liquid.

"Closest we got, kid," she said matter-of-factly, "take it or leave it."

"Thank you." Cassius took a long gulp. He shivered as the cold liquid worked its way down his throat, "I was hoping you could help me with something else..."

The barkeeper cocked one eye and crossed her arms. Cassius once again dug out his purse and set it on the bar.

"I'm looking for a man, a store owner, named Rory? I was told I could find him here."

The woman gave him a long, hard stare. She flicked her eyes down towards the purse. Cassius dug a silver coin out and slid it across the bar. The woman stood stock still and did not even look at the coin. Cassius sighed and pulled out two more coins, stacking them on top of the first coin. She snatched the coins up and made them disappear inside her shirt, before leaning on the bar and lowering her voice so that it was barely audible over the singer's warbling cry in the background.

"Rory's upstairs. Back staircase, turn right, last room on the right. Don't make any trouble, or I'll kick you out of here and have my boys break your legs for good measure, you hear?"

Cassius nodded, glancing towards the back of the room. He turned the mug of ale up and gulped the rest down, blowing out a long breath before standing. He pulled a last twinkling silver out and placed it on the bar, earning a quizzical look from the bartender, before stepping away.

A few hazy eyes followed him across the room, momentarily distracted from the stage and burning braziers, but quickly returned to their far more interesting activities. Behind a heavy velvet curtain Cassius found a staircase which rose up into the darkness above. He stalked up the stairs and found himself in a long, dimly lit hallway which stretched out to either side.

He could hear the muffled voices and noises of the patrons partaking in their entertainment, trying hard to ignore the sudden cries and groans which sporadically erupted from behind closed doors. The last door on the right was closed. Nothing set it apart from the others, but Cassius tensed as he slipped his hand behind his back and he grasped the handle of his knife once again. The Prince was especially thankful that the doorman had missed it. He put one hand on the door latch, took a deep breath and pushed into the room.

The Prince was surprised to find the razor thin man he sought reclining peacefully in a large easy chair which took up the majority of the small room. The man was smiling under his stringy mustache as he stared up at the ceiling with eyes glazed over and unseeing. A boy with golden hair, far too young to be in a place like this, stood beside the chair, hand placed on the man's shoulder. His brow was furrowed in concentration and little beads of sweat dripped from his face onto the floor. He looked up when Cassius entered but the Prince held up a finger to his lips and pointed to the man.

"*Rory?*" He whispered.

The boy frowned but nodded slowly. Cassius whipped the long knife out with a flourish, causing the boy's eyes to widen with sudden fear. But the Prince pulled a coin out of his pocket and pressed it into the boy's hand then pointed a finger towards the door. The boy nodded quickly and removed his hand from the man's shoulder, quickly scrambling out the door and shutting it behind him without another word. The man began blinking and groaning almost immediately.

"Aaron...wha...why did you stop...?" The man's voice was husky and halting, like he had woken from a deep slumber. The moment he looked over and saw Cassius looming over him, knife in hand, they became sharp all at once.

"Hello, Rory," Cassius grabbed the man by the collar and pressed the knife against his throat, "I have some questions for you."

Rory, blinking and casting a desperate eye around the room, sputtered, "I...who, who are you? Guards! Guards!"

Cassius pulled back and drove the fist closed around the knife's handle into the man's nose. Immediately a spurt of blood stained the thin mustache and flowed into his mouth. Rory coughed and cried out. Cassius dropped his fist into the man's nose again. The thin man whimpered and more blood and snot flowed out as tears welled up in the corners of his eyes.

"Argh! Stop it! *Please*!"

"Are you going to keep quiet?" Cassius pulled his fist back a third time.

"Y-Yes! Just stop it!" Rory was shaking as he held his hands in front of his face. The blood had dribbled down his face and was staining the fine silk shirt he wore around Cassius' clenched fist. The Prince shoved him backward into the chair and wiped his hand on the armrest. He stared hard at the man, knife still held loosely in his grasp, gleaming in the low light.

"Okay, Rory...where's Lawrence?"

"What are you talking about?" Rory's voice was muffled as he held his nose to try and stop the blood from pouring out.

Cassius sighed. He leaned forward and placed the knife, pointed down, on the man's bony thigh. He caught Rory's eye and applied the lightest of pressure. The man's thin clothes provided no resistance.

"Are you sure about that?"

"Ah, damn you! I...I can't, they'll *kill me*..."

"What makes you think I won't?" Cassius applied more pressure. Another spot of dark red bloomed from under the thin cloth, staining the man's pants as it spread out in every direction. He whimpered and grimaced in pain.

"Fine, fine! He left, days ago. The guards got word he was in the city somehow. They came to my shop, so he had to get out before they found him."

"Where did he go?" Cassius put a bit more pressure on the knife. The red stain on his pants grew.

"I don't know! Why would he tell me that?!" The man hissed through the pain.

"You're his partner."

"*No!* No, no, no...we, we're just in a temporary arrangement! I'm not part of the Blades, I don't even know what they're doing here! I just gave them a place to operate when they were in the city!"

Cassius pulled the knife out of his leg. Rory's shoulders relaxed, but then his eyes widened when the Prince pressed the knife against his throat once again.

"If you don't know anything...you're no good to me."

"Wait! Please, he...he said he was going South! The Broken Coast, the Crescent City! He...he's going there!"

"You're sure?"

Rory nodded frantically, trying desperately to push backwards away from the blade into the chair. Cassius raised one eyebrow.

"If you're lying to me, I'll come back here and gut you and that shopkeeper of yours like fish."

Rory shook his head sending little droplets of blood and tears in every direction, "I have no reason to! They already paid me!"

"And I can see you're using it well." Cassius let the man's shirt go and he collapsed into the chair. The Prince again wiped his hands and knife on the armrests, sheathed the blade and gave Rory a final grin, "I'll leave you to it then, try not to spend it all in one night."

He turned and headed for the exit, eager to be done with this place. But as he closed his hand around the door handle a chill ran down his spine and his entire body felt like it was covered in pins and needles. The room seemed to fall away and the light was receding into the corners of his vision. He tried to turn, but his mind did not seem to be in command of his body anymore. The voice, still muddled from holding his nose, spoke up behind him. It was jagged with untempered wrath.

"They told me the Baron might send someone..." Rory's tone was black and it seemed to be getting closer. Cassius stared at the wooden door, desperate as he tried to force his body to obey him, "to ask questions. Warned me to be on my guard. I guess it was foolish of me to think those common soldiers would be the last of it."

The Prince could feel the man's presence closing in. It seemed like he could practically feel the breath on the back of his neck as his mind raced.

"Funny, I *hate* to spill my own blood for a spell...but now that it's already so readily available..." The sound of Cassius's knife being slid from its sheath was like the hiss of a viper in the underbrush. He screamed in his own mind, but no words came out. Suddenly, the thin man was in his periphery. He could see the dark eyes staring at him from over the bloody mess he had left of the man's face.

The knife was in the thin man's right hand and he could barely make out the other holding a small, white shape which seemed to glow a bit. The thin man's eyes were like an animal's, dark and full of hunger, "I would normally slit your throat and be done with it, but we have this room all to ourselves for quite a while. I would hate to waste such a perfect opportunity for...*retribution*."

Rory licked his lips. He moved to slide the lock on the door shut. But just as his hand touched the metal, the door burst open. It shoved the thin man off balance and he tumbled into Cassius, sending them both to the floor in a tangle of limbs. A man in a leather jacket carrying a wicked looking club entered the room. He was so wide he almost obscured the face of the boy from earlier, Aaron, peering around him from the hallway.

Cassius suddenly felt his body freed from whatever hold was on it. He scrambled to free himself from the bony form of Rory, who was still trying to regain his bearings, and managed to get to his feet. But the big man was already on them, moving quickly through the small room.

As the leather clad man swung the club, Cassius ducked under the wide arc and tackled him. Landing astride the big man's body, he pushed up to his knees and threw his fist into the man's face again and again. He rained down blows until it was a mess of mangled flesh. There was a scream in the hallway, with loud voices and angry calls answering. His head snapped around and he saw Rory crawling towards the white shape, which had slid across the room and was lying under a window. Cassius made a mad dash towards him, partially crawling on his hands and knees as he tripped over the big man's legs.

He was on Rory's back in a flash, forcing him over and wrenching the figure out of his grasp. He had a moment to recognize it as a tiny figurine of a person, carved out of something white, he thought bone most likely, before raising it over his head. Then he grabbed the thin man by the shirt and brought the figurine down on his head. Blood erupted from his forehead in an arc as Cassius brought the figure up for another strike. Rory's eyes bulged and he kicked desperately, thrashing under the Prince's weight. But the figure came down hard, ripping the thin man's forehead open even further in a gruesome laceration. The Prince struck him three more times, until, finally, mercifully, the man's body stopped shaking.

As the last lights drained out Rory's eyes, Cassius let the now carnage-covered figurine drop from his grasp as he heard feet come rushing through the door. He turned and saw two more guards in the room, with more following behind.

"*Damn me to the Hells!*" He cursed, looking around frantically for an exit.

The rain was once again coming down hard on the window when Cassius threw himself through it. He burst into open air, emerging into the darkness through a cloud of water and shattered glass. The screams of the guards faded quickly as he plummeted down through the rain towards the black, roiling water below. In an instant, the ocean rushed up to greet him and he was crashing into the cold surf. Salt water filled his ears and mouth as he sunk into the darkness. The last thing he heard as he disappeared beneath the waves was the far off crashing of thunder as the storm raged overhead.

Chapter Fifteen

Bending With the Wind

Gray green water lapped at the hull as their vessel cut through the restless waters surrounding the Crescent Cape. The *Salt Stallion*, a sleek, fast moving vessel designed to outrun everyone from pirates to the Republic's Navy, was silent as it made its way south, skirting the edge of the shoreline by moonlight. A skeleton crew was manning the ship, with only a handful of figures on deck. Holton stood with his arms crossed near the prow, eyes fixed on the black horizon.

He had left the disguise of the traveling bard behind and was back to wearing leathers and simple traveling clothes, tattoos and scars once again visible in the dim light. Erin stood beside him, her brow furrowed and a frown permanently affixed to her face. She was chewing on her fingernails and he kept seeing her sneak glances at him. Finally, she sighed and relented, speaking up and breaking their long silence.

"Are you really sure about this, Holt?"

He nodded without looking at her, a stoic expression set on his face.

"It's just, we don't know anyone in the Broken Coast. We don't have any contacts, no partners, no safe houses. What if Lawrence is setting us up?"

"I don't believe he is." Holton said quietly, still staring out at the dark water, "He left Redwater in a hurry, that much is clear.

Somehow, word got out that he was in the city and soldiers were asking for him by name. We know that for a fact. He obviously has a lot invested in this venture, why risk everything just to try and screw us out of our payday?"

"Maybe he doesn't have the money?" Erin glanced up at him again, "*Double*? Double our price just to take the witch and the kids to Crescent City? Seems like we're buying a basket of spoiled eggs to me."

Holton snorted and turned to face her, "We've already committed the crime, Erin, what would you have us do? Leave the witch and her brood on the street, wish luck to smile on them? Then we'd have done this all for nothing."

Erin bit at her nails like a hungry dog gnawing on the bones of its last meal, "I just...I don't like it."

"It's not my ideal situation either, truth be told. But the job's the job. We gotta bend with the way the wind blows. Besides, if we show up and the eggs have turned, we can always kill the overdressed bastard. I'm sure we could make a great deal off those suits of his." Holton flashed her his toothy grin and she managed to smile weakly back at him. But the tension in her shoulders never relaxed, and she continued to devour her nails like they were the last meal on earth.

There was a noise behind them and they both glanced around. The pale face of Alice peeked out from under her dark hair as she watched them from the stairs that led below deck. She was pretending to read a small book she had picked up somewhere, but the pages had remained exactly in the same place as when she had opened it an hour ago. Erin gave the man next to her a smirk.

"She likes you, you know."

"The witch girl?" Holton rolled his eyes, "She's at least fifteen winters too young for me."

"Not like that, you goon." The blonde woman sighed heavily, "She looks up to you. Haven't you noticed she's always hanging around, asking questions, you know...?"

"I'm not the person those kids need to look up to." Holton shook his head, "I've got nothing for 'em but a lifetime of bad decisions."

"You mean your lifetime of stealing from the Northern Kings and the other high born? I think that's something most of us common folks could get behind."

"I've made a lot of mistakes, Erin. Those victories have come at a high price."

"We've all made mistakes, Holt. None of us would be here if we had many other options."

"I'm shocked, and here I was thinking it was my sparkling personality that kept this lot around." Holton grinned wolfishly again and she elbowed him in the ribs.

There was a long silence as the two stared out into the night. The wind coming in off the water was a relief from the muggy heat which hung in the air, even in the dead of night. Stars shone in the clear sky and the moon was large and brilliant in the black. Eventually, Erin sighed and spoke up again.

"What *is* the plan, Holt?" She asked quietly, "You asked us to trust you and we have, but now what? We pass the woman and kids off to Lawrence, then what, head back north? The heat on us will be unreal now. I don't think there's any way we can go back to robbing local lords after this."

Holton shook his head, "No, you're right. Even before this job, we were barely keeping our necks out of the noose. After this, it would be a miracle if we could stay ahead of the Law, even if we called in every favor we have and emptied our purses."

"So...what then?"

Holton stole a glance back towards the girl who quickly looked back down at the book in her lap. Then he went on in a quiet voice, "You know where they're taking them, right?"

"I've heard the Blades are staking their claim in the Lorrailia, right? Is *that* your plan? To go with them to the New World?"

Holton nodded, grabbing her hand and fixing her with his intense gaze, "Think about it, Erin, twenty four years ago a

bunch of mercenaries and thieves, just like us, beat the Federation *and* nearly beat the Empire! The two greatest powers in the
world. The Confederacy is independent now, like the Republic.
Things are changing, Erin, and fast. The New World, that's our
path out of this life."

Erin pulled back. Her eyes searched his face as she silently
turned over his words in her mind. Finally, she seemed to grasp
it, "This has been your plan all along."

"Yes. When the Blades first reached out to us, I wasn't going
to work for them...the jobs had too much risk, we had too much
to lose. But then they started talking about the New World, the
opportunity...the *wealth*. I've already made arrangements for all
of us, it was part of our deal for doing this job."

Erin stared out at the sea, face still troubled, "I don't know
Holt, you're staking everything on the word of a masterless
mage I wouldn't trust with a basket of sweet cakes, much less
all of our lives."

Holton nodded, "I know it's a risk. But we've been running
from one job to the next our whole lives. Never settled, never
able to sleep without keeping one eye open. We spend everything we make on one job to stay hidden until we can pull the
next one off. We need an exit strategy. Wouldn't you like to have
a home again? Like when we were little?"

"I can hardly remember our home."

"Well I do, and I'm going to make sure we have one again. If
it's the last thing I do, we are going to have a home again." He
put a hand on her shoulder. She swallowed her doubt, nodded
and managed to smile back at him. They watched the starlight
play across the water as they sailed south through the dark
ocean.

The *Salt Stallion* slid into the bay in the early morning
hours, skirting around the edge of the Crescent Cape

which shimmered like a jewel jutting out of the sea with its many lighthouses blinking at them in the semi-darkness. The thin peninsula stretched from the mainland in a curving arm and ran parallel to the western coast of the Southlands, a barrier which shielded the marshy deltas of the Broken Coast from the Lancing Ocean.

It was warmer this far south, and a heavy fog was rolling off the ocean and smothering the rocky peninsula. The pointed tips of hundreds of spires could be seen peeking through the fog, catching the first glimpses of morning sun as it rose over the mainland. There were already dozens of ships creeping along through the mist out towards the ocean, small vessels carrying fishermen and messengers and cargo away from the great port as Holton and his crew arrived in the bay.

The Crescent City sprawled over the entire peninsula, coming into full view as the mist slowly gave way to the sun. Compared to the overwhelming monotone of the Rothmount, the City looked as if someone had discovered paint for the first time and was intent to use every variation available. The buildings were tall stone structures clustered tightly upon terraced cliffs as they climbed upward at a precarious angle. These rose up and formed elevated patios and balconies under great spires of impractical height.

Large, arching supports and seawalls were used to reinforce the natural stone, which would have given the city the sensation of being one giant structure if it was not for the immense variety of colors. The city was painted in pastels of pink, yellow, red, orange, white, and blue, an almost alien world which had risen out of the gray green water to meet them. Standing on the deck of the ship, Holton noticed the look of shock on the children's faces and grinned.

"I guess none of you have ever been south of the Horn, huh?"

They shook their heads, dumbfounded. Louis, the makeup removed from his face so that his birthmark once again showed, spoke up, "There's so many colors!"

"The people of the Broken Coast still hold on to their lineage quite strongly." Mary said, explaining in the tone of a teacher, "Before the Federation absorbed the Broken Coast, it was home to a people known as the Wave Walkers. They wore brightly colored clothes and painted their homes to ward off evil. They believed the beasts of the deep sea were hungry spirits that hunted the shores at night and hated the light of day. So they wore bright colors to keep themselves safe, believing the colors would trick the beasts. They even painted their boats like that."

"But that's nonsense." Alice protested, "The sea monsters of old were all driven from our shores generations ago."

The witch nodded patiently, "Yes, but the traditions of old die hard, young one, and here, far from the heart of the Federation, they still persist."

"I think it's pretty." Madeleine exclaimed in delight, staring with wide eyes with wonderment, "Everything in the North is so dull and gray, and the Horn is nothing but red and brown."

Holton half listened as the children continued discussing the city, consumed by his own thoughts. As the *Stallion* docked, sidling up to a long wharf which stretched out into the bay, Erin collected the group and Holton paid the captain the remainder of their fees. The group disembarked onto the busy dock and made their way towards the city.

The streets of the Crescent City formed a tight, winding labyrinth of cobblestone that climbed up the cliff faces at sharp angles. Alleys and paths would often give way to sudden staircases or switchback paths to ascend a particularly steep section of the city. Many buildings had stairs which wrapped around their exterior without rails or siding, which appeared perilous to the uninitiated Northerners. There were thin bridges built between buildings of different heights, ostensibly connecting the lower levels of the city to upper levels in a web of elevated pathways.

Despite the often precarious angles, people still made their way up and down the byways of the city undeterred. There was a steady stream of traffic moving in every direction, flowing through the streets and bridges and rooftops without fear. The constant wind blowing off the ocean kept the heat from being unbearable, but seemed to always threaten to knock them right off the face of the city and back into the ocean.

As they made their way through the maze of colorful houses and shops, Holton noticed the children openly gaping at the equally vibrantly decorated people. The people of the Broken Coast wore brightly colored sashes and ponchos to match their city, adorned with brass, gold and bronze chains and rings. Many bore colorful tattoos which spread across their exposed flesh in a canvas of ornate colors and designs and some bore piercings in their ears, noses, or lips. He and Erin had to yank the children along and remind them each not to stare multiple times. Mary attempted to help them, but she too seemed a bit flustered by the new surroundings. She clung closely around her children, trying to watch everything and everyone at once.

Holton and his crew did their best to intercept the pushy street performers and vendors that attempted to ensnare the group, often in an unfriendly manner. On more than one occasion Holton's hand dropped to the hilt of his blade before a particularly stubborn salesman would get the point. Finally, after an eternity of climbing the streets and having to stop and ask directions multiple times, they reached their destination.

A three story building painted a dusty pink which had faded from the sun and sea salted winds and stood on the ocean facing side of the city. A few quick raps of his knuckles earned him an opened door and the annoyed glare of a large man holding an impractical looking barbed knife long enough to be considered a short sword.

"Nice blade." Jarryd commented off handedly, a smirk on his face.

The man cast a glare his way, then his dark eyes darted between Holton and the motley group assembled behind him, "Talk quick now, what be your business here?"

"Easy there, friend," Holton stared back at him evenly, trying to hold his attention, "we're here to see Lawrence."

The man shifted, recognizing the name, but he did not relax even a little and he kept the knife drawn, "What be your business with him?"

"Just tell Lawrence that Holton Hart is here with his delivery."

The man eyed them suspiciously for a moment longer. Then he slammed the door shut and the sound of a security bar could be heard as it slid into place. They waited outside in the relentless sun, sweating as much from it as they were from their climb through the city streets. Eventually, they could hear the sound of the bar being moved again and the man with the knife was back. He said nothing but motioned them all inside, holding the door, slamming it shut again behind them. Stepping into the interior was a bit jarring. Outside, the sun had fully risen and was mercilessly baking the seashore, but inside, the windows were shuttered and curtains were drawn.

The room was only dimly lit from the bit of light that slinked in from around with curtain edges and between the door frames. Low couches with plush cushions were laid out over the rug covered stone floor, where a half dozen other men sat lounging around a circular central table. A saucer occupied the center of the table and a low burning coal sat in it. The sickly sweet smell of something being burned coiled its way into their nostrils as the men led them past the sitting area. They earned the curious gazes of the men as they passed, but they said nothing as the knife wielding doorkeeper led them through another passageway.

The next room was something like an office or meeting room. Two chairs sat facing each other and shelves filled with books and trinkets lined one wall. The opposite wall hosted a desk made of highly polished wood, behind which sat a dark haired man in a fine gray suit. He looked up from the small ledger he had been writing in and smiled at them as they entered.

"Holton!" He proclaimed. He always spoke a bit too smoothly for Holton's liking, like everything was rehearsed at some point prior to their meeting, "You made it, I'm so glad."

The group had funneled into the room, Holton's crew spreading out casually and checking the windows and other doors while the witch and her children stood in a cluster near the entrance. Lawrence waved off the doorkeeper, who gave them one last glare and shut the door behind them with a resounding thud. As he went, Holton heard Jarryd mutter under his breath, "Careful not to cut yourself with that thing..."

Once he was gone, Lawrence turned to Mary, all broad smiles, "My dear, it is so good to see you. Tell me, how was your journey? Are you well? I do hope my associate here took good care of you and the younglings?"

"We're fine." The witch answered briskly, glancing around at the crew of hardened criminals and killers, "They were most gracious."

"Excellent!" Lawrence clapped his hands and pointed to the chairs, "Sit, sit, relax, I'm sure you are exhausted from your journey."

Holton glanced at the witch and she shrugged. The two of them sat, leaving only the one chair for Lawrence, but the rest of the group was left standing. Lawrence noted this and waved a hand. Suddenly, the door at the far end of the room swung open. He proclaimed, "If we could have a moment, please help yourself to anything you would like in the kitchen."

Holton exchanged glances with Erin and his other crew members, nodding to them. They gathered up the children and made their way through the secondary passage. Once they were all through the door it slammed shut with another wave of the dark haired man's wrist. Lawrence sat and faced the two seated across from him, one leg crossed casually over the other as he lounged in his chair. His grin returned and he was watching them with great curiosity.

"So..." he began, staring at Holton, then sliding his gaze to Mary, "how much have you told him?"

"Him? Nothing." Mary ran her fingers through her dark hair, fidgeting in her seat as she flicked her eyes back and forth between the two men, "I kept quiet, just like you told me to."

Holton watched the exchange with a curious eye. He noted how the witch seemed less settled now that she was amongst her supposed benefactors.

"That's good, the less people who know the details of our plans, the better." Lawrence turned back towards the thief, "No offense, of course. I must say, you have exceeded my expectations once again, Holton. You've completed your task and even managed to get all of the children here unharmed. First the College, now this...I made the right call, betting on you."

"Thank you." Holton grumbled. He was staring hard at the well dressed man as he waited expectantly.

Lawrence nodded, "As promised, you will have double the agreed upon total for your extra troubles. My man out there should already be pulling the marks out of our strongbox."

After he gave a quick nod to acknowledge the remark, Holton replied "Good, that's good...but I think we need to talk about the rest of our deal."

Lawrence gave him a quizzical look. Then he snapped his fingers and grinned again, "Ah, yes, you wanted safe passage to the New World, a place for you and your men."

Holton said nothing as he watched Lawrence with a suspicious eye. The dark haired man gave his goatee a few strokes and then again snapped his fingers and pointed at him.

"I know what we can do. We are in the period of...*rapid expansion* for our organization. We have quite a few more jobs that need the attention of someone capable, and you have more than proved yourself. If you and your companions would be willing to make this arrangement a bit more permanent, I think we could work something out for you in the New World."

"I thought that was *already* part of the deal..." Holton growled in a low voice. His hand twitched reflexively towards his knife but he steadied it with considerable effort.

"The deal was, you complete this job and we would *talk* about your passage to Lorrailia. Now we are, and I'm telling you what is required to make that particular dream a reality." Seeing the dark look which clouded the red haired man's face, he added, "Look, the New World is already being carved up quickly. New Oarenhiem is always on the cusp of another expansion and the Free Cities are in constant conflict. Cassel just doesn't have the manpower nor the resources to hold his Confederacy together, and all that's not even considering the issue of the natives..."

Lawrence gave him a significant look and overexaggerated a little shudder, "...the land isn't just free to anyone who wants it. Not anymore. But if you join us, become part of what we're doing, I can guarantee you that you'll have a place to call your own when all this is over."

Mary was watching them intently. He noticed her examining Lawrence's face from her perch on the chair with an unblinking stare that distinctly reminded Holton of a wide eyed Northern owl. She turned to face him and he was caught staring back at her before he grunted something and returned his attention to the matter at hand.

"I don't suppose I can get that in writing?" He said through gritted teeth.

"In fact, we would *insist* on a contract." Lawrence's smile seemed to ooze unsubtle self satisfaction.

Holton glanced again at Mary, who was still staring at him, eyes luminescent as she wore an implacable expression. He gave the dark haired man a hard stare.

"What *exactly* would this contract include?"

"Well...to start, we would need you to help collect another group of recruits for us. We are sending a ship across the Lancing

Ocean and we need to ensure all our charges make it successfully."

Holton cocked his head, "Would this happen to be another
group of children?"

Lawrence's grin widened as Mary shot him a look, "Why, as
a matter of fact, it is."

"What exactly are you doing with all these children,
Lawrence?"

The well dressed man shook a finger before him and made a
disapproving sound, "That, my friend, is a company secret, of
which you are not a part. Not yet, anyway."

There was a strange scent in the air. Holton identified it as an
herbal burning, coming from the room where the guardsmen
were sitting. He tried to ignore it and focus on the conversation
at hand. He already felt distinctly uneasy about this arrangement, but there were not many other options he could see laid
out before him.

Lawrence seemed to read the decision weighing heavily on his
face, "Look, Holton, if it helps, I give you my word we will do
our best to ensure no harm will come to these children. Why,
our mutual friend here is letting us use her little ones, aren't you,
Mary?"

The dark haired woman nodded slowly, but a troubled look
passed across her face for the briefest of moments. Holton noted
this and wondered at it, but he knew he would get no answers
without a commitment. He sighed.

"Show me this contract of yours."

T he setting sun had painted the horizon in a brilliant array of oranges and red over the water, putting even this
flamboyant city to shame. Many had gathered on the various
rooftops, balconies, and patios to watch the display and snip-
pets of laughter and conversation could be heard drifting on

the sea wind like birds riding the warm air. The dark figures of Holton's crew lounged on an upper deck of the Blades safe house which looked out at the ocean, all in various stages of their evening drinks.

Holton leaned back on the railing, facing his crew. A metal strongbox sat on the center of their gathering, lid casually flung open to reveal a small mountain of coins. They glittered in the colorful evening light, teasing the eyes and winking seductively at each of the thieves. Erin stared hard at the coins as she spoke, voice a bit husky with emotion.

"So...the Red Wolf's a mercenary now, eh, Holt?"

Holton sighed deeply, ran his hands through his hair and shook his head, "No, that's not what I would call it."

"Then what, *exactly*?"

"This...is just another job."

Erin snorted and tore her eyes away from the box to face him, "You know that's not true."

Taron, his drink held loosely in one hand as he sprawled across an armchair, pointed at him and complained, "Yeah, a job has a goal, an end...this ain't no job. What happened to stayin' outta politics, lookin' out for us and our own?"

Holton looked from him to the rest of the group. He set his jaw, "Look, you've all been with me a long time. You know me, I'm a practical man. We've run through every last drop of our luck in the North. We've avoided the headman's ax by inches about two dozen times over these last few years. We've kept from killing anyone that mattered too much, done our best to stay out of the spotlight, and that's kept the Northern Kings off our backs. But now? After this job, we can't just go strutting back there."

"But that doesn't mean we have to join up with the Blades." Jarryd interjected, stroking his mustache. He toyed with a knife, flipping it back and forth in his other hand absentmindedly.

"Right," Barney added, waving a hand out to the ocean, "there's a whole world out there, Holt. With this much money we could go anywhere, Oarenhiem, the Breach, Vinatieri...hell, we could just charter a ship to take us to Lorrailia ourselves, if that's where your heart's set on."

Holton nodded, "Yes, we could. But then what?"

He paused and let the question hang in the air. It filled the silence with a growing weight that was pressing down on all of them. He looked at each of them in turn as he spoke, "If we take this payout and run, we'll be back at the bottom again inside a year. We might have the coin, but we'd have to use every bit of it to start our new lives. Maybe you get lucky, use your share to buy yourself a nice little life somewhere, maybe a trader or maybe a farmer, aye?"

"We could start the operation over on a new continent." Barney offered, "I'm sure there's plenty to steal and set fire to in the New World."

The others looked at Holton, curious looks on their faces. He shook his head, "And find ourselves in this position a few years down the line? If that's what you lot want, you're welcome to it. Take your cut and go, I won't stop you. But that ain't why I got into this life. I ain't looking for half measures, I want it all."

He leaned over and took out a fistful of glittering coins, flicking them back into the chest one at a time. They made metallic clinks as they landed, adding emphasis to his words "I want a haul that makes this look like a log splitter's wages. I want the kind of fortune I'm never going to be able to spend...I want to be a *king*."

The men around him watched, equal parts surprised and entranced. Something else was in their eyes, the same thing Holton knew every man like them shared; the hunger. A deep, gnawing need for more. It was what drove them, deep down in their core and he knew it. He smiled, looking at them now, "Trust me, my brothers, what these mercenaries have planned...it's going to rewrite the order of the world, make rulers out of a lot of men, and I aim to be one of them."

Taron was sitting up straight now. His eyes had that sheen, like a wild dog ready to stalk down its next meal. He glanced at the other two men, recognizing the same look in their eyes. He nodded to each of them in turn and they all looked up at their leader.

"Been a while since I had a proper title." Jarryd said softly. He had stopped flicking the knife back and forth.

Taron stood and mimicked an ornate courtly bow, balancing his drink in his free hand, "We're with you, Holt, or should I say, *my liege.*"

"Good," he grinned his broad wolfish grin, showing his rows of teeth. He looked over to Erin, who hadn't spoken at all during his entire speech, "and you?"

She eyed him, brushing short strands of hair out of her face. She gave him a long look, letting the question hang in the air unanswered. The sun had almost sunk below the water's edge now, the last dying light of day disappearing behind the enveloping darkness. When she spoke, her voice was very quiet, almost a whisper, "We're not warriors, Holt. We're criminals, thieves. Whatever the Blades are planning, whatever they promised you, it's not going to come without bloodshed."

Holton softened a bit. His shoulders slumped and he looked around at his crew. "You're right," he began, taking on a quieter, resolute tone, "but that doesn't change anything. We have a chance here, Erin. A chance we might never get again. I'm not going to let that slip through my fingers...are you?"

She sat there staring back at him for another long moment, then she sighed and shook her head, "No, I suppose I won't."

"That's my girl." Holton reached over and clapped her on the arm, planting a firm kiss on her forehead, "I can't do this without you!"

"No, I don't suppose you can," she lightened a bit and cracked her first smile of the evening, "someone has to keep you boys from getting yourselves killed."

They all laughed and Taron poured another round of drinks. They toasted and talked more of the future, enjoying the night air as it blew a cool western wind over the city.

Chapter Sixteen

The Emperor

I t was the first pleasant morning in days as the rain had finally blown out to sea and left the peninsula in peace. Morning light streamed into the Grand Palace of Khanar through large windows decorated with geometric patterns of delicate gold and silver, filling the halls and casting out the gloom which had hung over the city for the past week. The multi paneled murals of landscapes and historical battles were bathed in brilliant light alongside large bronze statues staring down at the passers with lordly importance.

The palace was a buzzing hive of bodies at this hour, with servants and courtiers and various others rushing about as they began the day's activities. All wore summer clothes of fine chiffon and sheer decorated with ornate lace and stitch work. Few nobles were about at this hour, as the modern fashion was not to be seen in public before midday. As Juniper and her mother were led through the high arching hallways by a guard in gaudy armor inlaid with gold, the various denizens of the palace stepped to the side and bowed deeply until far after they had passed. Neither of the mages acknowledged their presence, simply passing by with their chins thrust out in cool indifference.

Both women wore thin dresses in the summer style of deep violet to denote their department within the Conservatory. Aria Faye wore her golden sun brooch at the clasp of her dress as well as a gold and jewel encrusted hair clip, painting an elegant picture and sparking a familiar sense of inferiority in her daughter. As they passed through a large, orderly waiting room with two rows of traditional low backed chairs, Juniper noted that there were more guards here, two standing at each entrance, faces shrouded behind their brilliantly polished helmets. They passed another set of doors, these massive and covered in golden filigree depicting the shimmering forms of a golden serpent winding across them, and finally entered the throne room.

It was an imposing site, one which Juniper had only borne witness to once before, when she had been formally given the task of being liaison to the Horn for the Summit Festival. The room was circular and tremendously tall, with a vaulted glass ceiling that let the light stream through into the chamber. There was only one entrance visible, the one they had entered through, and there were no other breaks in the walls as they climbed up into the heavens.

The smooth stone had been decorated with a breathtaking barrage of paintings, depicting the scenes from the Book of Wairdien. Mostly, these took the form of muscular men fighting demonic looking beasts or building great structures and beautiful women delivering food or water to the waiting mouths of hungry looking crowds. These were the Demigods, those that Wairdien, the one true god, had charged with enacting his will in the world. According to the scripture, sitting before them in the center of the room on a raised, gold and jewel encrusted throne, sat the last man to share blood with one of those mythical figures, the Emperor of Oarenhiem.

Emperor Devon Omari watched them with dark eyes, a sneer of cold command frozen on his face. His hair was slicked back and both it and his skin shone like from some oil treatment. He wore a long, flowing robe of rich jade, decorated with a scale like pattern. Jeweled rings sparkled on almost all of fingers and he wore a chain around his neck with the coiling serpent of the Empire emblazoned on a golden disk.

When they were about twenty feet from the platform, he held up a hand for them to stop. Both Juniper and her mother immediately dropped to their knees on the marble floor of the chamber, bowing with their foreheads touching the ground. They stayed that way for a long time, long enough that Juniper's knees began to ache and she struggled to keep from fidgeting. Eventually, the Emperor called out in a voice that was surprisingly high pitched and nasally, putting an end to their suffering.

"Rise."

Both women stood up immediately. The Emperor was staring at them, eyes hard like shards of obsidian, then motioned to a pair of the traditional chairs which sat before the throne. They sat cross legged on wide cushions, folding their dresses carefully as they bent down, and watched as he rang a small bell by the side of his throne. A portion of the wall, imperceptible as a door only a moment before, slid open soundlessly and a small procession of servants made their way into the chamber. They meticulously set out another cushioned seat and a table in front of the two women, laying out an assortment of small plates and bowls, each containing a small portion of food.

There were strips of fish, both sauteed and raw, set into orderly rows on little plates, cups of pickled vegetables, small piles of finely diced fruit, an egg floating in a bowl of light liquid, several tiny dishes of sauces and a bowl of lightly colored nuts. The servants set identical sets of food in front of each woman, deferentially bowing away once the display was finished and disappearing into the hidden exit door. Once they were gone, the Emperor descended the platform and sat on the cushion across from them making a casual motion toward the food.

"Please, eat. It is early, and we must all prepare for the day ahead."

"Thank you, your Highness." They both immediately began eating. They used dainty skewers and thin knives, making little bites by combining various portions of the food. The Emperor began with the egg, lifting the cup to his mouth and sucking the liquid down, a particularly loud slurping sound letting them know he had devoured the egg as well. He set the cup down and looked at them.

"So, tell me, what is the latest news from the House of Stone and Glass?"

Aria dabbed at her mouth with a thin napkin, putting on a face that showed a perfectly pleasant expression, "The Conservatory is well, your highness. The Department heads are managing to keep away from each other's throats, for now. The Hall of Illuminators have had a particularly successful year so far, thanks in no small part to my daughter."

Juniper inclined her head and gave the Emperor what she hoped looked like a shy smile. She tried to keep his eye contact but something about his gaze made her uneasy. She looked back down at her strip of fish and busied herself piling strands of fruit onto it.

"I have heard you put on quite the performance." the Emperor's direct address shook her back to attention, "Tell me, how was your trip to the Southlands?"

She took a moment, then replied diplomatically, "The *performance* went well."

The Emperor smirked and gave her a knowing look, "I'm sure you were in a hurry to get home. Those of the Federation are so backwards they might as well still be nomads living in caves and riding their horses across the plains. It's like going back in time, no?"

She swallowed, suppressing a smirk of her own, "Their customs were a bit...old fashioned. They were kind to me, for the most part. Unfortunately, there was an incident..."

"Yes, I had heard of these troubles." Juniper leaned in to see if he would elaborate, "It seems the great Baron Roth has trouble managing the keys to his own keep. Truth be told, I'm not sure how anyone manages to maintain order in that whole nation. All those Barons and Dukes and Lords, always rising and falling, vying for control, absurd."

"Quite, your Grace," Aria agreed quickly, "there's no stability."

"Exactly!" He thumped a fist on the table, speaking with a steady fervor that reeked of self satisfaction, "Look at the Empire, my ancestors received the holy writ of Wairdien three thousand years ago, and now? We're thriving! New Oarenhiem is expanding every year, and our people enjoy the fruits of our success! Stability! Tradition! Every man in their proper place! That's what real empires are built on."

"Indeed." Aria nodded solemnly, as if the Emperor was doling out sage advice and not the same trite propaganda Juniper had heard since she was a child.

"Look at your own family! You and your husband are both the descendants of long lines of loyal servants to the Dynasty. Has your dedication not given you everything you could *possibly* want?"

"Of course, your Grace, nothing fulfills my everlasting soul more than serving your will." She stole a glance at her daughter while the dark eyed man was putting together his next bite of breakfast, "In fact, that's why we have requested your presence. Something occurred while my daughter was on her trip, something you must be made aware of immediately. It could be of dire importance to the Empire."

The Emperor stopped eating and turned to face the younger woman, cocking one eyebrow. Juniper took a deep breath and tried to keep her tone as neutral as possible.

"The Princess, Valeria, approached me while I was there. She put on airs of friendship, at first at least. But eventually she revealed her true intentions. She believes there is a widespread conspiracy, one which seeks to undermine the Federation. She wanted me...to assist her. To see if I could find traces of it here, in the Empire."

The Emperor frowned. He took the bite that had been left on his fork and chewed for a moment, seeming to turn the information over in his mouth, tasting all sides of it. Eventually, he asked, "She believes this is the same group that raided the Hold? Stole the Baron's prisoners?"

Juniper nodded. He gave her another piercing look, "What information did she provide you about this group, exactly?"

"Well, your Highness, the Princess has found evidence of several mercenary groups being hired by an unknown benefactor across the North and the Southlands, the Burning Blades, the Houndstooth Company, others, I'm not sure how many. Freelance arcanists as well. She spoke about being opposed when she attempted to investigate further. At least one of her agents has disappeared already, others have been threatened." Juniper took a steadying breath, "I...agreed to help her. I thought this conspiracy, whatever it is, might pose a threat to the Empire...perhaps even to you."

The Emperor blinked and gave her a soft smile, "Oh, my child, if only all my people were as loyal and true as you and your family."

He produced another small bell from a hidden pouch in his robe and rang it. A well groomed servant seemed to materialize from some other point in the room, unseen behind the throne platform. He leaned over as the Emperor spoke to him in a softer, yet clear voice.

"Summon Chancellor Chale, to attend to me immediately, and have the Head Chronicler and Professor Payce come here at once too." The servant nodded and bowed as he retreated from the table.

The Emperor returned his attention to the women seated before him, "You have done well, Lady Faye. You have brought us very useful information about this potential plot to destabilize the Federation and you seem to have made an ally out of one of the most powerful people in the Federation and the North. I assume she has given you a way to stay in contact?"

Juniper nodded again and pulled out the small stone inscribed with golden inlaid patterns. She held it out for him to inspect and he nodded. She tucked it back into her interior dress pocket.

"I want you to stay in contact with the Princess from now on. Give her nothing of consequence, but keep your communication friendly. If she is right, we need to root out the snake in our shallows, but we must not allow them any more information. We need to know if someone in our government is involved in this cabal, and if they intend to try their tricks here as well."

A door, this time on the opposite side of the room, opened in the wall and two men and a woman entered, being led by a single servant. The first man was broad, appearing to have been stuffed into his fine robes with great effort, with a shaved head that was decorated with tattoos on one side, while the second was a stark contrast, so thin and frail he looked like he could be blown over at any moment by the slightest breeze. His eyes were unfocused and he seemed to be unaffected by the grand surroundings. The woman was mousy and wore her hair in an elaborate bun. They all fell to their knees and gave a deep bow once they were about twenty paces from the Emperor. He made a noise and motioned for them all to rise.

"Chancellor Chale," he called, addressing the large man first, "we have information about a group of conspirators operating in the North and the Southlands to undermine the Federation. They may have a presence here as well. Set your best agents on it immediately."

"Your Highness," the large man began, keeping his eyes downcast, "unfortunately, we have most of our agents set to the matters of the colonies already, per your request. We do not have the manpower..."

The Emperor did not even look up. A small flick of his wrist and the large man stopped talking. His eyes went wide. He stood perfectly still, not daring even to breathe. The others shrank away from the Chancellor. The mousy woman looked like she was barely containing her terror. Aria did her best to keep her face impassive, but even she was grimacing. Juniper watched him, fascinated. She could not begin to understand why the man had chosen to speak out of turn. The only person who did not react was the thin man, who continued to stare impassively at nothing.

The Emperor lifted his cup to his lips and took a long, loud sip of tea before speaking, "Chancellor, I did not ask for excuses, nor did I ask for your opinion. If you find the orders of your Emperor too taxing for you, I'm sure we can find a suitable replacement."

"*N-no*, your grace! My apologies. I will...figure something out."

"Excellent. You may let him go."

Suddenly, the air around Chancellor Chale shimmered and blurred. Two forms manifested out of the air, both wearing dark armor, devoid of the typical ornamentation of palace guards. Their faces were obscured by their helmets which sported demon faced masks, but both wielded longswords of darkened steel. One had the blade across the Chancellor's neck, pressing just enough to leave an imprint, and the other had the point in his back.

When they appeared, the mousy woman recoiled, throwing her hands up instinctively with a small yelp of fear. In a seemingly single motion, both soldiers sheathed their swords, turned to the Emperor and bowed deeply. Then, without a single word, both rapidly faded once again. They began to become translucent, then vanished altogether within a minute.

Chancellor Chale rubbed at his neck, looking from Juniper and her mother to the Emperor. The dark eyed man seemed to hardly notice, carefully skewering another piece of fish. After a moment of silence, he made a shooing motion, "You may go, Chancellor Chale."

The large man blinked. Then stood up straight, tried to regain some sense of dignity, gave a quick bow and strode quickly out of the chamber. The Emperor sighed, shook his head and looked from Juniper to her mother, "I hope that display hasn't put you off your breakfast?'

Both women shook their heads quickly. The Emperor nodded and turned to face the two remaining newcomers. He pointed to the mousy woman.

"Professor Payce, if you would." He motioned to her to come forward with one finger. The woman had gone so pale, she might have been mistaken for a Northerner. She scooted forward, barely seeming to move her feet more than an inch at a time. Juniper wondered if she would be as afraid as the other professor if she were run afoul of those guards. Their disappearing trick was one that stemmed from her own college's catalog, but their mastery of the skill was impressive even to a skilled arcanist like her. She was unsure if she would be able to counter it if called upon. When Professor Payce was standing beside the table, the Emperor cleared his throat.

"Professor, I need you to send a message to the Baron of the Horn. Your hand, if you please."

Professor Payce blinked a few times, her eyes wide, looking like she was doing her best not to dart for the exit. She finally managed to stammer, "Y-yes, your Grace."

She held out her hand and he took it in his. Suddenly, her eyes rolled and her head snapped backwards. Her back curled and she seemed to be mouthing words no one could hear. Juniper could feel the draw of energy from around the room. It caused the professor's body to twitch and vibrate erratically, so she seemed to be in the clutches of a seizure.

Then, as suddenly as it had begun, it was over. The woman's body stopped spasming and she lowered her head to look back at them. She was breathing slowly and ragged and she seemed barely able to keep her eyes open. The entire affair had lasted less than a minute.

"That will be all, Professor."

"It...it is, was, my pleasure to..."

He cut her off, mercifully ending her pitiful muttering, holding up a finger to his lips, "*Shhhh*...that will be all."

She nodded, her head bobbing lazily. She took a deep, shuddering breath and gave an unsteady bow, then scurried out of the chamber. Juniper could not help thinking of a rodent that had barely escaped the clutches of a snake. Once she had left, the Emperor turned his attention to the final member of the group. The thin man stood there with a blank expression on his face, seemingly nonplussed by the series of events. He walked forward when the Emperor beckoned him and continued to stare, seemingly at nothing.

"Chronicler," the dark haired man began, without looking at the frail man, once again picking at the food set out before him, "tell me where the Faye family stands currently."

The man spoke in a voice that was worse than all the lectures of every monotonous and uninspired Professor at the Conservatory by leagues, "The family has no outstanding debts to the Empire or private entities therewithin, no standing punitive actions from the Justice. Both sides of the family have been held in good grace by the Emperor for the past three generations with only a single notable mark of disgrace. Their eldest son defected from the Imperial Military and was later arrested during the colonial rebellion. The family disowned him after he was caught and given the Emperor's Justice. The incident has yet to be cleansed from their current standing, your grace."

Juniper noted the nearly imperceptible tightening of her mother's jawline, at the mention of her brother. She could see her lips thin out as she fought to keep her composure. If the Emperor noticed, he made no comment about it.

"I believe one sibling's service can forgive anothers trespasses. See that the mark against the family is stricken from the record." The Emperor declared dismissively.

The chronicler closed his eyes and tilted his head back. After a moment, he opened them and reported, "It is done."

"Good." He smacked his lips as he seemed to be enjoying a particularly tasty bite, "See to it there is also a note of favor for the Professor, for special services rendered to the Dynasty."

The thin man nodded again. But again only closed his eyes briefly, making no moves to indicate any recording of what the Emperor had said.

"Your Highness, you're too kind..." Juniper began but the Emperor cut her off.

"You've done the Empire a service, Professor. With any luck, we'll be able to play this situation to our advantage. If any tendrils of that conspiracy have taken root here in the Empire, Chale will rip them out and salt the earth they've sprouted from. Any developments will be reported to him going forward, and he will pass on any further instructions I have for you." He stood abruptly, wiping his mouth with a fine white cloth, "Now, I have other matters I must attend to. There is a meeting of my Advisors in progress, and I intend to make an appearance. You are dismissed, Headmistress, Professor."

Both women stood up, their meals half finished. Juniper noted that the Emperor had eaten nearly everything on his own plate. He had been far less distracted during their meal. Both women bowed deeply. Without another word, the Emperor turned and strode out of the room, his footfalls echoing in the massive, seemingly empty chamber. Once he was gone, servants emerged from the invisible doorways in the walls and began hurriedly clearing the food away. Juniper glanced over at the Chronicler before being led out of the room with her mother. He had bowed when the Emperor left, but now, he had returned to standing still, staring blankly. Just before they left the chamber, she saw a servant gently take him by the hand and begin to lead him away from the throne.

L aying in the mid morning sun which streamed into the courtyard, Juniper thought about how good the heat felt on her skin. She had changed out of the fine dress from her meeting with the Empire once she had arrived at her parent's house, adopting a simpler outfit with shorter sleeves and skirt. There was a greenhand who was failing miserably to hide the glimpses she kept stealing at her as she tended to their carefully crafted garden. She was shaping the bushes with a few motions of her hands, the branches gently bending and sprouting new leaves at her urging, and Juniper was mildly worried she might mess up the delicate topiary if she did not keep her attention on her work. But she was not so concerned that she bothered to cover up. She continued to read her book as she stretched out on the long, cushioned bench, enjoying the brief moment of serenity.

"You look comfortable." A soft yet steady voice spoke up behind her.

She glanced over as her father ambled toward her as best as he could while supporting himself on his white cane. Like most of those in Oaren, his skin was a yellowish gold, yet it had become pale due to lack of time outdoors. He wore his hair slicked back as the Emperor had, but it was less glossy and streaked with gray, framing his angular face. He wore the gray robes associated with his station, unadorned with jewels or lace. Only his eyes belied the tremendous wit and intelligence Juniper knew to be contained in that weathered appearance. They were still bright and sharp, always scanning, probing with an intensity that unnerved even his own daughter. As he eased himself onto the bench beside her, he winced, putting most of his body weight on the cane. Eventually, he was able to collapse onto the cushion and let out a relieved sigh.

"Is your leg bothering you?" Juniper asked, quickly sitting up straight as she placed the book on a side table.

"The storm didn't do it any favors the last few days ." He grumbled, sticking it out in front of him and flexing his foot back and forth. It was a move she had seen him do many times before, "But now that it's broken hopefully the heat will work all the stiffness out."

"Have you been back to the healers lately?"

"The war was more than twenty years ago, June, if something could be done for my pain, it would have been done by now." Her father did not sound bitter, just held a tone of resignation laced with a deep weariness. He put his foot down and turned to face her, "I heard your meeting with the Emperor went well today?"

"It did." She nodded, gently dropping the subject. She knew her father did not like to talk about his time in the New World, "He seemed pleased, said I did the right thing by agreeing to help the Princess..."

Her father made a motion for her to wait and called out, "Miss Maylee, if you could give us the garden for a moment?"

The woman stopped what she was doing immediately and bowed, "Of course, Chancellor Faye."

She turned and hurried out of the courtyard, leaving the bush she was growing half finished. It was meant to be a fish of some sort, but she had only finished the tail and half the body, leaving a headless sculpture. Juniper stared at it for a moment and thought about what kind of statement that might make to the court if they left it that way, but her father called her back to reality.

"As you were saying?"

"Ah, yes...the Emperor was pleased. He had the mark against our family stricken from the records, and he said we were in his favor."

Her father nodded slowly. He motioned for her to go on.

"He told me to keep in touch with Valeria, feed her information, but nothing of consequence. I am to report to Chancellor Chale directly."

Her father gave her a wry smile, "So, he's set the hound on finding us, eh? Chale can be...difficult, but he *is* excellent at his job. We must be careful how we tread from here on out."

Juniper considered this, pursing her lips and letting her eyes search the flagstones as she formulated her thoughts. "Why not ask the Chancellor to join us? Others have...and after what I saw today, I doubt he has much love for the Emperor. Having the Empire's hatchet man on our side would no doubt be a boon to our plans."

Her father shook his head, "Unfortunately, Chale is...limited, in his thinking. He is a true believer. Even if he hates the Emperor, he would never turn against him."

Juniper nodded but furrowed her brow. The sunlight was still radiant in the mid morning, bathing them in its warmth. Her father had his face turned towards it. She wondered to herself how long it had been since he sat out here. How much time was he spending in his study, pouring over cases, working on his plans. She was silent for a time. When she finally spoke up, her voice was soft, hesitant, almost like a child. She hated it, but she struggled to overcome the fear that was filling up her chest.

"What if he finds out, father? What will happen to us?"

Cristos Faye turned to face his daughter. His eyes were like dark wells, set against the pallid skin in stark relief. She could see the sympathetic gaze there. But there was something else, something deeper. It was hard, unyielding, a deep set iron which would not be moved.

"If he discovers our plans," her father began, his voice even, steady, "we will be ruined. Our family will be shamed now and forever. Everyone who shares our bloodline would be killed. We would be lucky to escape with our lives, then, even if we flee across the ocean or to the south, we would be hunted. We would spend the rest of our days running, as would any children of our line."

Juniper swallowed hard. She knew the truth, but to hear her father speak it so plainly was like a knife in the guts. She could feel it twisting and tearing at her inside, shivering with the sudden onset of self doubt. She began breathing harder, her muscles seeming to contract.

"But you know, as do I, that we have no choice."

Juniper looked up at him. He was staring at her, his eyes softer than they had been. He was grasping the handle of his cane so hard his knuckles were white.

"I've told you the truth. You know what that...*man* did, all those years ago, during the war, to our people. His *own* people. To us. You know what he continues to do. Something has to be done. If we let him keep expanding the Empire across the New World..."

Juniper took a deep breath, held it, and blew out slowly. The same breathing exercise she had done hundreds of times since learning them as a girl in the Conservatory. She met her father's gaze evenly, steeling herself. The doubt was not gone, not entirely, but it was overcome with that familiar sense of righteous fury she had felt years ago, when her parents had first brought her into their confidence. When they had told her the truth about the Emperor. She nodded, not quite ready to speak.

Her father gave her a warm smile. He put a hand on her shoulder and squeezed it, "Good. We need you committed to the plan Juniper, your mother and I, and the rest of us. It's going to take all of us, together. After all, we're only going to get one chance to kill our false god."

L ater that evening Juniper sat in her childhood bedroom, stooped over her desk working on a sketch with colored chalks. Most of the furniture had changed over the years, but the massive wall painting of the skyship was still there, vibrant even in the low light. The familiar shelves of paints and pens and papers were like a balm to her mind which was still reeling and anxious from the day. She let herself become engulfed in her work, unaware of the time passing as she scribbled away.

The breeze fluttered through her open window, rustling the papers and blowing a lock of hair loose off her ear. She stained her ear with a smudge of chalk as she tucked it back, matching the color on her hands and clothes. A knock came at her door. She ignored it, staying bent over her desk, absorbed in her work. The knock came again, and a third time. Finally, the door cracked open.

"Juniper?" A voice she did not expect came fluttering in, light and gentle as the morning. She spun around and saw the round face of a young woman, auburn hair spilling around her face in bouncy curls, peaking in. As she entered, Juniper noted that she wore a fancy dress, suited for court, with a low cut which revealed the smattering of freckles across her shoulders and chest. Her pale skin was kissed by the sun, pink in the face and tan in the shoulders. When she saw Juniper, her face lit up and she threw the door open the rest of the way, "Oh, you *are* here!"

"Kali!" Juniper shot up out of her seat and was across the room in a few quick strides. The chalk sketch lay forgotten on the desk. They embraced, holding each other tightly. Then she pulled back and kissed the young woman. She lingered, drinking in her familiar scent and the feel of her soft lips. When she finally leaned back, still holding her around the waist, Juniper smiled broadly as she took in the young woman's face, "What are you doing back? I thought you were supposed to be gone until winter?"

Her face became clouded. All the humor seemed to flow out of it as her shoulders slumped. She took a half step back and looked Juniper in the eyes with clear concern.

"There is a problem with the operation." Kali hugged herself across the stomach.

"What? Kali, what is it?"

"There's trouble on the frontier. The natives have started pushing back harder than expected. Several of the outer settlements have been destroyed. But that's not all, there's also the rebels. They've been far too active lately. There have been riots daily, all across the colonies. They even took Toryo, declared the whole town independent."

Juniper furrowed her brow, "Lord above! They can't just wait until the end of the year? I thought all this was being handled? What are we paying all these damn mercenaries for if they can't keep the colonies under control?"

Kali shook her head, "They've done everything they can. We've been talking to all the leaders, trying to get them to understand, but they've been pushed too far. There's nothing we can do to get a handle on it anymore. I came back with one of the emissaries from Sylar's Bay. June, the Steward sent a message urging the Emperor to move up his visit to the colonies to assist with the rebels. They want him to come at the end of the season"

Juniper turned away. She closed her eyes and took a long, deep breath. She held it in for a moment. Then it all came erupting to the surface at once. The constant fear, the ever-mounting doubt, the unspoken frustration. Her scream echoed around the room. She yelled so loudly it caused a small flock of birds to flee from her parent's courtyard in a panic. She was so angry her entire body was shaking.

Tears flowed, washing warm lines from through the chalk which smudged her face. She tried to wipe them away but they kept coming, streaming freely dripping off her chin and staining her dress with little dirty smudges. Suddenly, a freckled arm wrapped around her waist from behind. She felt the warmth of Kali's body press against her back, the gentle touch of her cheek on hers.

"*Shhh...*" the young woman whispered soothingly as she nuzzled her face to Juniper's, "it's going to be okay, June."

"But...what are we going to do, Kal?" She hated how her voice felt, whiny, lost, like a little girl. Ridiculous, but she could not help it, "Things just keep going wrong..."

"I know, but we're going to figure this out."

Kali's hand, soft but surprisingly strong, grasped her chin, turning it sideways towards her. Her lips found Juniper's and they met for a long moment, not wanting to separate. The taste was familiar and comforting, even more so than when she had walked into her room for the first time after being gone for so long. When their lips finally came apart, Juniper found the tears had stopped. She opened her eyes to find Kali's fierce gaze on her.

"We can't lose faith now, June. Not after everything we've been through." She smiled, softening a bit, "We're in this together, remember? Until the end."

Juniper nodded. She took a deep breath and leaned her forehead against the other woman's, "Until the end."

CHAPTER SEVENTEEN

HIGHER LEARNING

"**A**gain!"

Jayce winced at the sound of the instructor's voice cracking over the room like a whip. He held out his hand towards the perfectly spherical metal ball resting on a cushion on the table in front of him. He struggled to keep the tremor in his arm under control. Sweat was already pouring down his face, soaking his shirt and forming a small puddle on the table.

He clenched his teeth and extended his focus towards the ball. It was like trying to force himself to fly. No matter how much he strained, how hard he tried to apply his will to the sphere, the metal ball sat shining on its perch, unmoved. He tried to feel it, to reach out and grasp at the internal essence of the thing, the way he did when he manipulated the water or the winds. But it showed no signs of yielding.

Around him on either side were other students, all younger, seven in total. They sat at a long table, all facing towards the front of a long room, each with a metal sphere before them. A couple of the others had managed to lift their balls, causing them to float in the air. The rest, including him, had not managed to lift theirs at all. They were all sweating, breathing hard, some, especially the younger ones, looked close to tears.

A pot bellied man with jowls that jiggled with every step and a harshly receding hairline stalked back and forth in front of the table. He wore a suit of fine blue cotton and white trim which would have looked fanciful on any other man. However, he managed to make even such a garment appear sloppy, wearing the shirt unlaced and letting it come untucked, complemented by the heavy grease stains on the sleeves and front of his coat. He stared at the young ones before him with deep set, glassy eyes that peered out from his pudgy face. He reminded Jayce of a particularly unpleasant wild hog.

"Come now, *children*," he gave Jayce a pointed look as he passed him, "this metal is challenging to manipulate, true, as it is far from the earthly components. But to be a true Arcanist is to master one's self, to overcome those natural impulses and exert one's will, regardless of the subject."

As if to add emphasis to his statement, the pig-like man lifted his hand. All the metal balls flew into the air. They gathered together, forming a small cluster which rotated slowly in the air before him.

"Take one." He commanded, speaking in a voice that was full of barely concealed contempt, "Take one and you may go. I will end your lesson for the day."

The students looked at each other, hesitating. But one boy held out his hands and let out a low growl of effort. One of the balls quivered, moving away barely an inch from the cluster before snapping back into place. The flabby man laughed.

"Good effort, young master, but not good enough. I will reward your effort though!" He flicked his wrist and that same metal ball, about the size of a grapefruit, flew out of the bundle. The boy had no time to react before it hit him in the chest with such force it flung him backwards out of his chair. He landed hard, headed snapping back and thudding off the stone floor. Several other students went to check on him. Jayce stood so he could see over their crouching forms. The boy had had the wind knocked out of him, gasping for breath as tears streamed from both eyes.

"You have your ball, Master Thatcher. You may go now!" The teacher's voice came from behind them.

Jayce turned to face him. He was grinning broadly, jowls flopping back and forth as he turned towards the new challenger.

"Arcanist Allegheny," Jayce said through gritted teeth, "if I understand the task, we must get one of those balls from you to be successful, correct?"

The pudgy man nodded, clearly enjoying himself, "But I doubt you could do much to manipulate one of these, Master Acosta, you couldn't even move yours..."

Jayce cut him off, raising a hand and pulling at the latent energy in the air around the room. It was like gathering dozens of strands of string into a bundle and weaving them together to form one, cohesive whole. A violent blast of air tore through the classroom and collided with the balding man, sending him careening backward in a tumble. The metal balls fell to the floor in a clatter of jangles and thuds and rolled in every direction. Jayce caught one with his foot as it rolled by.

Arcanist Allegheny stood in a huff, straightening his coat and combing down what was left of his hair. "That was cheating! You were supposed to be manipulating the *ball*, not the air!"

Jayce gave the man a smug grin and spat out, "You did not specify what method we were to use, Master Arcanist."

The mage's frown cut deep grooves into his face, jowls vibrating with unvoiced fury. Then, suddenly, a wicked little smirk wormed its way across his face. When he spoke, it was with a wheedling voice that inspired an instinctive urge for violence, "Well met, Master Acosta. You got the best of me, but I suppose I should have expected it. You settled, your kind has always been known for their tricks. A *true* Arcanist would have stuck to the lesson, but I suppose I should have known a weather witch would find a way to weasel out of the hard work."

Jayce's veins ran cold. A pulse of energy ran through his body as he instinctively began reaching out for closest sources of power. He became aware of the air in every inch of the room, feeling the slight change in the atmosphere as all the bodies tensed for an upcoming conflict. Even the moisture that was slowly evaporating from the table and floors and the skin of his classmates emanated a small pulse of energy. The pudgy man stared at him, beady eyes gleaming in their sunken sockets. He licked his lips, "Would you like to test your will against mine, Master Acosta?"

Jayce stared at him, his breathing hard as he weighed the options in his mind. He took a breath and forced himself to relax. His focus retracted. Once again inside the confines of his own body, he could feel his heart beating in his chest. He willed himself to give the fat man a grin and replied, "No, I wouldn't want you to sully your hands on my *kind*."

With that, he spun on his heel and was out the door, striding out before he cost himself his place here at the University, leaving a room full of students and one disheveled teacher staring after him.

I t was midday in the city of Asaldon. The sun hung over the city like a brilliant chandelier, casting its light across the plains and driving any memory of the shadows left by the storms. From the balcony overlooking the gardens, he could see the streets spread out around him like a web, intertwining in infinite patterns and disappearing into the labyrinth of buildings. Beyond the city, the wind blew through the fields of wheat and barley which stretched relentlessly in every direction, dotted intermittently by a farmhouse or barn.

The Sovereign's Road stretched south away from the city, bisecting the countryside with a clear line of gray stone that disappeared over the horizon. Jayce could not make out any figures at this distance, but he was sure there would be hundreds of farmers toiling away in the heat. He leaned on banister and wondered if any of the local stormspeakers ever stared up at the massive city, imagining what it must be like to attend the University, to get away from their homes and families, as he had. He sighed deeply, letting his head droop low onto his arms. His mind drifted back to the ocean, to the gentle sway of the ship under his feet. The stone balcony suddenly seemed very alien, like he had wandered somewhere that made him uneasy down to his core. There was a mad moment where he wondered if there would be any ships leaving for the Breach out of Asaldon's port this time of day.

But then the conversations he had at the Hold came back to him and cast those daydreams aside without regard. There were people in the garden below. He could hear workers tending to the plants, a few students chatting, the gentle bubble of the fountain. He closed his eyes, basking in the sun like one of those great sea lizards on the rocky coast of Oaren he had been so fascinated by as a child.

"Enjoying the view?"

Jayce stood up and whipped his head around. Andrea, Headmistress of Apprentices, stood behind him a bit, arms folded across a cream colored dress. She wore her hair up and tidy as always and her glasses shone brightly in the sun. Jayce did nothing to hide his eyes as he rolled them back to the gardens below. The silver haired woman moved to stand beside him, posture stiff as a statue as she cast her gaze on him, sunlight reflecting in her glasses.

"I heard you had an...*issue* with Arcanist Allegheny earlier." She had no notes of malice nor disapproval in her voice, only spoke with a frank dispassion that seemed to betray a sense of boredom. Jayce did not reply. He continued to stare out at the gardens, shoulders slumped.

After waiting a moment the Headmistress spoke again, a note of annoyance in her voice, "You understand, I hope, that assaulting anyone, especially a member of the faculty at this establishment, is heavily discouraged? That if the Arcanist sought to, he could have you disciplined for this incident?"

"I was only completing the task I was assigned, Headmistress Whistler." Jayce grumbled, giving her a sideways look.

"Yes, well," a look of annoyance flashed across her face before it was once again concealed by her stoic mask, "the Archmage might see it differently. Fortunately, Arcanist Allegheny has elected not to pursue the matter any further. Lucky, for you, and me."

"For you?" Jayce blinked.

Andrea gave him a sideways look, "*Yes*...I am the Headmistress of Apprentices, Jayce. I am responsible for you and your actions while you are a student here."

The thought had never occurred to him, and the realization must have shown on his face, because Andrea gave a long, exasperated sigh.

"Jayce," she began, clearly attempting a placating tone she was not comfortable using, "I know our first meeting last cycle wasn't as fortuitous as the spring rain on the seeded fields, but understand, I am not your enemy. My job, my purpose in this place, is to help young people along their path."

As she spoke, her expression softened somewhat. The hard lines around her eyes and jaw faded and Jayce thought he could see a very different woman peeking through the stony visage. She was looking out over the gardens now too, her unfocused gaze far away.

"When you came here, I tried to dissuade you because I knew what your time here would be like. Do you think you're the first person to come here, wealthy benefactors pushing you through our doors? Many people leave the University after months, sometimes even *years*, disappointed."

"I don't understand," Jayce finally blurted out, pushing off the banister and turning to face her, "I can control the wind, I can move a ship through the ocean, but I can't lift a metal ball!

These *children* can figure it out, but I can't. None of the reading I've done, none of these classes or teachers can explain it to me."

The Headmistress closed her eyes. She breathed out, then turned to face him. Jayce almost took a step back when he saw the hardness that had reformed in her eyes.

"Then let me make this clear for you...you will *never* be an Arcanist. When a child is born with a talent for the Art, no matter how great or minor, all the potential for what they might achieve with it is already inside them. Some are able to move plants and make them grow, some may walk in the shadows or bend light and some can even heal flesh. With training, they can grow and develop, maybe even accomplish some impressive things. But they will never be *true* Arcanists. Someone who has the true Gift can manipulate the forces of the world in its purest form, no matter where it comes from. That's why we call you settled, your abilities will always be base, simple, lacking the ability to reach any higher."

Jayce stared at her. He was vaguely aware of his nails digging into the meat of his palms as he clenched his fists, using every bit of his willpower and managed to remain silent as she pushed on.

"These lessons you've been attending, they are not to teach you magic. They are to weed you and those like you out of our University. We are looking for the exceptional. But your skill is limited and it always will be. When you use your Gift, you are moving on instinct, the way a man treads water when he falls into a river. It is simply part of your nature. You will never be able to touch the forces of creation, to manipulate the world in a way that lasts. You will never be able to achieve the High Art."

She let her words hang in the air. Her face was not scornful, only frank, meeting his gaze evenly and without any hint of pity. For one of the only times in his life, he struggled to form the words to even respond.

"Does that mean you're going to throw me out? Expel me?" He managed. The thought of all his failed attempts to learn anything about the Heist of The Hold and how it would look if he was thrown out of the University within a single season. The thought of returning to Valeria and the Baron made him shudder like a dog soaked after a rainstorm.

Something like a smirk cracked her stony face, "Of course not. We are happy to keep accepting the Roth's patronage. You will simply continue to attend the *lower level* courses until you quit of your own accord. Or make a mistake large enough that we are forced to release you."

He found he still had nothing to say as the woman gave him one last look, lifted her chin and strode back inside the University, leaving Jayce alone, staring after her at the great monolith of stone and metal which shone brightly in the midday sun.

S itting in front of the massive statue of Oswald Uther, the founder of the University, which loomed over the central courtyard, Jayce felt very small. The statue's gaze was hard and seemed to suggest a deep well of contempt for the unwelcome guest in its house. He had wandered the halls of the University and its grounds for hours after his conversation with the Headmistress, trying to piece together a plan for what to do next. He had ended up here, sitting on an uncomfortable stone bench, in a sort of daze as he recounted everything over and over again, wondering what if there was a way out of this predicament where he got to retain some measure of a life.

"Are you waiting to see if he moves?"

The voice shocked him so badly he jumped. He glanced around quickly and saw a young woman standing beside him. She had a fair complexion and her golden hair framed an angular face which held a slightly mocking smirk. She wore work clothes and had dirt and bits of sticks and leaves all over her, hands sheathed in heavy leather gloves.

"Wh-what?" Jayce stammered, his brain still consumed in a roiling cloud of confusion.

"The statue," she clarified, pointing up at the founder, "I've heard them say he moves if you watch him long enough...eyes follow people around the courtyard, stare at you while you're not looking, that sort of thing."

He could only stare at her dumbfounded. She rolled her eyes and rubbed her gloved hands together, "Not much of a talker, are you?"

He fumbled the words in his mouth before finally managing to throw out, "Maybe...I know better than to talk to strange women."

"Worried I might be a witch looking to lure a wayward child away from his mother?"

He cast a significant look around the courtyard, "Seems to be the right spot for it."

"Fair enough." She cracked another grin and started to turn away from him, "I guess I'll leave you to it then."

"Wait," Jayce tried to straighten up, "you're one of the gardeners here?"

She cast a look down at her dirty clothes, "What gave me away?"

"Are you...a Greenhand?"

"Not me, I've none of the Gift, as far as I know. But my master is one, do you want me to get him for you?" She cast a thumb over her shoulder and pointed towards a figure across the courtyard. Jayce leaned over and saw a man so thin he wondered if he might disappear if he turned sideways making small motions over a circular bush, causing it to shutter slightly as new flower petals bloomed under his touch.

Jayce shook his head, "It's alright. I shouldn't distract him from his work."

The girl cocked her head to one side, "But you were happy to distract me, huh?"

"I, uh...you came up to me first." He managed lamely.

She laughed. It sounded like a bell ringing out in the early morning to announce the break of day over the long night.

"True enough, I suppose. What do you want a Greenhand for anyway?"

Jayce bit his tongue, suddenly realizing how foolish he must seem. He cast his gaze aside and mumbled, "I just...wanted to ask him about the mages in this city, outside the University I mean. I was wondering what kind of work someone might find."

The girl took a moment to think this over, looking at him oddly, then brushed her hair back over her ears and sat beside him on the bench. Jayce was taken back by this for a moment, but recovered, giving her a look of his own.

"What is your name?" She asked him.

"Jayce," he began, "don't you have to be getting back..."

"I'm Lyra," she interrupted. She was staring at him with her brilliant, bright eyes, making it hard for him to think clearly, "so, you're quitting the University?"

"No!" He said, a bit more forcefully than he intended.

"Being expelled, then?"

"No, nothing like that. I'm just weighing all my options." Jayce found he had a hard time meeting her gaze.

The girl pursed her lips and plopped her chin on her up-turned hand, which rested on her knee, "Well, this is a big city, the biggest, some say, I'm sure there are lots of opportunities for a former University apprentice. What did you have in mind?"

Jayce sighed, "I was a Stormspeaker...before coming here, I mean..."

"Stormspeaker? Well there's plenty of call for those!" Another smile broke out across her face. Jayce found it hard not to stare at the little dimples that had formed in the corners of her mouth, "They always need good help out on the Lake, especially the ships that take the channel to the sea. Then there's always the fields. They're going to need weather workers for the end of the summer season."

Jayce briefly thought about living out his days in a little home by the water, helping fishermen bring in their catches, or disappearing into the countryside, calling down rain for farmers and keeping the frosts at bay. Perhaps with a pretty gardener girl he met during his time in the city. Then he shook his head, "I don't think that life is for me. Besides, I have too many promises to keep here."

"Oh, what sort of promises?"

His shoulders slumped a little, "I'm here by someone else's blessing, they're paying my tuition. They're spending quite a bit of money for me to be here. I wouldn't want to let them down."

Lyra, scrunched up her nose, "Seems like a pretty poor way to live your life, just being what someone else wants you to be."

Jayce gave her a sideways glance, "You're certainly a straightforward one, aren't you?"

She shrugged, "Never known another way to be."

He grinned and shrugged his shoulders back at her, "I got a good deal, all things considered. It was the fish I was hunting after all, I just didn't expect it to be quite such a beastie."

"You sound like one of the boys down at the docks."

"I worked on a merchant vessel, my whole life, in fact, before coming here."

"Ah, well you're a long way from the ocean, sailor."

"I am that..." he trailed off, not sure what to say next.

They sat in silence for a moment. Then Lyra abruptly stood and motioned back towards the thin man, "I should be getting back to work. Elias doesn't like to be kept waiting."

Jayce nodded. As she turned to go, he called out, "Lyra?"

"Hmm?"

"Would you...like to get together sometime? I'm new in this city, and I could use someone to show me the ropes, help me get my legs under me, sort of speak?"

She smiled, looked around, then nodded, "Sure, we should be done later this evening. Want to meet back here?"

Jayce nodded, "Looking forward to it."

She gave him another smile and spun around, striding back across the courtyard and leaving him to watch her go.

The sun had just started to make its first steps towards the horizon, still hanging high over the western skyline of the city, when Jayce began making his way from the dormitory towards the courtyard. He had washed and changed, shaved the stubble from his face and attempted to put together something resembling a presentable outfit from his meager wardrobe. He considered calling on Lucian to borrow a suit, but felt that might be a bit much. It was only an outing with a girl he had just met, after all, not a royal dinner appointment.

As he passed the groups of students and teachers that cluttered the hallways, he had a lightness in his step he had not felt in ages, the burdens of secrets seemingly moving off his shoulders for the briefest of moments. He might not know what the future held for him, but for this one moment he had something to look forward to and he was determined to make the most of it.

However, he had a stop to make first. He had resolved to apologize to Allegheny, no matter how distasteful it would be. He knew the man could make his life even more of a hell than it already was, so he decided a bit of diplomacy would be for the best. His father always said the ship with the biggest cannons was the one with the right of way, after all, and he was in a good enough mood to eat a little shark skat if it would help him in the long run. He approached the instructor's door and was preparing to knock when he heard familiar voices speaking. It took him a moment before he recognized it, but when he did, it brought the weight of the world crashing back onto his shoulders again.

The first voice was Allegheny, with its obnoxious note of self satisfaction. But the second was the unmistakable halting whine of Breyer, the master Arcanist of the Hold. He struggled to hear what they were saying, but then the voices became louder and he saw the knob starting to turn. He flew down the hallway, skittering around a corner. When he had caught his breath, he looked around in time to catch sight of the sloppy Arcanist walking away from him and speaking in low tones, seemingly to himself. But Jayce noted he was carrying a package wrapped in a blanket under one arm that was half hidden by his robes.

The older mage disappeared behind the bend of the far hallway and for a moment, Jayce considered ignoring it. But then the many failed attempts at espionage he had tried during his short stay here came back to him and he cast a last, mournful look towards the courtyard. He slipped down the hallway behind the muttering man, trying his best to appear unassuming.

As Allegheny continued his muttered conversation he shot furtive glances at every passerby and glared at those he passed, earning him a wide path through the University's halls. Jayce dared not get closer. Even though he could not hear the details of the man's seemingly solo conversation, he managed to keep the Arcanist in sight as he wound his way through the labyrinthine halls, staying a turn or so behind, ducking into alcoves when there was a long straightaways in case he happened to check over his shoulder.

Eventually, Allegheny reached a set of wide stairs and descended, making his way into the underground levels of the building. Jayce followed, trying not to make a sound as his boots plodded along the cobblestone steps. The Arcanist continued his trek through the basement, moving through the dimly lit halls with the confidence of a man who had walked this path many times before, until he reached a large double doorway with large doors of dark wood. Allegheny knocked twice and the door opened from the inside. Then he entered without further word and the door shut with a click behind him.

Jayce swore silently and hurried up to the doorway. He looked around but found no easy answers for how to get through the door without risking drawing attention to himself. He turned and followed the wall to where it turned, hoping for a side entrance. He found none, but near the place where the wall turned again he found a small grate. Smooth grooves were cut along the edges of the floor, places where water could flow into and be directed out if the basement was washed or flooded. The iron grate was tiny and covered the area where one of these grooves flowed through the wall. Jayce could not even fit a hand through it, but when he lay down on the floor he found he heard voices on the other side.

"-and the Baron still has no idea who it was that informed the Blades of his prisoners?" Allegheny was speaking. Jayce could imagine his sneering face snorting out every word.

"No, of course not." Breyer responded. Jayce noted the man seemed significantly less timid and hesitant now than he had been in the Great Hall, "The Baron and his bitch of a daughter are, erm, still chasing their tails. They seem to believe that Oarenhiem is the most likely perpetrator. If not for my, erm, interference, that entertainer would have taken the witch's place in the dungeons."

"It wouldn't have been a great loss," a new voice, one Jayce did not recognize, male, self-satisfied and smug, "her parents are the most important piece of the puzzle. But still, better to avoid anyone discovering stone solid evidence of the collusion until the absolute last moments."

"Or not at all." Breyer spoke up again, "It would be quite embarrassing for the Federation if word got out that the Senate was involved. To that end, we still have the Prince to deal with."

"Quite right," another new voice, female, speaking Herron with an accent that curled the i's and dropped the r's. It was familiar, like his father's accent, but somehow a bit off, "we've gotten word he killed the shopkeeper in Redwater and is still in the wind. We don't know what he got out of the man first. For all we know, he's still on the trail of Lawrence and the witch."

"He is tenacious. But perhaps we can use that idiot to pull attention away from us." Breyer said thoughtfully, "The Baron's been in a blind rage since the Prince left. He has been combing the Horn for any sign of his son and seems to have forgotten all about looking for the traitor in his court. If we can find him, we can use him to keep the Baron's attention off of our operation."

They were talking about Cassius. Jayce remembered how even Lucian had been unable to laugh it off when they had received word the Prince had stolen away from The Hold. Valeria had sent word demanding he tell her anything he knew about her brother's plans. But the Princess was disappointed. He still had not heard from the Prince since leaving Rothmount.

"We'll just have to set a trap for him," the prideful man was speaking again, "If the prince is still following the trail, he'll end up on the Coast. We'll have our agents prepare something special, a surprise which he won't be able to squeeze his way out of this time."

"Won't that send the Baron on a warpath...?" Allegheny inquired.

"Against whom?" Breyer interjected, "The Blades are the only group they know for a fact are involved, and the mercenaries will be mostly off this continent by the time we enact our plans. If we catch the Prince while he's on his fool's errand, there will be no proof of the perpetrators. The Baron will bluster and, uh, may even make some rash decisions, but there will be nothing for him to sink his teeth into."

"Besides," the woman's voice spoke up again, "if all else fails, the Baron has two sons. If we get rid of the elder Prince, from what I've heard the younger will struggle much less on the line."

"I'll make the arrangements," the unknown man said, "if the Prince is still on our trail, he will be dealt with. Once that is handled, Lawrence will be able to ensure the shipments can continue uninterrupted. We should only need a few more and the project is almost finished."

"Are you sure you'll be ready in time?"

"No need to worry yourselves," the man replied dismissively, "the Ceaseless Scions will be ready to move when the time is right..."

Jayce blinked. He needed to tell Lucian. He needed to tell the Baron. What he was hearing could mean the difference between Cassius' life and death. The voices continued speaking but he had heard enough. He pushed up to his feet and fled down the hallway, using all his self control to keep from sprinting through the dimly lit corridors of the University.

CHAPTER EIGHTEEN

DINNER PLANS

He was late. The sun was well and truly setting now, painting the horizon a bright shade of pinkish red as it relinquished the sky to the oncoming night. Lyra stood in the courtyard under the great statue of the bearded sorcerer, as she had for over an hour, waiting with her arms crossed as she tapped a foot. She was wearing a pale yellow dress, cut short as was the trend in this year's summer fashion. She had found that in addition to helping her blend in with high society, it served quite well for keeping the attention of potential suitors of all ages. With her hair done up, she could have passed for a student on a casual glance.

Unfortunately, the man who minded the gates knew her for the gardener's assistant and eyed her from his post, arms folded as he leaned against the little guardhouse in the compound's wall. She had been granted leave to wait for Jayce here, but she knew a non student would only be given so much grace. Technically, she had no business being here. Elias's contract was to maintain the grounds and gardens of the University, a task achieved easily without ever entering the main building or staying past day's end. She wished she had not let her mark out of her sight in the first place. She was no stranger to waiting, but this was starting to get on her nerves.

The merchant sailor had taken the bait she had so carefully laid out, following her crumbs like a marsh rat follows morsels of cheese. He was wonderfully predictable, a trait she greatly appreciated in a mark. Stringing along eager men was like a dance to which she knew all the familiar steps. But now her mark was late, and that was something she had little patience for.

After considering her options, she had almost made the decision to go home and wait for another opportunity to approach her quarry. Then, she saw a man come rushing out of the building at an erratic pace, part running, part walking, muttering as he went. It was Jayce. He looked haggard, clothes disheveled. She turned and strode across the courtyard at an angle so she would intercept him right as he reached the gate.

"Hey! Did you forget about me?"

Her voice seemed to jolt him into awareness of his surroundings again. He looked around and saw her, noticing her for the first time. She noticed the manic look in his eyes, surprised at how off balance he seemed. It took a moment before recognition flashed across his face.

He stammered and stumbled as he tried to walk and talk at the same time, "Lyra! I, I'm sorry...oh, our evening...I forgot..."

"What's the matter, Jayce? What happened?" She caught his arm but he grabbed her hand and whirled to face her. Her free hand dropped instinctually to the dagger she kept strapped on her thigh, safely out of view beneath her dress.

"I can't talk now, not here...it's too dangerous." He hissed and cast a wild eye around the courtyard.

"*Dangerous?*" She asked, casting a feigned look of worry about.

He nodded rapidly. His breathing was heavy and he could not stop looking back towards the main building. She pulled her hand away from her concealed weapon with considerable effort and put it on his shoulder.

"Hey...just calm down, okay?" She spoke in a low, soothing voice, "Is there somewhere we can go that's safe?"

He nodded again speaking in a low, urgent voice, "I need to get to the Consul of the Horn, *right now!*"

Lyra stood for a moment. She had no idea what had frightened him, but she had a hunch it was tied to the true reason for him being here. She was not about to let this opportunity to get to the truth of the matter slip away.

"Alright then, let's go."

W ithin the hour they had reached the broad row of lavish estates that made up the housing for the delegates from the Baronies and various other nations. As they passed under the multicolored banners, Lyra could feel the harsh gaze of the various guardsmen that watched them from the gates. She adjusted her dress and stayed close to Jayce, who barged past the guard in front of the Horn's delegation with barely a word. The estate was even more gorgeous on the inside than out, decorated in fine tapestries the likes of which would be worth more than her weight in marks. Jayce spoke a few words to a bewildered servant who directed him towards the back of the house.

They passed several beautiful rooms and a few more servants who busied themselves getting out of his way before reaching an open outer deck. A handsome man with a short beard and a suit that looked like it was custom made sat with a striking, red haired beauty eating dinner at an outdoor table. There was also a young girl. She was perhaps in her seventeenth year, a bright brunette with a lighter complexion then common and large honey colored eyes. She bore a striking resemblance to the well dressed man across from her. When Jayce entered, the man waved to him and a broad smile broke out across his face.

"Jayce, so good to see you..." he trailed off when he saw the expression on the younger man's face. He immediately stood and faced them, all pretense of the welcoming host gone in an instant, "What's wrong? What happened?"

Jayce looked from the handsome man to the woman, then to the girl and back at Lyra, "I've discovered something, and it's what we've been looking for."

The handsome man's eyes widened. Then he nodded and snapped his fingers at the servant who stood at attention off to the side, "Leave us. Shut the doors, turn away all callers."

The servant nodded and left them, pulling the doors to the deck shut as he left. Once he was gone, the man indicated they should all sit and introduced himself as Lucian Roth, Consul of the Horn, and the woman as his wife, Lady Marigold of the Northern Kingdoms. The girl was their daughter, Mariana.

"And you, my dear, are?" Lucian asked pointedly.

"Lyra..."

"She's a friend..." Jayce interjected.

Lyra noted the young noblewoman was staring at her intently. She whispered something to her mother and the two of them gave Lyra an appraising look. Mariana pointed a finger at her with a grin, "Have we met before? You look *so* familiar..."

"I-I don't think so, I'm just a gardener." Lyra lied, trying her best to put on the effect of a flustered commoner. She had, of course, recognized this couple and their daughter the moment she had walked out onto their elegant veranda. She had seen the Lord and Lady multiple times at events around the city, lavish parties and such, that she had attended on the arm of some lesser nobleman or merchant's son. She had even held brief conversations with Mariana a number of times before. The girl was a well known socialite around the city and they often traveled in interweaving circles. But that was a different Lyra, and she could not afford to lose her advantage now that she was so close to learning more.

"She works at the University," Jayce attempted to assist, "We are...friends."

"*Anyway*," Lucian pointedly interjected, "what were you saying about your discovery, Jayce?"

Jayce shook himself and made a visible effort to refocus himself, "Ah, yes...I was on my way out to meet Lyra here, and I heard Breyer at the University."

"*Breyer*? Are you sure?"

Jayce nodded quickly, "Yes! I went to Allegheny's office to apologize for an incident that happened earlier and I heard the old man talking inside. They must have been using something to communicate, like a sending stone, because Allegheny was carrying a parcel when he left, and he was still talking to Breyer. It seemed suspicious so I followed him. They went into the cellars and had some sort of meeting. I wasn't able to see all the people but I could hear them. There were at least four of them, including Breyer and Allegheny. They were talking about the heist of the Horn. They spoke about the conspiracy. They mentioned the Senate, it seemed...like some of them were a part of it."

Lucian slowly leaned forward, elbows on knees, a look of deep concern on his face, "Jayce, are you sure about what you heard?"

Jayce nodded again, more deliberately this time.

The handsome man's eyes went wide and he cast a glance over at his wife. She had a finger on one side of her face, staring hard at the young man. She cast a significant glance at the younger woman seated beside her. Mariana leaned over and whispered something to her father.

Lucian nodded and cleared his throat, "Perhaps we should have a bit more privacy for the remainder of this conversation."

Lyra looked over at Jayce, "I can leave if you want me to..."

The young man gave Lucian and his wife a pointed look, "She's not part of this...there's no harm in her knowing any of this. I trust her."

Lucian and Marigold exchanged a look. The Lady raised her glass to her lips and took a pensive sip while staring at the young woman.

"I'm afraid," Lucian began gently, "that I am going to have to insist. No offense intended of course, miss."

Jayce looked as though he was going to object, but Lyra cut him off, "I understand, my Lord."

Lucian nodded and waved a hand towards the house, "If you go inside, the servants will show you towards the sitting room. Jayce can collect you there when we're done."

She nodded respectfully and stood. Before leaving the table, she leaned over and kissed Jayce gently on the cheek. It was a quick motion, so sudden that the young man barely had time to react before she was moving towards the door. She paused before leaving, took a last glance back at him, smiled and waved. He grinned widely back at her, momentarily struck silent. The delegate had to snap a few times to draw the young man's attention back to the conversation at hand. As she went through the door, she slipped her hand out of her pocket, grasped around a gray sending stone. She had slipped its twin into Jayce's coat pocket, where it was patiently waiting for her to find a quiet place to eavesdrop on the rest of the conversation.

Once she was sure she was alone, standing in the family's lavish sitting room with low couches and an ornate fireplace, Lyra spoke the awakening words into the stone. These were special sending stones, they neither glowed or grew hot when they were activated. They had cost Hector a fortune, but they had proven invaluable time and time again. Lyra grinned, remembering how she had convinced him to buy them from that old mage whose hands shook from the drink, as she eagerly held the little stone up to her ear.

The delegate was speaking again, his tone severe, "-this is even more serious than we thought. The High Senate is composed of the most powerful Lords of the Federation, like the High Justice and the Lord Imperator...then of course, there's the Sovereign himself. If they're involved, even a single member, we have to assume our enemy has resources to counter any move we make. We need to move carefully, and quietly, because at this level, we have to assume we're risking everything by moving against this coalition."

Lyra felt the sudden sensation of the earth falling away beneath her. Like missing a step and falling into a hole she had not known was there a moment ago. This was not what she had expected. This was a plot that went straight to the highest halls of power in the land. She found that she was trying to quickly decipher what she was hearing while also not missing any information.

"There's more," Jayce took a steadying breath, "they talked about Cassius. Apparently, he's still on the trail of the men who breached The Hold. They said he's causing problems for them and that they're planning something for him. It sounded like they were going to abduct him, or do something to get him out of their way."

Lady Marigold let out a noise somewhere between a gasp and a hiss. Lucian swore. Lyra noted he was suddenly sounding very different, all the casual swagger gone from his demeanor.

"Oh no!" Mariana's voice, high pitched and whiny, cut through, "Not Cas! We need to do something, father!"

Lyra heard the Lady make a hushing noise and Lucian spoke gently, "We will, darling, I won't let anything happen to your cousin. Jayce, did you hear anything else, anything at all?"

"They mentioned a name, the Ceaseless Scions. It's not familiar to me, but it sounded important. And they talked about the Broken Coast, it sounded like that's where a major part of their operation is. I think that must be where he is headed."

There was a silence for a moment, then Lucian spoke up again, "I'll do some digging into that name, and I'll reach out to some of my contacts at the Coast. They can keep an eye out for Cassius, and they can look into what the Burning Blades are doing there. Once we know more, we can figure out our next step."

There was a pause.

"That's it?" Jayce was incredulous, "They're going to kill Cas! Lucian, we have to do *something*!"

Mariana began to speak up in protest as well but Lady Marigold cut her off in a quiet, even voice, "What would you two suggest? That we march an army to the Broken Coast and turn over every alehouse and tavern until we find the Prince?"

Jayce was silent, but the Lady pushed on, "This coalition is much more serious than we initially believed. We have to face the facts that we might be dealing with a covert operation on behalf of members of the High Senate, maybe even the Sovereign himself..."

Lucian cut in, "We need more information before we act. If I take this to the wrong person...it could be all our heads."

"Instead of just mine, you mean." There was no response from the noble family. Jayce added in a low voice, "You...you want me to go back in there, don't you?"

There was a long moment of silence. Even listening as she was, Lyra could hear the tension which held a stranglehold on the conversation.

"I can't..." Jayce said, his voice full of desperation, "if they find me out, they'll kill me. I'm not a spy. I'm not even a real mage! They don't *want* me there!"

"Jayce...we need you to do this. I'll work on rooting out more information in the Senate and the Tribunals, but that may not work out. I hadn't heard anything about this conspiracy until now, and I have friends at every level of the political game. The University has always been notoriously closed off. They protect their secrets and hold their cards close to their chests, but they're also the only ones we can be sure have some part in this whole affair. You are the *best chance* we have to uncover this plot." Lucian's voice was soothing, measured. Lyra thought it was probably what he sounded like when addressing the Senate.

"And don't forget, it's the best way you can help your friend."
Marigold was quick to add.

Lyra felt a tugging in her chest. She felt for the young merchant, foolish as he was. There was something unsettling about
the way he was being coerced by these two far more experienced
players of the game. She quickly squashed that feeling and tried
to refocus on the conversation.

"Fine, what do you need me to do?" A resigned tone perme-
ated the young man's words, still ringing with resentment.

"Find evidence, get more information...the same as before."
Lucian still spoke in his placating tone, "We just need a *little*
more before we can act."

"Don't worry, there's no reason to suspect they uncovered
your eavesdropping, is there?"

"None other than it being a school for *magic*..."

Marigold gave a small chuckle, "Well, we know they certainly
don't have the answer for everything. Otherwise, you wouldn't
have made it here to tell us what you heard in the first place."

"That's quite comforting..."

It was only a little while later when Jayce collected her from
the sitting room. They left the Consul's house together, declin-
ing the couple's repeated requests that they stay for dinner. Jayce
was quiet for a long time afterward. They wandered down the
streets of Asaldon in the dark of the evening, the amber glow of
witchlights illuminating the streets. The largest city in the land
never slept and even in the late evening, there were lots of people
about.

Many stores still remained open, light spilling out from their
doors open to attract passers. Taverns and alehouses attracted
small crowds and the sounds of music and laughter could be
heard from their gently glowing windows. A few street performers and beggars staked their claims on corners and particularly desirable alleys or parks. Jayce seemed not to notice any of
this, lost somewhere in the recesses of his thoughts. Lyra waited
as long as she could before trying to gently get him talking.

"So, that sounded...serious..."

Jayce looked at her and blinked. He seemed to have momentarily forgotten she was there, "Yeah... I'm in something of a strange position."

"Anything you want to talk about?"

He shook his head, "I can't, at least, I guess I'm not supposed to."

"What if I guess at it? Then you won't be telling me."

Jayce looked at her, his blue eyes shining in the witchlight. There was a hint of amusement in them, peeking through the distress, "Well, I guess that would work..."

"Alright," she took a moment and collected her thoughts. She decided it was time for a gamble, "the Roth's are paying for you to attend the University."

He nodded solemnly.

"But their money came with conditions. They want something from you in return. Information, from what it sounded like. They need an inside man in the school."

Jayce blinked in surprise, then nodded again. He regarded her with something that looked like newfound respect. Maybe a bit of suspicion. She made a mental note to keep her risks measured as they turned down another street lined with cafes and trinket shops.

"But I didn't understand that bit about a conspiracy or the High Senate, and something about a *heist*? I'm guessing that's all the information they wanted to keep me out of." She tossed her hair back and blinked up at him.

He took a long moment, seeming to turn the conversation over in his mind. He looked back over his shoulder, the way they had come, then back at her, gently putting his hand on her shoulder to stop her. They were on a less busy area of the street now, the closest cluster of people seated before a restaurant about thirty paces back. He ran his hand over his short hair, shaved close to his scalp with sharp line work, a Republic style, and gave her a long, thoughtful look. Then he sighed.

"Ah, dark skies be damned," he cast another glance down the street, "you might be the only friend I have in this city, and I need someone to talk to about all this. But you have to swear not to repeat any of this to another soul, ya?"

She made an X across her chest with her fingers, giving him the most innocent smile she could muster. He grinned and led her toward a park, where they promptly found a bench and he launched into his tale.

"I nteresting." Hector mumbled, sausage juice running down the corners of his mouth. He was seated on a stool at the counter of his butcher shop, eating a late dinner of sausages and hard cheese with flatbread. He wore his heavy leather apron and had his sleeves rolled up past his elbows, hands still stained from the day's work. This butcher shop in the Lower End was the place Hector had started out, a tiny, grungy store in one of the last places in town anyone would want to buy meat. He had inherited it from his father and had operated it for years while running his burgeoning criminal empire from the back. Now, all this time later, he still came in every few days to work the counter, or process meat, or sharpen the knives.

The criminal wiped his mouth on a filthy rag and raised a meaty finger to point at his protégé, "I told you you could do it, didn't I?"

Lyra nodded. She leaned against the window which faced out towards the street with her arms crossed, resting her head against cool glass. She had her eyes closed and was doing her best to settle her mind. She felt like it had been a churning river during a particularly rough flooding season, threatening to overwhelm her and pull her under.

"Did you have to bed him to get him to trust you?"

She slowly opened her eyes and gazed at him with a stare that could cut through stones. He grinned and shrugged, then speared another sausage with his knife, "So he's just particularly stupid then?"

"He's not stupid...he's *isolated*." She felt an instinctual rise in her, but she squashed it down quickly, "The position they've put him in...it's more than just difficult, it's incredibly dangerous. Still, he didn't tell me *everything*, just that there was a heist and that the Roth's suspect someone in the University to be involved. If I hadn't planted the stone I'd still be in the dark about a lot. Hell, I still don't know what was stolen from The Hold."

Hector nodded thoughtfully as he chewed his sausage. He made a motion with his knife, "The boy will be lucky to last out the summer if he keeps digging. Those mages, they're a crafty bunch...and they don't like sharing their secrets. If he pokes around long enough he's bound to put his hand in a rattrap, and you know what happens to rats in this city."

He slammed a meaty hand onto the table. Lyra jumped a bit then swore under her breath. The big man let out a low belly chuckle and wiped his mouth again, "Okay, so now we know what he's doing here. What's your next move?"

"Move?"

"Yes, how are you to turn this to your advantage?"

"I'm *not*." She turned to face him and put her hands on her hips, "This is bigger than some trading company trying to make plays or a squabble between noble houses...this is the High Senate, the *Sovereign*. We should get out of this now, while we can still make a clean break."

The criminal made a clucking sound with his tongue, "Come now, my flower, you're not getting the shivers are you? Think about the payoff this could mean if we play it right."

"Or the consequences if we don't." She made a wave around the room, "All *this*? Everything you've built? It all comes down if we attract the wrong attention from the Senate. Even you can't fight the Legions."

"Perhaps..." The big man nodded sagely as if he was seriously considering her counsel, "But, opportunities like this don't come around often. It would be foolish not to at least consider the possibilities. I didn't get all of *this*, as you put it, without taking some risks. You should remember that."

Lyra stared at him, her eyes flashing like shards of steel glinting in the light.

"Have you given any thought to the reward we might get if we assist in rooting out a plot against the crown? What having a family like the Acosta's or the Roth's indebted to us might mean?"

She blinked. The thought had not occurred to her. A frown was cut in her face as she narrowed her eyes and tried to think of the possibilities in her head.

"If this plot goes as far up the ladder as the merchant's son believes, we are talking about treason of the highest order. This is the sort of thing that fells entire houses, brings low some families...while it raises others."

"And...what of the Roth delegates fears that this might be a shadowy hand of the Sovereign himself?"

"In that case," Hector's golden eyes glinted fiercely, "we'll cut the boy down before he does any damage and hand him and all his cohorts over as traitors to the Federation. It'll be the deepest, darkest cells in Silence for him, that statesman and his wife, and who knows how many others. We get the favor of the Sovereign, a reward that is sure to be due *and* we'll have the inside track on the severe fall from grace of one of the most powerful families in the Southlands before the competition."

Lyra had to give it to the big man, he could sniff out a score like a bloodhound and he could see all the angles. She shifted her weight, crossing her arms over her chest.

"So you want me to get closer to him?"

He nodded. He swirled the last bit of his bread around his plate, soaking up all the leftover gristle and fat, then bit off a chunk. As he chewed it, a thoughtful grin spread across his glistening lips. He pointed the dripping roll at her, "If you play this right, you might even find yourself in the position to buy your own territory from me. I know you've had your eyes on the Stag's Head District."

She blinked. There was a long moment of silence as they stared at each other. She walked across the room and leaned against the corner. She eyed him. He was a hard one to read, clever like an alley cat and twice as slippery as one.

"Free rein?"

"Minus the standard tax that everyone pays." His eyes gleamed, "But otherwise, you can run your own business. Think about it, girlie; a crew of your own, choosing your own marks, running your own jobs."

"What would it run me?" She did not even try to hide the suspicion in her tone.

"For the Head? Those people have deep pockets and high connections. I'd charge anyone else two hundred thousand marks, but for you? I could let it go for half."

She swallowed hard, "That's a king's ransom."

"...or a Prince's."

She considered it for a moment. Then she held out her hand, "Deal. If this plays out and we make the profit you seem to think we will, we'll have that easy."

He grasped her hand, enveloping her much smaller one in his meaty fist. He shook it once and grinned, his smile wide and wolfish, "There's the wildflower I know, the one with all her thorns intact."

Despite herself, she grinned back at him. Outside, she could hear the street cats yowl in their alleys and dogs baying at the full moon. She knew the cut purses and pickpockets would be making their rounds on the fashionable streets. A crew of thieves were meant to be hitting houses on the Upper East End, as most of the residents would be attending a concert in the public gardens. Two girls had been sent as servants to the Lady

Hargreaves's dinner party and would return with pockets full of fine jewelry from her boudoir.

Despite the late hour, the city was still alive and, with it, Hector's network of criminals, busy at work. She was just playing her part in it, same as she had since she was a girl. But for the first time, she could see a way out. It was like the slivers of light which filtered through the street grates and into the sewers, but she had learned to find her way with less than that long ago. She was not going to let this opportunity slip away.

CHAPTER NINETEEN

THE COAST

The dark enveloped Cassius like a cage. Every breath was like sucking in a mouthful of water, the air was so thick with salt laden moisture. He had lain in the hull of this creaking ship for nearly a week while it bucked and rolled under the ever present churning of the ocean. His escape from the *Captain's Clutch* had not been without its price. The window shards had carved long gashes in his left leg and both arms. When he hit water, he had been dazed, staying under far too long. He swallowed what he assumed to be a few buckets of seawater as he struggled in the current.

By the time he washed ashore, bleeding, shivering, and vomiting up his last weeks worth of meals, he was on the verge of collapse. He had ended up near the wharf and had managed to drag himself to a dockmaster to ask after a ship headed to the Broken Coast. He worked out a deal with the Captain of a moderate sized merchant ship to hitch a ride south, costing him all of his remaining marks. He was fairly certain the Captain assumed him to be a criminal running from the law, but if he had suspicions about the man bleeding all over his lower deck, he kept them to himself.

The past half cycle had given the Prince significant time to think while he bandaged his wounds and drank rotgut liquor in the dark. He cursed over the loss of his good knife and regretted not being able to go back and recover his sword and other effects. Worst of all, he had left Rearden behind. He had paid the stablemaster handsomely, but it would not buy him long. The thought of his long-time companion being sold off was painful to his heart, but there was nothing he could do about it now. He put it out of his mind and considered everything he had learned in Redwater, turning over what Rory had told him again and again.

There was little doubt left that Valeria's theories about there being a greater conspiracy were valid. The shopkeeper was obviously well paid, and whatever entity had hired him was still making moves. The man he was following was clearly more than capable as well. He was resourceful and connected. Avoiding the soldiers would have been a difficult task, given they had his name and description from Jayce. A man like that would disappear quickly. The Prince had drastically underestimated his quarry in his first attempt, nearly costing him his life. He knew he needed to move more carefully this time. As the hours rolled by, a rough plan took shape in his mind.

After a few days of recovering, he could stand the dark no longer and had begun venturing onto the deck. So when the ship reached the Crescent City he was standing at the prow watching the ship's Stormspeaker and helmsman working together to guide the boat into harbor. He enjoyed the sun and the wind on his face, a welcome change from the dank stillness of the hull. The city's explosion of colors decorated the coastline like someone had taken a paintbrush to the cliffs themselves.

Cassius turned and looked towards the other side of the inlet, towards the western coast of the mainland. The Farian forest, an expanse of wilderness and marshes which stretched from the southern tail of the Horn down the western edge of the continent until it hit the barren scrubland of the Fiery Expanse, formed a stretch of unbroken green which ran in both directions as far as the eye could see. There were a few clusters of homes and docks which dotted the shore, mostly huddled around river mouths where their flat-bottomed barges could venture inland, but the majority of that side of the bay was a marshy wilderness.

Once the ship had made dock, he said his brief farewells and departed, moving through the crowd as inconspicuously as he could manage. A few cast sideways glances at his bandaged arms and leg, but none stopped him or attempted to speak with him. He imagined that he cut a rather foreboding figure. Once he reached the city proper, he tried to gather his bearings. He had been to the Broken Coast many times in his youth, assisting his father in his campaign against the pirate lords that raided up and down the western coast of Evardene, but the layout of the Crescent City was still alien to him. The barrage of colors and smells and strange sights was disorienting. Even the layout of the city was strange. There were sudden stops and level changes, people climbed rail less exterior stairs, scaled rooftops and rickety bridges to move between various sections of the city. He figured out the correct way the best he could manage and set out, careful to avoid catching anyone's eye for too long as he slinked through the crowds.

It took Cassius over an hour to find his way to the Lighthouse. Named for the massive tower which erupted from the sea of colorful buildings and dwarfed every other spire surrounding it, the Lighthouse was a long, narrow castle which straddled the point of the craggy ridge the city was built upon. It was built largely of white stone, but the giant plates of brass roofing made it shine like a gem in the midmorning sun. It was the seat of power for the Candor's, the Broken Coast's ruling family, who were cousins of the Roth's by multiple marriages.

He worked his way around the perimeter until he found an estate that looked familiar. The estate was large and separated from the other structures with a small gated courtyard in the front. Two Legionnaires in brass armor adorned with white sashes and carrying wicked looking scimitars stood guard by the gate. As he approached them, lifting his hands and calling out long before he was in striking distance.

"Hail, sirs. I am here to call on Nadine Navarre." He tried to look as unthreatening as possible, fully aware the lengths of bloodied bandages and days of hard travel probably were not helping his case.

Both guards dropped a hand to their swords immediately. One stepped forward, face scrunched up with contempt, "Our nobles have no time for beggars."

"Tell her that her cousin is here to see her. Tell her I would very much like to see her collection of seashells again, especially the pink one with the stripes."

For a moment, he worried they might not deliver the message, but then one whispered something to the other and turned to head inside. The remaining guard stood there, hand firmly clasped on the hilt of his blade, eyeing Cassius like a hungry hawk. It was tense a few minutes until the guard returned, leading a half dozen more armed men. Hidden amongst them was his cousin, Nadine, one of the Jewels of the Broken Coast.

The youngest of his aunt's four daughters, the last to be unmarried, she was a radiant beauty that seemed to dull anything in her near vicinity. They shared the rich brown eyes of their maternal family, but where Cassius was broad and of a lighter complexion, due to his father's blood, Nadine was slight and her skin was a deep hue of bronze, accented by her raven dark hair and the multiple jewels she wore in each ear. When she saw him, a broad smile broke out across her face.

"Cas!" She ran past the guards, who moved to stop her a moment too late, throwing her arms around his neck. She was a head shorter than him, but she managed to yank him down to her level with the whole of her body weight with her impromptu hug.

"Hey, Nad." He did his best not to grimace as she strained the cuts on his shoulder and the extra weight caused his leg to scream in protest, "It's good to see you."

"Of course it is! Welcome to the Coast!" When she finally released him and leaned back to look him over properly, her smile melted into a frown of dismay, "What happened to you?"

"It is a long story. May I tell you over a drink, maybe some food?"

T he interior of the Navarre estate was lavishly decorated, all delicate silk, tall mirrors, golden furnishings and stained glass. Watercolor paintings of the coast and ships at sea lined the walls, along with portraits of various familial relations, most of which Cassius could not have named to save his life. The second floor sitting room where they took their meal was bathed in light and airy with all the windows thrown open to the morning.

Nadine had gotten the servants to bring them a large platter of smoked fish and oysters, bowls of light curries and heavily seasoned flatbread, as well as two large carafes of wine. She had also called for one of the servants to redress his wounds, and the elderly woman was still in the process of cleaning Cassius' leg when the food arrived. He leaned over from his spot on the low couch and poured himself a large goblet of pale spirits, gulping down about half on his first drink. The old woman clucked at him, shaking her head in disapproval.

"Wine won't help your wounds heal, sir Lord."

"It's not for my leg," he gave Nadine a grin, "my head needs some care as well."

The woman gave him a withering look. She fingered some thick salve out of a pouch and smeared it on his cut. It was cold at first, then his leg began to tingle and go numb almost immediately. He breathed out through his nose, then smiled.

"My thanks, goodmother."

She snorted and began wrapping the wound in a new dressing. Once she was done, she tied it off and collected her kit, wrapping them back up in a roll and gave him a look, "You won't lose the leg. But try not to get in any more knife fights."

"I told you, it was just a little accident."

The woman rolled her eyes but shuffled dutifully out of the room. Once the door had closed behind her, Nadine turned to stare at him, her eyes fixed on him.

"What *happened*, Cas?"

The Prince ignored her, reached over, grabbed an oyster and slurped it down noisily. He took another long drag from his cup, he wiped his mouth on the back of his sleeve. His cousin watched him evenly, a look between amusement and annoyance playing for ground at the edges of her face.

"Are you not going to eat?" Cassius asked, motioning to the platter.

"I had a late breakfast."

He shrugged and tore off a piece of bread. He dipped it in the curry and stuffed it in his mouth.

"Cas," Nadine leaned forward, her tone gentle yet firm, "I know you ran away. We received word from the Horn days ago. Did you come here because you thought I was the least likely to turn you in?"

Cassius swallowed hard. He tried not to let the guilt show, "The thought had crossed my mind. I am your favorite cousin after all, right?"

The noblewoman rolled her eyes and pushed her fingers through her dark hair, "You do understand the moment my parents come home, my father will have the guards take you and ship you back to your father? What would you have done if he had been home?"

"I took a chance...and besides, I hope to be gone long before they return."

Nadine put a hand on his, voice dropping low, almost conspiratorial, "What are you doing, Cas? No more nonsense, you know you can talk to me."

The Prince sighed and finally met his cousin's gaze, "There's something coming, Nad. Someone's making moves, huge ones. We're not sure of their goals, but whatever they are, it doesn't seem like it'll be good for any of us. The Horn, the Coast, the whole Federation."

Nadine nodded slowly. She rubbed her shoulders as though a chill had gone through her, "So you're...what? Trying to stop them? Alone?"

"Someone broke into The Hold during the Sun's Summit..." Her eyes went wide at that, but he pushed on.

"...they broke some prisoners out of the dungeons, one's *I* didn't even know my father had. They were well prepared, knew our defenses, got through them like they were nothing. The only way that could happen is if they had a connection on the inside, someone feeding them information."

"A traitor?"

Cassius nodded, "I'm on the trail of the thieves. I tracked them to Redwater and found they had fled here. But that's all I've got. I *need* to find them, Nad. We need to know how they got in, who hired them. But most importantly, we need to stop them. They killed people, Nad, our people. We have to stop them before they hurt anyone else again."

Nadine looked sideways, biting her lip. Cassius felt a new wave of guilt wash over him. He knew the position he was putting her in, how it would play out when her parents found out. Besides, she was so young, barely more than a child really. He almost told her not to worry, that he would go and handle the matter on his own. But she spoke before he could.

"What do you need, Cas?"

Cassius hesitated, but then he gave in, "Have you heard of a mercenary group called the Burning Blades?"

It was a few hours later when Cassius was getting ready to depart the Navarre complex. Nadine had gotten him new clothes, seen to it that he was given a traveling satchel with more food, water, a change of clothes and fat purse nearly overflowing with Federation marks. She had also acquired a new sword for him. It was a falchion much like the one he was used to carrying, but with a more ornate crossguard that bore the image of a great shark bearing its teeth across it.

"Is this one of your fathers?" Cassius asked, eyeing the blade. They stood in the courtyard once again, guards at a respectable distance, "Don't you think he'll miss it?"

"He's unlikely to even notice it's gone." She made an exasperated noise, "I swear, the older he gets, the more he likes to collect weapons and the less he uses them. I don't think this one's even been used on the training grounds."

"I suppose a man could have worse vices. At least he's not trying to marry you off to one of the local Lordlings."

"My mother has that handled all on her own, thank you very much." She rolled her eyes, "I swear, the woman would marry me to one of the gators if he had the right titles."

Cassius grinned and sheathed the sword. He held out his arms and gave his cousin a great bear hug, lifting her off the ground a few inches.

"Thank you for this, Nad. You've no idea what it means to me."

Nadine gave him a warm smile, but it was quickly overcome with a look of apprehension, "I'm happy to help, just...are you sure you've thought this through? Why not wait for my father? He can send more men with you, or maybe you can talk to Baron Candor?"

"There's no time, Nad. Every minute that passes the trail gets colder. Besides, who knows what your father or Baron Candor are going to want to do? They might be more interested in playing the grand game...like some others..."

"Valeria?"

Cassius nodded. Nadine sighed and crossed her arms, "Just, don't do anything rash, come back before you get yourself in the deep waters? Do we have a deal, Cas?"

"Deal. Oh, and before I forget..." he reached into his pocket and pulled out a letter, "This is a letter I wrote earlier for the Sovereign. It explains everything. I promised Julius I would tell the Sovereign if I couldn't stop all this myself. If I don't make it back..."

Nadine took the letter solemnly. She looked up at him, almost seeming on the verge of tears, "Cas..."

"It's just a precaution." He smiled, doing his best to encourage her, "Don't worry about me."

He gave her a kiss on the forehead and ruffled her hair, pushing it into her face, the way he had done when they were children. That drew a snorting laugh from the young woman and she pushed him away playfully. He took one last look at her, then turned and marched towards the group of people who were waiting at the gate. They wore civilian clothes but their weapons and manner marked them as soldiers to his well trained eye. The officer, a tall man with a dark beard and piercing dark eyes, turned to face him. He stood tall, with his shoulders held back proudly and had a sword similar to Cassius' dangling loosely off his belt.

"You're Captain Sebastian? Nadine told me you know where the Blades are operating out of?"

He nodded, regarding Cassius with an appraising look. When he spoke it was with a deep voice, thick with the accent of the island tribes, "I believe so, my Lord. I spoke to my men and they say the mercenaries are operating on the North side of town. They've been dropping lots of marks in the taverns and whorehouses. Several of my guards have been approached, offered money for their service, but none have taken the offers. They must have a safe house somewhere over there."

Cassius nodded, "Any idea what they're up to in town? Heard about any contracts, know of anyone hiring them?"

The Captain shook his head, "No, my Lord, none at all. It is strange for the mercenaries to be about without a known contract. The men tell me they've been here for many seasons, which is even stranger yet."

"Seasons..." Cassius considered for a moment, "that is odd."

"Perhaps, we'll be able to sort the matter, eh Lord Roth?"

Cassius gave him a grin, "We shall see. You're sure you and your men are up for this? I know Nadine gave me leave of her personal guard, but I won't force anyone into this."

Sebastian grinned back at him, the motion doing nothing to erase any of the severity from his face, "Oh, I think you'll find we are always up for routing men of low moral character."

He shook the man's hand, waiting as the Captain called together his group of guards. The cadre was small, four including the Captain himself. There was a young man with tan skin and dark hair cut close to the scalp on the sides and two women, one with her hair in a series of braids tied up and the other with a religious tattoo on the side of her shaved head. They had shed their armor and white sashes in favor of outfits that allowed them to better blend in with the local populace, but the Prince could pick out concealed weapons on all of them. They all nodded wordlessly to him. Turning and giving one last wave to his cousin, he motioned for Sebastian to lead the way. He fell in easy step with the group as the Captain led them out into the bustling crowds of the city.

As he made his way across the steeply sloping streets, Cassius had to admit it felt good to once again feel the weight of steel on his belt. He took the cobblestones in long strides and moved confidently, barely feeling the wounds in their fresh bandages. Street vendors hollered and performers beckoned but they paid them no mind, making their way to the northern district within the hour. It only took them a short time to reach their destination, walking downhill from the ridge line with the confident pace of locals. Sebastian led them to an alehouse which was the last place one of his guards had reported seeing members of the Blades.

The *Maelstrom* was the sort of place you might expect to pop up in a child's tale of pirates and plunder. It was a three story boarding house with a tavern which encompassed the entire first floor. There were few windows and the filthy exterior looked as inviting as the open maw of a dragon's cave, broken mugs and busted furniture and stinking drunks littering the alleys around it. Men and suggestively dressed women loitered about, despite the early hour, leaning on the side of the building and leering at passers with a wary eye. As Cassius passed under the single sign, a faded black mug with the tavern's name emblazoned across it, he returned the looks of the locals with a cocky grin, knowing anything less could mean issues for him in a place like this.

The Captain silently instructed his cadre to take up positions around the area with a few quick hand motions. The young man strode over and leaned against a wall on the other side of the street, pulling a flask from his pocket, and both women disappeared down side alleyways to opposite sides of the building. The Prince found himself impressed by their disciplined demeanor, needing minimal instruction to be deployed in position. Sebastian wordlessly motioned for Cassius to follow him inside, through a door that was half off its hinges from what he assumed was the result of repeated bodies being hurled out of it.

The interior of the place was much the same as the exterior. The place was visibly filthy, with more broken furniture than not, and it stank like sour ale and old blood. A thin layer of haze filled the air despite the opened windows, as various tables burned braziers while others smoked rolled tobacco or pipes, giving off a dizzying array of different scents and pungent odors. It was surprisingly busy. Men and women milled about, taking up the darkened corners of the room and lounging in easy chairs and tables. Cassius counted roughly two dozen sets of eyes turned towards them as they entered. They ambled easily through the room and seated themselves at the low bar. A few of the patrons cast sideways glances at them, but with the new clothes and gilded blade Nadine had gifted him they blended into the scenery fairly well. They turned back to their drinks without much fuss.

Once the barkeeper eventually found his way over to his newest customers, Cassius ordered an ale for him and Sebastian and they proceeded to sip their drinks in silence for a while, letting the general murmur of the place build back up after their entrance. He fingered at a splinter which had worked its way partially free of the bar top, using his nail to liberate it from the saturated wood. Eventually, he caught the barkeeper as the man passed him empty handed, hoping it was the best time to bend his ear.

"Would you spare a moment," he said, keeping his voice low. He put a hand on the bar top, pulling it back to reveal the twinkle of a silver coin, "I'm not familiar with the town and am looking for employment..."

"I don't need no more bouncers..." the barkeeper grunted reflexively, his ruddy face covered in a sheen of sweat under his frizzy black hair. Then he saw the coin and turned to face him.

"I don't doubt that," Cassius cast a glance to his side. Two ferocious looking men sat at the edge of the bar, each eyeing them. They both wore clubs at their belts and carried a slew of scars that screamed volumes about their histories of violence. The Prince had seen them the moment he had entered and kept one eye on them the entire time they were there, "but you misunderstand. What I want is information."

The barkeeper wiped his face on the already filthy sleeve of his shirt and leaned in heavily on the bar top. He cocked one eyebrow and inclined his head a bit, a listening gesture if ever there was one.

"We've just returned from down south, working to protect the shipping lanes. We need to find work now that we're back. I hear tell there's profit to be made for fighting men in this town. You know anything about that?"

The barkeeper reached out and slid the coin out from under Cassius' hand, carefully slipping it into his pocket without a word. Then he looked back towards the young Prince.

"Down south you say?" He gave Cassius and Sebastian a suspicious eye, "Whereabouts?"

"The Outer Isles mostly. Pirates are giving the merchant ships hell, some say they're losing one in every ten now, and from what I saw, I'd believe it."

"What port did they have you fellows working out of?"

Sebastian cut in, "Hag's Head mostly. But we did stints in Black Bend and Ghal as well."

The barkeeper seemed to relax a little. He took a pointed look at the bandages peeking out from under his sleeve and collar, "You sure you're up for another job, lad? Looks like you've been in your share of storms already."

The Prince shook his head with a grin, "Ain't got much choice. The islands took most of my earnings before I'd even caught my ferry back to the mainland. You heard about the hospitality they've got out there, aye?"

The barkeeper slapped the counter and let out a bark of laughter that made the men at the bar glare up at him from their cups as he finally cracked a wide grin, "That I have, may have even partaken myself once or twice in my younger days. I do know how it goes, lad. I may be able to help you after all." He looked suspiciously back and forth down the bar, "There's men that come here on the regular with an outfit that's been working here in town the last few months. They've been looking for like minded folks to join up. You might be able to earn some marks with them."

Cassius cast a look at the table, "This outfit got a name? Any idea what kind of work they've been up to?"

The barkeeper shook his head, "No idea what work they've been doin', they been pretty tight lipped about it. But they say

they're with the Blades, and I believe 'em. They've been in here every night spending marks like they're burning holes in their pockets. Tried to tempt my boys away a few times, but I keep 'em in the coins, right boys?"

One of the rough men at the end of the bar inclined his head slightly, still staring at Cassius, hand loosely resting on the butt of his club.

"How will I recognize this group when I see them?"

The barkeeper rubbed his chin, "Oh, you'll know them. They make an awful ruckus every time they're in here. One of 'em has a short beard and shaved head, loud as hell, always singing and carrying on. Fellow likes to start fights. Can't miss 'em, guarantee he'll let you know he's with the group before you have to ask."

Cassius gave him a quick nod and thanked the barkeeper, paying for another round of drinks. Once the man had shuffled off, he turned to Sebastian. The look on the Captain's face reminded the Prince of one of their hunting hounds when it was on the trail.

"What's the move here, Sebastian?"

The Captain sipped his drink, speaking in a quiet, thoughtful manner, "We can't approach these men. I am too well known in these parts, as are most of my soldiers, and you...well, you're the Prince of The Horn. We have to assume someone in the Blades will be able to recognize you. But I can set Mateo in here. He's the newest of the guards, least likely to be recognized."

Cassius chewing his lip, "We can watch the place, find somewhere to hunker down. Then we would be at hand in case things go badly."

The Captain nodded. They finished their drinks and exited, reconvening with the rest of their crew to lay out their plans.

I t was long after dark when they finally found their marks. The Legionnaires had rented a tiny room in one of the upper levels of a flophouse across from the *Maelstrom*. Mateo had been stationed inside the tavern while the rest had crammed into the room and all took turns watching the front door through their single window. The day had crept by at an insufferable pace, the room hot and stinking of old piss and sweat. They spoke little and smiled less.

Cassius attempted to inspire comradery by passing out the meager rations Nadine had had packed for him, but they mostly ate in silence. He learned the woman with the braids was named Camila and the one with tattoos was Lucia. Both were hardened veterans who had served the Barony for their entire lives, assigned to Nadine's personal guard only within the past few years. By the time Sebastian called them to the window, it was well past midnight, with the moon already beginning its descent. He pointed wordlessly down at the street.

Mateo was outside. He was smiling and clapping backs with a bearded man with a shaved head. There was a group of other men lingering about, all hard looking with weapons readily at hand, casually drinking large mugs of ale or laughing as they shouted stories at each other. The group slowly began to make its way down the street, many stumbling and struggling to keep their feet under them. Mateo clasped hands with the bearded man, exchanging a few more words. The man slipped him something with his free hand. Cassius thought he saw the flash of metal, but could not be sure at this distance. Once the bearded man had followed his comrades down the street and was long out of sight, Mateo strode across the street and a few moments later they heard a quick series of knocks at the door.

Camila opened it and let the young guardsman in. He stank of liquor and his loose shirt was drenched in the stuff. He had the kind of cocky grin only the young can manage plastered across his face.

"Report." Sebastian demanded in an even voice.

"The guy's greasier than a gator's ass." Mateo said, his rolling coastal accent hard to understand as his words stumbled over each other. He wiped his hands on a rag he yanked off the table, "His name's Taron. He was throwing marks around and trying to start fights with everyone in there, singing over the performing lady they got. When one of the other fellows had finally had enough, I managed to step in before any of the other goons. Got a whole tray of drinks spilled on me for my trouble, but Taron appreciated it. He asked me if I was looking for work, gave me this..."

He dug out a silver coin from his pocket. It held the image of a blade engulfed in fire on the upturned side.

"Storms and serpents, boy!" Sebastian murmured. He clasped the young man on the arm, "You did it!"

Mateo grinned and flipped the coin. It spun up into the air and Cassius caught the image of a skull emblazoned on its backside for the briefest of moments before he noticed a strange sheen across its surface. Then thunder crashed through the room. There was a blinding flash and in a split second, everything went white.

Chapter Twenty

PROBLEMS

I n the dark of the night, the High Conservatory was like the ancient castle of a long dead king, all darkened alcoves and unsettling visages staring down at you from the paintings and statues. Despite it being like her second home, Juniper did not like wandering the halls at night. It had not earned its nickname, the House of Glass and Stone, by accident. She felt a chill run through her, crossing her arms over her chest and holding herself as she padded down the lonely corridor.

She was deep in the main building now, on the lower levels which burrowed their way down into the mountain. This was far from her mother's department, where the glass domes and windows let in cascades of light and showed panoramic views of the city and countryside as it sprawled in every direction. She felt her pace quicken, keen as she was to get to her destination.

She reached a massive set of iron doors, masterfully crafted with intricate detailing which looked like it would have taken a half dozen men a year to construct. She grabbed the knocker, which was warm to the touch, and banged twice. The sound echoed around the cavernous halls and Juniper checked in every direction to be sure she was not followed. One of the giant doors swung open enough to reveal a man in his middle years, his face and short hair darkened with soot, peaking out at her through large round spectacles. He was an inch shorter than her, which was a rarity as she was not particularly tall, and his face was sweaty and flushed over his heavy apron and long work gloves. When he saw her, his eyes immediately went wide.

"Juniper, what are you doing here?" He demanded immediately. He looked around the halls, mimicking the motion she had just made, then waved to her urgently, "Hurry, hurry! Get in here before someone sees you."

Juniper shuffled inside and was hit by an immediate wave of heat and a cacophony of smells. The acrid scent of cut steel was offset by smoke and cinder, with the earthy notes of raw ore and split wood and burning iron accenting the entire affair. There was a stuffiness to the air which felt oppressive, and she immediately felt like she could not draw in a full breath. She had entered a massive workshop, one which stretched out in every direction and disappeared behind shelves and models and an endless array of every tool ever conceived by humans.

Small groups of people clustered around tables or red hot forges all around the space, working at their various tasks with intense focus. Some hefted tools and did the heavy physical labor, while others etched delicate patterns into their own projects. A few manned the forges and waved their hands over them to cause them to flare up, their glows suddenly becoming much brighter or changing color for a few moments. Juniper saw various pieces of work she recognized, and many others she did not. The short man led her through the circus of craftsmen, limping slightly, towards the back of the shop, to a small office tucked away in the far corner.

He ushered her inside and shut the door, checking again that no one had managed to follow her inside. The office was like a miniature version of the outside, with half finished projects and design plans cluttering every corner. Tools were hung on the walls along with magical devices and instruments. The only thing that denoted it as an office was the large standing height desk flanked by stools in the center of the room. The man stripped off his gloves and apron and tossed them on the table, hefting himself onto one of the stools. Once there he crossed one leg over the other, stripping off his boot.

In place of his right foot he had a metal prosthetic. It was crafted out of segmented bronze and had several pieces which were designed to rotate and move with his steps. As Juniper sat across from him, trying to fake an air of ease which she could not get herself to feel no matter how hard she tried. He ran his hands over his face, smearing the soot and dust, then pulled out a small pointed tool from his pocket. He began fiddling with the foot, chewing his tongue as he did.

"This damn thing. Sometimes I think it would be better to have gotten a peg leg and been done with it." He glanced up and pointed at her, "You're sure you weren't followed?"

"No, of course not." She waved a hand in front of her face, "Even the Imperial Guards can't hide from me if I'm looking for them, remember?"

He gave her a frown, grumbling, "That you know of..."

Juniper shrugged, "Dean Ghibli, I trust you as the foremost Artificer in the Empire and, as such, I would never dream of questioning your expertise. Please consider it professional courtesy to assume that my knowledge as an Illuminator is of similar quality."

"But, unless I am very much mistaken, I believe your mother is still the Dean of that particular college, yes?"

Juniper felt a thin smile work its way across her face as she inclined her head. The short man grinned, revealing a crooked smile marked with several gold teeth back at her. Then his eyes softened as he looked her over from behind his massive spectacles, "Come now, don't pout. It is good to see you, my dear."

She smiled, genuinely this time, "It is good to see you as well, Jiro. My mother sends her regrets that she could not come herself. But her movements attract far too much attention and we are too close to the endgame to take unnecessary risks."

He eyed her, gears seeming to turn inside his head even as he started turning one of the bronze screws on his false foot, "There's a problem with the plan, isn't there?"

She shook her head, "Not yet, and hopefully, not at all. But the plan is going to require some adjustments."

"What kind of adjustments?"

"The Emperor has received some troubling news. There is too much rebel activity in the colonies. During my most recent meetings with Chancellor Chale, he mentioned the Emperor has decided to move up his visit to the colonies...to the end of the season."

"*The end of the season*?!" The man's tool slipped and he cut a shallow groove into the metal of his false foot, "Damnit!"

He slammed the tool onto the table and put his foot down, turning his full attention on her. His expression was grim.

"That's not going to work, June." He shook his head, sending small droplets of dirty sweat scattering across the table, "It's not possible."

"It's going to have to be." She leaned forward, doing her best not to be distracted by the sweltering heat and assault of banging and crashing which was still headache-inducingly loud within the office, "We are *not* going to get another chance like this anytime soon."

"Then we're just going to have to call the whole thing off. I'm telling you, this simply can't be done that soon."

"We can get you more funds, if that's what it takes."

He shook his head again, looking to the ceiling like he was with frustration creasing his aged face, "You don't understand, it's not about the money. It's...here, come with me."

He stood suddenly, not bothering to pull the boot back on as he strode past her, his foot clinking on the stone floor. She followed him back out into the unending fray of the workshop, past the various workers as they went about their crafting. He all but shouted over the noise as he led her further along into the shop.

"Do you remember your primers on Artificing from your time as a student?"

"Of course." She had to move to avoid a shower of sparks from a forge as one of the workers banged away at a piece of metal with an overly large hammer.

"Then you know, it's not like the other disciplines of the High Art. We use magic to alter the very nature of the material we are working with. It has to be done bit by bit, layer by layer. This is not a process that can be rushed. Any minute mistake could mean a failure of the entire system."

They moved out of the main workshop and into a narrower chamber filled with desks. There were less people here, most of them writing out plans or fiddling with tiny details on delicate machines. The walls were littered with design plans and drawings, new ones hung over the old, obscuring nearly every inch of stone. Few of the workers even looked up as the Dean clopped past, the metal sound of his odd steps ringing in the relative calm. They were fixed on their work with furious intensity.

"Then more people, perhaps?" Juniper suggested, close on his heels as they strode through the desks.

The Dean let out a noise somewhere between a snort and a grunt. He reached the back wall and began thumbing through a ring of keys he dug out of a pocket.

"I already have all the best craftsmen on the continent here, working for me. Who else would you hire to hurry the project along? They'd have to come from Vinatieri, we've no one qualified left in the whole of Evardene. But shipping someone up here from down there would take months...time we simply don't have. Not on the schedule you're proposing."

He found the key he was looking for and jammed it in the lock. It clicked open and he led her down a set of winding stairs, further underground. The stairs seemed to go down forever and Juniper began to feel a sense of panic creep in as the walls seemed to close in around her. She hated the lack of windows in this place, the crushing feeling of thousands of tons of rock overhead. When she was sure they would never reach the end of this eternal staircase, the ground rushed up to meet them and she found herself on a flat surface again.

They were on a small landing before another door, this time a large bronze affair with several reinforced bands across it. It shone in the dim light and seemed to almost beckon them inside. Jiro again fished out his keys and slid one into the door, turning it with a click. This time, Juniper could hear the answer of mechanical gears and tumblers sliding into place. Once the door was open, the Dean led them inside and quickly shut the door and locked it behind them.

The room before them was long with an arched ceiling. It was outfitted similarly to the workshop upstairs, only far more organized and with only a handful of people. They were all working at different stations, each with tools and fully absorbed in their individual tasks. None so much as glanced up from their tasks when the newcomers entered. Jiro led Juniper to the first workstation where a young woman was painstakingly shaving almost imperceptible slivers of silver off a coin with the aid of a large magnifying glass that was held by a stand.

"This is Ashlyn. She's one of the finest and most trusted Professors in my department. She's been working here, in my private lab for almost a year, just on this project."

The girl paused and looked up. Her dark eyes were sunken and she looked drained in every conceivable notion of the word. She tried to smile at Juniper but all she managed was a slight twitch at the corner of her mouth and a bare inclination of the head. Jiro clasped a firm hand on her shoulder and waved at the room.

"These are the most talented Artificers in the land, and the ones I trust beyond the shadow of a doubt. They have been killing themselves to make this happen...as have I. If we try to bring someone else in now...it'll never work. The risk of discovery alone is too great, but the idea of trying to bring someone new up to speed on what we've been doing? Inconceivable. We'll just have to find another opportunity"

Juniper frowned. She watched one of the men as he was fixing a metal rod to a long piece of metal with several other rods already attached to it. The man was holding a tool which emitted a flame which was burning so intensely it was bright white and caused a searing sound when he touched it to the metal. It hurt Juniper's eyes to look at it, so she looked back to Jiro, who was busy conversing with Ashlyn in low tones.

"What if you had more power?"

"What?"

"More power...the machine is meant to increase the user's ability to use magic, right?"

Jiro crossed his arms and gave her a disgruntled stare, "In the simplest possible terms, yes. Less increase and more...*broaden*."

"Semantics." She rubbed the side of her face, "When crafting spells, we create a framework upon which magic will take shape. The hardest part of it is anticipating the exact amount of power needed, because once begun, the spell is going to draw in what it needs, regardless of where it comes from."

"Your point?"

"When designing the machine, you had an idea of what you'd be working with? How much fuel you'd have, in a manner of speaking. What if we could increase the amount of power you're working with? Could you skip ahead?"

He gave her a long, level look. His gaze was calculating, curious, "You're talking about sacrificing efficiency? Burning through twice as much fuel for the same end result."

She nodded. The look on her face was intended to be stoic, but she could hardly help the slight pride she felt in finding a solution that the Dean of Artificers had missed. But the look on his face gave her pause. It was harsh in a way that she had never seen before.

"That...is *not* going to work." The Arcanist hissed through clenched teeth.

"Why?"

"June...you can't be serious, think about what you're suggesting. The cost of using this machine already...and now you're talking about doubling it, maybe *worse*?" He shook his head fervently. The others in the workshop had taken notice of the changed atmosphere between them, finally looking up from their work.

Juniper crossed her arms. She set her jaw and fixed the Senior Arcanist with a frosty look, "You know what's at stake, Jiro. We need to make this happen, not next season, not next year. Now, by the end of the summer."

Jiro met her gaze with a smoldering stare that was rapidly building into full blown fury, "I wasn't comfortable with this before...Harnessing is a dark discipline, it was forbidden and buried away for a reason. But despite everything you convinced me, you and your mother. But this...this goes too far."

"Jiro...you knew the costs before we started."

"Every man has a limit, June. If this is the path you intend on going down, you can find someone else to craft your machine for you."

Juniper considered his ultimatum for a moment. The other professors were all watching them now. No one moved, no one made a sound. The workshop was deathly still. She took a deep breath, sighed and looked up.

"You know we cannot do this without you, Jiro. Your level of craftsmanship can be found nowhere else in the world. We simply have no other choice."

Jiro let out a long low breath, shoulders slumping as the tension that had built in him began to release. Then he grinned, his gold teeth shining in the dim light.

"Don't worry, June," he began, speaking in a fatherly manner once again, "we will find another way. Even if that means delaying our plans for another season or two, or even a few years, we will-"

Abruptly, he stopped. Suddenly, all the Artificers in the room began to cry out and make wild movements as they flung their hands in front of their faces. There was a crash as one of the professors fell over onto his desk, sending the metal instruments he had been using scattering across the floor. The room was in chaos in a matter of seconds. Only Juniper and Jiro stood still. Jiro's eyes had gone unfocused, staring at nothing. A hard look had spread across his face and he was grimacing as he spoke.

"So you got all of us then. How did you manage a veil of this complexity without any of us noticing?"

"Because I didn't cast it."

Beside her, a figure slowly took shape out of thin air. As the veil dropped, Aria Faye once again became visible, although neither Jiro nor any of his professors could tell until she spoke.

"Jiro," Aria said, her voice reproachful, "I had hoped it wouldn't come to this."

"You crafty old *snake.*" Jiro growled. In a move so fast it surprised Juniper, he reached into his pocket and pulled something out. It was a gray, metal cylinder. He squeezed it and in an instant it expanded and folded out of itself until it formed into a rod in his hand, appearing at first glance to be a fairly standard piece of metal. But then the end began to glow red hot, heat wisps rising off of it menacingly.

"I don't know what your plan is, Aria. But I promise you, blind or not, I'm not going to make this easy on you."

The two women glanced at each other. Aria held up a hand, an entirely unnecessary gesture, Juniper thought, as the man was still blind as a bat, "Peace, Jiro. I have no desire to make an enemy of you."

"You have a funny way of showing it."

"Don't be dramatic, it's only a simple veil over your eyes. I just needed you to use your ears for once and *listen.* As my daughter tried to explain to you, we simply cannot do this without you. In light of our many years of friendship, I would prefer you acquiesce willingly. But there is too much at stake, too many lives on the line, to let you derail this entire plan because of your ethical preoccupations."

Aria stepped over to where Ashlyn was flailing around on the ground near her desk. The girl was crying, desperately running her hands over face and trying to fumble through the words of a spell to break the enchantment on herself. The older woman leaned down and said a few words in a soft voice, almost a whisper.

Ashlyn sucked in a sharp breath. Then she let out a high pitched screech. Juniper felt her guts turn to liquid. The woman screamed and screamed, slapping at her face and eyes, kicking and writhing around on the ground. Jiro looked around wildly, his blind eyes searching in vain.

"What did you do?!" He demanded, starting to walk forward, his glowing rod stretched out before him.

Aria spoke without looking at him, "Nothing permanent, not yet anyway. She's seeing some of the most horrible images I've collected over the years. Hearing them too. It's nothing she won't be able to get over...in time. But as I'm sure you remember from your studies, Illumination is the study of *all* the senses, of which sight is the most basic. I can do worse, to all of them. You know that I can."

The glow at the end of the rod slowly started to die away. It faded until it was once again gray metal. The man's shoulders slumped, "What do you want?"

"Finish the machine." The older woman turned away from the manic professor on the floor and snapped her fingers. The master Artificer blinked, eyes refocusing. He glanced at his pupil before fixing on Aria with a gaze that was brimming with barely contained hate. She returned his look levelly.

"If I don't?"

"You'll have to explain to the Emperor why all your top Professors went insane in one night."

"So it's mutually assured destruction then, that's the tactic you're using?"

Aria stood and stalked over to the short man. The look on her face was terrible to behold. Her usual composure vanished. When she spoke, it was in a low, ferocious voice that quivered with a cold hate. It sent a shiver down Juniper's spine.

"That man took my *son* from me, took yours too, in case you've forgotten."

"I haven't forgotten, Aria. But losing our children doesn't give us free rein to inflict that pain on the rest of the world. We didn't start the Scions to take other people's children away from them, we wanted to avenge our own." Jiro replied, his face dark. But the older woman was undeterred.

"We are doing what's necessary. After all these years, we have found a way to *finally* make him pay for his crimes, and I will use any means I need to ensure it does not slip through my fingers."

With that, she waved a hand at the rest of the room and all the professors stopped screaming. They began blinking, looking around the room with unfocused eyes. Ashlyn stopped writhing, but the sounds of her sobbing still echoed around the halls. Aria gave Jiro one last, withering look.

"*Finish the machine.*" She hissed at him. Then she turned and stalked out of the lab, Juniper hurrying along behind her. As they went back through the bronze door, Juniper could still hear the heavy sobbing of the girl who still laid on the floor. She shuddered, wrapped her arms around herself, and did her best to control her racing heart as she followed her mother back out of the Artificer's domain.

J uniper shook awake with a start. It was too hot. The inside of Kali's room felt like one of the saunas on the Steaming Isles. She lay in Kali's bed, clothed only in a chiffon night dress, as she watched her lover sleep. She had not rested well that night. Her dreams were full of the screams and the images of the blind professors wandering around in confusion and terror.

She could not get the sound of Ashlyn wailing out of her head, nor the look in her mother's eyes when she had menaced Jiro.

She could not help but think about all the times the Master Artificer had sat at their table and ate with them when she was a child. He had brought her paintbrushes and pencils and little toys he made which walked across the floor or floated through the air. He had even spoken for her when she was raised from Initiate to Professor. She knew he had found some solace in being a mentor for her after the death of his own son during the war. He was a friend, or, at least, he had been. She was not sure what he would be now. It was unlikely they would ever be anything close to what they were.

She tossed the covers off of her and shuffled across the room, bare feet on the imported Vinatierian rug. She threw the window open and felt a slight relief as the sensation of fresh air greeted her. It felt good on her skin, raising goosebumps all along her bare flesh. She breathed the scents of night in deeply as she stared out over the darkened city. A few lights dotted the sea of buildings, but for the most part it was quiet and still. She stared out over it, lost in thought for a long moment. Then, a soft voice called her back to reality.

"June...what are you doing?"

She turned and saw the form of Kali silhouetted in the moonlight. She lay in the bed, half covered in the fine sheets, her pale skin was luminescent against the dark and Juniper felt herself flush as she stared at her. She smiled softly, trying to banish the thoughts from her mind.

"Nothing, just getting some air."

She shuffled back across the room to the bed, sliding back under the sheets. As she laid her head on the pillow, she stared into Kali's eyes, her face framed in the red cascades of her hair. She felt her breath catch in her chest.

"I wish this night could go on forever." Juniper said, her voice a hoarse whisper. She felt the tightness in her chest constricting like a snake crushing its prey.

Kali nodded, "It's been a long few cycles. I've missed you."

Juniper kissed her. It was a lingering, sad kind of kiss. When she pulled away, she spoke with a bit more sureness in her voice, "If...when, this is all over, my father said the Empire will change. We'll have a representative body, like the Federation, or the Republic. The old beliefs won't hold the Empire in a vice. In Republic and Vinatieri, people like us can be together, even marry. Soon we can finally be free to be together..."

Kali's face became a show of sorrow. She closed her eyes and tears welled up in the corners and she buried her face into the pillow.

"What? Kal, what's wrong?"

She shook her head, face still in her pillow. When she finally looked up, she seemed to be breaking down, all the grace and self assuredness she had once had gone as she collapsed into a sobbing mess.

"I'm promised, June."

It took her a moment to comprehend what she had said. She stared at the woman beside her for a moment which seemed to stretch out for an era. When she finally spoke, she could not bring herself to do more than croak a single word, "*What?*"

Kali stared back at her, misery mutilating her typically beautiful features, "I received word today. I didn't know how to tell you, after you came back from the University you were so upset and I just...it was all my father. He's been insisting, saying since I had graduated from the University and was a full fledged Medicinist, I had no excuse not to marry anymore. I had nothing to say, no case to argue. My family has debts, we're still in bad standing with the Emperor after my grandfather's transgressions. I tried, I argued and fought, I even cried and threatened to join the Acolytes, but it didn't do any good. I had hoped I could hold it off until after the Scion's made their move, with the Emperor dead, maybe things would be different. But my father has enacted his plans..."

Juniper felt like she was watching the conversation take place from somewhere else, somewhere hundred a thousand leagues away. This could not be happening. Not now, not after everything else. Not after all her sacrifice.

"...he's promised me to some old lord in the New World who has a large freehold on the western edge of the New Oarenhiem. His wife died giving birth to their last child. He's looking for a new bride and has pledged my father a great deal of money, enough to clear our family's debts." Kali's voice had an obvious note of disgust, her face contorted into a mixture of fury and pain, "I'm sure he'll expect someone who can raise his children and probably give him a whole host more. June, I don't want...I can't..."

Kali's mouth was moving but she could not find the words. Juniper stared at her, unable to find her own voice. Her mind had stopped working. She stood up from the bed, suddenly.

"I...I'm going to fix this..." she stammered, hardly able to formulate her words, "Kali, I'll handle it..."

She knew that Kali was trying to get her attention, calling out from behind her, but she could not face her. She grabbed her dress from where it hung on the closet door and wrapped it around herself before rushing across the room and out into the hallway, ignoring Kali's voice as it vanished behind her.

ACT III

Consequences & Rewards

STAGHEART PRESS, LLC

Chapter Twenty-One

New Recruits

The flash was so bright that even the light which filtered through the cracks around the door frame was blinding. In the hallway, Holton and mercenaries he had been given command of were poised on either side of the door, weapons at the ready. The moment the light faded, he nodded to one of the men and he smashed his heavy boot into the door near the lock, immediately knocking it free of the frame with a resounding snap. The Northman had a hatchet in one hand and a long knife in the other as he breached the threshold. His group of mercenaries poured into the tiny room, hefting their clubs and short swords, eager to begin the festivities.

Inside were five people, the boy from the tavern, two hard looking women and a man, all of whom he recognized as soldiers doing a bad job of disguising themselves as commoners, as well as a handsome young man with dark hair and a short beard. They were all blinking and crying out, blind and deafened, struggling wildly as the flood of mercenaries pinned them down, disarmed them and bound them in ropes and gags. It was all done in a matter of moments, so quickly they had barely begun recovering by the time they were being dragged into a line on their knees.

He grabbed the single chair and sat before them. By the time he sat, the effects of the coin had worn off and all the prisoners could see him. The rest of the mercenaries crowded around the room with amused looks as they settled in to watch. He grinned down at the prisoners, taking his time as he looked at each in turn.

"Let me explain the mess I find myself in." He scratched at his beard, freshly trimmed and washed for the first time in ages, "We received word that we were being followed, to expect trouble from the eldest Roth Prince. So we paid off all the barkeeps and such to let us know if someone was asking about us, we stationed lookouts all over town. Hell, I've even had my man make a damn fool of himself every night, spouting off about our organization to anyone who would listen, just in case you happened to make it this far."

He glanced behind him to where the man with the shaved head had wandered in and was leaning against the fractured door frame. He gave Mateo a crooked grin and a little wave.

"You took the bait nice and easy too. But what I did not expect was for you to bring friends...and that, well that puts me in a damned awkward position."

He held the gaze of his prisoners for a moment longer. Then he settled on the Prince, he noted the rage and indignation barely contained behind the young man's eyes, "Lord Roth, you brought these good people here when I was only expecting to host one guest. What do you think we should do with them?"

One of the mercenaries ripped the gag out of the Prince's mouth. He spat, a mixture of blood and spit, splattering the floor a foot in front of Holton's boot, "What are you doing here? What are you doing with the witch and the kids?"

Holton whistled, "I've got to give it to you, you're either very brave...or very foolish."

He struck out without warning. A smacking sound cracked through the air as he backhanded the Prince across the face, almost sending him to the floor. The man's mouth immediately began to bleed even more, dribbling red down his chin and onto the floorboards. When he looked up, the eyes that met Holton's were full of palpable defiance despite the obvious odds stacked against him. He gave it a moment but the young lord did not break his gaze.

Holton sighed. He made a motion to one of the men who stood behind the prisoners. The grim man whipped out a curved knife and grabbed one of the women by her braids, pressing the blade against her throat so hard he immediately drew a long, thin line of blood. It dribbled down the hilt and stained the yellow body wrap she wore as a shirt with tiny red drops. The Prince's eyes went wide and he gritted his teeth.

"I hope we've established the order of things now." The thief pulled out his dagger and held it levelly, about three inches from the Prince's nose, "But in case you haven't gotten it, let me make this clear. I would rather kill you, here and now. But, against my own better judgment, a higher power wants you alive. He seems to think you might be valuable in case things go wrong. So you need to be kept alive, but the rest of your companions have no such protections. So you're going to work with me, all nicely, or I'm going to start cutting throats."

The Prince maintained his defiant look, never breaking eye contact with Holton. He refused to speak but managed a stiff nod, his head barely bobbing up and down. The red haired thief motioned and the mercenaries crowded around, yanking the prisoners to their feet and ushering them out the door. As the Prince was roughly shoved through the doorway, the last of the prisoners to be escorted out, he turned and gave Holton a fierce last look.

"You'd have never taken us in a fair fight. What kind of man are you?" He spat at Holton.

"I am what I need to be." The thief responded simply.

The Prince was pulled from the room and manhandled down the hallway. Holton took one last look around the room, knelt down and retrieved the coin Taron had given the guardsmen. He stuffed it in his pocket and followed his prisoners down the stairs and out into the humid air of the evening.

There was something about these stifling mangrove swamps that set Holton at ease. The others whined and cursed, complaining about everything endlessly day and night, looking for every chance to slink off to find a shaded spot and hide. He was constantly having to corral them like lost sheep. Since joining the Blades, he had been charged with the annoying task of playing nanny to this group of feckless mercenaries. But he could manage. Unlike the rest of them, the constant biting flies and the unending chorus of bullfrogs and crickets that warbled through the trees all day and night barely bothered him. Even the danger of the great snakes and lizards that waited in the murky waters to catch you unawares hardly weighed on his mind.

Truth be told, as he stared out into the early morning mists hanging over the marsh, he thought about how it was similar to the evergreen forests of the North in many ways. Danger lurked around every corner, waiting for you to let your guard down. The conditions were harsh, driving the weaker ones out quickly and leaving a cadre of only the toughest and most stubborn bastards. It felt a lot like home.

The rest of his group seemed to be adapting similarly as well. Erin was sitting at the other end of the pier, leaning against a foundation pole. They had drawn the last watch together and were awaiting the full sunrise before waking the others. She wore her hair tied up and had shed her coats and leathers, wearing only a pair of loose fitting cloth trousers and a wrap around her chest in the local fashion.

Even in the dim early morning light, he could see the tattoos across her back, flames and a wolf's skull decorated with runes from the old language, which mirrored his bare left arm and shoulder, as well as a series of smaller tattoos portraying birds and flowers on her chest and arms. She hosted her own smattering of scars, none so horrific as the jagged one across her chin, but still an impressive collection in its own right. He stared at the history which had been mapped out across her body, the old feelings of guilt creeping back through the murky fog of his memories.

"Stop staring." Erin's voice brought him back to reality. She was looking directly at him, face impassive.

"Sorry," he muttered quietly. The constant buzzing and croaking that formed the swamp's ever present ambiance made it hard to hear his words, "guess it's been a while since I've seen...all of it. Just remembering..."

Erin cast a glance down at herself. Then she nodded towards him, "Guess we can't all go around parading ourselves like ladies of the night, can we?"

Holton snorted. He was shirtless, exposing his own canvas of decorated and disfigured flesh. Looking appraisingly at himself, examining the lines inked into his arm, "I suppose not."

"Back when we got these," she put a thumb over her shoulder toward the wolf on her back, "did you ever think we'd be here? Working with mercenaries, holding a Prince hostage, involved in...something like *this*?"

"Honestly? Back then I thought we'd be dead before the end of the season."

Erin cocked an eyebrow, "Truly?"

"Truly."

"Then why join up at all?" She sat up a little straighter, "Why were you so eager to join up with Bill and the rest?"

"What choice did I have?" Holton scratched at his beard, casting a glance over the murky water as a particularly loud bullfrog punctuating the stillness of the morning, "I was barely in my tenth year, it was the middle of winter, the farm was gone, everyone I knew was dead...and I had a baby sister to take care of."

"You could've gone to one of the towns, Hog's Hollow, Gavinport, maybe found work..."

"What work?" His mocking tone earned a frown from Erin. But he pulled back, his voice gentle once again, "I was a goat herder, no skills, no trade, and you...you were barely off our mother's tit. Nothing was waiting for us in the cities but the whorehouse for you and life on the streets for me."

"But Black Bill was better? Being with the *crew* was better?"

"The city would have been an early grave, more than likely, for both of us. At least we lived with Black Bill."

"I suppose..." she looked out over the swamp, "However long that holds out has yet to be seen."

"Do you want out? I can pay you your share now, if you want."

Erin gave him a hard stare, "You think I'm going to abandon you?"

He shrugged, "I wouldn't hold it against you."

She shook her head, a strand of her strawberry blonde hair coming loose from the bun and dangling out in front of her face, "I was with you before you were the Red Wolf. I stuck with you for all those jobs that made you famous. I stuck with you when you killed the old man. I'll stick with you now. Better or worse, we're in this together."

He scooched across the wooden platform so that he was next to her. He threw his arm around the shoulder, grinning down at her, "I'll stick with you too."

She was the one that snorted this time, "Sure. Don't worry, I'll make sure you don't get us too deep in the greens without a way out."

Holton shrugged again, "If it doesn't work out, we can always kill everyone and run."

Erin's eyes went distant as she stared off into the swamp, "Same old plan as always."

They were silent for a moment after that. They listened to the swamp sounds and watched the mist swirl around the trees and dance over the dark water. Finally, Erin spoke up again.

"Seriously, Holt, we need a plan. Our position here is too unsteady. We need leverage in case things go to shit."

"Don't worry, Erin, I'm working on something for that."

B y the time the sun had fully risen and burned off the
last wisps of fog from the swamp, the camp was a bustle
of activity once again. Men and women were toiling away in
the summer heat, sweating and swatting flies off themselves.
A steady stream of cursing filled the air, punctuated with the
occasional threat. They were in the process of unloading several
flat bottom river boats and packing their cargo into a large storehouse, the single structure which sat on the elevated platform.
In the depths of the marsh, it was almost impossible to tell
the storehouse and platform were here unless you happened to
stumble right up to it, hidden as it was amongst the thick copse
of trees and underbrush. Whoever had built it had known what
they were doing.

"Hey!"

A familiar voice called out just behind him. He turned and
saw Alice, hair done up in a similar manner to Erin's, sweat
beaded all across her face and bare shoulders. She looked remarkably slight in comparison to the hefty forms of the mercenaries unloading the barges only a few feet from her. She had
her hands on her hips and was staring at him, face screwed up
in frustration.

"We've been in this swamp for almost a cycle and you keep
filling that storehouse with more people. Now we've even got
to share it with prisoners! You said it was only going to be a few
days. Are we ever going to get out of here?"

Holton sighed, "This should be the last shipment of goods.
Now, we're just waiting on Lawrence's man to bring the next
group of recruits, once they're here we'll load you all onto the
ship with the gear and head west."

"So you have no idea how much longer it's going to be?"

Holton shook his head. Alice threw up her hands and made a
frustrated sound, "Can we at least go back across the Bay to the

city? You all get to come and go, after all. It wasn't so horrible and hot there."

"Sorry, girlie, boss man says it's too dangerous for you lot or the witch to be there, in case someone sees you and puts the pieces together." He grinned wickedly at her, "I'm sure you'll manage. You survived the deepest, darkest dungeons of The Hold, after all."

She rolled her eyes and turned to stalk off, muttering something unintelligible. But she stopped mid step and turned stare towards the swamp. He followed her gaze and frowned when he noticed another flat bottom boat gliding through the trees towards their little hideout. It was small, little more than a fisherman's skiff, nothing like the large cargo boats he had been expecting. A dark skinned man with deep set eyes that reminded him of an ancient bloodhound disembarked and approached. He spoke in the slow, rolling tones that the natives of the swamp all seemed to have inborn.

"You're Holton?" He rumbled, stripping off his floppy hat and fanning himself with it.

He nodded and the man continued, "I'm s'posed to pass on a message to you, from the man Carrigan."

Holton breathed out a long, low breath through his nose. Carrigan was the agent he had been waiting on. His counterpart, the one who was bringing the last of the recruits for Lawrence's master plot.

"Master Carrigan wants me to relay that he will be here tonight. He was having some trouble with the locals in Wren's Hollow, but he has resolved the issue." The dark skinned man drawled his way through the message without any perceptible change in expression.

"Anything else?"

The man slowly shook his head. Holton thanked him and palmed him a silver mark as he shook his hand. He turned and saw Alice, arms folded, still watching him. She had a curious look on her face.

"Does this mean we're leaving?"

Holton gave her a look and strode past her towards the store-house. She fell in step behind, walking quickly to keep up.

"Should we get packed, are you going to disguise us like minstrels again?"

He ignored her, throwing open the doors and walking inside. The building was a single, massive room, packed with crates and sacks, all stacked up in haphazard piles throughout the area. There was an area of cots set up against one wall where the witch and her two other children sat. They were going over the details of some scroll work, all looking up when he entered. Against the opposite wall, a row of cages were arranged in a row.

His prisoners sat there, still bruised and battered from their eventful night. They also looked up, staring at him as he walked across the great room. The Prince sat in the corner of the last cage. A stream of dried blood still stained the corner of his defiant grimace, marking the blow Holton had dealt him. He watched them pass but Holton ignored his prisoner and moved over to a large desk where several maps had been laid out. He ran his finger along one until he found what he was looking for.

"Wren's Hollow..." he murmured under his breath, wheels turning in his mind, "that's only a few hours upriver from here. What's taking this fool so damned long?"

Alice was at his shoulder, peering down at the map. She made a clucking sound, "Don't enjoy when someone makes you wait, hmm?"

Holton gave her the hardest stare he could manage, but it did nothing to deter the girl's look of smugness. She turned and glanced at the Prince, her little smirk slipping away. He was still staring at them, eyes hard shards of hate embedded in his face.

"I wish you would've killed him." Alice said in a voice a little too loud to be considered a whisper, "He would have taken us back if you hadn't caught him."

Holton nodded, "Probably would've been the best call. But we had higher orders. We need to keep him alive, for the moment at least."

Alice leveled her gaze on him, "Who would think that would be a good idea? Was it that creepy sorcerer, the one with the greasy hair?"

Holton pointed a finger up toward the ceiling, "Higher...someone above Lawrence. The magician wanted him dead as much as you do."

Alice scrunched up her nose and made a face, "I don't like this. I know Mother Mary made a deal with these people but I don't trust it. She won't tell me what me and the others are meant to do, only that what we're doing is important and we'll get a big reward at the end."

"Don't you trust her? Isn't she your *mother* after all?"

Alice snorted, "Hardly, that's just a title. She just...adopted all of us. I ran away from home when I was in my ninth year. My da was...a bad man..."

The thief noted how she suddenly became very interested in studying the wood grain beneath her feet. He took pity on her and interjected, "You think she'd toss you out like bad bathwater after you've served your purpose?"

"She's no white witch from some children's story." Holton stole a glance at the woman, who had gone back to her lesson with the two other children. When he looked back Alice was still staring at him, "She saved me from the wild and the cold, but believe me, she'd sell my soul to save her own skin."

He grinned, "Better get used to that, girl. Stay in this game long enough and you'll find out for yourself, everyone's playing their own angle. No one shares more than they have to. All you can do is look out for you and your own, nothing more, nothing less."

She nodded slowly. She was watching him, and he wondered vaguely if she was trying to read his thoughts. Could witches do that? Some of the stories said so. But he had learned not to put much stock in legends and folktales. He clapped a friendly hand on her arm.

"Better get some rest, I have a feeling it's going to be a long night."

He turned and left her, striding across the storeroom again. The Prince watched him go, eyes still harsh. Holton met his gaze evenly for a long moment. As he exited the building, he grumbled under his breath, "Damn nobles, always more trouble than they're worth."

Night had enveloped the marsh like a flood which drowned out the last gasping breaths of sunlight. The bullfrogs were singing and the night time buzz of flying insects was like a symphony. The only light visible under the canopy of trees came from their little man made island. Holton waited on the peer with a small group. Erin was at his side, as were the rest of his group. He already had his misgivings about this man they had been tasked with meeting and he was not so confident in the mercenaries Lawrence had put under his command. If things went awry, he wanted to know it was his own crew at his back.

Eventually, they saw a tiny flickering light appear out of the wooded swamp. As it grew closer, they could make out the shapes of a series of boats, flat bottom barges, riding low in the water. There were men and women moving around the deck, silently keeping the course as they poled the boats along with long sticks and oars. Eventually, they reached the deck and Holton's crew helped them tie off.

Once the boats were moored, the men from the boat stood waiting, leaving the two groups staring at each other in the gloom. Holton was just about to ask where the man in charge was when his question was answered for him. A man who was short and so slender Holton could have mistaken him for a woman at first glance stepped onto the deck. He had blonde hair and an angular face that screamed of proper breeding, even more so than his fine clothes and the deep red cloak he wore. He managed to glance down his nose at Holton's crew, despite his disadvantage in stature, and the thief could feel himself being weighed and measured. It immediately set his teeth on edge.

"You're the brigand Lawrence told me I was to meet?" The man asked, a disapproving grimace plain on his face.

Holton stepped forward. He dwarfed the man, in both size and stature, "I am, and you've kept me waiting."

The man turned his frown into a thin smirk and his brilliant blue eyes shone in the darkness at the sudden challenge, "Please excuse my tardiness. It was...unavoidable."

"I'm sure. Do you have the recruits, Carrigan?"

"Indeed." He snapped his fingers, thin, bony looking things that were near translucent in the firelight, and a figure appeared from the interior of the boat's cabin. She had brown hair cut like a man's and patterned tattoos down one arm. A wicked looking curved blade hung from her belt and she stood at the angle which told Holton she knew everything she needed to know about how to wield it. She made a general motion to the men on the deck.

"Come on, you slugs, I can't move all this cargo by myself you know."

Holton glanced at Carrigan, who simply stared back, the thin smile still stuck on his face. He motioned to his men and Jarryd and Barney stepped gingerly onto the gently swaying boats. They followed the other men inside and there were a few moments of pregnant anticipation. A few men came shuffling out, carrying large pieces of cargo covered in blankets between them, unloading them onto the pier. Then Jarryd came hurrying back out from the cabin, shuffling over to the side of the boat. Holton walked over, leaning down so they could keep their voices low.

"Better come have a look at this, boss." The Oaren said, his tone dark. He gave Holton a severe look over his mustache which spoke volumes.

Holton nodded and stepped down into the gently swaying vessel. He followed Jarryd, ducking inside the cabin. It was already crowded, with several men shuffling around each other as they awkwardly tried to maneuver large bits of cargo around the cramped cabin. This was made more difficult as each was tightly covered in a thick blanket, obscuring any potential handholds. The thieves pushed themselves against a wall, allowing two men to heft one of the pieces of cargo past them and out into the night. Holton gave his man a quizzical look, but Jarryd just motioned for him to follow. They made their way over to one of the cages, where Barney was waiting. He had cut a slit in the tarp and peel it back for Holton to see.

Beneath, cold iron bars formed a cage, inside which lay the unmoving body of a young boy. He was perhaps in his thirteenth year, sandy hair swept over his face. He was so still Holton initially thought he was dead, but after a moment he saw the barest movement of his chest as he took a breath. Holton stared at the child for a long moment before taking a step back and surveying the rest of the cabin. There were six cages in total left inside. But Carrigan had brought three boats.

The red haired thief wheeled on his heel and stalked outside. He was vaguely aware that Barney and Jarryd followed closely behind, but his whole attention was focused on the man in the red cloak. The blonde man stood on the dock, smirk still on his face as he watched Holton leap up on the dock and approach with mild interest.

"Where did these children come from?" Holton demanded, sticking a finger in the man's chest. He was only a foot or so in front of the man and could smell the floral notes of scented water on him.

"A few came from Asaldon, but most came from the farm towns and little villages of the Dawn Plains and the Broken

Coast." His nonchalant tone made Holton want to grab him by the throat, "Honestly, it's hard to remember at this point."

"You kidnapped them."

"That's what I was paid to do, yes." He looked Holton up and down, "What? Don't tell me you have some *moral* quandary here? I was told you were a ruthless cutthroat, a lawless criminal...wasn't that why we hired you?"

"I was told the children wouldn't be harmed." Holton managed to growl through his gritted teeth.

Carrigan shrugged, "They haven't been...at least, not much. Just a simple sleeping spell to keep them sedated."

Holton felt a hand grab his shoulder. He glanced and saw Erin, who shook her head at him. He gave Carrigan a last, murderous glare and spun away from him. He stalked off down the pier, leaving the mercenaries to finish their business in the fading lamplight.

CHAPTER TWENTY-TWO

ANGLES

Lyra subtly shifted so that a bit more of her leg was showing from under the side of her dress, pretending not to be aware of it as she reclined on the park bench, eyes closed as she basked in the warmth of the morning sun. It was a brilliant morning in the city and she and the young sailor had decided to enjoy it in one of the city parks. They had been spending a great deal of their free time together since the night she had tagged along to the Consul's house. It had not slipped her notice that he had wanted to be as far away from the University as often as possible.

So she had taken on the role of his personal guide and they had spent their time wandering the streets, shopping, enjoying parks and little airy cafes; anything to get away from the oppressive shadow of the school where he was being forced to reside. He spent much of the time lamenting his position, which she listened to with the patience of a confessor, ears pricked for any important detail. When she was not listening to him vent his troubles, he often insisted that he needed to study. Today he was nose deep in a thick, leatherbound book entitled *Gorman's Glossary of High Art*, but she kept catching him stealing glances at her that were supposed to be subtle.

When she readjusted her dress, she opened her eyes slightly and again caught him staring at her out of the corner of his eye.

She snapped her fingers at him, "If you're just going to stare at me we can at least do that somewhere more interesting."

His eyes snapped up to her face and he saw for the first time she was staring at him. He immediately looked abashed, then tried to cover it up with a smile that was full of false confidence, "You're not making it easy for me to concentrate. What did you have in mind?"

"You've never shown me around the University. I've been on the grounds tons of times, but never inside beyond your tiny little room. Could you take me around?"

Jayce's expression immediately slipped. His brow furrowed and he wore a frown that looked like someone had spit in his porridge, "I don't know, Lyra. We're not supposed to have visitors really, and it's pretty dangerous for me there right now. You know what all is going on."

"I know, I was thinking maybe I could help you out a bit. You haven't found out anything more about your mystery have you?"

He shook his head. The look on his face spelled out self doubt as surely as an outright statement, "No, and there's been too many close calls. I don't want to put you in danger..."

"Don't worry, I can take care of myself. I'm a woman of the New Age after all," she indicated her fashionably short skirt, "you're not a man of the old credences, are you?"

"No!" He shook his head again, more vigorously this time, "I'm sure you're capable...it's just..."

"You worry too much." She stood up suddenly, smiling down at him from behind her cascade of blonde locks, "Besides...I'm sure there's lots to see in a school for wizards. Maybe we might even have time to see your room?"

That was the key to erase the last traces of apprehension on his worried face. He grinned and stood, taking her hand in his free one and striding across the park back towards the looming figure of the school in the near distance.

The grounds were littered with students enjoying the gorgeous day. Small groups lounged on the lawn, reading or making light small talk, some displaying minor examples of their Art. As they made their way across the grounds, one young woman was directing a translucent flock of birds in a graceful arc over the grounds, while a young man made a crowd of other students laugh by taking on the image of a particularly old and crotchety member of the staff.

Most of the young men were in the fashionable light summer shirts of pastel coloring, while many of the girls were dressed similarly to her, short dresses with floral designs or simple patterns displayed. Various tones of skin were in full display in the sunlight, accented with delicate gold and silver jewelry. She would have been willing to bet she was not the only lady here working over a partner. As Jayce led them to the entrance to the main building, she noted several of the women examining her with an appraising eye. She felt the familiar sensation of entering the fine parties of in the wealthier neighborhoods of Asaldon on the arm of some well-to-do youth.

Jayce led her across the building's threshold, walking through an extra wide set of double doors that were thrown open to let in the day, she felt something bristle across her skin, like the cool morning air after the warmth of the house. But as quickly as it had come on it was gone, leaving her wondering if she had imagined it. Jayce had not seemed to notice, as he was still strolling along without so much as a break in pace. She knew the rumors, that the University was enchanted with ancient magic that kept out thieves and spies.

Every once in a while, an enterprising burglar would go missing and people would always say they crossed one of the mages. There was never any confirmation of the supposed curses that protected the school, but most of the criminals in Asaldon did their best to avoid any work that brought them into direct conflict with the mages, just in case. She considered this, trying to recollect any of the stories that might have any validity, as she followed Jayce around the school, half listening to his somewhat sedate tour.

The school was massive, perhaps the biggest building in Asaldon aside from the Sovereign's Palace itself, and it took them ages to wander their way through it. He led her through the massive Grand Hall and kitchens, the apprentices halls and living quarters, around several living spaces and past many classrooms. All were well furnished in richly detailed, if outdated, furniture and fine wall tapestries and paintings. Finally, they reached the library. Lyra had seen libraries before, in stores in the wealthy parts of town as well as the private quarters of wealthy merchants and minor nobility. Some of the guildhalls and temples had small collections of books related to their respective area of expertise. But the library of Uthersanctorum was like nothing she had ever experienced.

It spanned five floors of the school, from the ground level to the highest story that was not part of one of the towers. Each floor was lined with rows and rows of shelves, stretching out into the distance. There were fields of desks and tables where students were engrossed in their studies, often with a mess of books and papers strewn about before them. There were large maps and intricate diagrams displayed alongside shelves of ancient looking scrolls and spindly models of machines of which she could not guess the purposes. There were other objects displayed as well, pottery and bones and jewelry all adorned with scrawling writing she could not decipher. In the center, a circular atrium spanned the entire five story height of the library, in which the reconstructed skeleton of a great, winged dragon was suspended as though in flight.

She stared at it, mind suddenly overwhelmed by the spectacle of it all. The dragon's remains were unlike anything she had ever seen. She realized Jayce was staring at her and a sly grin had slid across his face.

"So, is it what you expected?"

She did her best to maintain her persona while staring at the floating behemoth, "Th-this is amazing! I've never seen so many books in one place...and *this*! Where did they get a dragon?"

"It's the one that was King Remus killed in the Farian Forest, the last dragon seen on Evardene in a thousand years." Jayce kept his gaze on her, "After it was slain, the Arcanist's Guild had it brought here for study."

She managed to tear her eyes away from it long enough to give him a sideways glance, "Did they learn anything from it?"

"Nobody knows. The rumor is they learned how to stop them from breeding, which is why they disappeared from this continent. But they kept all their findings a secret."

"You couldn't find out? Not in all these books?"

"No, this is the general library. All the big secrets are kept under lock and key."

She blinked, "There's...more?"

"Of course," Jayce waved a hand, "all of this is general knowledge, basic magic, histories, sciences, philosophy...some of it is rare, even valuable, but the really dangerous stuff is kept separate. Many of the teachers have private collections, but there's also the Stacks."

Seeing her quizzical look, he went pointed down.

"The Stacks are another section of the library...underground, in the cellars. I only found out about them because I was looking around for my...other duties." Seeing her nod sympathetically, he went on, "There's an area that's always guarded, night or day, and has a big iron door with great giant locks, like a vault. I asked some of the other students about it until one finally told me. He said it's where they keep all the theoretical information about the High Arts, all the things they haven't quite worked out yet, and all the stuff they have worked out but is too dangerous to leave lying around where anyone could just pick it up."

Lyra considered this for a moment. She pursed her lips, "People keep saying that, the *High Art*, what exactly does that mean?"

Jayce's brow furrowed and he was quiet for a moment. When he finally spoke, his words were measured and deliberate, as if he was reciting them from a memorized speech, "From what they tell me, when someone manipulates the world around them, moving the energies of the world as they naturally occur, that's called the Low, or Base, Art. They say it's done instinctually, the way a fish swims or a horse runs. Most people who have the ability to practice magic can only perform feats of the Low Art, like Greenhands or Fireweavers..."

"...or Stormspeakers?"

"Yes." He seemed to have trouble meeting her gaze, "Their...our capacity to use magic, is limited. We can only affect certain things. That's why they call us settled. But High Art is spellcraft and enchantment, when you take the energy in the world and manipulate it in its raw form, creating something new. It's true magic."

"You didn't know that before you came here?"

Jayce shook his head, "Knowledge about magic is limited outside the great schools. I tried to learn from books but it was hopeless. Everything I knew before I came here I learned from my mother and she had no formal education. She was against me coming to learn from true Arcanists actually. I suppose she was right..."

Lyra was quiet for a long time. She turned the idea over and over in her head and found herself speaking before she realized it, "You know, I saw a Stormspeaker quiet a hurricane once."

Jayce met her gaze finally. He could not quite keep the curiosity out of his eyes.

"It was a long time ago, and I was a little girl. I was out on a ship, far out in the ocean. My da, he was bringing us south after my ma died, looking for work in the capital, you see. Well, anyway, the storm hit us real hard, it seemed like it came out of nowhere at all. A great spinning wall of water was pulling us in, howling and spitting and throwing wind in every direction.

My da tied me to a railing, then went to help and try to get the rigging under control. That was the last time I ever saw him."

"Lyra..." but she ignored him.

"I was a mess, barely in my eighth year, crying myself blind and screaming until I was well past hoarse. But I saw him...the Stormspeaker, I mean. He was tall, with a great big beard and a heavy cloak, just like a wizard in the old stories. He was holding up his hands and shouting while all the others were running about the ship, getting cast overboard and all. He screamed and was shaking and I could see his face was red like fire. Finally, he made a great big sweeping motion and the hurricane just...went away. I don't know how else to describe it. It was coming towards us one moment, then gone the next. Everything calmed down real quick after that and before we knew it, we were just floating on the sea again, like nothing happened."

"What happened to him? The Stormspeaker, I mean."

"He died. Just collapsed, right there on the deck, all pale like death himself, eyes were wide like saucers. I never forgot his face."

They were both silent for a long time, staring up at the ghastly creature which soared above them. Only the gentle rustle of pages and scratching pens and the occasional mutterings of a preoccupied student punctuated the oppressive weight of silence that pressed down on them.

"So you've been here ever since?" Jayce asked finally.

She nodded, "The captain kicked everyone off the ship once we got to port, never gave me a second glance. I had no one here. I begged for a while, stole for a while longer."

"Hey, at least you found your feet eventually, right?"

"Yes, I suppose so." She stared up at the massive skeleton's empty eye sockets. They seemed to be staring back at her with a hunger that had somehow survived the turning of ages and threatened to swallow her whole. She was so caught up by them she only noticed the merchant had put his arm around her when he pulled her close and held her against him. To her own surprise, she let him hold her for a long time, letting the memories sink back into the depths once again. Eventually, she pushed away and looked him in the eyes, taken aback once again as she noted their sparkling blue hue, so bright against his dark skin. He smiled at her and she felt an unfamiliar warmth as she recognized sincerity in his expression. She smiled back despite herself.

"You know Jayce, you really shouldn't let these people's opinions wound you so deeply. You have nothing to prove to them."

He shrugged, feigning indifference, "It's just, I wanted to come here so badly. I fought for it, begged for it. Hells, I defied my own parents for it. But now, I wish I could be somewhere else. I thought it would be different. It's not just about my magic, my limitations; it's the *people*. They're so cruel and greedy and conniving...did you know how many students I've seen break down since I've been here?"

She shook her head, glancing around at the library where several were writing feverishly in their notes.

"More than I can count, and they don't care. The ones that can't *get it* are kicked out, not given a second thought. They just disappear. It's madness."

"So leave." Lyra made a motion towards the door, "If you hate it that badly, just go. The Roth's only own you because they're paying your tuition. If you drop out they'll have nothing on you."

"It's not that simple. Cassius is my oldest friend, and he's in danger. If I can figure out what they're up to, maybe I can save him. Then of course, we still don't know what they're really doing. It could be something terrible. Why else would someone break a witch out of prison?"

Lyra blinked, "A witch?"

"Yes...I suppose I never told you. But it doesn't matter much now, I've told you everything else. The men who broke into the Hold freed a witch and her coven. They were awaiting transport here, to be imprisoned in Silence. The only people who knew were the Baron himself and his advisors, and some of the staff of the University. That's why the Roth's thought someone here was involved, and they were right."

Lyra was lost in thought for a long moment. She could feel the tendrils of an idea struggling to grasp together and form a coherent being.

"Lyra, what is it?"

She felt the sudden spark of realization hit her like a flash of light, "The missing children!"

"Missing...what are you...?"

"Children have been going missing in the city, several were last seen near the University. The rumors are that they had magical talent, Jayce!" She was speaking quickly and struggling to keep her voice low in the relative silence of the library.

"I don't, what does that have to do with..." Jayce's eyes suddenly gained piercing clarity as he finally came to the same realization, "You think it's the same people! They didn't want the witch, they wanted her kids!"

Lyra nodded, "Whatever this conspiracy that you're investigating is, children with the Gift are part of it! These people are collecting them from all over the Federation. Hells, I'll bet some of the children that are kicked out of the school itself get taken as well."

Jayce considered this for a long moment, looking around the room in contemplation, "But how does that help us? I've been shadowing Allegheny since I saw him talking to Breyer and he hasn't slipped up at all. Not a toe out of place that I've seen."

Lyra pursed her lips and spoke slowly, trying to be patient, "If we know what they're after, we can figure out what they're going to do. Maybe, set a trap for them, catch them in the act. Isn't that what Lucian wants? Evidence, proof of who's involved?"

Jayce furrowed his brow, seeming to shrink back from her, "Set a trap? Lyra, these are the most powerful Arcanists on the continent. We can't *trap* them."

Her lips curled into a wicked smile, "You just can't see all the angles."

I t was late in the evening when Jayce met her at the door to the University grounds. Guests were not allowed past nightfall so she had to depart earlier in the day, promising to return to help him enact their plan. Luckily, it had given her an excuse to leave him and send a runner to report to Hector, as well as stock up on essentials. She had a feeling this job was going to become far more hazardous fairly soon, so she had brought her full kit with her. She had ditched the eye catching dress in favor of a more mundane dress of gray woven wool, one that would allow her to more easily sink into the background and was wearing her golden hair under a simple working woman's wrap. She could have easily passed for one of the serving girls who did the laundry or prepared meals in the school, assuming someone spared her a second glance. When Jayce saw her, he did a double take.

"Not what you expected?"

"Just impressed. Even those old crone rags look good on you."

She gave him a smirk which she only half had to force and followed inside. They passed a guard who eyed her in a way that spared no confusion as to what he assumed was going on. She eyed Jayce suspiciously.

"What did you tell the guard?"

"That I had a beautiful young woman from town who wanted to come see me. I let him fill in the blanks. A few marks in his pocket and he was happy to look the other way."

She grumbled about what way he could look as they approached the main building. There was something foreboding about the school at night. The massive towers and flying arches that looked so regal and mysterious in the daylight appeared daunting in the gloom. Lyra had spent many nights amongst the city's nighttime skyline, but somehow the behemoth before her now stood out like a beast that dwarfed all others in its kingdom. Even the distant form of the Sovereign's Palace far beyond the University walls to the east seemed like it paled in comparison when standing in this imposing shadow.

As they walked across the threshold, Lyra felt the need to silently steady the rising beat of her heart as it threatened to crush her ribs against the wall of her chest. She anticipated the strange sensation on her skin that she had felt this morning, but it never came. She barely had a moment to wonder about it as Jayce led her deeper into the darkened halls of the school.

As they made their way towards the inner recesses of the school, Lyra noticed the occasional muffled voices coming from behind closed doors. It sounded like the unmistakable droning of lectures. As they passed a closed door from which yet more incoherent noise could be heard, she gave Jayce a quizzical look.

"Night classes," he answered curtly, "certain classes are only taught at night."

"Why?"

He shrugged, "Not sure, I guess some teachers only want to teach then. They set the schedules, we just have to operate around them. A few classes are only ever offered in the dead of night. "

Lyra thought about protesting, stating that made no sense from a logistical standpoint, but it seemed like a fruitless effort. She knew next to nothing about the dealings of mages, only that they were best left to their own devices. She trailed behind her guide, finding it hard to keep her sense of direction in the maze of similar seeming halls. But then, suddenly they were at their destination. Jayce ducked into a side hall off a main thorough-

fare, taking Lyra by the hand. The look in his eye brought her
to full attention.

"Okay, Allegheny's office is right there around the corner. He
should be in there, he always works late." Jayce's tone was low
and urgent, "Are you sure you want to do this? You don't have
to, I can figure out what they're doing some other way."

Lyra gave him a small smile, swallowing her own doubts and
putting a hand on his cheek, "You're cute when you're anxious.
Don't worry, I can do this."

"He's a cruel bastard, Lyra, and he's clever. Don't let him get
any hint of who you really are."

Her smile faltered for a fraction of a second and she felt the
nagging twist of her stomach, "Trust me, I can play a part."

She started to turn away, but then stopped. She turned and
grabbed Jayce by the shirt and pulled him into her. She gave him
a long, lingering kiss, feeling the surprise melt away as he relaxed.
His eyes were still closed when she pried herself away from him,
and when he blinked them open she gave him a quick grin and
moved out into the hall. She wiped her mouth and thought
with a sense of satisfaction that if he was an easy mark before,
he would be like clay in her hands now.

She was in front of the great door to the teacher's office in
a manner of moments and there, facing the dark hardwood,
everything became suddenly very real. She took a long, deep
breath and raised her hand, rapping on the door with soft, timid
knocks. After a moment, the door was swung open to show a
plump figure in a gray shirt and red suit pants.

The Master Arcanist was the opposite of what Lyra envi-
sioned when she thought of a teacher at the University. His suit
was of masterful quality but any of its fineness was squandered
by the wearer's sloppy and unkempt appearance, with his wrinkled and heavily stained clothes only accented by the sheen of
greasy sweat across his chubby face. His skin had the kind of
sallow, loose appearance she recognized from the smoke houses
in the worst parts of town and his eyes were watery little spots

of darkness which leered at her in a way that made her think of the dead fish at the dock markets. He grinned when she looked up at him, revealing his rows of small, graying teeth.

"Here for the nightly cleaning, young miss?"

"No-no, my Lord." She injected a slight tremble into her voice and did her best to play up her nervous ticks, tugging at her hair and glancing down anytime they made eye contact, "I'm here to ask your help. It's my brother..."

There was a glint in the pudgy man's dead eyes, like a snake that catches sight of a rodent unawares, "Your brother? Come in, dear, let's see what we can do."

He placed a hand on her shoulder which immediately sent shivers down her back and steered her into the room, closing the door behind them. The Arcanist's office was lavishly decorated, with several ornate paintings and shelves full of expensive looking trinkets and richly bound books. He led her to a small sitting area, two leather chairs and a small love seat centered around a fine table of silver and glass. He motioned for her to take the couch and drug a chair over towards her after she sat down, sitting uncomfortably close. He grinned at her, tongue darting over his lips briefly as he stared at her, glassy eyes locked on her.

"What seems to be the trouble, my dear?"

She swallowed hard, only halfway having to play up the character beats now. This man made her skin want to crawl off of her and get as far away as it could get. She stared at her hands as she started talking, stealing quick glances up at his sallow face.

"L-like I said before, my Lord, it's my brother, Micah. There's something, something not quite right with him. He...does things, strange things...no one can explain..."

"Like what?"

She did her best to remember the story of a young boy whom Mother Moore had taken under her care only a few years prior, "Well, he makes the cats go mad around him. T-they follow him around sometimes and gather at our doorstep, even when father shoos them away. They just sit there and stare at the door, sometimes a few, sometimes a dozen, more even! There's other things too.."

"Go on..." the Arcanist had a slight smile on his face that was unnerving, but Lyra ignored it as she pushed on.

"Sometimes...sometimes we can hear him talking, even when his mouth is closed. We can *feel* his thoughts." She forced tears to well up in her eyes, a trick she had learned years ago, making herself shake as she shortened her breaths and dug her fingers into the leather of the couch, "He...talks to me in my dreams. But when I wake up, he's still there, sound asleep."

"That all sounds very frightening."

"Yes..." something in his tone was off, he sounded almost amused, "I-I was hoping you would bring him here, maybe you could help him. The others in our borough, they think he's cursed, a witch born."

Allegheny steepled his fingers and pressed his lips together. His grin became a line so thin his lips practically disappeared and he leaned in close enough for Lyra to see the tiny lines of pink in his eyes. She could smell his foul breath and it took every bit of her experience and training not to recoil in disgust.

"I believe I can be of assistance, girlie. Just let me get my things and you can take me to-"

The door to the office came open with a jolting snap and both of them turned to see what had caused it. Two men, both in University cloaks, held Jayce by the shoulders. He was slumped between them, with a stream of red flowing down his face from an open wound in his right temple. He was groaning and did not look up. The first spoke up, "Master Arcanist, this student was hanging around outside, wouldn't tell us what he was doing here so late..."

Allegheny looked from the limp form of Jayce to the girl seated before him, small eyes seeming to sharpen as he began to put the strands of the scenario together for himself. He examined Lyra with a sudden intensity and he spoke with acid in every syllable, "So...did your brother's episodes begin before or after young master Acosta hired you?"

Lyra reacted on instinct. She immediately lashed out at him, raking her nails across his cheek. He spat curses as angry red lines sprouted up from his cheek. He reached out blindly to grab her but she was already up and back from the couch. She whipped a knife out of the concealed slit in her dress and flung it at him as he was bellowing the beginnings of some spell in a language she did not understand. It buried itself in his shoulder and he abruptly stopped his conjuring to scream in agony, clawing wildly at the hilt. She did not waste the moment.

Spinning on her heels, she sprinted towards the doorway where the two men held Jayce. She barreled into the first one, falling to the ground on top of him in a tangle of ropes and skirts. She flipped over the student's flailing form and landed on all fours with a sort of feline grace. Jayce was crumpled to the ground and the second student was gaping open mouthed as he looked from Allegheny to the woman who had just tackled her way into the hallway.

Lyra took a fraction of a heartbeat to weigh her options. Then Jayce rolled over and made a swinging motion with one arm. A sudden *whoosh* of air filled the hall, blowing Lyra's hair into a tangle all in her face and knocking the second student backwards into the wall. She started to move to grab him, but he waved a hand at her.

"Go!" He croaked, barely able to get the words out, "Get out of here! Now!"

He was trying to get up on his hands and knees, but Allegheny had made it to the doorway and put a foot on his back, forcing him back down onto the stone. Lyra swore as she turned and sprinted in the opposite direction. She heard shouts and angry voices behind her. Suddenly, she felt a wave of hot air break over her and force the air from her lungs.

A massive burst of fire had exploded against the wall just as she rounded the turn down a side hall. She coughed and forced herself to keep moving, taking turns at random, flying down hallways and leaping down whole sets of stairs. She ran until she was covered in sweat, heaving her breaths in through burning lungs as she struggled to find a place to stop.

She ducked into the open door to an empty classroom, slamming it behind her. She fought hard to control her breathing. Her heart was hammering in her chest and she felt like she was going to throw up, but she fought to keep the acid that was running through her entire body at bay as she listened at the door. She counted to one hundred, then one hundred again.

After she had not heard a sound for what seemed like an eternity, she let out a long, low breath and let body uncoil. She looked around at the empty desks and multiple darkened diagrams of bodies. They depicted various bodily systems, from a bare skeleton to a detailed illustration of an eye, for what she assumed were medical purposes. Aside from their unseeing looks, she was utterly alone in the empty room of the massive University.

CHAPTER TWENTY-THREE

RISK & REWARD

The barest hint of morning had peeked over the horizon when Juniper arrived at her family home. In her rush, she had not done her hair nor her makeup. She had crossed the city on foot and was sweating, making her thin dress cling to her in a way most unbecoming for a lady of her station. She did not care. She made her way inside the gates and flew through the estate to her parents suite in a matter of moments. She rapped on the door with her knuckles, the echoes of her knocks filling the silence of the sleeping house.

For a few moments, there was nothing. Then she heard the sound of shuffling footsteps and a lock sliding out from a bolt. The face of her father peered out of the gloom at her. Even now, moments after being woken in the middle of the night, he appeared alert, eyes bright, searching her face then scanning the hall. Cristos's face grew concerned when he saw the state of her.

"Juniper? What's going on, is everything alright?"

She shook her head. Something about the sight of her father broke the barrier which had erected itself when Kali had told her the terrible news. She felt hot tears well up in her eyes and the breath caught in her throat. Her father saw her expression and he pushed the door open, revealing the voluminous and ornately decorated bedchamber her parents shared, and motioned for her to come in. She entered without a word, letting her father close the door behind her.

As she sat in her parents small private den, on a low couch with them facing her, Juniper took a moment to compose herself. She closed her eyes and did the breathing exercises she had been instructed on since the day she had turned five years old, as instinctive now to her as eating or sleeping. Her parents gave her the grace she needed, not interrupting. After a few moments, she finally reopened her eyes, seeing the concerned looks of her parents as they sat across from her, holding hands and murmuring to each other in low voices. She searched for the words before finally forcing them out all at once.

"Kali has been promised."

She did not know how long it took her to tell her parents everything, but once she had started, it spilled out quickly. Her thoughts ran over each other as she scrambled to explain the issue. She spoke about their time at the Conservatory, how they had become close and how they had relied on each other during the hardest days of their respective programs. She told them how that friendship had blossomed into something they had not expected, but once it was there neither could ignore it. She told them how their relationship had grown over the years and explained how now Kali was on the verge of being ripped away.

When she was done, there was a long silence. Juniper suddenly felt very unsure of herself. The situation with her and Kali had never been directly addressed between her and her family. She found she had a hard time meeting her parents eyes. Juniper wanted to look up, to stare defiantly at those judgmental glares, but found it more difficult than she would have believed. When she heard her father finally speak, the softness in his voice was surprising.

"Juniper, we know you and Kali have been...close, since your time as students," his words were slow and deliberate, "and I'm sure you are especially distraught to have this happening now, at such a chaotic time."

Juniper blinked, "You...knew?"

"June," Aria cut in, voice mirroring her father's, low and soothing, "you and Kali have spent all your free time together since you were at the Conservatory. You both shunned any suitors who attempted to court you. Besides, people in our circles talk and I am a Dean. It was not the secret you think it was."

Juniper was still processing this, trying to calm the swarming storm of thoughts in her mind, when her mother spoke up again.

"That said, I must ask, what would you have us do?"

She took a breath and gathered her thoughts, "I...was hoping you could speak with Kali's father. He is forcing this union to pay off his familial debts. If you could get him to put it off until after the plan is complete, when the Emperor has fallen..."

Her mother cut in, voice taking on a slightly harder edge, "June...if we intercede on this, the lord your friend is promised to will want an explanation. He will not simply accept a canceled union with a powerful family. It will draw attention to Kali and the rest of the Rhee House. The position our plans are in is already precarious. We simply cannot afford any unnecessary risks."

"*Unnecessary...*" Juniper could hardly comprehend what she was hearing. She spoke through gritted teeth, "But, what about everything I've done? The risks I've taken..."

"Juniper, you've done quite well," her mother spoke with a maddening sense of calm, sounding just like she did speaking to one of her students, "but we are all simply pieces of the greater plan, and you know what's at stake here. You know the consequences if we are found out. No one person's needs or agenda can be allowed to overshadow the greater goal, as we had to explain to the Dean yesterday."

Her thoughts raced through her head, every attempt at keeping herself in control lost to the flood of righteous fury that was roiling up from the pits of her stomach. She was nearly ready to slap the self satisfied look off her mother's face when her father cut in again.

"Juniper," he was still sympathetic, voice calm and understanding, "it's more than just the plan. Your mother and I have known many people who have enjoyed similar *persuasions* as you and continue to do so. Many of my colleagues in the Courts and several of your mothers at the University. We bear no animosity towards you for your personal choices. But, as everyone knows, at some point, we must put our personal desires aside in order to do what is best for your House."

She looked at him, eyes narrowing. She was shocked to see a sort of pity on his face. The old statesman's eyes were full of resigned concern which for some reason unsettled her more than if they had been full of rage. She looked from one to the other, her voice creeping louder against her own desire, "What do you mean?"

"June," her father spoke slowly, softly, obviously taking great care with his words, "at your age, you must know that most unions are born out of obligation, to further the standing of one's House. Love is for children. True unions are born of cooperation and grow with time. Your mother and I hardly knew each other when we were wedded, but here we are now, three decades later, with our lives built and you, our wonderful daughter, here before us. We have supported each other, been partners through all our pains and successes. What you and Kali have, it's just a fleeting passion, a flash in the hearth. Your mother and I chose to give you your space, and we had hoped that you would come to accept your responsibilities on your own, without being pushed into a union as your friend has been. I know this is difficult for you now, but you must trust us. In time you will see this is for the best. "

"So you would have me abandon Kali?!" She was near yelling at this point. She could not help herself as she dug her nails into her palms.

He sighed heavily, "You are not abandoning her, June. She is performing her duty to her nation and her family, as we all must. It is a far greater purpose than the whims of any one person, especially now, with such adversity facing us all."

Juniper could feel the tears begin to well up in her eyes, despair building in her chest at the sudden realization of her position, "I thought we were trying to change the Empire? Why are we even doing all of this?"

"To depose a tyrant." Aria's voice was flat and she stared hard at her daughter, "To get revenge for your brother."

Juniper found herself unable to speak. She looked from her mother to her father, seeking some refuge from this new, inhospitable reality she found herself in and finding none. She was both furious and heartbroken. She had held so much hope inside of her, like a burning core that kept her warm in the coldest depths of her desperation and helped her see a destination in the darkness. But now it had been extinguished, in a matter of minutes, and by those she thought would understand.

She swallowed a hard lump down her throat and reflexively forced herself to take steadying breaths. The tears dried up in her eyes as she reforged the steel foundation of her will again. She forced herself to adopt a neutral expression, looking at her parents and gritting out the words she knew they wanted to hear.

"Yes...yes, of course you're right. I suppose I should have accepted that far sooner than now. I think with everything that's happening so fast, the plan, all the problems, I just...didn't want to face it."

"We understand." Her mother said immediately. She reached out and took Juniper's hand in her own, "This has been so difficult for everyone. But we *will* figure it out. We will be free of the Emperor and his tyranny soon, and your brother will be able to rest in peace."

Juniper forced a slight smile onto her face and hurriedly excused herself from their chamber. She did not go to her quarters. Her mind was reeling from the meeting and she felt like the walls of the estate she had once found so comforting were crowding around her, like the labyrinth under the Emperor's palace. The sense of constant pressure she always felt on her increased tenfold, coiling her gut into a knotted mass. She needed to find a way out. She practically fled her parents estate. Dawn had broken and the spindly clouds floating off the ocean were painted with an array of oranges and yellows that seemed to mock her dark mood with their brilliance.

She wandered the upper terraces of Khanar, aimless as she considered her options. The beginnings of a plan began to take root in the recesses of her mind. She found herself back at the Rhee estate before long. Kali was in a casual house dress, seated alone at a small table in the courtyard, an untouched breakfast before her. She wore a worried concoction of deep frown lines and dark circles under the eyes. She still had wet lines from where tears had run down her cheeks. Juniper walked over to Kali, wordlessly wrapping her arms around her as she stood to greet her, pulling her into a tight embrace. After a long moment of enjoying the scent of the rose scented oils she used in her hair, Juniper pulled back and looked her in the eyes.

"I'm not going to lose you, Kali. We can't rely on anyone else anymore. I think it's time you and I start working on our own plans. Don't you?"

Kali's eyes grew wide. Her mouth hung open for a moment before she finally found the steel inside her and nodded. When she spoke, her words were set with old iron Juniper had always found so endearing, "What are we going to do?"

"Well, I figure, if they can work out deals with our allies, why can't we? All we need is to carve out our own little slice of the cake."

That evening, Juniper left Kali's home and made her way through the streets of the upper city just as the sun was beginning to dip behind the mountains in the west. She followed the route to the Conservatory quickly, the steps familiar from the years of finding her way to Kali's home so many times before. The rising sun was glinting brilliantly off the domes, nearly blinding as she approached. There were a few small groups of students still about this late, clustered in nooks and claiming tables to study at. A few servants were making their rounds, preparing the classrooms and workrooms for the next day's activities.

No one she recognized saw her as she wound her way down into the bowels of the University. She followed the same path she had only the day before, deep into the heart of the mountain. She felt the heat building as she approached the massive double doors of solid iron, rapping the knocker against the metal with a resounding clanging. The wait seemed like an eternity and she found herself rubbing her arms despite the heat emanating from within. Suddenly, the door was flung open and she was met with the bespectacled face of Jiro, Dean of the Artificing, staring at her with a hard set jaw.

"Juniper? What are *you* doing here?" He asked flatly, neither angry nor afraid.

"I need your help." She replied, in the most forthright tone she could muster.

The man snorted and began to close the door. She caught it with her foot, which pinched into the soft leather of her shoe painfully, holding his gaze with imploring eyes, "Please, Jiro, there's no one else I can ask. I *need* you."

He stared at her, artificially magnified eyes squinting as he assessed her from behind his large spectacles. She could practically hear the gears and pistons clacking away in his head. Finally, he made a motion and allowed her to follow him inside. The workshop was silent and still. Half finished projects littered the tables and floors, left in pieces which she could only guess at the final product of. It was a far cry from the frenetic pace of the place she had visited so recently. Only the forges were still active, glowing faintly and emitting constant heat from the magma from deep below.

She followed the old man into his office once again, taking the same seats they had previously. This time, there were no pleasantries, no banter from long time friends. Jiro sat with his arms crossed and stared at her with flinty eyes that held no compassion, only a sort of grim curiosity, and said nothing. Juniper took a long, slow breath and spoke in deliberate, careful tones.

"Jiro, what happened the other night...that wasn't my idea."

"No, I don't suppose it was." His expression did not change, but remained impassive.

"For what it's worth, I'm sorry."

He spit a bit of phlegm onto the floor and maintained his stony silence. She got the message.

"Look," she breathed finally, dropping all pretext of apology, "I need to know, what are the details of this deal you've all worked out with the mercenaries and the Blades? How are you going to split up the New World when this is all over?"

Jiro gave her an odd look. This was not at all what he had expected and it was written all over his face, "Your parents haven't told you?"

"They've told me the basics. I know the Ceaseless Scions came up with the plan, my mother's agents stole the secrets of Harnessing from the Winter Palace. That we reached out to those in the Federation first, and that they're providing us with much of the money and resources we needed to pay the mercenaries and set all this up. What I don't know, what they never told me, is what was promised. What the Federation is getting for their part in all this, what the mercenaries are promised. Most importantly, what are we going to be left with?"

Jiro leaned forward, baring his golden teeth at her, "Upset you're being left out of the grownups plans?"

Juniper sighed, letting her shoulders droop, "No. I don't care about the plans. I've only gone along this far because of my parents. When my brother died in the rebellion, I was only a child. The truth is, I barely even remember him. I know him and the others, like your son and Lysler's daughter, all died trying to liberate the colonies from the Emperor. I know the Emperor has done terrible things, committed crimes against his own people. But the truth is, I was only involved because I knew it was what they wanted from me. But that's not enough anymore."

Again, a ripple of surprise spread across Jiro's face. He stared hard at her.

"Somewhere deep down, I thought, foolishly, I suppose, that if this revolution succeeded, if the Emperor fell, that things would change. But I know now that I was wrong. There won't be a place for...someone like me here, even after he's gone."

She watched as he tried to work through her words. The raw contempt had been replaced by some of the usual mischievous curiosity. He was considering her, the mind clearly whirring away under the soot and grime.

"Ah, this is about...you and Kali, then?"

Juniper blinked at him and, for the first time since their previous, nightmarish encounter, she saw some of the familiar warmth return to his gaze. It reminded her of the way he used to look when he watched her play with the little toys he made for her as a child.

"You two were, let's say, not as discreet as you may have believed when you were students here." He smiled, "I think anyone with eyes could see what was between you two."

Juniper sat rigid for a moment, her mind racing at the thought of other members of the Conservatory, her colleagues and superiors, knowing about her and Kali. But then she reasoned that it was of little consequence at this point, "Yes, we need to find a place to go, once this is over. Somewhere we can be together, somewhere outside the Empire. We've already discussed our situation. If we run now, we'll be running forever.

We're too valuable, the Imperial agents will chase us until the day we die rather than risk us serving another nation. So we can't run away, not now, not when we're so close. But...we need a contingency plan. We need to know where we're going to end up when all this is over. Because we can't stay here. That I know for certain."

The short man leaned back in his chair. He rubbed his hands together and pushed his spectacles up with the back of a knuckle. He coughed awkwardly and seemed to have a hard time finding the words. The arcanist strummed his fingers on the table, "Have you talked to your parents?"

Juniper gave him a look. He held up his hands defensively, "I was a parent once. You might be surprised what they'd be willing to accept from their own child. How much leniency you might actually have."

She shook her head firmly, "They're not going to help us."

Jiro sighed, "Well, regardless, you need to understand, the contracts we have with all those mercenaries, and the agreements we have with the Federation, they're not ironclad. They are ever evolving with the times."

Juniper put her elbows on the table and her head in her upturned hands, staring at him. Jiro sighed again.

"Alright, I'll do my best to explain...the agreements have several contingencies, depending on how things work out. Both our friends in the Federation and the various mercenary groups we hired have agreed to help us eliminate the Emperor. The mercenaries are simply our muscle, they are helping to keep things in the colonies under control so that there isn't a full blown revolt before we've gotten our shot, and they are collecting the necessary resources for our plan to work effectively. Our partners in the Federation are providing them cover, allowing them to operate as they need to on the mainland, and helping us fund this whole operation. Until the Emperor dies, that is roughly the extent of both entities involvement in our plans."

"I more or less knew all of that." Juniper said shortly, "What are they *getting* for their part in the operation?"

"Patience." Jiro commanded as though she were an unruly student. Juniper rolled her eyes but stopped speaking, "Once the tyrant is dead, the Empire will be in chaos. The Emperor has no legitimate children, no declared heir, and there will be a power gap. We, that is, the Scions, will take advantage of that opportunity to demand an abolishment of the monarchy and establish a republic, a change which is sorely overdue in this nation. Meanwhile, our colleagues in the New World will use this as an opportunity to unify the colonies."

"Won't that be incredibly difficult? The Emperor has been trying to quell the rebellions for over twenty years."

"He had been his own worst enemy in that endeavor. His tactics are inhumane. His own people despise him. They will gladly accept a change of regime. Besides, if there is resistance, we will still have the mercenaries, as well as the full strength of the Federation. Our southern neighbors have been looking for a way to retake their position in the New World ever since its own colonies declared independence. All they need is a foothold, ports to dock in, a way to maintain supply lines for their campaign. Our allies have assured us that if we can provide them with that, they can guarantee us the support of their standing Legions."

Juniper cocked her head, "So, that's what the Federation is getting out of all this. But what are the mercenaries getting out of all this, just money?"

"Ah, therein lies perhaps your fathers most impressive feat of political sorcery yet. We are paying them, of course, but it is a pittance compared to the scope of the task. Once the dust is settled and both nations are reclaimed, their reward will be freedom to stake claim to take any new lands West of our settlements. The mercenaries are to be raised to freehold barons of any lands they acquire for us. It is a stroke of genius, is it not? These mercenaries will grow our own nations for us!"

Jiro's amusement was lost on Juniper, who sat dumbfounded. She had known whatever devil's deal her parents had made to make their dream of revolution a reality was surely to be awful. But she had never suspected this.

"You...your plan is to retake the colonies, only to commit them to more conflict? That's the whole reason they're revolting in the first place! The colonies are tired of the Emperor forcing them into conflict after conflict, and you're going to drag them into open war against the Free Cities and then, after all that, an extended campaign against the native's?"

The amusement fell from his face as he recognized her reticence. He held out his hands in a helpless gesture, "Juniper, the colonies are already in conflict. Almost half of the border towns are in open revolt against the Empire, and they are all fighting off the native's on a daily basis. If not this, their only fate is to continue to suffer. At least our plan will offer a resolution. If something doesn't change soon, the Emperor will sail the rest of his army to the New World and attempt to personally quell the rebellions again...and we all know how that will end."

Juniper sat in silence for a long moment. The stillness of the workshop outside of Jiro's office was eerie compared to the typical buzz of activity. She silently searched inside herself, trying to process what she had just learned.

"This whole plan is a gamble." She breathed finally, "A terrible, stupid gamble. A million things could go wrong."

"What is the alternative, Juniper?" Jiro's voice was soft but his tone firm, "We all live in a cage, a gilded one, but a cage nonetheless. You can't be with your love, just as I can't stop manufacturing weapons. Your mother will never be allowed to stop training his spies, outfitting his soldiers. Your father will never be able to practice true justice. We are all trapped by the will of the Emperor, and the only way out will have to be won in blood."

She took a breath and steeled herself. She knew he was right. There was no other way, "Alright, Jiro. If this plan succeeds, there will be big changes. The Free Cities...once they are under Federation control again, they'll be safe, free from Imperial Law. Your partners are going to have some influence there, yes?"

"I would imagine so."

"Can you strike a deal with them? They'll be redistributing everything once the Cities are retaken, surely. There will be lots of lands and titles up for grabs. Surely they can find a place for us? Somewhere we'll be safe."

"Seems awfully risky. Why not run to the Breach or Vinatieri?"

Juniper set her jaw, "Why should we run? Why should we run and hide like rats? After all we've done for the cause, why shouldn't we get a reward?"

Jiro inclined his head, "I see your point. I suppose I could speak with them. But why would I risk it? Where is my incentive?"

Juniper paused for a moment, considered, then leaned in and said in a low voice, "Jiro...you want your revenge, for the other night? Just imagine how much it would upset my mother if you help me."

The older man stared at her from behind his spectacles, artificially wide eyes watching her closely. Then he broke out into a wide grin, showing off the false teeth that glinted in the dim light. His gaze held something that might have been admiration.

"Clever." He rubbed his chin, thoughtfully, "You really have grown up haven't you? But I'm sure you understand, you are asking me to risk quite a bit, just for a bit of revenge. I will need more if I am to do what you ask."

Juniper hesitated. His tone implied this was a consideration he had since the moment she had shown up at his doorstep. The short man eyed her with an unnerving, analytical fascination. She recognized the clinical curiosity of a scientist and could not help but recall the animals he kept to test new prosthetic designs on.

"What do you want?"

His eyes gleamed with victory, "I want you to wield the machine."

"*Me?*" She asked incredulously, "Why me?"

Jiro sighed and again drummed his fingers on the table top, his face being overtaken by a wistful look, "When our little conclave first came up with this scheme, all those years ago, it was always assumed that your mother would wield the machine when I finished it. She is the most naturally powerful arcanist amongst our number, and she has the discipline to manage such a burden. She has shown a knack for it when we have tested the prototypes. But now...I cannot trust her."

The depth of sadness that filled his eyes surprised Juniper. He removed his glasses and rubbed at the bridge of his nose and she thought he suddenly looked like he had aged a few dozen years. His stooped posture seemed more pronounced, the lines on his face deeper than she had ever noticed before. When he looked back up at her, the desperation he had in his face was something horrible to witness.

"This machine...if it works, it will change the course of history, June. I *need* to know whoever I give it to will wield it for a righteous purpose. I cannot put that power into your mothers hands. Not anymore. If you don't do this for me, I will have no choice but to destroy the machine, damn the consequences, and all our plans will be for naught."

She stared at him, words caught in her throat. She fumbled as she tried to think of the right thing to say, stuttering like a child at her first lessons. Finally, she just nodded. Jiro grinned grimly.

"I'll see what I can do for you and Kali, June. But know this, this entire endeavor may yet fail. If this machine fails or if the Emperor catches wind of what we're doing..."

Juniper shook her head, "We'll make it work, we'll find a way. We have to."

O nce she left Jiro's workshop, she made her way back
up the twisting halls and passages, out of the mountain
and into the Conservatory proper. It was mid morning by that
point, and she found herself wandering the sunbathed halls
in a daze. She passed classrooms where professors lectured on
various subjects, groups of students and faculty who clustered
in groups and chatted without paying her any attention. She
found herself wondering if she had made the right decision.
What was going to happen if the plot did succeed? What would
happen if it did not?

She could not decide which would be worse. If they succeeded, she and Kali would be fugitives, never to return to the
Empire. The familiar halls of the Conservatory would be closed
to her forever. She would likely never see her parents again. But
if they failed, Kali would be gone. Spirited away to the estate
of some nobleman, never to be hers again. Not to mention the
issue that was her own fate. She closed her eyes at the thought.
It was too much to consider, too many possible problems.

She turned down a hallway and saw that there was a crowd
forming up ahead. Curious, Juniper made her way to where she
could see and noted they were all gathered around a classroom.
The students had all been put out and the only figures inside
were two cloaked figures, one in Alchemist's red and one in
Medicinist's white, the former flanked by a pair of armored men
wearing the black and yellow uniforms of standard city watch.
Juniper immediately recognized the figure in red, Lee Lysler,
who was standing with a handful of papers clutched in one
hand. He held them out accusingly.

"Admit it, Zane!" He proclaimed, his voice carrying across
the crowd like a professional playwright, "You are a conspirator!
A traitor! You've been helping the rebels this whole time!"

"I-I have no idea what you're talking about!" The other man,
a professor in the Hall of Medicinist's, looked around frantically. His eyes were bulging out of head as he tried desperately

to figure out his next move, "I've never seen those documents before!"

"Lies! They were found in *your* office, this is your signature, is it not?"

"I-I don't know how that got there, I d-don't know what's happening!" He looked manic, like a man on the verge of doing something very dangerous. His fingers twitched as he stepped back from the Dean of Alchemy and his accompanying guardsmen. One of the guards took a step forward, reaching a gauntleted hand out for the professor. He let out a yelp and threw up one of his hands, putting a hand on the man's unprotected face.

It took a second before anyone knew what was happening. The watchman yanked his head back in surprise, but when he did, not all of his skin came with it. A vaguely hand shaped patch of exposed muscle and tendons stood out sharply on the watchman's face. The professor held a thin sheet of pink flesh in his outstretched palm, removed through some ghastly trick of medical magic.

The watchman stared at the professor for a moment before seeming to recognize what had happened, then immediately dropped to his knees and began to wail as he clawed at the exposed part of his face. Zane shook the skin off his hand, eyes widening even further, growing impossibly large as he stared at the watchman, then at Dean Lysler, then at the crowd of onlookers.

"I-I...I didn't mean to..." he stammered, backing further away from them. His back was almost to the rear wall by that point. He pointed at Lysler and practically screamed, "Y-you! You're trying to frame me!"

The Dean rolled his eyes and reached into his pocket. He pulled out a small, glass vial filled with yellow liquid, popping off the top with one deft flick of his thumb, "Let us end this charade, shall we? If you won't come quietly I will have to make you come."

He swiftly swallowed the vial's contents in one, quick gulp and grimaced at the taste. Then he turned to face the other professor. Several things happened at once. Zane cried out and raised both his hands, charging wildly for the Dean of Alchemy. The Dean, meanwhile, began to move much more quickly than Juniper would have guessed would be possible for a man his age.

He ducked out of the way of the professor's hands with seeming ease, grabbing the professor by the shirt and hurling him into a nearby desk with bone crunching force. Zane landed in a heap, too stunned to do anything but moan as he rolled on the floor. The other watchman had not even had time to react, only pulling out his sword after the professor had landed on the ground.

Dean Lysler took several deep breaths in through his nose, as if he was trying to calm down. Sweat beaded on his forehead and his face was beat red. He reached into another pocket and pulled out a similar vial to the first, but this time the liquid was silvery. He made his way over to the professor, who lay cradling his arm and trying not to move. Another popped top and the liquid inside began to evaporate, leaving a wispy trail of silvery gas dissipating behind it. He forced under the other man's nose, holding it there until the liquid was gone. The professor's eyes rolled and he was unconscious before his head hit the ground.

"That's it then." Lysler said, matter-of-factly, "He'll be unconscious for the next twelve hours or so. I'll leave you to take him in, shouldn't be much of a problem for you now."

He cast an unsympathetic gaze on the watchman who still rolled on the ground holding his face, and he pointed towards the crowd, "You there, take him to the infirmary. I'm sure they can do...something for him there."

Two students rushed forward and helped the injured man to his feet. Then they awkwardly led him through the crowd, disappearing quickly down the hall. Lysler took one last look around the room and seemed to decide his work was done here.

He fixed his cloak and strode towards the exit. As he passed her, he gave Juniper a quick look over.

"Faye, if you would be so kind, please let your mother know our little issue has been resolved." With that, he broke from the crowd and strode off down the hall, leaving the students and faculty to stare at the wreckage he had left in his wake.

CHAPTER TWENTY-FOUR

CONSEQUENCES

E ven in the dead of night, the heat in the marshlands was oppressive. Cassius could barely keep the stinging sweat from his eyes as he cursed under his breath, struggling to keep quiet despite the effort. He had been blindly sawing at the binds behind his back for hours, rubbing the ropes against the rusty nail he had found sticking out of the floor of his cage, painstakingly cutting through one strand at a time. His wrists were raw from the effort and he could feel the warm trickle of blood running down his hands. Finally, after what he was sure was hours of work, he felt the last strands start to give and he yanked hard, ripping the ropes apart. He brought his hands around the front and saw the angry indentations in his skin, the bleeding abrasions from where the constant rubbing had done its damage.

He rubbed at his wrists for a moment, trying to bring some life back into them as he cast a glance around the storehouse. Unconscious figures were scattered around the space, some snoring or murmuring in their slumber. No one was paying the captives any attention. He crawled over to the side of his cage and hissed at Captain Sebastian through the bars as loudly as he dared. The Captain was dozing in a sitting position, head lolled against his chest. Eventually, Cassius was able to get his attention. The bearded man glanced around, eyes sharp despite being woken in the dead of night. He caught sight of the Prince and crawled over.

"Cassius?"

Cassius showed him his free hands and motioned for him to turn around. He was able to reach through the gates and untie the Captain quickly, as he did he relayed his plan in a hushed tone, keeping one eye on the figures outside their cages.

"I heard them talking earlier. Whoever they were waiting for is here now so they're going to be shipping out in the early morning. Wherever they're going, it sounds like it's a long journey. They're going to begin emptying the storehouse and making trips across the bay to a ship. If they're smart, they'll move us last, and hopefully most of the men will be out by the time they come for us. If we get everyone freed we can jump them when they open the doors. Then we can make a break for the boats. With any luck we can get across the bay and get the city watch to head them off before they're able to get away. Just wait for my signal."

The Captain looked apprehensive. He stared at the Prince, eyes narrowed in the gloom. His hoarse whisper carried an air of urgency in it, "Prince Cassius, are you sure about this? The bay is no small crossing and we are so few against so many. If we are caught..."

"I understand your hesitation Sebastian," Cassius whispered back, putting a steadying hand on the Captain's arm through the bars, "but we *need* to do this. Whatever these men are planning is a danger to the entire Federation. I know it. We cannot allow them to leave the Broken Coast."

The Captain eyed him for a moment, then nodded curtly, rubbing at his own wrists. He turned and crawled across the cage toward the far end, where Mateo was laying, passed out on his cot. Cassius watched as he roused the younger man and relayed the plan, freeing him in turn. The rest of the cages were too far for him to see in the darkness, but he saw Mateo crawl off and disappear across his cage once he was free.

Eventually, Mateo returned and nodded to his Captain, who turned and passed the nod to him. Cassius turned and crawled back over to his cot, hiding the town rope under his blanket. He sat with his back against the rear bars and put his hands behind his back, careful not to let it show that he was free. Then, he took a deep breath, settled in and waited.

T he mercenaries began to empty the storehouse before the first light of dawn. They worked efficiently, moving boxes and barrels out of the storehouse with surprising haste, leaving the building mostly empty within an hour. Eventually, Holton came to escort the witch and her coven out. As they were loading up their small bundles of possessions, Holton cast a glance at Cassius.

"Comfortable, my Lord?" He asked, his beard offset at an angle as he smirked at the nobleman.

"Where are you running to now, Hart? Further south?" Cassius called back, ignoring his jibe, "You know there's nowhere you can go that's far enough to escape the noose."

The red haired rogue snorted at that, "Oh, I don't know, I think you'll find you're very wrong about that, Prince."

With that, he turned and left the room, the witch and her three children in tow. A few moments later, a handful of men entered through the same door. They made a beeline straight for the cages. The man who had tricked Mateo the other night, Taron, they had called him, was in the lead. He still wore an obnoxious grin plastered across his face. He waved to the prisoners, making a point to give the young soldier a wink. The men began opening the cages, starting with the one closest to the door first.

The soldiers had all had the foresight to rewrap the ropes around their wrists, at least giving the initial impression they were still bound. As they were hauled to their feet, the mercenaries did not even bother to check the constraints. All the soldiers were led out and stood in a row one by one. Then, one of the men walked over and opened Cassius' cage, stalking over to the Prince and yanking him to his feet. A puzzled look came over his face when he felt the give in the Prince's arm as he pulled on it and he looked around his side to double check the bindings.

"*Now!*" Cassius roared and leapt on the man. He tackled the man into the cell bars, causing him to slam his head into the iron with a resounding thud. He heard the others make their moves, but he was too busy slamming the man's head into the bar a second, third and fourth time to see what had happened. Once the mercenary's limp body slid down to the ground, blood pouring from the wide gash he had opened in the back of his head, he looked up. Of the five mercenaries that had come to get them, only two remained standing.

Taron and a large man with tattoos down his arms were backing away from the prisoners, blades drawn. The rest lay in crumpled heaps on the ground. Lucia was cradling one of her arms, a jagged gash freely bleeding through her fingers, and Mateo sported a freshly bloodied nose, but otherwise the soldiers looked unharmed. They spread out in a semicircle, advancing on the two remaining mercenaries with grim expressions on their faces. Sebastian and Camila had taken weapons off the bodies of the fallen men, holding them before them with menace. Cassius yanked a knife off the belt of the man whose head he had just bashed in and joined his companions.

"Tell us where Holton's taking the witch." Cassius demanded in a low growl, "Then, maybe, we'll let you live."

Taron grinned back at him, even his sudden shift in fortune not able to strip the expression from his face. He cocked his head, "What a *generous* offer, my Lord. Allow me to make a counter..."

Suddenly, he reached over and shoved the tattooed mercenary forward with a hard shove, forcing him into clumsy combat with the five advancing prisoners. As Sebastian and his cadre cut the man down with relative ease, Taron turned and bolted for the door. Cassius took off after him, sprinting with every ounce of strength he had in his body. He pumped his arms and covered the ground to the door in a fraction of a moment, reaching the fleeing man just as he broke the threshold. He dove into the open air of the muggy, half darkened swamp, catching the mercenary in a full bodied tackle.

"*Holt!*" Taron was screaming as Cassius made contact, "The prisoners...*oof!*"

The two landed in a jumble on the boards of the deck. They both scrambled to get themselves into a better position. Cassius was partially on top of the other man, and managed to get his arms free and raise his knife up for a killing blow. But Taron had managed to hold on to his knife as well, and he was quicker than the Prince. He sliced out with the blade and carved a gash into his left arm. Cassius felt the instant searing pain as he cried out and his vision went white for a brief moment. But he kept his wits enough not to drop his own knife.

He used his bloodied arm to pin down Taron's knife hand and brought his own blade straight down into the mercenary's chest. It went through the man's leathers and shirt with little effort. Dark red blood bubbled through his clothes as the knife buried itself up to the hilt with a sickening squelch. Taron's eyes went wide and he tried to cough. It sounded wet and strained. He spat blood and tried to grasp at the blade with trembling hands. But Cassius yanked the knife out and stood, watching as life began to drain from the man's eyes, leaving him sputtering and shaking.

A terrible cry brought him back to reality. He had been so focused on stopping the fleeing mercenary, he had not even noticed his surroundings. He looked up and saw the platform was empty, except for the single boat that bobbed in the water just before him. For a brief moment, he was confused as to where the sound had come from, then he scanned the marsh beyond the dock and saw a shape quickly disappearing into the treeline. It was a small ship, with several figures clustered on it, floating down a channel.

He noticed a single, red haired figure standing on the stern of the boat, leaning out as far as he could, without falling into the swamp. Even in the dim light of the early morning, Cassius could see the figure staring at him from across the dark waters. He stared back, watching until the boat was hidden behind the trees and the low hanging fog, lost in the marsh.

Captain Sebastian and his soldiers joined him out on the dock in a few moments. They stared at the dead man at his feet, then quickly began making the last boat ready for travel. Cassius stopped them with a word.

"He saw me." The Prince said, "Hart, the leader. They know we've escaped. Once they gather more men, they'll be coming back for us."

The Captain looked over to him and cursed under his breath. He rubbed the back of his head and paced back and forth across the dock.

"There's nothing for it." He said finally, "If we wait here, they'll capture us again, or worse."

Cassius nodded in silent agreement. He motioned to the boat, "We have to try and make it back to the city. Does anyone know these swamps?"

Mateo raised his arm, "Aye, I was born to the Marshlanders."

"Can you find us a route around them?"

He gave it a moment's consideration, "It'll be tough. There's many of them, few of us. About even chances we're caught and killed, I'd say."

"That'll have to do." Cassius set his jaw and set about helping them load up the boat.

M inutes later they were shoving off from the hidden storehouse into the marsh. They used paddles and long

sticks to edge their way through the murky water, doing everything they could to stay silent and take advantage of the early
morning fog. They all crouched low, with Mateo at the prow,
his nose quickly swollen up from his injury, eyes squinted as he
tried to guide them through the swamp with hand signals and
sharp, hissed words. The songs of night bugs and frogs filled
the air, helping to mask the small plops as their paddles hit the
water.

They slid across the swamp at a snail's pace, breath caught
in their throats as they listened for any sound of discovery. In
their minds, every rustling bush was a cadre of mercenaries
descending on them from out of the fog and every stray branch
shaking was the whisper of a bowstring loosing an arrow into
their unprepared backs. Cassius found himself inadvertently
holding his breath multiple times, having to force himself to
stop as he tried desperately not to make a sound.

After what seemed like hours, the tree cover began to light-
en. They saw the sky begin to peer through the canopy as it
became less an impenetrable blanket and more a smattering of
leafy clouds above them. The smell of salt air became more
pronounced and Cassius thought he could hear the rhythmic
sound of waves breaking gently on the shore. They kept paddling and pushing their way through the fog, a mad hope rising
in their chests. Then, suddenly, the sound of a voice froze their
hopes like a cold front moving in on an unsuspecting valley.

"Search everywhere!" A harsh command, cried across the
open water, sounded as if it was coming from eerily close, "Do
not let them across the bay!"

They all froze in position as the muddled glow of torchlight
rolled through the fog not forty paces before them. They had
no light on their boat, so the fog and underbrush of the marsh
kept them hidden as a boat slid noiselessly across the open water ahead of them. They could just make out the outlines of
figures moving back and forth, conversing in low tones as they
peered out into the darkness. For several long, heart stopping

moments, the boat remained in front of them, its slow, monotonous pace keeping it in position to see them for painfully long. Finally, the light mercifully moved beyond their vision, far to their left, and they all let out a collective sigh. Camila looked from Mateo over to the Captain.

"Are we good to be moving on?" She whispered.

But a sound brought all their heads snapping back around. A second cluster of bobbing torchlight was passing into their field of vision. It followed the same trajectory as the first, strafing silently across the bay in a slow, deliberate fashion. They all watched it, silent and staring as they held their breath and waited for it to move beyond their range of vision. But suddenly, it stopped and turned back the way it had come, doubling the time they had to sit in utter silence. Once it was beyond their vision, the first light became visible again on their left, bobbing into view.

Captain Sebastian cursed under his breath, "Damn these mercenaries, they're keeping too tight of a patrol on the shoreline. Even if we get past them, the chances they won't see us once we're in the open water are close to none."

"Can't we wait them out?" Lucia asked, her voice low and urgent as she cradled her now roughly bandaged arm, "They'll need to catch the tide if they want out of the Bay in any reasonable amount of time."

The Captain shook his head fervently, pointing up toward the sky. It was beginning to lighten up, the sun peaking ever so slightly out of the horizon, "The sun will be up in a matter of minutes, it'll burn away the fog and the light will surely let them see us with ease. Even if we retreat into the swamp further, they're likely only waiting for the light to begin their push inwards to root us out."

"What if we retreat?" Mateo asked. He pointed back the way they had come, "I can get us upriver. Maybe they'll give up if they can't find us in time."

The Captain gave Cassius an inquiring look, but the Prince shook his head, "No, we know too much now, if they leave us alive it'll ruin their whole operation here. They won't leave until they've run us down. Even if that means delaying their departure."

The soldiers all looked at him with grim expressions, but their faces were resolved, the truth of what he said settling in like a lead weight. For a moment, they all sat in silence and watched the torchlight float through the fog ahead of them, the hushed, urgent voices of men hunting their prey carrying across the water to them. Finally, it was Mateo who broke the silence.

"I can lead them away."

"What?" Lucia and Camila gave each other an incredulous look. Cassius only stared at the young man.

Captain Sebastian set his jaw and shook his head, "No, I forbid it."

Mateo turned a piercing look on each of them in turn, "What's your plan then?"

An uncomfortable silence fell over the group as they all failed to meet each other's eyes. Mateo's gaze fell on the Prince until he met the young soldier's eyes, "You said these people, whatever they're planning, it's dangerous to the whole Federation, right?"

Cassius nodded, managing to croak a response, "I believe so."

"Then that's it then." He went up on his knees suddenly and began unstrapping his cloak and removing his heavy boots, "I'm the only one who knows anything about the swamps, I'm the only one who has any chance of leading them away and not getting snagged up faster than a minnow in a snake hole."

He stripped down until all he wore was his pants, which he rolled high, and a length of rope which he wound across his chest. He looked out over the dark water and took a long, low breath. The Captain got up to his knees quickly and put his hands on the young man's shoulders.

"It's been an honor to be your commanding officer, Mateo Rueza. May the Lady of the Deeps grant you passage through her waters." The look in his eyes was some unknowable mixture of pride and anguish that hurt Cassius to bear witness to.

The young man nodded to the two women, both of whom looked like they might be close to tears themselves. Finally, he gave the Prince a final look. The young man nodded solemnly to him and Cassius could do nothing but nod back, feeling a swell of pride for the soldier in his chest. Then, without further hesitation, Mateo slid from the boat's side and sank into the murky water with a soft plop. They watched as he swam silently into the forest, taking long, slow strokes with his arms and legs underwater like a frog, until he was swallowed up by the darkness. Then he was gone. In the silence that followed, they waited and watched.

The sun rose steadily. The fog began to burn off as it became brighter and brighter in the swamp. Cassius and the others cast nervous glances towards the torchlight of the roving patrols, which were rapidly becoming unnecessary. The Prince was beginning to wonder if the young soldier might have met some misfortune, one of the giant swamp lizards or massive lurking snakes perhaps, when suddenly, a noise rang out, far to their right.

At their distance, they could tell it was shouting, but it was indistinct and they could not make out any noises. But the commotion had its intended effect. The bobbing glows of torchlight began to move up the coastline towards the sound, abandoning their tight patrol lines. The Captain gave them all a curt nod and they all bent their paddles to row feverishly towards the bay.

As they broke the tree line and felt the first waves break on the bow of their boat, they cast their glances towards the right. A small cluster of the torchlights bobbed up and down far down the shoreline, flanking a much larger glow. From their position, it looked like an entire boat had gone up in flames. Cassius had no idea how the young soldier had managed it, but he was grateful for the distraction. They paddled away from the shoreline and the sun climbed higher in the sky, the last tendrils of fog dissipated. The small river boats had no sails, so they paddled hard, knowing that without the dark or the cover of the fog and tree line, it was only a matter of time before they were spotted.

It was not long before they were all sweating, chest heaving as the rhythmic paddling began to take its toll. Cassius felt his hands begin to ache. His palms were raw and tearing, the salt air doing nothing to help soften the rough wood as it ate into his skin. He felt like his lungs were on fire and every muscle in his body began to ache from the exertion. He cast a glance around, checking on his companions. All of them looked as bad as he felt, sweat pouring off of them as they fought to keep their paddles moving. They were all weakened from their days of imprisonment and it was showing starkly on all their faces. He bent his head and worked his arms harder, ignoring the screaming protests of his muscles.

"They've spotted us." Captain Sebastian's voice cut through his exhaustion induced stupor. He glanced back and saw a trail of small ships following them, the closest about two hundred paces back.

Cassius cursed under his breath and began paddling harder. They worked furiously as they all cast glances back at their pursuers, trying hard to focus on the task at hand. He did not know if it was an hour or ten minutes before the closest of the ships got within range of theirs. Both shores of the bay, the green of the marshlands behind them and the colorful cityscape of the peninsula in front, looked about equal distance.

But as the first of the arrows rained down and embedded itself in their aft, Sebastian announced they needed to take cover. The women tried to protest, but the Captain simply stated the obvious; the ship was going to catch them before they reached the shores of Crescent City, and if they were shot through with arrows before they reached the shore, they would do no good to anyone. They resigned themselves to their position without enthusiasm, dropping their oars. They had no bows or cannons to return fire with, so the Captain ordered them all to arm themselves and take cover, waiting until the ship got within boarding range to strike back. They listened to arrows thudding into the deck as they hid in the under cabin or below the wooden awning, doing their best not to flinch when one sailed particularly close.

Eventually, they heard screams and defiant cries which signaled the boat was close enough for a boarding party. Footsteps sounded on the deck and Sebastian gave the signal for a counter attack. Cassius broke from under the awning to see a few men armed with curved swords and hatchets had leapt over to their boat from the small pursuit vessel that had sidled up beside them. He let out a roar and hurled his paddle like a javelin at the closest man. It rocketed through the air and crashed into the large man's barrel chest, knocking him off the deck with an unceremonious yelp of surprise followed by a splash.

His only other weapon was the knife he had used to kill the grinning mercenary earlier, so he leapt at the closest of the remaining mercenaries, eager to close the distance before they were ready. However, the man was quick and he managed to raise his sword in a defensive arc and fend off the Prince's initial attack, metal crashing off metal with a loud clanging sound. Around him, the others had advanced on the boarding party. Camila wielded her paddle like a staff, taking quick swipes with both ends at a man armed with a hatchet, keeping him at distance. Lucia, arm still injured, held a knife in her good hand and was dancing back and forth, with the last of the mercenaries.

Captain Sebastian stepped forward with his paddle and swung it in an overhead arc, crying out as he brought it down on the head of Lucia's opponent. It broke the oar in half, but the man collapsed into a twitching mound on the deck. Immediately, he stepped forward and swung the broken half of the oar at the mercenary Cassius was engaged with. The man deftly stepped to the side, but it gave the Prince ample opportunity to duck down and take a low swipe at his body. He heard the satisfying cry of pain as a crimson spray stained the deck. The man stumbled backward, casting a glance back toward the boat he had come from.

But that momentary lack of focus gave Cassius time to step forward and drive his heel into the man's gut, sending him tumbling backwards over the side and into the water. He looked over in time to see Camila crack the final assailant across the face with the blade of her paddle, sending him to the deck with a sort of dead weight that made Cassius doubt if he would ever get up again. When he looked back the Captain and Lucia were already across the narrow ravine between the two boats and advancing on the single remaining mercenary who had been left to keep the pursuit boat steady.

They made quick work of him, with Sebastian driving the broken shard of his paddle through the man's guts and Lucia kicking off into the bay. Cassius and Camila joined them. Captain Sebastian was sporting a new wound across his forearm, but other than that, they had managed the first boat full of mercenaries without issue. Cassius said a quick prayer of thanks under his breath and looked pointedly back towards the rest of the advancing ships. The closest one was perhaps fifty paces out and closing fast.

"We have no time, Captain," he said breathlessly, "do we run, or fight?"

Sebastian cast a glance backwards. He took a deep breath and gave Cassius a hard look, "Running will not avail us any longer. We fight."

Cassius nodded and quickly salvaged a bow and some arrows from the deck. He began sending arrow after arrow at the oncoming boat, with Camila joined him with another bow and they bombarded the ship. She gave him a vicious smile over her shoulder, but despite their combined efforts, the ship was upon them in moments. Cassius watched as it suddenly turned, the broadside facing them all at once, and a half dozen men popped up, each wielding a heavy crossbow.

"Down!" He screamed and flattened himself against the deck with his hands over his head. A breath later the harsh thud of crossbow bolts splintering wood deadened all other sound around him. It was over in a second and he looked up, ready to return fire. But then he saw Camila, laying on the deck with the rigid shape of an arrow sprouting from her abdomen. He crawled over and put a hand on her arm, she looked at him, pain and confusion clouding her face before looking back down, wide eyed at the bolt. She whimpered and let out a sob before a sudden cry brought Cassius back to his senses.

He looked up just in time to see a heavyset, mountain of a man bringing a club down towards his head. He rolled across the deck to get out of the way, the swaying of the boat disorienting him as he tried to leap to his feet. Luckily the big man seemed thrown off as well. He swayed unsteadily as he tried to heft his club for a second swing. Cassius managed to get his wits about him enough to realize he still had the knife in his belt, so he yanked it out and hurled it at the man.

It hit with the hilt first and bounced off the man's forehead with a loud thud. It was not the intended outcome, but it confused him long enough. Cassius leapt at the mercenary, but despite hitting him with all his weight, the large man did not fall. Rather he dropped his club and grabbed the Prince with both arms around the back and squeezed with all his might, lifting him off the ground. Cassius gasped as he felt his ribs crackle and something pop under the pressure. He struggled against the bear hug, but it was no use. The big man only closed his vice like arms tighter and tighter until Cassius thought his chest was going to cave in.

In a last, desperate ploy as he saw spots appearing in his vision, the Prince pulled his head back as far as he could and drove his forehead into the big man's nose as hard as he could. He was rewarded with the sound of a sickening crunch. The big man let out a yelp of pain but did not let go. He snarled and squeezed the Prince tighter than he thought possible. Cassius let out his own cry as he felt something shift out of place in his back and brought his head back again. He whipped it forward into the big man's nose for a second time, earning another scream of pain. This time, the big man let go, hands instinctively flying to his face. Cassius dropped to the deck in a heap, gasping for breath, and watched as the heavyset mercenary stumbled backwards, hands grasped around his freely bleeding nose, cursing as tears of pain streamed down his cheeks.

Cassius wasted no time as he scrambled to his knees, ignoring the pain that seared through his whole body, and charged the big man. With one swift motion, he swooped down, grabbed the knife and drove it into the man's chest. The big man's eyes went wide as he stumbled backwards with a gasp and tumbled off the side of the ship. The Prince immediately turned to check on the rest of his companions. Captain Sebastian stood with a spear he had acquired somewhere, fending off two men with fluid graceful arcs. Lucia was standing near the aft of the ship, a sword in her good hand as she fended off two more men on her own with short, stabbing flurries. As he heard the large man hit the water, Cassius flew across the deck.

He ran for Lucia, bending to grab the big man's dropped club mid sprint. He lifted the massive weapon overhead and brought it down on the back of the first mercenary, feeling a crack as he dropped the man with a single blow. Lucia took advantage of the momentary distraction and stepped forward, slicing the second man across the chest. He screamed but then she ran the blade through his throat, silencing him before he fell beside his comrade. The two exchanged a brief glance, before rushing to aid the Captain. They engaged the remaining mercenaries in combat, turning the odds. Cassius felled his opponent, shattering his face with a massive blow from the club, just as Sebastian ran the last man through with his spear. Lucia turned to Cassius, a word half formed on her lips, when a deafening boom echoed out across the bay.

The roar of fire filled the air. There was a flash and Cassius instantly dropped down to the deck once again, a sudden wave of flames roiling over him. Only his quick reflexes had saved him. He felt the heat singe the back of his neck and the exposed flesh of his arms, then it was over as quickly as it had begun. He blinked, vision hazy from the burst of bright light. Then he smelled the scent of burning flesh and saw a shape writhing on the deck before him.

It was Lucia, a massive, blackened wound on her chest with tendrils of smoke rising from it. Her lips were curled back in agony as she screamed in pain. He looked back and saw a third boat had come upon them in the confusion, with several figures on deck ready to board their vessel. One, a young Northman with a scar on his cheek, held an outstretched hand which still hissed with flickering tongues of fire. The fresh wave of mercenaries poured onto their vessel and beside him, Sebastian raised his spear to begin fending off the first of the new wave of attackers.

Cassius brought his club up to defend himself when he saw the tall, tattooed form of the Red Wolf leap from the prow of the encroaching vessel, a hatchet in one hand and a long knife in the other. He was across the boat instantly, bringing his hatchet down at the Prince's head. Cassius raised the club to defend himself, but Holton struck out with the blade in the same movement. The Prince tried to shift his body out of the way, but the thief caught him on the side and he felt the immediate searing pain as it opened a fresh wound.

He cursed and brought the club down in a swift counter. But Holton was so fast, spinning to the side and immediately unleashing a flurry of strikes with both weapons. Cassius was caught off guard by the ferocity of the assault, barely managing to avoid the sharp ends as they tore at him. He was breathing heavily, exhaustion and waves of pain starting to take their toll. There was a cold rage in the thief's eyes, his teeth set in a snarl as he struck out again and again.

Then the ship lurched and Cassius miss stepped, letting Holton catch him with a wicked slice across his upper thigh. The Prince cried out in pain and swung the club in an upward arc, wildly trying to drive the Northman away from him. But the swing was too slow and put him in a poor position. Holton danced out of the way, his maneuver leaving him next to the Prince's exposed flank.

In one motion, the thief drove the knife into his leg all the way to this hilt. A flash of white hot pain ripped through Cassius and his vision blurred. He dropped the club and fell to his hands and knees immediately, crying out in agony. He fought to stay conscious as pain overtook every faculty, overwhelming his senses. He tried to turn around but felt fingers grasp his hair from behind and pull his head back. He felt Holton face come in close beside him, hoarse voice barely a whisper as he spoke into his ear.

"I *told* you there would be consequences if you gave me problems."

A moment later a figure was dragged into his field of vision and put on its knees. Captain Sebastian, bloodied, bruised, one arm badly deformed, stared back at him. He appeared to be barely staving off the black embrace of unconsciousness. The Captain tried to speak, but his voice came out in a bubbling gurgle.

"Don't..." Cassius cried out. But it was too late.

An Oaren man with a thin mustache dragged a knife across Sebastian's throat. A flood of crimson streamed forth and flowed down his neck and chest, soaking the Captain's clothes and pooling on the deck. Cassius tried to cry out but he was shoved down hard, knocking the wind out of him. He felt a weight on his back and knew the Red Wolf was still on top of him. He heard the thief's voice growling in his ear once again.

"They say I can't kill you," the man spat, his tone full of cold fury that sent a chill through the Prince's spine, "but I can't let what you did to my man go unpunished..."

Suddenly, he felt his left arm grasped and yanked to the side. From his view, face flat on wood, he could see a hand grasp his wrist and force it flat on the deck. Then the hatchet came down. At first, he did not register what had happened. The dull thud rang out amongst the chaotic sounds and shouts of the men around him. He was still in shock at seeing his comrades fall, his plan gone to ruin.

Then, once the hands holding his arm down let go, he saw the bloody stump and everything came rushing in at once. His eyes widened and he felt the bile rise in his chest. He screamed as he never had before as they lifted him off the deck and tied a burlap sack over his head, plunging him into darkness.

Chapter Twenty-Five

The Conspiracy

J ayce shook awake with a jolt. He was disoriented and could not remember where he was or how he had gotten there. His head was throbbing. Waves of nausea washed over him as he tried to get his vision to adjust to his new surroundings. The room was nearly pitch black, with the exception of a small glow from a single witchlight embedded in the ceiling above him. He tried to turn his head and suddenly realized he was locked in place, strapped to some sort of chair. He shook and yanked at his bindings until his wrists and ankles ached. There was no give at all. His eyes darted around the dark room, desperate to find some sort of answers. All he could see was plain stone walls, with no windows and no doors.

It was cool and musty, which was unusual since it was the height of summer. He could smell stagnant water. In his panicky reasoning, he worked out he must be underground, most likely somewhere in the basements or subbasements of the University. Then things began to come back to him. Lyra was in trouble. He tried to reach out and grasp at the tendrils of energy in the air around him, desperately hoping he could figure out something to do with them. But a sudden shock of pain seared through the back of his mind and broke his focus. He yelped in pain. The lingering ache in his head was like he had been whacked with something heavy and hard, causing his vision to blur and fresh waves of nausea to flow over him.

"Ah, you're awake." A familiar voice came from somewhere behind him. He glanced around as much as his restraints would allow him to, finally seeing a figure stroll into his vision, pushing a small cart. It was Allegheny. He had discarded his usual coat and wore only an under tunic and pants. Jayce saw with some satisfaction he was sporting a bandage on his shoulder and another on the side of his face.

"Looks like you had an accident?" He asked, working as much spite as he could muster into his voice.

The arcanist shot him a look of annoyance before recovering his composure. He grinned with utter contempt at his prisoner, "Oh, don't worry. I'll be sure to take my recompense in kind once your friend gets here."

So they had not caught her yet. Jayce breathed a sigh of relief. He watched as Allegheny came to a stop in front of him, rubbing the bandaged side of his face. The cart sat ominously at his side as they stood in silence for a moment, staring at each other.

"Just so we're both clear on your situation," when he spoke there was a disconcerting tone of anticipatory glee in his tone, "you cannot escape. That chair senses every time you start to manipulate your life force and it will punish you for it. We are quite far underground and no one knows you're here. I can do whatever I want to you, and no one will ever know. Are you getting a *clear* picture of your situation?"

Jayce felt a chill run through his body. He knew first hand that this man had a wicked streak of cruelty that ran through him and the thought of being alone with him, without any chance of rescue, sat in his stomach like a stone. He thought desperately for some way out, some way to redirect his attention.

"So, you and the other's...you're in league with the Blades?" He spoke quickly, stumbling over his words, playing for whatever time he could, "Helping them steal children with the Gift?"

"Steal?" He snorted as he turned to the cart, "The children we have spirited away came from the gutters. Destined to become laborers, factory workers...without us, their Gifts would have been meaningless. We *saved* them."

"But now?"

"They will serve a grand purpose." He spoke with a fervent passion which took Jayce by surprise, eyes taking on a faraway look, "They will power our engine of change and reshape the world in ways you cannot even imagine."

He tried to recover as best he could, his mind racing, "What are you talking about?"

He gave Jayce a sneer. He pulled a small leather roll out of the cart and spread it out on top. The sheen of metallic instruments gleamed in the low light, like teeth in the night. Jayce eyed them, a sense of dread mounting.

"It's nothing you have to concern yourself with." He pulled a blade so long and fine it was almost a needle out of the roll and held it out in front of him, examining it with fondness, "We are going to drag this world into a new age, one where all this nonsense of nobility is left in the past, and only those of us who deserve to rule will have the power."

"So...you're not doing this for the Sovereign?"

Allegheny whirled on him and made an unpleasant sound somewhere between a snort and a laugh, "The *Sovereign*? That dullard couldn't even begin to comprehend the genius of our plans. No, no, Master Acosta, we have no need for someone as insignificant as that figurehead. Now, hold still."

He approached Jayce with ill intent written plainly across his visage. Jayce tried to squirm, to slip his bindings, but the leather wraps around his wrists and ankles were as tight as manacles of cold iron. He tried to reach out again, grasp at the stagnant air around him, the moisture on the floor, anything. But he was again hit with pain so blinding it nearly sent him unconscious. But he managed to hold on, pure terror keeping him awake as he watched Allegheny raise the blade towards him.

"No, wait...what are you...*argh*!"

A fresh stab of agony washed over him as he felt the sharp end of the knife cut into the flesh of his hand. Jayce screamed and squeezed his eyes shut as he writhed and shook, desperate for the pain to end. The teacher sunk the blade in a few more inches, the searing pain doubling over as he pushed it further and further. Finally, he stopped.

Jayce opened his eyes slowly. The blade sat there, protruding from a small pool of blood which had welled up on the back of his hand. He was shaking and covered in a cold sweat, breath ragged in his chest. Allegheny had turned and was pulling a second thin blade out of the roll.

"Wha...what in the Hells are you doing?" Jayce croaked out in a hoarse whisper. Between the throbbing ache in his head and the burning pain in his hand, he found it hard to focus on the flabby man.

The teacher turned to his prisoner with a slightly too wide smile that was more unsettling than the slender knife in his hand, "You wanted to know about our plans for the children, no? I'm just giving you a personal lesson."

He stalked over to Jayce with the knife raised, a grin still wickedly plastered across his face.

"Wait, wait, wait!" Jayce screamed, voice raising an octave.

But it was no use. Allegheny cut him off as he drove the blade into his other hand, another well of blood oozing up to the surface. He screamed again. By the time the Arcanist stepped away again, all the adrenaline had been burned out of his body and he was left exhausted. He felt like he could barely manage to keep his head upright. Allegheny watched him, a viscous look in his eyes. He was not even trying to hide his sadistic enjoyment, which gave Jayce the anger to muster a wordless snarl at him.

"Still got some strength left in you, I see. That's good. You wouldn't be of much use to us if you didn't survive the procedure." He strode over to the cart and pulled yet another blade out of the roll. He came back and held it in front of Jayce's face, waving it back and forth, "Any guess as to where this one goes?"

Suddenly, the clink of a lock pulled his attention away. He stood up straight and cast a harsh glare over Jayce's shoulder, "What do you want? I told you I was not to be..."

He trailed off and his eyes narrowed. Jayce tried to turn but the chair kept him frozen rigidly in place, so he kept watching his teacher. The fat man set the blade down and raised his hands, showing his open palms.

"Step away from the chair." A woman's voice, clipped and nasally, replied. Jayce felt a twang of hope jump in his chest. He saw a form enter his periphery and was taken aback. It was Andrea Whistler, Headmistress of Apprentices, approaching with one trembling hand held out before her grasping a small wooden wand decorated with gold inlay. In the low light, her glasses gleamed sickly orange like the eyes of an oversized cat, "What is this? What are you doing to this boy?"

An oily smile still saturated Allegheny's face as he replied, voice lowered to barely more than a whisper, "Just a bit of practical instruction, Headmistress."

"H-Help me..." Jayce managed, staring wide eyed at her, "He's insane!"

She cast a look down at him, eyes wide as they lingered on the blades sticking out of his hands. She gave Allegheny a sharp look, "I always thought you were up to something! All those former apprentices that you taught, just gone, families asking questions, never any sign of them. I could never find any proof, I had my suspicions...but *this*. Are you trying to bind him, Stellan? Have you been practicing *Harnessing*?"

The jowls on the teacher's face waggled as his dark little eyes darted around the room, landing on Jayce, then to the headmistress, then to the cart at his side. He gave her another stomach turning smile, his tone wheedling.

"Andrea, come now, you have no idea what we're on the verge of accomplishing. We're going to change the way things work. Let me show you." He waved a hand dismissively at his prisoner, a look of disdain on his face, "How many failed students have you seen walk out those gates during your time as Headmistress? Hundreds, at least, likely more. All that potential, just *wasted*. Imagine what we could do if we could actually wield all that wasted power, put it to some use. There's no reason to worry about the boy, he's nothing, just another settled conjurer of cheap tricks...no one will miss him."

For the briefest shadow of a moment, Whistler looked unsure of herself. Doubt fluttered across her features and the tip of her outstretched wand dipped ever so slightly. Jayce stared in disbelief. He shook violently at his restraints.

"Don't listen to him!" He cried out, face contorted in pain and desperation, "*Help me!*"

Her gaze snapped to him. The faraway look was wiped away almost immediately as she straightened up, her wand trained on his chest.

"No, this is *wrong*, Stellan. You are going to let this boy go and we're going upstairs to have a chat with the Archmage. I'm sure he'll have something to say about this." The note of steel in her voice was surprisingly harsh coming from the small frame. She stared at the pudgy man like a hawk eyeing its prey.

Allegheny snorted, his eyes narrowing as he gave her a sly look, "Andrea, come now, do you really think Octavius was in the dark about this?"

"No..." her voice was barely more than a whisper, "He wouldn't, he *cares* about the students..."

"Only the ones that matter." Allegheny's voice was ruthless as he cast a dismissive glance at Jayce, "He was more than happy to let me work on my own *projects* as long as I stuck to the practitioners of the Low Art."

She shook her head, "You're lying."

The teacher spread his hands wide, "Find out for yourself. We can go speak with the Archmage and you can be brought into the fold. You can be part of something great."

The shadow of doubt crept across her face again. This time, she let the hand holding the wand drop to her side entirely. Jayce could feel his heart slamming against his chest as his chance of escape slipped away like a fresh fish back into an endless ocean of hopelessness. He swore and blinked the tears out of his eyes, a harsh tone creeping into his voice as he whispered a growl at the two teachers before him.

"You are all *monsters*." They both looked up at the interruption, seemingly seeing him with fresh eyes, "Every goddamn one of you! What gives you the right..."

Whistler stared at him, face shifting between several emotions. She seemed to have lost the ability to keep her typically neutral expression and was struggling to regain control of her features. There was a tense moment where no one spoke. Then the Headmistress made a choked noise that sounded like she was trying to suppress a whimper. She turned back to Allegheny.

"I can't be a part of this...I can't..." she whispered, voice cracking.

"It's alright, Andrea." He spoke in a low, soothing voice. His gray teeth gleamed dully in the witchlight, "You don't have to be."

Allegheny thrust his hand out and one of the needles shot from the cart through the open air. The sound of clothes ripping and the sudden sound of liquid hitting stone pierced the silence. Whistler let out a gasp. She turned and Jayce saw the long, thin blade had sprouted from the woman's side. He cried out, but it was no use. Her eyes went wide as she dropped the wand and grasped at the blade's handle, letting out a low cry of pain. Her hands could not get a grip on it, as blood had already slicked the handle and darkened the dress she wore with a rapidly growing splotch of crimson. She stumbled, looking up at Allegheny with shock.

"Y-you'll hang for this..." she coughed.

"Only if they find your body."

Her lips curled into a defiant snarl as she threw her hand out at him. A beaded bracelet on her wrist he had never noticed before glowed brightly in the dim light. Gold tinted fire erupted from her hand, roaring into life in an explosion which instantly filled the room with light. The heat was immense. Jayce recoiled from the flame, jamming his eyes closed. For a few seconds, the bellowing of fire filled his ears and he felt searing as the small hairs on his arm and the side of his neck burned away. Then, as quickly as it began, it was over.

When he blinked his eyes open, there were spots swimming in his vision. It took a moment to readjust to the dimness of the basement room. When he did, he saw the Headmistress slumped on the ground, head hanging over her chest. At first, he thought she might be dead, but he noted the barest movement in her back which proved she was still breathing. Jayce scanned the room as much as his restraints would allow, but Allegheny was gone.

"Headmistress," he called to her, desperate, "can you hear me. Andrea!"

She jolted slightly, letting out a little whimper. Her head turned and he saw she was pale as a whitefish in the sun. The wound had taken its toll. Her side was covered in blood, staining her dress in a large patch of deep red. She stared at him, eyes unfocused as her head bobbed.

"You need to free me! I'll get us out of here!"

She dipped her head in the barest fraction of a nod and began to crawl over towards him. Her progress was painfully slow and she left a trail of crimson streaks across the stone floor behind her. He gritted his teeth as he watched her, silently willing her to move faster. When she finally reached him, he could see she was covered in a sheen of sweat, every part of her shaking badly.

As she tried to undo the clasps on his hands, she struggled to work the latches. Her trembling fingers were slicked with blood and kept slipping off the metal. Jayce kept glancing around the room. He was worried Allegheny would materialize out of the darkness like some dreadful specter.

"*Shit...*" Andrea cursed in a whisper as her fingers slipped off the clasp for the third time.

"Just focus," Jayce fought hard to keep his voice calm, "you can do this. Did you see what happened to Allegheny?"

She coughed, a bit of blood mixed with her spittle dribbled out onto her chin. He could see she had only moments before she slipped into unconsciousness, "I think he must've gotten away...no way that was hot enough to incinerate his bones."

Finally, Jayce felt the tension on his wrist ease up. He wriggled his hand free from the loosened belt and immediately reached over to undo the other hand, then the binds on his head, waist, and ankles. He was free in a matter of moments, standing up and taking a quick survey of the entire room. It was just a windowless stone circle with minimal furnishings and two doors which were both on the rear wall. The right one sat ajar, leading out to a dimly lit hallway. No sign of any waiting masochistic mages lurking in the dark.

Jayce yanked the blades out of his hands, wincing and biting back the gasp of pain that came with each one, then stooped to check on Andrea. As he had predicted, she was already slipping into unconsciousness, her head leaning against the chair and eyes almost entirely closed. He shook her slightly and her gaze slid over to him sluggishly.

"I'm going to get us out of here." He reassured her, doing his best to inject courage into his terrified voice.

He bent down and struggled with her mostly limp form for a bit trying in vain to lift her. But she was heavier than he would have guessed and his hands were weakened from his wounds. He cursed, wiping blood on his pants, trying to regain some of his grip. He finally managed to get her to feet, one arm draped across his shoulders. She yelped in pain as he lifted her. Her head lolled and she leaned so hard against him it was hard to take even a single step.

"Come on, we have to get back upstairs."

She grunted and they shuffled out into the hallway. It was incredibly slow going. He was essentially carrying her along and he quickly began to tire, his own wounds draining him. He had no idea where they were, any sense of direction was entirely lost to him down here. It seemed like whatever this part of the University had been at one point, all it was used for now was storage. Every open room they passed was stacked with boxes and barrels or old furniture.

Every time they reached an intersection he would have to shake Andrea to get her out of her stupor and she would vaguely motion to him to take this hallway or that. He did his best to keep them moving, praying to all the gods he knew of they would make it out before Allegheny crawled out from wherever he had disappeared to. He was terrified Andrea would pass out before they got out, leaving him to navigate this dungeon on his own.

"Andrea, come on, stay awake now...how did you find me down here?" He asked, keeping his voice low.

"I...had people watching...for months now..." she slurred her words between gasping breaths, barely managing to walk as she clung to him, "...I've always been suspicious...one of mine saw you being taken...followed him down here..."

Jayce thought about this for a moment, questions formulating in his mind, "Does anyone else know?"

She shook her head weakly, "No...needed evidence...he's a Senior Arcanist..."

Jayce set his jaw and redoubled his efforts, doing his best to drag her along beside him. They finally reached the stairs which rose up into the darkness. He pulled her along as they made their slow way up the steps. Finally, they reached a large, heavy door which was mercifully unlocked. Jayce shoved it open and they stumbled through. It took a moment to adjust to the brighter surroundings, but it quickly became apparent that they had found themselves inside a library.

Unlike the central library on the main building, this one was low ceilinged and cramped, with the shelves of books tightly packed together in rows filling the long, narrow room and lining the perimeter walls. Several books were bound to the shelves with chains and there were even a few cases which locked away small collections. The walls bore no adornments nor fantastical displays. There were only a few tables, clustered at either end of the room with shaded witchlight lamps, gently glowing in the gloom. There were no windows and only a single door at either end of the long room. No one was there and it was quiet as a grave inside.

Jayce shivered. He guessed it was the private library that the Senior Apprentices whispered about, but something about it made his hair stand on end. He looked to Andrea, who vaguely motioned to his right. They shuffled along through the stacks of books, Jayce eager not to linger in the strange library. They reached the door and he paused for a moment, sure he would find it was locked. He yanked at it and said a silent prayer of thanks as it opened. As soon as he opened the door, he saw a man standing there facing away from him. It was a senior student, standing watch. As the door clicked open the man turned around and was frozen for a long moment in silent bewilderment, staring at the two bloodied figures that had emerged from the room he had been guarding.

"H...Headmistress? What happened?" He gasped.

Jayce heaved the limp form of Andrea into the man's chest, nearly knocking him over. He was shaking now, feeling the exhaustion hit him all at once.

"Get help." He managed to croak before collapsing to the floor in a heap at the man's feet.

J ayce and Andrea were laying in beds beside each other in the Medicinist's Hall. The large room was full of empty cots and shelves of equipment, everything meticulously clean and organized. She was asleep but breathing, her skin still pale as a ghost. Her wounds had been bandaged and there were multiple Arcanists in Medicinist's white hovering like looming spirits around her bed. Jayce was in the process of having his hands bandaged by a single student but he was captivated watching the work beside him. He stared at the unconscious form of the Headmistress as he replayed the night's events in his mind.

She had saved him, that much was true. Without her, he surely would have been dead, or worse. He still was not sure what Allegheny had been trying to do to him, but whatever it was it had horrified Andrea. But not so much that she had not hesitated. Twice. The moments were brief, but Jayce remembered them as if they had stretched on for hours. Remembering the look of uncertainty in her eyes had been something that sent chills through his spine. The revelation that Allegheny, for all his cruelty, was not so alone in his views, that perhaps the other Arcanists shared them to some degree, was a sobering thought. He needed to get to Lucian. He needed to find Lyra.

The sound of soft voices and a door closing pulled him from his contemplation. There was a figure standing at the entrance to the clinic. He was tall and rail thin, with a slightly hunched posture and a hook nose that gave him a birdlike appearance. He wore a pale blue suit with a long, embroidered cloak, an older style that was long out of fashion. His hair and pointed beard were iron gray and so well oiled they shone even in the low light. Jayce had only seen the Archmage of the University a handful of times during his short tenure here, but he recognized the man instantly. He sat up as straight as he could manage in bed, starting to swing his legs out to stand, but the old man waved him back down.

He made his way over with a purposeful stride, his ornately carved walking stick punctuating his steps as it clacked along on the stone. He approached Andrea's bed first. He spoke to the lead Medicinist in hushed tones and then the white clad figures quickly gathered themselves up and marched out of the room in orderly fashion. Once they were gone, the Archmage touched a hand to Whistler's face and spoke a few soft words that were unintelligible even to Jayce at this close distance. She seemed to tense for a moment, then relax. The old man took a moment longer at her bedside, sighed and turned to Jayce. His eyes were a pale shade of off blue, so faded they almost matched his suit. He approached Jayce's bed and stared at him for a moment, silently taking stock of him.

"So, you're the one Stellan abducted." He said, his voice carrying a surprisingly high, whistling tone that was just a bit off putting.

"Y-yes, Archmage," Jayce managed to stammer, "he kidnapped me, took me to some place in the basement and tried to perform...some sort of ritual on me."

"Let me see your hands." The old Arcanist commanded.

Jayce held out his hands and the Archmage turned them over a few times, examining the bandages. He mumbled to himself as he did it, tracing the lines of the bandages with a gentle caress. Finally, he let Jayce's hands drift back down to rest on the bed.

"Ah, yes, of course...it appears Master Allegheny was attempting a Harnessing ritual. Almost successfully as well, judging by your wounds."

"The Headmistress said the same thing." Jayce furrowed his brow, "I've never heard of that discipline before. May I ask, what is Harnessing, exactly?"

The Archmage gave him a long, hard look before speaking, folding his hands over the head of his cane, "An apprentice such as yourself has no business knowing, but considering the circumstances...I will tell you. It is one of the forbidden disciplines of High Art, and it is considered especially distasteful. It is an ancient, dangerous magic whose secrets have been locked away since the time of Old Uther himself. Even what limited *history* we have concerning the art is restricted to only the most senior of Arcanists."

Jayce frowned, "But why is it so restricted?"

"Because it breaks one of the Arcanist's Guild's Cardinal Laws, set down over fifteen hundred years ago; that the sanctity of one's own magic shall not be infringed. That the innate power of those with the Gift is theirs and theirs alone to wield."

"Are you saying..."

"Yes, Master Acosta, Harnessing allows you to wield the magic of others, against even their own will."

Jayce slouched in his bed, leaning his head against the wall. He stared at his bandaged hands, and thought back to the conversation with Allegheny in the University catacombs. It all started to become clear, finally, the pieces seemed to come together to form the terrible picture he had been trying to see this entire time. Lyra was right. Whatever this conclave of Allegheny's was planning, they were using Gifted children to power it.

"What could one do with a power like that?" He half asked himself, his voice barely a whisper.

"Quite a bit, in fact." The Archmage fingered the top of his cane thoughtfully, "No matter how much we might try and pretend otherwise, each of us is limited by our nature. We can train and study and practice, but at the end of the day, we are all still mortal men. Our bodies can only wield so much power, withstand so much punishment. But if you could use the power of others and distribute the toll amongst two practitioners, or even a group, you could push the limits of magic itself."

His tone caused Jayce to look up. The expression on the Archmage's face was not one of scholarly interest, nor was it rational consideration of a concerned party. What Jayce saw on the old man's face was hunger. The raw, desperate yearning for power that was like a gaping pit. His eyes were fixed on Jayce, widening with a tinge of mania behind the pale blue gray. Jayce recoiled.

"H-he said you knew...that you didn't care..." Jayce stammered as he began to edge away from the old man.

"Oh, I *know*. How could I not? Within these halls, I am sovereign." A grin spread across his wrinkled face, contorting his features until he hardly resembled the picture of scholarly dignity that had entered only moments before, "When the Oaren Arcanists approached us, telling us they had rediscovered the lost art of Harnessing, not just legends and myths, but the actual rituals of old, and offered us to share in their secrets, how could we not jump at the opportunity?"

Jayce glanced over to the other bed, desperate for some sign of deliverance. But the Headmistresses form was still. Too still. Jayce saw with some horror that she was no longer breathing. He stumbled to the floor in a heap of sheets and pillows and desperately wrestled his way to his feet as the Archmage rounded the corner of his bed. He did not run, just stalked closer at his same, steady pace.

"But we're *your* students! How can you do this to your own kind?!"

For the first time, anger spread across the old man's face. He sneered and gave Jayce a look like he was an insect that had dared to crawl across his dinner table, "*My kind?* You are no Arcanist, boy, and you never will be! You are just a cheap magician, destined to serve peasants and scrounge out a living performing for pennies! The highest destiny you could ever hope for is this, to be part of something greater than yourself. You should be *honored*!"

Octavius reached out for him but Jayce was already pulling on the tendrils of energy in the air around him, winding them into a whirling blast of wind which erupted from his hands directly into the old man's chest. It moved him a few paces backwards, but then he stopped. Jayce stared in confusion, but then he saw. The old man's cane. It had begun glowing the moment Jayce had hit him with the wind. Somehow, it had absorbed the energy he had instilled into the air, leaving it harmless and still once more. Jayce gritted his teeth and reached out, grasping for anything he could sense nearby.

There were jugs of water scattered around the room, some for drinking, others for cleaning the patients and the Medicinist's tools. He pulled at the familiar inert energy contained within each of them, reminded it of the waves and storms of his home out on the ocean. It all came at once, shattering the containers as jets of water shot through the air towards the Archmage from a dozen different directions at high speed. But the old man stood his ground. The staff glowed again and the water lost momentum the moment it came within a few paces of him. The water sloshed across his cloak harmlessly, dripping onto the floor in a large puddle which soaked the stones. The old man clicked his tongue. He looked up at Jayce, gaze harsh like cold iron.

"Nothing but a purveyor of cheap parlor tricks." His tone was mocking, vicious and full of contempt, "You don't deserve the little power you have, better for someone like me to have it then it be wasted on the likes of...*Argh!*"

He yelped and writhed in sudden pain. He turned to the side, hands clawing at his back where a scalpel had sprouted out of the cloak near his left shoulder blade. A short, blond figure darted out from behind him. It was Lyra. She rushed over and grabbed Jayce by the hand.

"We need to get out of here, *now!*" She demanded, yanking him by the arm to get him moving.

It took a breath for him to get his bearings, trying to shake off the shock at the rapidly changing set of circumstances, but he forced out a stiff to nod. He found his feet and started to follow Lyra out the door. But as they exited, he took a second to glance back at the room. Octavius was cursing, desperately trying to grasp at the scalpel. But it was Andrea he was more concerned with. Her limp form lay on the bed, unmoving, eyes half open. He stared as long as he could, hoping desperately to see some sign of life, some small spark. But she lay perfectly still. He turned and dashed out after Lyra.

He took the lead as they sprinted down the halls. It was still nighttime and the University was blanketed in darkness. They passed no one else as they found their way to the main exit. By the time Jayce led them out into the courtyard and they rushed towards the gatehouse, they were both panting and covered in sweat. The doors were surprisingly unlocked and the guards sitting in the gatehouse only cried out at them as they rushed up to the gate and pushed out into the open city street. Jayce began to run towards the street of delegation houses but Lyra caught him by the collar.

"This way!" She hissed at him, yanking him in the other direction.

"Why...?" he started to protest, but she yanked him so hard he nearly fell over.

They sprinted down the street a few dozen paces until they came to a mule drawn cart. A single man, dark haired and incredibly slender, sat in the driver seat. Jayce recognized him as the lead gardener Lyra worked for. She nodded to him and he stood, reaching down to give them a hand up.

"Lyra what in the Hells..."

"*No time!*" She bodily shoved him up the steps and into the back of the cart, "We'll talk later!"

He relented and ducked down into the back of the cart. There was a small, well hidden hatch which revealed a false bottom, narrow enough that two people might fit in if they lay close and completely flat. He wedged himself in and Lyra squeezed in beside. The dark haired man piled foul smelling sacks on top of the trapdoor and then retook his seat. With a quick crack of the reins the cart began to creak along the cobblestone street, slowly building up speed as it wheeled away from the University and disappeared into the early morning hustle of the Asaldon city streets.

CHAPTER TWENTY-SIX

DUTY & DESPERATION

Juniper found herself unable to sit still as she waited in the opulent office her mother had claimed as her own when she took over as the Dean of Illuminators. Encompassing the highest room in one of the perimeter towers of the main building, the office was large and circular, with windows looking out on the rest of the Conservatory in almost every direction. The office consisted of a sitting area with a low table and chairs and a circular fireplace where a warming stone sat dark, a desk with ornate filigree worked into the amber wood and a small private library with several shelves filled with annotated books and various trinkets.

She paced back and forth, ignoring the panoramic views which sprawled out before the Illuminator's Tower, absorbed in her own thoughts. She bit at her nails, ran her fingers through her hair, cursed under her breath, and paced some more. Being stuck in the room alone was maddening. She felt wild thoughts scratching at the corners of her mind, snapping and snarling at the few remaining scraps of her rapidly fraying nerves. When she finally heard the telltale click of the office door opening nearly cried out in relief. Her mother came in, dressed in her official robes, carrying a small satchel in one hand and a steaming cup in the other.

"Oh, Juniper, what are you doing here?" Her mother asked, tone pleasant as she made her way over to her desk.

"Dean Lysler brought the City Watch to arrest one of the College of Medicinism's Professors today." She blurted out, "A man named Zane. He...wanted me to tell you your problem was taken care of."

Her mother took the information with a slight nod of approval, "Excellent, Lee worked quicker than I expected."

Juniper blinked. She bit her lip, watching as her mother unpacked a few papers and books from her satchel and sat at her desk. Finally, she managed to formulate the question that had been eating at her insides like a nest of worms.

"He was innocent, wasn't he?"

"What do you mean, my dear?"

"You know what I mean, the Professor, Zane, he wasn't part of any of this, was he?"

"Of course not." She glanced up from her papers, "We couldn't sacrifice one of the actual members of the Scions, could we? The Emperor will interrogate him. If he actually had any knowledge to extract about our operation, he would have it excised in short order. But we need Chancellor Chale and the Emperor to think he is making headway in rooting out those who have sympathies with the rebellion. We need to keep him off our trail and make his visit to the colonies as planned."

Juniper felt like the floor had fallen out from beneath her, "You...framed him? But the Emperor will torture him. Mother, he'll kill that man..."

For the first time, Aria Faye stopped rifling through her pages of notes and set her books down on her desk, turning her full attention to her daughter. She indicated the seat across from her own. Juniper thought briefly of protesting, but she decided against it. She sat without a word and stared at her mother, wishing she could see a way in which the woman before her could make sense of this newest horrible revelation. But the look in mother's eyes was not one of concern nor one of sympathy.

Her eyes held only the deep set iron of determination that had become so familiar to her.

"Juniper," her mother began, tone icy, "you are no longer the girl who grew up in these halls, playing in the courtyards and hiding beneath this desk. You are a grown woman. When we told you of the atrocities the Emperor committed you begged to be part of our plans. You joined this conclave of your own volition, you understand the stakes."

The two women held their gaze for a long moment in the silent office. The morning light streamed in through the walls of windows and bathed the room in a golden cascade. Juniper leaned forward, her tone low and deliberate as she met her mother's frigid intensity.

"I never signed up to frame innocent men, to torture our *friends*."

"What did you think? That we would topple the tyrannical dictatorship that has reigned over our nation for generations without getting our hands dirty?" She gave her daughter a withering look.

"This is too far, mother. We cannot sink to his level..."

"*His level*?" Aria's tone rose several octaves, "You think this about principles? We are deposing a monster and you want to worry over moral quandaries? I thought you were smarter than that, Juniper. You're just as bad as Jiro!"

"Jiro is right!" Juniper retorted. She found herself standing, voice echoing around the large office as she nearly shouted at her mother, "What use is overthrowing the Emperor if you're just going to be as bad as he is?"

Aria stood, fury overtaking her face as she matched her daughter's intensity. Her face was contorted by lines and the mask of calm she usually wore had melted away to reveal the core of rage that burned inside her.

"How *dare* you? I am nothing like that monster." She hissed, "The Emperor used his foul magic to bind your brother and wielded him like a weapon. He made him and the others murder their own people, crush their own uprising. Then he cast them aside." Tears welled up in the woman's eyes. She shook and looked like she was on the verge of collapse, waves of grief wracking her body, "Han was such a good boy, always so strong, so smart. When we found his body it was so warped and atrophied I didn't even recognize him at first...my own son. The Emperor didn't kill him, he *destroyed* him."

"You...you never told me..." Juniper whispered, "I knew he killed the others who led the revolt but I never..."

Juniper stared at her mother. The expression of absolute dismay that was painted across the older woman's face quelled her own fury. She felt herself deflate as the will to fight left her and was replaced with a flood of horror and pity. Silence slipped into the space as the two struggled to meet each other's eyes. When Aria spoke, she looked not at Juniper, but at the small, gold framed portrait on her desk.

Though it faced away from her, Juniper knew it was the same family portrait that had always been there. It had been commissioned just before her brother was sent on campaign to the New World and, while it portrayed her as a small child, he had once cut an impressive figure in his perfectly pressed military uniform. But his face had been marked out after he had been publicly declared a traitor and now there was only a black mark for her mother to stare at.

"I never wanted you to know, Juniper. I never wanted you to know what they forced your brother to become. The Imperial family has used the secrets of Harnessing to keep their hold on this Empire for generations. Until we stole that tome from the Winter Palace, no one understood how it worked. They suppressed the knowledge, killed any Arcanist who got too close to the truth. But now we know. We have an opportunity no one in this Empire has ever had before, and likely never will again."

Juniper watched her mother. The anger had gone out of the regally dressed woman all at once and now there was nothing but a quiet, worn desperation in her voice. Her eyes were haunted, still staring at the defaced picture.

"Every day we wait is another day he gets closer to rooting us out, another day he gets closer to discovering who stole that knowledge. He's so close already, we've barely avoided discovery a dozen times over. Once he finds us, we lose our one chance, and if we fail, no one will get the chance again. He will kill us all and destroy our work, then he'll bury the knowledge of Harnessing so deep it'll never be found again." She took a breath, steadying herself, "That is why we cannot delay. We cannot miss our chance, not for anything."

Juniper only stared at her mother, trying in vain to form words that would not come. For an unbearably long time, the two sat in silence. Aria turned her gaze slowly towards her daughter. Her expression bore no anger, only a resolute lack of empathy that was difficult to face without cringing.

"Juniper, you have long passed the time of questioning. It is time to choose. When we make our move, we can have no dissenters. Are you with us? Will you do what is necessary?"

Juniper sat quietly for a moment. She thought about the convulsing form of Jiro's apprentice, of the terrified face of the professor they had framed. Then she thought about the previous night and this morning. Of her promise to Jiro. Of Kali, her soft smile lighting up her face.

Juniper forced a small smile and nodded, "I understand. I'll do whatever it takes, mother."

I t was early afternoon when a knock came at her office door. She had been sitting at her desk, staring at her stacks of paper while barely being aware of hours passing by as she thought back over all the events that had transpired. An untouched cup of tea sat on her desk, long cold besides an untouched saucer of delicate pastries. The sound shook her out of her stupor and yanked back to reality. She stood up, nearly knocking over a stack of books as she rushed to the door. She cracked it open and was taken aback. Her father stood in the doorway. He wore his formal court robes and a silver chain to complement his white walking stick today. She saw the look on his face and immediately knew something was wrong.

"What's happened?" She asked.

He did not answer, but indicated she let him into her small office. She closed the door behind him, locking the latch. He rejected her offer to help as he limped into the small sitting area and sank into one of the low chairs. She sat opposite him, immediately leaning in, eyeing her father. He took a moment to adjust his unwieldy formal robes and prop his leg into a position of comfort, then he turned to face her.

"I...was called to a meeting with the Emperor today." He said in a slow, deliberate voice. His face was stony and set in a look of permanent disgruntlement.

"The Emperor? For what?"

"I was there in my official capacity as High Justice. He brought several of the senior Chancellors to a private meeting. Chale was there as Head of Intelligence, as was the Defense Chancellor and the Provost of the Conservatory. He wanted to talk about certain growing threats to the Empire." He made a face, "Perhaps *talk* is the wrong word. He demanded answers. After we framed that professor, I thought he would be content. But it seems finding confirmation of collusion with the rebellion efforts within the capital itself has only provoked him. He's redoubling his efforts to crush the rebellion. He is recalling more of the army to maintain control of the Empire immediately, as well as increasing his search for more sympathizers. This was our mistake, we acted too quickly. We were not aware of the new intelligence he received earlier this week which ties Oarenhiem to the mercenary companies operating in the New World."

Juniper's eyes widened. She began to breathe faster as she felt her heart race, "He knows?"

"No, not everything. It seems Chale has been performing his duties rather well." His tone was bitter, "His agents have managed to extract some information from someone tied to the Burning Blades. Luckily, it wasn't one of their key members. He knows they were hired by someone in the Oarenhiem Empire, that they are being deployed in the colonies for various tasks. But he doesn't know who hired them, or what their ultimate purpose is. However, this still complicates things."

Juniper ran her fingers through her hair, letting out a long, low breath. She held her head in her hands and stared at the floor, trying to get her racing mind to slow enough so she could get a handle on it. When her father pointedly cleared his throat, she looked up.

"There's more?"

Her father nodded, "The Emperor has made it known he will be conscripting several of our best Arcanists, both from within the military and from outside, to assist in these efforts to stamp out the conspiracy. Amongst other things, he wants to send some of our Arcanists to the New World to help with the effort there. I put forth your name, and the Emperor and the other Chancellors agreed you would be an excellent candidate, especially given how you have handled the Roth girl."

His words hit her like he had dumped a bucket of cold water over her. It took a moment to register, but when it did she had a visceral reaction. Her stomach tensed and she immediately felt light headed. The idea of being pulled even further into all of this made her feel like she was going to vomit all over her tiny office. She groaned and wrapped her arms around her stomach.

"Why would you do that? Father, I can't..."

"June," he interrupted, his tone soft but firm, "you cannot say no to this. It is a direct request on behalf of the Emperor. You are already involved, feeding the Princess misinformation and reporting to Chale about your conversations. They all see this as just the next logical step, a potential move to elevate your standing with the Emperor. Any other Arcanist would climb over the bodies of their fellows for this opportunity. If you refuse to do this, it will be extremely incriminating."

"But what am I supposed to do?" She exclaimed, desperation creeping into her voice, "It's one thing to lie to Valeria by way of message stone once every other week, but this? This something else entirely! You want me to play the role of a spy, one who is hunting herself! How am I supposed to make this work?"

"*Listen to me!*" His tone caused her to pause. She looked at her father and for the first time noticed the creeping tendrils of fear that had wormed their way into his face. She could see the way he was blinking too often, how his eyes darted back and forth around the room, his white knuckled grip of the chairs armrests.

"Father...?"

"This situation is getting out of our control. Things are happening too quickly, the Emperor is figuring things out. He is a hairsbreadth from uncovering our entire conclave. If that happens, Juniper, we cannot protect you."

She sat in silence as he sighed and placed a heavy hand on her knee, "Your mother...she is so consumed by this hatred inside of her. She thinks only of making the Emperor pay for what he did to our son. But I won't sacrifice the life of one of my children for the memory of another. I won't see the evil that took Han from us inflicted on you as well. You *will* go to the colonies. If we are discovered at least you will be out of the Emperor's immediate reach. You can seek shelter with the rebellion. If we fail, I have arranged that notes of our plan be leaked directly to the Emperor..."

Juniper's eyes widened in horror but he pressed on.

"It is to provide certain assurances," his face was set in a grim expression, "so the mercenaries and our other allies will have no recourse but to side with the rebels in the worst-case scenario. This goal is too important to die with us. If we are discovered, the Emperor will slaughter who he believes is involved, without mercy or hesitation, and they all know it. By doing this I am giving the rebels a fighting chance even if our plan fails. So, you being there will give you at least some small chance of survival, whichever way this goes."

Juniper had a difficult time coming up with the words. She stared at her father, feeling for the first time in her life like she was seeing a stranger. Her mind still seemed to be struggling to grasp everything that had happened in the past few hours and was now clamoring to handle this new information.

"Jiro asked me to wield the machine when he finishes it." She blurted out after a long moment. She did not know why she said it, just that she needed to tell him, "He said he can't trust mother with it anymore."

Cristos blinked in surprise, then he nodded with the slightest crack of a grin at the corner of his mouth, "Of course he did. Crafty, that one. I suspected he would find some recourse after what your mother did to him. But, perhaps it is for the best."

"For the best?" She stared at him incredulously.

He shrugged, "As I said before, your mother is so focused on revenge at this point I doubt she would have the clarity of mind to wield the weapon effectively against the Emperor when the time comes. I am no Arcanist, but from what I understand it is going to take a massive force of will just to operate Jiro's device, much less use it in combat. But Juniper, I have to ask, are you sure you're up for it?"

She blinked at him, "What do you mean?"

"You know what the cost is going to be. Are you sure you can handle having something like that on your conscience?"

"It doesn't seem like I have much choice, do I?"

He gave her a small, sad smile, taking her hand in his, "Oh my blossom, you always have a choice."

She looked at him, her mind still reeling from the flood of information.

"Besides, we'll only get a chance to use the machine if we make it until the Emperor's visit to the colonies, assuming the old tinkerer finishes it in time. Jiro can still get what he wants if we send you now, rather than at the end of the season. Besides, that will give you some more time with your friend before her wedding."

If Juniper thought she was surprised before, the last words from her father shocked her more deeply than she thought possible. She looked at him and saw the strangest expression on his face. He appeared to be lost in thought, his gaze unfocused and a small smile creeping across his face.

"I know you are angry about the situation, June. I know what it is like to feel that you have no choice in your future. There was a serving girl in our house who I thought I loved when I was a young man. We were...close, like you and Kali. But my father had her sent from the city the same night I was promised to your mother. I never saw her again after that and never got a chance to say my farewells to her. But that was the way of things. Our people have never been romantics. Now, since this move needs to happen anyway, and Kali is to return to her family soon, I had hoped this might also give you a bit more time together...to bring your relationship to a gentler close, than mine had."

"Father..."

She could think of nothing else to say, only staring at him as he looked out the window. His usual stoic demeanor seemed softened, the hard lines on his face less severe in the midday sun. He was quiet for a long time after that as they sat together, listening to the birds chirping outside in the Conservatory's courtyards below.

It was nearly dark before Juniper caught up with Kali again. Her family's estate was smaller than Juniper's and placed on a lower level of the city, but they still always managed to find quiet corners in which to hide away. They had commandeered a small study to hide away from the rest of her family who still remained in Khanar, a smattering of siblings who worked in the government and some elderly grandparents too old to make the move to the New World. They lounged on a long, low couch with the remains of their dinner laid before them on the table.

In the low light of the office, surrounded by shelves of medical texts and fine looking, outdated surgical instruments encased in glass, Juniper felt some of the tension that had been roiling inside her slowly slipping away. She leaned on Kali's shoulder, the other woman's hair loose and spilling all down her chest. Juniper was running her fingers through it, pulling out the tangles she found with delicate little tugs. Kali spoke in a low voice, her words slow and deliberate.

"So, what *happens* when you get to the colonies? I know they want you to help quell the rebellions, but what does that mean for you?"

Juniper took a deep breath. She desperately wanted to talk about anything other than this, but she knew she could not hide from it.

"I don't know, Kal. I suppose there'll be a lot of interrogations and investigating people suspected of being sympathizers."

She was quiet for a moment. Then she said in a quiet voice, "What will you do if they bring you an actual member of the Conspiracy? June, they're not going to make you torture anyone, are they?"

She stared blankly at the wall. She did not respond, but the answer hung in the air between them.

"Oh god, what if they bring you one of us?" Kali's body stiffened under her, and she could hear the fear creeping into her tone.

Juniper sat up and turned to look her love in the eye, "If that happens...I'll deal with it."

Kali stared at her, then slowly nodded. Juniper could tell she was still hesitant, but she let the question die and took her hand in hers. She caught her eye and gave her a pointed stare.

"It's too late to worry about keeping our hands clean, Kal. We have a plan, Jiro will hold up his end of the bargain. We just need to focus on doing what we need to until we can get out on our own."

Kali shook her head, her auburn curls bobbing back and forth around her head, "I don't know June, this is such a risk. Why wait until after the conclave is exposed? If the plan fails the Emperor will be on a warpath. Why not just go now? We could be halfway across the world."

"...and go where? Where could we go that would be safe if this plan fails?"

"I have friends in the south!" Her voice had a desperate edge to it, "The Broadwater Republic, the Emperor couldn't chase us there even if he survives the assassination attempt."

"Come on, Kal," Juniper kept her tone calm, trying to soothe the other woman, "we've been over this, you know that wouldn't work. We'd be political refugees. The Merchant Lords of the Republic are no better than pirates, they'd trade us back in a heartbeat if it got them some coin in their pockets. Even if we fled all the way to Vinatieri, they wouldn't risk an international incident for the lives of two women."

"You don't *know* that."

"I do. My father works directly for the Emperor, I've heard the stories. He's vindictive and the other nations do what they can to avoid conflict with him. It's a no win scenario."

"Then what about after he's gone? Why do we need to rely on Jiro, why can't we just break all ties with the Scions and go once the Emperor is dead?"

Juniper paused at that. She considered this for a moment before shaking her own head, "Then what, Kal? We spend the rest of our lives looking over our shoulders, hoping our parents don't come after us? We just end up as refugees, with no home, nothing to our names?"

"We would have each other. Wouldn't that be enough?"

"That's not fair. You're being unrealistic." Juniper crossed her arms.

Kali closed her eyes and let out a low breath. She sat for a moment before opening them again and speaking in a tone which was deliberate and measured, "Juniper, I know you think you can solve this problem. That there's an answer where everything works out for us and we get to be together without sacrificing all of this-" she waved a hand around the room, "but I don't think there is. Sometimes you must sacrifice part of the body to save the whole. We are going to have to make hard decisions here. If we don't make a decision, I'm afraid it will be made for us."

Juniper let out an exasperated sigh and shrugged her shoulders, "What do you suggest we do then?"

"Let me reach out to my contacts. At least I can try and get something set up for us in case everything goes belly-up."

She sighed again but nodded. Her reasoning was sound, even if Juniper felt it was ultimately pointless, "Just be careful. You know how close the Emperor is to uncovering this entire thing."

Just then, a young man with quaffed hair the same color as Kali's and a sharp goatee came bursting through the door, not bothering to knock.

"Rami," Kali admonished, "don't you know how to knock?"

Rami gave her a look and turned to look at Juniper, "There's someone from the Ministry here to see you, Faye."

"The Ministry...who is it?" Juniper asked apprehensively.

Just then, a broad figure in a formal robe strode past the young man into the office. Chancellor Chale cast a severe look over the two women before giving a slight bow to Rami, who bowed back, much more deeply, and backed out of the room, closing the doors behind him. Juniper felt her shoulders tighten as she shot a look to Kali, who sat stock still, eyes transfixed on the man who had stood before them. He raised an eyebrow at Juniper, then indicated the mostly empty dishes spread out across the table between them.

"Having a late dinner, Professors?"

Juniper swallowed hard and forced herself to speak, "Y-yes, Chancellor. We were both working most of the day and only recently got in. Are you hungry? Why don't you sit and I'm sure the Rhee's chef's could..."

He interrupted her, waving a dismissive hand, "No, thank you, I won't be here long. I presume your father has informed you that you will be going to the colonies soon?" She nodded. Her mind was racing again, she felt her stomach churning inside her as she fought the impulse to grab Kali and bolt from the room.

He looked Kali up and down, "I suppose you'll tell her eventually anyway, so there's no point in telling you to leave. Just know what I'm going to say now is considered an Imperial secret, so if you reveal this to anyone outside this room, there will be...consequences."

Kali nodded vigorously. Chale reached into his robe and pulled out a scroll case. It was a black leather tube with a simple clasp. He handed it to Juniper, who took it and gave him a quizzical look.

"That is all the information we have on the rebellion, their strongholds, leaders, allies. It has taken a lot of work on behalf of my agents, so don't let it fall into the wrong hands." He crossed his arms and stared at her, gaze intense, "We know there are sympathizers who are funding them here in the Empire, but we haven't been able to figure out who. We guess they're some of the same people involved in this conspiracy. We're so close. We know the same people that hired every decent mercenary company they could get their hands on were also the ones behind the break in on the Roth's stronghold, and we have evidence they've been behind other crimes around the continent. They're working on *something*... something very big, I can feel it. The pieces are there, we just need to get the last part of the puzzle."

He pointed a thick finger at Juniper, and in the moment she could not help but recall the cold, dark eyes of a shark she had seen swimming past the ship on her journey to the Southlands.

"Your work with the Roth Princess has been exceptional. The Emperor is impressed, and he has decreed that you will be leading the team of Arcanists we send to the colonies. We are counting on you to figure this out, Juniper. We need to stop these traitors before they can enact whatever it is they're plotting. For the good of all of the Empire."

She just nodded again, words escaping her. For the briefest of moments, she thought she had misheard him. But a glance at Kali showed that her eyes, as big as saucers, were fixed on the tube, confirming she was not mistaken. Chale looked her up and down, a little smirk worming its way across his face.

"I can see you're hesitant. Look at it this way, find the traitors and you can make your own way. The Emperor will be in your debt. You can ask for anything. Titles, positions of privilege, maybe even a piece of land in the New World...somewhere close to your *friend*."

Juniper blinked and her mind reeled as she tried desperately to catch up. The Chancellor stared at them both for a moment, still with his knowing grin, then grunted in satisfaction. He made a curt goodbye, then strode out of the room in a swirl of robes, letting the doors to the study slam shut behind him. Once he was gone, they stood in stunned silence for a long moment.

Finally, Kali looked up at Juniper, eyes still wide, "Did he say, *leading* the Arcanists?"

Juniper groaned and buried her head in her hands, letting the black tube fall to the ground and roll away from her.

CHAPTER TWENTY-SEVEN

THE RED WOLF

S tanding on the deck of the *Dancing Sabre*, a sleek, modern Vinatierian designed ship made to cut through the high seas, Holton watched as the sailors and mercenaries moved around him on the deck. In addition to sails, it had a large, wheeled paddle near the rear and, strangely, the hull was made of metal. Some part of his mind remembered someone mentioning the paddle was run on steam, but he had a hard time believing that something so large and heavy could be moved without magic being involved somehow. He had never been aboard one of these new ships and still had a hard time believing it floated, but it seemed sturdy enough as the men made last minute adjustments and triple checking the ropes and rigging.

Despite this, a sense of nervous tension hung unspoken in the air amongst the crew. The familiar feeling that always haunted the last moments of a job, when the slightest mistake might ruin everything. He considered changing after the Prince's little escape attempt, as there was still fresh blood on his robes and under his nails, but he felt losing focus for even a moment would be a mistake. Besides, there would always be time for niceties later. He tried to keep his eyes on everything at once, watching the men, eyeing the shore for the approach of harbormasters or the city watch, trying to keep track of where that damned red cloaked mage and his woman were. Motion at his side told him

Erin was there, her voice low, barely containing the tremble of emotion that was just beneath the surface.

"It's official now, Lawrence is late." She said, her voice a low growl. When Holton looked down at her, he saw that she was holding back tears.

"Erin..." he began, but she shook her head.

"No..." she interrupted, "he's gone, ain't nothing going to change that. None of your words or speeches, no thoughts, nor prayers. Taron's just another former crew mate now."

Holton nodded silently. He put an arm around her and pulled her into a tight embrace. He felt her tears dampen his shirt and found his own eyes begin to water, "He wasn't just any crew mate. We'll all miss him something fierce, Erin."

She pulled away, looking up at him with pain in her eyes, "Why didn't you kill the bastard? After what he did...*why*?"

Holton ran his hands through his hair in frustration, "I did what I could, you know that. They want him alive."

"Sure, *they* do." Erin wiped her face on the back of her sleeve, eyes growing hard, "I hope all this is worth selling our souls, Holt. I truly do."

She turned without waiting on his response and stalked across the deck. He watched her go and cursed under his breath. He thought about going after her but then turned and walked back towards the aft of the ship. This was not the time to lose focus. The stress was getting to everyone. Men bickered about insignificant details and shoved each other, casting nervous glances towards the shore. The morning had come and gone and they were still here, far past the scheduled time for departure.

Lawrence was late, and had left them sitting on a boat full of captive children, a fugitive witch and her cohort and a kidnapped Prince. The harbor was busy, but sooner or later someone would notice them sitting there without departing for too long. Holton was about to go speak with the first in command when he spotted a single figure running along the dock. It was a young boy, barely out of his child years, that he recognized as one of the messengers the Blades employed in the city. Holton strode down the gangplank and caught the boy as he made it to the ship.

"What is it, lad?" He demanded as the boy, soaked in sweat and puffing heavily, struggled to speak.

"Th-they caught him, Sir. The City Watch, they found our safe house somehow, struck just before dawn. They brought a mage of their own. Killed most of the men up there, but they clapped the mage and a few others in irons, drug 'em up to the dungeons. If I hadn't been out on a run I would've been right there with 'em, or worse. Got back just in time to see 'em bein' dragged off, followed to see what they'd do with 'em, then came here proper fast."

His street slang was hard to follow but Holton got the gist. He ran his hands through his hair and rubbed the back of his head vigorously, then remembered himself.

"Good work," he told the lad, clapping him on the shoulder, "do you know if there's any other high ranking Blades in the City?"

The boy gave him a look, cocking his head slightly, "Well...just you, sir."

That threw him off for a moment, then he recovered and nodded to the boy. He turned and saw Carrigan and his partner had appeared behind him. The mage cocked his head and looked at Holton with an odd grin.

"It appears our mutual friend is going to miss our journey. Pity, but we should leave with all due haste I think. Can't risk being here if one of those that got caught spilling our secrets to the watch."

"Don't be a fool." Holton growled, "How do you expect to get paid if we leave Lawrence behind? He was the only one who knew what the hell we were supposed to do with all these kids. What are you going to do, show up in the New World and start asking if anyone wants a few dozen kidnapped children?"

"The trade is not so unique as you might believe," Carrigan said, an amused tone in his voice, "I'm sure I could find *someone* willing to pay for this cargo, especially given their Gifted nature."

Holton felt something inside his guts twist at the implications the odd man might be hinting at. He kept his gaze locked on him, "No, we're getting the mage back. Without him all this was for nothing."

Carrigan shrugged his shoulders. He cast a look at his partner, who stared impassively back at Holton, giving away nothing. The red cloaked man looked back at him, "Do what you must, but we need to move this boat if we're going to avoid the suspicions of the harbormasters."

Holton nodded, "Agreed. We'll have some of the men take the boat out to sea and anchor out of sight. We can stay here and use both our crews to work on breaking Lawrence out, then we'll meet up with the ship once we have him."

"Unfortunately," he replied quickly, voice dripping with feigned regret, "as much as I enjoy the idea of watching you work, I cannot be part of this little rescue attempt. I must stay with the cargo to keep them under my spell, you see. But I will lend you my men, and my second in command."

Holton eyed the brown haired woman, who stood with her hand resting casually on the pommel of her sword, as she stared at him with her dark eyes. He nodded, "Let's get to work then."

It was late afternoon as their group huddled in one of the narrow alleyways which had a view of the Watchhouse. It was an ancient fortress near the northern edge of the city, facing out to the ocean. It was squatter than the buildings around the rest of the city and was not painted in the same bright colors, tan brick left natural and unadorned except for a massive crest of the city which was cast in iron and hung on the outer wall.

No other buildings butted up to it, leaving the area around it an open field to watch for anyone approaching. The doors looked solid enough to stop a cannon and were heavily reinforced with wrought iron. A contingent of guards patrolled outside in their brass armor and white sashes, obviously on high alert after the morning's excitement.

Holton watched them, trying to assess the fortress for weak spots, looking for any exploitable lapse in the guards routine, but found none. He turned to his men. Erin, Jarryd and Barney stood near him, all waiting with their usual calm. Kacey and the rest of Carrigan's men, five in total, loitered a short distance down the alleyway, casting furtive glances over at them and nervously fingering their weapons. Holton had time to assess these men over the past day and had come to the conclusion that they were not thieves, as his men were. They were too anxious, too jumpy and ready to pull their weapons at a moment's notice. They were dangerous, that much was obvious. But they were enforcers and soldiers, which made this that much more complicated.

"Alright," he said, voice low, just loud enough that the other group could hear him, "let's go over this. This place is too well fortified for a frontal assault. We don't have the manpower to take them head on..."

"You might be surprised..." Kacey began, but he cut her off.

"We *don't* have the manpower. This isn't a debate. We also don't know where Lawrence is being kept, and according to the locals, that fortress had five levels of dungeons that run down below it. So even if we break in, we're going to be fumbling around like rats in a maze. So the best chance we have is to get someone inside who can search unnoticed for as long as possible, or persuade someone to show them where the mage is being held."

"How do you propose to do that, boss?" Jarryd asked, stroking his mustache.

"Easy, I'm one of the most wanted men in the country right now. They'll take me prisoner if I let them."

"But then how will you escape once they lock you up?" Kacey asked, a note of obvious doubt in her voice.

"Don't worry. I've got that covered." Holton shot Erin a glance and kept going before Kacey could raise another objection, "I'll find Lawrence, but I'll need an exit once I do. That's what I need you all for."

"How do you expect us to do that if we can't make a direct assault?"

Holton took a breath, "I need your crew to make a diversion. Something big and flashy, we need to empty out that guardhouse as much as we can."

"We can do that." Kacey snorted, "But that still won't get you out of there. No matter what we do they'll still leave a contingent there with you."

"I know, don't worry. I can handle it." Holton looked to his own crew, "Erin, I'm going to need you and the boys to get our exit plan figured out. Remember the job at Blackwater?"

"Alright, Holt." Erin stared at him for a moment, "But are we sure this really is the *best* option?"

"Don't see much other choice. We don't know how much they know. If we wait much longer they might extradite Lawrence back to the Horn, or maybe even the Capital. Hell they might hang him as a traitor. If we lose him, this is all over. We need to get this sorted out and we're on borrowed time as it is."

Erin shook her head, "This is a *bad* idea, Holt."

He grinned, "Only if it doesn't work."

H olton ducked out of the alleyway and into a rundown nearby alehouse, the kind of place where patrons were already deep into their cups despite the early hour, giving Erin a moment to get to the Watchhouse before beginning the first step of his plan. He sat with a clear view of the door and once he saw her talking to the guards, he scanned the room for his target. He found a man that looked like he might have had a boulder somewhere back in his bloodline and swaggered up to his table. The big man eyed him with suspicion as he casually gulped down the last of a flagon of ale, wiped his mouth with his hand, then smashed the cup over the man's head without.

The entire alehouse was in an uproar in an instant. Weapons were drawn, men were shouting and drunkenly stumbling to their feet and the sound of furniture breaking and glasses being shattered filled the air. It lasted only a few moments, as the guards were already inside the building before any real damage could be done aside from a few bruised eyes and bloody noses. Holton stood in the middle of the room, hands over his head, grinning as he saw Erin scamper away outside while the guards were distracted.

The guards rounded up most of the patrons and marched them all off to the Watchhouse in shackles with surprising efficiency. This was a standard procedure in every major city across the land, so Holton was not surprised when they were all patted down, had their weapons and purses taken, and were chucked into an outdoor, communal holding cell in the courtyard. He listened as the men around him argued and scuffled, shoving each other and claiming their spots on the ground. All the other men were still angry, casting dark glares at each other around the cage. He leaned up against the cage bars and waited. It was not long before a new watchman, a high ranking woman denoted by the large embroidered clasp on her sash, strode out to observe the new prisoners. She walked up and down the bars, sizing up the prisoners. She paused when she reached Holton.

"What's your story, red?" She asked, eyeing the tattoos on his exposed arms, "We don't get many Northerners this far south, heard it hurts that pretty skin of yours."

"Just passing through." Holton muttered, keeping his eyes pointedly facing away from her.

Another guard at her side spoke, "The other prisoners claim he was the main agitator, Lady."

"Is that so?" She gave Holton a hard look, then gave a curt command to the same soldier, "Bring me the book."

He bowed and quickly rushed off. A few moments later he reappeared with a thick tome, frayed and heavily worn, with papers sticking out at odd angles and pages dogeared and denoted with a dozen different types of markings. She flipped through the book, rapidly turning over whole chunks of pages. Then she found what she was looking for. She read aloud, "Holton Hart, also known as the Red Wolf; outlaw, kidnapper, thief, murderer. A wanted man in every Kingdom in the North as well as having a warrant here in the Federation. I thought you looked familiar, we got word from the Capital to watch for you weeks ago."

She held the book up to show a rendering of him that looked significantly exaggerated in the teeth and ears. He eyed it with disdain, "Doesn't look like me at all."

She turned the book back around and reread the description, "Red hair, extensive tattoos...this is you alright. Gods above, of all the things I expected today, finding a notorious fugitive hiding out in my city wasn't high on the list. Get him out of there, take him to one of the cells and chain him up."

He groaned and grumbled and plead innocence as they hauled him out of the cage and dragged him through the courtyard and into the fortress itself. Inside, they passed kitchens and offices and caches of weapons and armor before finding their way to a stairway which led underground. Holton let himself be roughly handled down three flights of stairs until they finally found the designated cell and tossed him in. He waited for the cell door to clink shut and for the footsteps to fade into the distance. Then he quickly got to his feet and took in his surroundings.

He was in a long, narrow room with cells on each side. The opposite wall had tiny slits through which light shone through, letting him know they were on the ocean facing cliffside. His cell was small with only a cot on the floor and a small bucket to piss in for accommodations, but it did not matter. He had no intention of staying here. He stood, silent for a moment, listening, doing his best to ignore the groaning or snoring shapes which occupied a few of the cells around him. Then he heard it. The scratching of tiny feet. He glanced over and saw a tiny creature coming down the stairs at the end of the hall. It was a big, gray rat.

He knelt down and held his hand out. It took a moment as the little creature scampered towards him in quick, sporadic little bursts, but he waited patiently, letting it work its way across the room in its own time. Eventually, the mouse climbed into his hand and he gave it a gentle stroke on the head. He did not know where his gift with animals came from, nor did he care to find out. It had always just been like this ever since his days as a goat herder in the far North above the Sentinels. It was enough that he understood them, and they, in turn, understood him. He whispered to the creature, continuing to stroke its small head. Then he gently turned it over to reveal a set of pins and a small silver rod that were tied to the creature with a nearly invisible bit of twine. He pulled them loose and placed the rat on the floor, giving it a last pat on the head and letting it scamper off into the gloom.

Holton spent the next few moments fiddling with the needles on his cuffs, finally earning a click which signaled his freedom. Then, he reached both hands through the bars and blindly picked the lock to his cell. It took longer than unlocking his manacles, but after several moments of twisting and turning and cursing, he was rewarded with the sound of the door clicking open. As he strode out into the hallway, he listened carefully for the sounds of approaching footsteps. Fortunately, it seemed like there were no guards anywhere close.

He began his search by checking all the cells on his level, quickly scanning the huddled shapes for any signs they might be the man he was searching for. They watched him pass with curious, wary eyes that reminded him of caged animals. Many held out their hands and called out for him to let them out of their cells, but he passed on, hastening to find his quarry. Some yelled angry jeers and slurs after him, calling him white belly and paleface, but he ignored them. It took a long time to search every cell, but eventually he concluded Lawrence must be on a lower level and found the staircase. He padded down, careful not to make a sound in the dimly lit corridor. He could hear muffled voices while he was on the stairs, but he was not sure if they were from below or above. He descended painstakingly slowly, constantly expecting the face of an unsuspecting guard to pop up from the gloom below. Finally, he found his way to the next floor down.

Much like the floor above, the next level of the fortress consisted of a long hallway with rows of cells on either side. Unlike the previous floor however, no windows could be seen, leaving the room much darker than the one above. The only light came from amber witchlights which glowed faintly in the ceiling above. Holton gave himself a moment to adjust to the light and started his search. The voices he had heard in the staircase were quite a bit louder now, and he suspected he was hearing some of the prisoners speaking to each other.

Carefully checking each cage as he went, he moved down the rows as he got closer to the voices. Eventually, he recognized one of them. It was Lawrence. Holton approached the block of cells where the voices were coming from. Lawrence was standing, leaning casually against the bars of his cage as he spoke loudly to the men in the cages around him. They were laughing.

"-and that's when I finally realized," Lawrence was saying as he approached, "she wasn't a healer at all...she was another of those bloody magyar!"

The men around him gave up a chorus of laughter, slapping their knees at what was apparently the punchline of quite the amusing story.

"Having fun?"

Lawrence glanced over, noticing for apparently the first time that Holton had materialized out of the gloom. He threw his arms up.

"Holton Hart, as I live and breathe!" He grinned, showing off his too bright teeth which gleamed brightly, even in this low light, "You are indeed worth every mark and penny I've paid you, Sir."

Holton approached the gate door and cast a quick glance around at the rest of the men who had fallen silent and were eyeing him from their cages, "Seems like you could use a hand?"

"An astute observation. Yes, I would very much like to get out of here before they decide to interrogate me."

Holton pulled the lockpicks out of his pocket and got to work on the mages cell door. As he worked, he asked, "So, what happened? You have a traitor in the crew?"

"I'm not sure," Lawrence replied in a low voice, "the Watch did seem to know an awful lot about our operation."

Holton glanced up at him, "Not good, Lawrence. That means they were tipped off."

The mage nodded, "They were in a hurry to get us out of the safe house as well. It seemed like they knew we had a large presence here in the city."

The lock clicked and Holton yanked the door open. He motioned for Lawrence to follow him, but the mage held his shackles up and pointed to the ceiling. Holton saw a ring of ruins and interlocking circles inscribed into the ceiling, and noted matching ruins were carved into the shackles. He swore under his breath and reached into his pocket. He pulled the silver rod out, the same one he had used back at The Hold. He held it up to the shackles and it rapidly grew warm, sending the familiar buzzing sensation up his arm. He turned it and the lock on the shackles clicked open. Lawrence shook them off and let them fall to the ground.

"One day you're going to have to give me back that skeleton key." Lawrence said, eyeing the rod, "That is an extremely rare little artifact you have there."

Holton snorted and shoved the key back into his pocket with his lockpicks. He motioned for Lawrence to follow and led him back out of the cage. The men around him called out but the mage only gave a cheeky wave and smirked as the two escaped down the hall. Holton led the mage up the stairs and back towards the surface, painstakingly hugging the wall and creeping along, listening for any sign of someone coming down. They began to hear the sounds of frantic, panicked voices coming from up top after they had passed the third floor. As they slowly climbed, they found that the voices grew louder and louder and were soon joined by the sounds of slamming feet and clinking metal.

"Seems like the girl did her part."

Lawrence raised a quizzical eyebrow, but Holton just shrugged and motioned for them to keep going. They approached the main floor and sidled up to the door, listening to the ruckus outside. It sounded like everyone was rushing out of the Watchhouse all at once, with men cursing and screaming at each other to move as furniture screeched along the floor and things crashing down onto the stone. The commotion was over quickly, leaving a lingering silence which hung in the air. Holton counted silently, overexaggerating the mouthed words so Lawrence could see them clearly. When he was done, he nodded and slowly pushed the door open.

As expected, the Watchhouse was a wreck. Desks and chairs had been overturned everywhere, plates and mugs scattered along with flurries of paperwork which had drifted to every corner of the room. There were three men left behind in the chaos attempting to clean up some of the mess left behind by their comrades. Two were junior looking watchmen and the third was a senior officer with a large gut which hung heavily over his belly. This last man was closest to the door, with his back turned to them.

Holton motioned for Lawrence to wait and slinked out from the doorway in a half crouch. The men were talking, the older barking orders at the two younger, and so none noticed as he stalked up to the fat man on silent feet. In one fluid motion, he snatched the man's knife from his belt and held him from behind, pushing it into the elder watchman's neck. The man gasped and the other two finally looked up, noticing him. Their hands flew to their swords, but Holton clicked his tongue at them.

"Nah, nah, none of that now boys. Not unless you want your superior here sliced from ear to ear." For emphasis, he pushed the knife hard against the man's flesh, drawing a thin line of blood which slid down the blade and dripped off the crossguard. The man gasped and stuttered as he managed to voice a command.

"D-drop your weapons!" He demanded, "*Now!*"

The two younger guardsmen looked at each other, hesitated for a moment, but then pulled out their swords and tossed them over towards Holton.

"Good lads. Now, I assume you've got some spare sets of irons laying around here?"

Within a few moments, the three were bound and gagged and stashed in a closet. Holton stole their uniforms, instructing Lawrence to change into one, following suit and changing into one himself afterward. They each took a sword and strapped them to their belts, doing their best to make the ill fitting clothes look as natural as possible. When they exited the Watchhouse, he could hear the far off screams and clanging metal, letting him know some sort of battle was happening nearby. It was sunset and the city was bathed in red and orange. He also noted a few tendrils of smoke worming their way into the skies to the east of them.

They quickly made their way across the courtyard and strode towards the main gate, past the large cage where the drunks were being held. A handful of guards still stood by the main entrance, eyes all cast towards the area where the smoke was rising. Holton and Lawrence strode past them, turning the opposite direction of the way they were looking, trying their best not to attract any attention. They had made it about five steps away from the massive outer door when a voice called behind them.

"Hey, where are you two going?"

They locked eyes for a brief moment, each man considering their options in their own mind, before turning to face the remaining watchmen. Only four of them had remained to watch the gate. One of them was striding over to where they stood with a dark look in his eyes.

"What are you two doing?" He asked pointedly, eyeing them both up and down.

"Going on patrol..." Holton lied smoothly.

"Patrol? Have you not seen what's going on over there?" He pointed to the smoking tendrils emphatically, "We need every available man there, *now!*"

Lawrence started to speak when a shout cut him off, "*Hey!* That's the rat that got us all locked in here..."

The men in the cage had taken notice of them. Some had apparently recognized Holton, pointing and shouting angrily at him. The watchman looked from them to the prisoners and back again, eyes narrowing. Holton moved like a snake. His knife flashed out and slit the man's throat, sending a spray of red across the cobblestones. The guard's eyes widened to saucers as he stumbled backwards, gagging and coughing on his own surprise. Holton was running before the man's body hit the ground.

"*Run, damn it!*" He shouted at Lawrence as he grabbed the stunned mage by the arm and yanked him along, dashing across the open street which separated the watch house from the rest of the city. A crossbow bolt whizzed past his ear and bounced off the wall of one of the houses with a snap, shattering on impact. A second skittered across the stones between them, missing Lawrence by a fraction of an inch. He cursed again as he sprinted, pulling the mage along as fast he could.

Men were shouting behind him and he could hear their footsteps as they ran. A last bolt slammed into one of the wooden doors nearby with a thud just as they reached the line of buildings, ducking behind a massive stone wall. Holton pulled his sword from the sheath and waited for a moment, then as the first guard rounded the corner he took a low swing and cut one of his legs out from under him.

Blood spurted out and covered the wall as the man collapsed in a screeching heap onto the ground. The next guard was fast approaching and Holton turned and yelled at Lawrence to run. They sprinted down the alley and around another corner, quickly getting lost in the twists and turns of the streets.

The winding alleyways, crisscrossing bridges and multi leveled terraces of the Crescent City were a maze of discordant colors and sounds. Street vendors cursed and women carrying large baskets screamed and swatted at them as they scrambled past, slipping down the crowded, tightly packed streets. It was slow going, the mage lagging behind as he huffed and puffed, desperately trying to catch his breath. Holton tried to maintain his bearings but he found it was incredibly difficult, ending up facing the ocean when he thought he was headed towards the Bay several times.

He ended up relying almost exclusively on always choosing the descending path, hoping he would be able to find his way to the port when he was closer to the shore. Guards nipped at their heels the entire way. He had wounded the first unfortunate watchman, hoping it would slow them down as they tried to get him medical attention, but they had rung the alarm bells and raised the alarm throughout the city. Somehow they had gotten word out in a shockingly rapid time, so every time patrol would spot them they would cry out for them to identify themselves, then sprint after them when they did not respond.

Holton dragged Lawrence down several side streets and zigzagged back and forth, barely managing to lose their pursuers several times. As they ducked into an alley behind a row of shops, narrowly avoiding a group of watchmen as they rushed by, Holton held up his hand.

"Wait for them to get further along." He turned to look at the wheezing mage who was drenched in sweat and bending over, "Can't you magic us down to the docks?"

Lawrence took a deep breath and coughed, "Only if you want us to get filled with arrows as we float through the air."

Holton grumbled about magic being worthless and glanced out into the alleyway, "Lose the uniforms and armor. They're looking for watchmen now, if we're in plainclothes we'll have an easier time."

Lawrence nodded and they stashed the armor and swords behind some crates before making their way back out into the street and joining the general flow of people. They came close to several more patrols, but none stopped them. Neither of their clothes had been too far off of the local populace, so they more or less blended in. By the time they finally found their way to the port it was long past nightfall. Holton led the way to the slip where the *Sabre* had been parked earlier. A smaller boat floating there, with Erin and his crew waiting aboard. Kacey and her mercenaries were nowhere to be seen. When they saw him approaching, Erin called out.

"Oy, took you long enough!"

Holton did not reply as he grabbed Lawrence's arm and steered him onto the boat. He sat the mage down and waved his hand over his head in a circular motion, whistling. Like clockwork his men began the process of shoving off and moving in the open water. Lawrence watched with quiet fascination, clearly impressed by their efficiency. After they had gotten a good distance out into open water, the mage leaned back in his seat and crossed his legs, looking like a smug cat that finally got hold of a troublesome mouse.

"So we're to meet up with the *Sabre* then?" His tone had regained some of the usual confident demeanor as he surveyed the crew, "I'm guessing you anchored it near one of the barrier islands?"

Holton whistled and the ship lurched to a stop as Jarryd and Barney stopped rowing. Lawrence glanced around, confusion mounting on his face. Holton sat down across from him, gazed fixed on his face with a dark expression.

"We need to talk."

CHAPTER TWENTY-EIGHT

DARK DEALINGS

The basement of *Garner's Imports & Exports* was dark, cold and smelled like old meat, sweat, and stale smoke. Everything had been washed down, the worktable wiped spotless from the day's gore. The laborers had all departed, leaving their blades and instruments hanging from the suspended rack on the ceiling. They gleamed in the witchlight, wickedly sharp instruments which evoked a sense of foreboding even in someone as versed in the building as Lyra. She knew they were often used for more than just butchering the livestock brought in from the countryside, and, sitting here for hours in the cramped space, it was hard not to imagine the times a living body had been strapped to that table.

She had spent most of the night lost in thought, perched on a chair near the door as she waited for the telltale click of the lock to signal someone had finally returned. However, despite her fraying nerves, she had to admit that Jayce was faring much worse. He had spent the entire night alternating between sitting with his head in his hands while muttering unintelligible gibberish and pacing the room in frantic little bursts while arguing loudly with himself. He had recently taken to simply laying his head against the wall and staring into space. He looked so broken Lyra worried his mind had started to slip from all the stress.

She had explained away having the cart and the hiding place, stating she had reached out to friends before they had attempted their subterfuge with Allegheny. At the time, Jayce had been so distraught and off balance that he had simply accepted the lies and misdirection and fallen in line. But since they had been locked in this room together, he had slowly begun to recover some of his wit.

He had been watching as she gave direction to the men who came to check on them. He had commented on how familiar she was here, how she retrieved salted meat and wine from a pantry and had pulled new bandages and poultice from a shelf for his hands. His gaze was becoming ever more and more suspicious as the time dragged on and she kept catching him sneaking furtive glances at her when he thought she was not looking. Finally, as they saw the first signs of daylight that were starting to edge over the rooftops in the distant east, the sailor burst, unable to contain his questions any longer.

"Lyra, what is going on?" He demanded, his voice hoarse and strained from everything he had gone through in the past day, "Who are all these people? How do you know them so well? What are we doing here?"

Lyra looked over at him. She let the questions hang in the air for a bit. Her mind ran through a series of scenarios and she attempted to think through the potential for each of her options. She considered attempting to prolong her ruse, but ultimately saw little point in it any longer. Still, she needed him. She wandered over and sat beside him, taking his hands in hers. She met his gaze as she responded, her tone soft yet direct.

"My name is Lyra, but I haven't been honest with you about who I am or what my intentions are. I work for a man named Hector. This is his place of business, one of many he operates throughout the city." She spoke slowly and deliberately, trying to keep her voice as calm as possible.

"Doing what?" He cast a look around the dimly lit basement, "What kind of business operates a processing room in the middle of the night?"

Lyra took a deep breath. She tried to keep her tone level and conversational, "Hector works in imports and exports. He works with tradesmen all across the Federation and beyond and has his ventures in many different fields..."

"So crime, then?" Jayce interrupted flatly. When she stared back at him, face impassive, he shook his head, "So...working with the gardener at the University was just a cover?"

"Yes. I needed to get into the University and it was the best and fastest way we could find."

"You were there for..."

"*You*, Jayce," she said emphatically, "we received information that the Roth's had sent someone to the University, and that person was a member of the Acosta Company. We didn't know more than that, but we had suspicions that there was something major taking place, and we needed to know what it was."

Jayce blinked. He considered this for a moment, his eyes searching the ceiling as his mind struggled to keep up, "That's why you approached me that day...Oh, Gods, I should've known better. I'm such a fool."

"Don't be so hard on yourself. You're no covert agent, Jayce. I figured that out the first day I met you." She smirked in a teasing sort of way but he was in no mood for her attempts at levity.

"But you are, right? You're...a con artist? You were playing me to get information?" He ripped his hands away from hers.

"I was." She did not deny it. She leaned back in her chair, watching him with curiosity.

"How can you be so calm?" He spat, "I thought I knew you, knew what you were about, but clearly you're not the person I thought you were. To *use* someone like that..."

"No more than you did."

"I-what?" He stared at her uncomprehendingly, blue eyes searching her face for some hidden meaning.

She waved a hand nonchalantly over her gray servant robes, "You thought I was a gardener's aid, no? Not even an apprentice Greenhand, just a common hedge minder. Can you honestly tell me you planned to take me with you when you were a full blown Arcanist? Were you going to take me with you when you went back to the Roth's? What about when you went home to the Breach and that great Acosta fortune?"

"Well...I suppose I was..." he muttered, but the indignation had been replaced by an air of doubt and apprehension, "I had no intentions of leaving you..."

"Oh, surely you had no *intentions*," she ladled on sarcasm as thick as the fat renderings off an oily everlasting stew, "no one ever has bad intentions. But if you're honest with yourself, you know the truth as well as I do. If I were the person you thought I was, you'd have had your fun with me until it was time for you to leave this city, then you'd have been off without a spare glance backward."

"Lyra, it's not...I'm not like that...you *mean* something to me."

"Oh really?" She cracked a crooked grin as she saw him squirm under the unrelenting pressure, "Tell me, how long after we met did you go buy the purple root powder? The one you didn't even bother to hide, in the tin by your bedside?"

He froze. His mouth moved but no noise came out. There was a look of panic about his eyes that she relished almost as much as she had the sensation of stabbing the ancient wizard earlier the same night.

"No...can't risk having a child with some poor peasant girl, can we?"

"But...that's not..." his voice was desperate, pleading, "you don't want a child with me, we've only just met..."

The look she gave him withered any scrap of pride he had clung to. His face fell as she responded, "Of course not. But do you really think that is the point? You never brought it up to me, never mentioned it. Not once, why is that? Did you think your gardener girl was holding on to hope she might be blessed with an Acosta child? That I was looking for a golden ship to sail me out of my lot in life? That I might not be as willing to keep entertaining this relationship without that hope?"

She could see on his face that he at least had the decency to admit the truth to himself. Even if his affection for her had been genuine, it was always secondary to his own desire. He hung his head, dejected. She waited for a moment, letting him wallow in the revelation of his own

"Don't worry, at least you're in good company. All you merchants and new nobility are the same. You get your feet out of the marsh and you can't wait to pull the ladder up behind you." She gave him a sideways glance, "Do you know how many men I've had try and court me, only to be hiding their use of purple root powder or silphion tea?"

"You're wrong about me, Lyra. I'm not like that. I just...needed to focus on my studies right now..." Jayce cocked his head, as if a thought suddenly occurred to him, "What exactly is it that you do for this Hector, Lyra?"

"A lot of things." She answered bluntly, "None of that is important to you right now. What is important is that you understand the situation you're in and that you listen to me, that's why I'm telling you all this."

Jayce snorted and shook his head, "Why would I listen to you?"

"Because if you don't, you'll likely be dead before you see your next dawn."

He stopped giving her that look that said he was going to be as obstinate as possible and unfolded his arms. He paused for a moment and then nodded to her in acquiescence. She leaned forward and stared him straight in the eyes.

"Listen closely, because you're only going to have one shot at this. The men that have been coming and going have told me the University is already scouring the city. They've offered a king's ransom in Federal Marks for you. They say you tried to kill the Archmage..."

"*What?!*" Jayce exclaimed, eyes going wide.

"*Shh*...listen for once, you dolt." She hissed, putting a finger in front of her lips, "I've been listening to you bitch and moan for half the season, you should be able to manage for a few moments."

He shut his mouth. Looking terrified and sullen all at once.

"The man I work for has no compulsions about returning you to the University. In fact I'm sure he would do it gladly. So your only chance is if we can convince him that you're worth more alive and under his protection than sold off to the highest bidder. Do you understand?"

Jayce nodded slowly. She could see the wheels turning slowly in his mind.

"We know now that the Sovereign is unaware of the plot. From the Archmage's own mouth, this conspiracy is operating without his knowledge. Therefore, we need to convince Hector that getting you in front of the Sovereign is the surest way to ensure he is bathed in riches and treasure. That is the only way we can be sure he won't take you straight back to the University as soon as he gets here."

For a moment, Jayce was silent. Then his eyes lit up, "What about Lucian? I'm sure if you just get me there he can figure out a way to..."

Lyra's expression gave away the truth before she could, "They've already taken your friend, Jayce. The Legionnaires arrested him and his wife on suspicion of collusion to commit the murder of the Archmage."

The young man's face fell. He stared at her, utterly lost for a moment. Then he took a breath and attempted to collect himself, "What about Mariana? Was she taken as well?"

"They didn't mention the girl."

He was about to speak when the door burst open. The broad form of Hector stood in the doorway, two of his bulky retainers shadowing him to either side. He wore his typical work clothes and bore no signs of being woken. She wondered, as she often had before, if he had even been to sleep. The large man was always about, always alert, as long as she had known him. His golden eyes gleamed in the low light as he strode up to the pair of them, a harsh grin on his face. He eyed Jayce for a long moment before turning to Lyra, placing a massive bear like paw gently on her shoulder.

"I see you've brought us a golden goose, my dear." His voice was a low, purring rumble in his chest, "Well done, we shall make quite the feast tonight."

Jayce tensed but Lyra held out a subtle hand. He relaxed slightly, never taking his wide eyes off the big man, but he sat at the edge of his chair and seemed ready to bolt at a moment's notice. Lyra turned her attention back to Hector, who had observed this exchange with a small grin on his face.

"Lyra, what did you promise this boy to get him to come here?" He cast a glance at his men with a wicked grin, who both loomed behind him like malevolent gargoyles menacing the exit, "I knew he was a fool, but surely he's guessed at your ruse by now?"

Lyra smirked, "I've already told him everything, but only to make this deal go easier."

Hector raised one of his bushy eyebrows, "Deal? The only deal I intend to make tonight is for this boy's hide."

Lyra shook her head, "You're not thinking through all the angles, Hector."

"Enlighten me."

"We found proof of a secret cabal within the University tonight."

"That is no great surprise." The big man scratched at his dark, wiry beard, in a distracted manner, "Sorcerer's spawn secret societies like snakes give birth to their wicked offspring."

"This one is committing some grand plot with Oaren-hiem, without the Sovereign's knowledge." Lyra said pointedly,

"They're the ones that have been spiriting children away from the capital."

Hector stopped scratching and looked over at Jayce for the first time since the conversation started, "Is that what you were hoping to find, boy? What the Roth's sent you here for?"

Jayce nodded. He had a thin sheet of sweat across his brow and had his eyes locked on Hector like the man would be on him if he so much as blinked. The big man considered this. He rubbed his mitten like hands together and muttered to himself.

"The rewards would be great, uncovering a plot so treasonous, and with such important players, But the risks..."

Lyra waited a moment before interrupting his musings, "As of now, the people in this room are the only ones in the city who are aware of this conspiracy and are in a position to tell the Sovereign of it. They've already gotten to the delegate from the Horn. Jayce has only one hope if he is to get to the Sovereign, and that's you. I'm sure he would be *eternally* grateful to you if you chose to help him."

She shot Jayce a look. He stuttered for a moment before getting his footing in the conversation, "Oh, uh, yes...of course. I'm sure the Sovereign would be grateful for your helping me get word to him as well. But I and the Roth's would of course be in your debt..."

"-and the Acosta company as well?" Hector cut in, his eyes shining as he stared at Jayce, "I'm sure they would be pleased that I saved their only son from these devilish traitors."

"Y-yes, I'm sure they would be." Jayce said, apprehension coating every syllable as he spoke.

The big man took hold of his shoulder suddenly. Jayce looked like he was on the verge of a complete breakdown as Hector pulled him in close so that he was looking directly into his golden eyes.

"How would you feel about being partners?" He asked with a tone that spoke volumes about what the alternative would be.

Jayce swallowed hard, "Technically, the company is not mine. I cannot by rights make you a partner."

"Not yet, boy. But in time, it will be, and when that day comes you will remember those that made sure you lived to get there, yes?" He held out one of his massive hands and waited expectantly, eyeing Jayce.

Jayce sat there looking hopelessly lost. He shot a desperate glance at Lyra, but she only watched with arms crossed expectantly. A look of resignation crossed his face and he sighed, reaching out and shaking Hector's hand with less enthusiasm than if the big man had offered to cut out his kidneys with a butter knife. Hector grinned and clapped the Stormspeaker on the back.

"Don't worry my boy, I see big things on the horizon for us, big things indeed."

D ay was just beginning to break over the city. Lyra watched as golden streaks cut through the darkness and pierced the layer of fog that had rolled in from the lake. She stood on one of the loading docks of Hector's warehouse, watching the men who were already busying themselves with their business of piling goods into the carts for delivery. She held a large mug in her hand, inhaling the steam as it wafted floral notes up from the tea. There were birds singing in the distance and she could see the smoke coming from the bakery chimneys, earthy scents of cooking bread and pastries mixing with the city scents. Women were emptying chamber pots and waste water into the street. No sewers in this part of the city. The witchlights were slowly beginning to dim and would be out within the hour.

She listened to the sounds of the city as it woke up from the summer night and sighed, letting herself relax for the first time in days. Just then, Hector ambled up beside her. He held an apple in one hand which he was noisily chewing. Lyra found herself fascinated as she watched him, as he seemed utterly incapable of taking a single bite without sending a new spurt of juices all into his beard and down his hand.

"That appears to be the juiciest apple I've ever seen." She commented flatly, shaking her head, "Are you going to clean yourself up after you're done or should I have one of the boys get a bucket and horsebrush?"

Hector snorted and gave a grunting sort of laugh with his mouth full. He quickly devoured the last bites of the apple before hurling the core out into the street. It exploded into a mess on the cobblestones.

"Now why would you go and do that? There's perfectly good bins in here for trash."

Hector wiped his mouth on the back of his hand, then wiped his hand on his pants. He spat and turned to her, "Why do you want me to save that boy?"

"What?"

"You heard me, girlie." He pointed one of his sausage fingers at her, "You could have taken him back yourself, got the coin and bought your precious territory from me. Could've started your own thing. But you brought him here, served him up to me on a silver platter."

Lyra paused for a moment before recovering smoothly, "I knew the score would be bigger if we can get him to the Sovereign. Enough to buy any territories I want. Hell, I could start up my own business in some other city with this payday. But I can't get him to the Sovereign myself. You're the only one with the resources to pull something like that off, especially with that bounty on his head. Half the city will be looking for him, not even counting all the damn Arcanists."

Hector nodded, his golden eyes searching her up and down. For a long moment, he said nothing. They listened to the men grunting and cursing as they worked. Finally, Hector spoke up, his tone carefully neutral.

"The boy's not going to have an easy go of it." He said, casting a glance back towards the building. Jayce was asleep in a hidden storeroom, locked away where Hector kept his most illegal goods stored safe from prying eyes and watchmen's searches, "He's soft, like a lamb fresh from the tit. This isn't going to be easy. It's going to be dangerous and take a lot of grit too. If they've got any sense at all, these damned sorcerers are going to keep the Sovereign on tight lockdown now that they've lost their man."

Lyra nodded, "But you can do it, yes? Get him in front of the Sovereign?"

He chewed on his thumbnail, eyes roving over the cityscape endlessly, "I might, if some things go right for us, and some others go wrong for the wizards. But it'll be tight. Better if we take the easy route and just give him up now, lose out on the big payday but save ourselves the headache."

"You did tell me I needed to take risks if I wanted to get to where you are."

Hector grunted at that, "Did I? Must've been in the cups that night."

Lyra gave him a look and he sighed. He looked up to the brightening sky and spoke aloud to it, "May all the God's curse me for the day I decided I needed daughters and not just more blockhead sons."

Lyra smiled. She took a long sip from her tea and looked back out to the city, enjoying the moment. She was roused when she realized Hector was staring at her again.

"What?"

"Of all my flowers, you're the most lovely. So it pains me indeed to tell you this. You're going to have to make a choice here, girlie. You can't have it all."

"What do you mean?" She could not keep her tone from turning indignant as she turned to face him.

"The boy." Hector nodded towards the building, "There's a great chance this goes badly for him, even if we manage to get him in front of the Sovereign to tell his tale. There's going to be a lot of people after him after this. He won't be safe. Chances are, this ends bloody for him, one way or another, unless he leaves town, most likely the Southlands altogether."

She wanted to protest, to deny her interest in him. But it was pointless. Something had taken root inside her, no matter how hard she had fought it. She thought to argue that Hector was wrong, and that she could root out all the conspirators in this mage's shadow game. But the part of her that was cold and dark and hard knew better than that. Hector had been her mentor for nearly fifteen years and he had rarely been wrong about this sort of thing.

Hector went on, undeterred by her furrowed brow and frown of disapproval, "If you want your own territory, run your own crew, carve out a part of this city for yourself, you'll have to choose. Maybe that choice will be made for you, but if it's not, you need to be prepared."

He gave her a small, pitying smile before turning and starting to walk back over to the other workers. She reached out and grabbed his arm, "But, couldn't I just take the coin and the boy and start anew somewhere?"

"Aye, you could. But are you sure that's what you want?" He gave her a steady look, golden eyes searching her face, "After all you've sacrificed, after the work you've done here? This is *your* city, Lyra. Do you want to give that up? Can you?"

Lyra was silent for a while. Hector patted her on the shoulder and walked away. She turned and stared back out at the city, her mind not as peaceful as it had been only moments before.

L yra arrived at the shack in Wetrun without squelching boots this time. It had not rained in days and all the streets were dry packed clay. The children were playing in the morning sun and people busied themselves as they hurried up and down the byway. She slipped out of the traffic and approached the front door, nodding to the two burly men who manned their posts on the porch. One grunted and opened the door for her, just as always. She went in and was immediately cast into dim light which took her eyes a moment to adjust.

Once they had, she searched the tiny home for Mother Moore, finding her seated in an easy chair in the corner. She was sipping tea and nibbling on a plate of biscuits, both of her ancient hands wrapped around the steaming cup as she brought it to her lips. When Lyra caught sight of her, she approached cautiously, worried she might startle the old woman, who had yet to acknowledge her presence in the least. Her milky eyes seemed to stare at nothing.

"Mother Moore?" Lyra said gently, kneeling beside the old woman.

"Little Lyra," she said, her voice as smooth and strong as ever, "you've found the children?"

"I...sort of. There is a...cabal of sorts at the University. They are stealing away children with the Gift in secret. We don't know for what purpose yet, nor how far this corruption goes."

Mother Moore was silent for a long moment. She took a sip from her tea and set it down, raising her shaking hands to Lyra's face. She held them there for a moment, then took a deep breath. Her rheumy eyes suddenly focused on Lyra's, appearing silvery and clear like coins polished to mirror brightness. Then Lyra felt herself tumble backwards into darkness. She felt like she was free falling, tumbling backwards endlessly through a barrage of colors and sounds.

She recognized some memories and feelings of the past few days. Other things were alien to her, events she had not witnessed, sensations she had no names for. She felt like she came unglued in time and was desperately seeking for her something solid to grasp on to. She had no idea how long it lasted, but when she finally became aware she was back in her own body, she felt herself shaking and covered in a cold sweat. She was still kneeling on the floor and Mother Moore was staring at her with her milky eyes.

"What was that?" She breathed, struggling to stand as she backed away from the old woman. She could barely speak as she felt like the wind had been forced out of her lungs.

"I just took a look inside, dear. This is too important to leave to the fickle whims of half memories and partial recollections."

She fought hard to recollect herself. She had known Mother Moore almost her entire life, seen her work minor miracles and healings for dozens of the Wetrun's citizens, but she had never seen her do something like that. It was an experience that made her reconsider everything she knew about the old woman.

"What did you see?"

The crone shook her head in disgust. She made a clicking sound with her tongue and spoke like she was sorely disappointed, "Children playing with their grandparents knives."

"But what does that *mean*?" Lyra moved so she was in front of the old woman. Her eyes had returned to their typical unfocused milky white, but with what she knew now, she wondered exactly how much the woman actually saw.

"*Harnessing...*" she said the word as though it were a curse, "They've found the old secrets of that dark magic and they're trying to resurrect it."

Lyra blinked, "Why do you care? Aren't you a witch?"

The old woman waved a hand in a dismissive gesture, "There are all kinds of forbidden magic, dear. Those stuffy old men in their towers and grand halls think they know so much, but the truth is their rules and regulations restrict them as much as they do everyone else. But Harnessing is something else entirely, that magic should have stayed buried wherever it was."

She considered this, still not entirely recovered from the experience of having the old woman in her head. She took a deep breath, "Alright then, if it's so dangerous, what are we going to do about it?"

The old woman blinked at her. She motioned to a stool which sat against the wall to her side, "Sit, Lyra. Things are moving very quickly now and we have much to discuss."

CHAPTER TWENTY-NINE

LEGACY

Lawrence blinked at Holton and his crew, who had all gathered around, watching the mage with predatory focus in their eyes. The mage licked his lips as his eyes darted around the ship like a cornered animal looking for its way out. He glanced back towards the shore, only a small cluster of flickering lights in the darkness now.

"Holton, what is this?"

The red haired thief sighed and ran a hand over his hair, rubbing the back of his head, "It's like this, Lawrence, you've paid well so far, far more generously than any other employer we've had in the past. Up until recently, this partnership has worked out for both of us...but we have certain concerns."

"Such as...?" Lawrence eyed him, suspicion playing across his face.

"Well look at what just happened, Lawrence. You were caught and we were all in the dark about what your plans are or where we're going. Hell, we don't even know who we're working for and you're our only point of contact. You left us with no other option but to rescue you..."

"-for which you'll be *handsomely* rewarded..." Lawrence interrupted, but Holton pressed on.

"See, that's not enough anymore. Understand, one of my men died just a day ago. Because some unseen employers insisted we capture the Prince, not kill him like I wanted to. Then, when he broke out and murdered one of my men, you again insisted we *still* keep him alive." Holton leaned forward, placing his elbows on his knees and getting close enough to smell the pungent mixture of sweat and perfume that still lingered on the well dressed mage, "I'm at my wits end here Lawrence. I need more information."

The mage's eyes flicked between the thieves and Holton could see the calculations spinning in his mind. He gave him a grim smirk.

"Wondering if you can fight your way out of this?" He asked, tone mocking, "Let me help you out, you can't. See, I figured you mages out a long time ago. You have lots of power, but you're not like a weather witch or a Fireweaver, you can't do it quickly. That is, unless you have your little toys, but they took all those off you back at the prison, didn't they?"

Lawrence's eyes widened and for the first time since he had met the man, the mage seemed to struggle with what to say next. The boat gently buffeted back and forth on the waves, the night air breeze cool as it cut across the open ocean. Finally, he managed to croak out a few words.

"You are...more resourceful than I gave you credit for."

Holton smiled, letting menace fill his toothy grin, "Let's start off simply, what are you doing with all these children?"

Lawrence swallowed hard, "Holton, we've been over this, everything is on a need to know basis..."

Holton felt his hand drift towards his belt, as he did his best to keep his anger in check. His voice held onto its civility by a thread, "I *need* to know, Lawrence. These aren't recruits. These are prisoners. You told me they weren't going to be hurt."

"They haven't been. A little sleeping spell, maybe a bit of rough handling, but none of these children have seen any real pain." Lawrence argued weakly, face taking on a pallid tone.

"You're avoiding the question."

Lawrence cast a glance around the small boat, but found no allies in the hard faces of the crew of thieves. He sighed and turned back to Holton. The last traces of his cheeky grin were gone and he was left looking glum and defeated. Finally, he managed to find his words.

"I suppose, given your contributions, I can make some allowances." He licked his lips again, pushing his fingers through his disheveled tangle of dark hair, "We need the children for their Gift."

Holton blinked, "The children are mages?"

Lawrence snorted, "No. An *Arcanist*, what you insist on calling mages, are trained for years at one of the Universities. They are not even settled, practitioners of the Low Art, like a Stormspeaker as you say. They simply have the talent for the craft, the innate ability required to wield magic."

Erin cut in, "If they can't do anything, then what could you possibly need them for?"

Lawrence sighed, "I don't know how to explain this to you, it requires a deep understanding of the laws and concepts of magic that we simply do not have time for me to teach you."

"Try." Holton growled.

Lawrence grimaced, "Fine. There is an Arcanist in Oarenhiem, a genius artificer. He has discovered the secrets of Harnessing."

"Secrets?"

"Yes," Lawrence said, clearly frustrated as he rushed through his explanation, "there are nine disciplines of magic, the High Arts. That is what the various Universities teach. But there are also disciplines that are forbidden. The arts that are too dangerous to study or teach, ones that violate the cardinal principles of the Arcanists Guild."

"You people have a guild?" Jarryd commented nonchalantly.

"It's just a loose association of the major Universities from across the world. But they created a set of cardinal principles after the First War of the Southlands and they each enforce the rules within their own domains." He had a distinctly uncomfortable look, "Too many Arcanists messed around with powers that were outside of their control during that conflict, desperate for anything that would give them the edge. It was decided after that there were lines we should never cross."

"But you're going to now..." Holton observed, unable to keep the edge out of his voice.

"We have a...*unique* opportunity." Lawrence lifted his chin, defiant, "After the Cardinal Principles were created and many types of magic were outlawed, their secrets were lost over the generations. No one knows how most of those magics were done. Only the highest authorities have any real knowledge of them. But this artificer and his coalition have unearthed the secrets of Harnessing somehow, and they are going to use them to overthrow the Emperor of Oarenhiem."

"So...you're using these children as a power source?" Erin asked, a look of disgust on her face.

"More or less. Imagine one Arcanist with the power of two, or three, or ten!" His eyes were distant at that moment, all the apprehension melted away. They reminded Holton of many of the criminals he had known in his time, full of dark intent. Lawrence spoke like a starving man describing the banquet of his dreams, "A man with that kind of power could do anything. The world would be his for the taking!"

"And you're going to be that man, are you?" Holton interjected, knocking him out of his stupor.

Lawrence blinked, seeming to remember himself, "No, of course not...I'm just saying, the possibilities are endless. No, there is a powerful Arcanist who has spearheaded this entire operation. I'm sure she will be the one to wield the weapon, once it's completed."

There was a pause. Holton mulled this over in his mind. When he spoke, it was with slow, deliberate emphasis, "What happens to the children when you do this?"

Lawrence looked back at him, brow furrowed in incomprehension, "What do you mean?"

"Will they survive the process, Lawrence?" Holton demanded, his tone flat.

"I...why do you care?"

"Just answer the question." Erin cut in, voice harsh.

"I don't know," he admitted, shrugging his shoulders in a manner that made Holton want to wring his neck like a chicken, "does it matter? Holton, you and your crew are going to be nobility after this. What I promised you still holds. Once we've retaken the colonies, the New World will be ours for the taking. We are all going to be kings in our own nations."

Holton paused. He looked at Erin, then to the rest of his crew. He furrowed his brow, considering his next step.

"Where are we going once we get to the New World? Who's the buyer? I need a name, Lawrence."

Lawrence smirked, "If I tell you that, what's to stop you from cutting me out of this deal?"

"Good faith." Barney interjected, his tone flat. He had a dark look on his face and Holton thought he caught the hint of sparks at his fingertips.

"You're going to need to trust us, Lawrence." Holton said in a low voice, meeting the mages gaze with his own, "A good crew runs on trust. Without that, you have nothing. Things have gotten more complicated. The stakes are higher now. We need to know we're all on the same side. If you can't trust us, after all this, we can't work together."

Lawrence took a moment. He stared at Holton, the calculations running behind his dark eyes. He sighed again.

"I suppose I have no choice. The plan is to meet up with the Blades contingent in New Oarenhiem. They have a stronghold there. The man in charge of the Blades is named Royce, Royce Broderick. He's the only one that communicates with the people in Oarenhiem directly, they're the ones that want the children, so he's the man we need to see."

Holton took a breath. He put a hand on Lawrence's shoulder and gave him a grin, "That wasn't so bad, was it? No need for all this cloak and dagger. From now on, we're going to be open with each other, right?"

Lawrence nodded, silent as he stared at the red haired thief. Holton made a motion and the men all began rowing again. Lawrence attempted to conceal the sigh of relief he breathed as he turned and faced the forward of the boat again. He glanced back towards the city.

"I'm glad we were able to make this work. You are quite impressive, Holton. I'm amazed you were able to facilitate such a rescue with such a small number of men."

"Oh, we had help," he said casually, standing, "Carrigan lent us his crew as well. They provided our distraction."

"Really? Are they...meeting us with us at the *Sabre*?"

Holton glanced over at Erin, who inclined her head. He shrugged, "They were supposed to meet us at the port. I'm not sure what kept them, but hopefully they'll make it before we shove off."

The *Sabre* had been anchored off the cost of a small, un-inhabited island outside the Bay, just off the coast. The men had kept the lights to a minimum and the ship was near silent so Holton and his crew were nearly upon it before they found its foreboding form in the gloom. Once they had clambered aboard and roused the crew, Lawrence took command without missing a beat.

"Alright gentlemen," he said, voice once again carrying his signature swagger, "now that that little delay is behind us, we are shoving off as immediately. We do have a schedule to keep."

"Hold on," a voice called out. Carrigan moved through the crowd, still wearing his red cloak, a dark expression on his face, "where are my men? What happened to Kacey?"

Holton and his crew still stood nearby, busying themselves as they finished unloading the boat before casting it adrift out to sea. He motioned back towards the city, "They never met us at the port, must've hit some trouble. They were our distraction, so mayhaps they got caught up before they could make their exit."

Carrigan frowned, considering the thief for a moment. He turned to Lawrence, "We need to go back and get them. We can't leave them behind."

The mage looked from him to Holton and back again. His usual smirk widened into a full grin, "Carrigan, so glad you were able to keep the ship safe while I was gone, but I'm afraid we won't have time for that. We're too far behind schedule already."

Carrigan's frown deepened and he turned to cast an accusatory glare at Holton and his crew once again, "You did this. You left them behind."

"It's not our fault your crew couldn't handle a simple assignment without being caught. Maybe you should've been with them to hold their hands." Erin snapped back at him.

Carrigan looked like he could spit. He fumbled, silent words forming in his mouth as he tried to speak. Finally, he turned back to Lawrence, seeming to come to a conclusion, "This doesn't change our deal. You still owe me, for their share."

Lawrence nodded, keeping his expression pointedly blank.

The mage seemed satisfied. He nodded back, cast one last suspicious glare at Holton's crew, then turned and stalked back across the deck. Lawrence gave Holton a curious expression, seeming to consider the thief for a long moment, before turning and beginning to give out orders to his men, striding across the deck.

T he ocean waves beat rhythmically against the hull as the *Sabre* cut through the dark water of the Lancing Ocean. Holton and his crew had made their quarters in one of the lower rooms, hammocks swaying as snores filled the air. Jarryd and Barney had passed out as soon as they were able to lie down, exhausted from the day. Erin sat beside Holton on the floor, head on his shoulder as they passed a bottle of liquor back and forth. She had just finished a large gulp and wiped her mouth on the back of her hand as she spoke, a slight slur in her speech as she struggled not to stumble over her words.

"Where in the world did you find Icefellers this far South, Holt?"

"You like it?" He took the bottle from her and took a long swig, "I thought it would be an appropriate celebration, assuming things worked out tonight."

Erin adjusted her position a bit, voice dropping a few octaves, "Things did work out alright, didn't they?"

Holton made a face, "Sure. We got what we wanted, right? The Watch moved on the safe house after you slipped them that information, just like we planned. We got what we wanted from the mage and he's none the wiser. We even managed to clear out most of Carrigan's crew. It's a shame we couldn't get rid of him too, but at least he's just one person to deal with if we need to. Plus, you saw what happened up on deck, Lawrence doesn't hold our colleague in the best of regards currently. Where did you send Kacey and the others by the way?"

"Told them the exit plan was to meet up at a port on the other side of town. Then Jarryd dropped a hint to the Watch that there were some smugglers working over there, planning a big operation, gave them Kacey's description and everything. I'm sure they ran right into the Watchmen's arms. Just like Blackwater..."

Holton snorted. He held up the bottle and clinked with an imaginary tankard in front of him, "To another job well done."

Erin was lost in thought for a moment. She made a motion and Holton handed her the bottle back, "Have you thought much about what he said out there, about the children?"

"No, not really."

Erin pushed off of him and looked him hard in the face. Her expression was disapproving through the haze of alcohol, "*Not really*? He said those kids won't survive whatever this thing is they need them for."

"He said he didn't know." Holton corrected, but his tone lacked conviction.

Erin snorted. She took a swig from the bottle and swayed a bit, keeping her glazed eyes on her brother, "You know what that means. You know how these people are. These kids are as good as dog meat if we hand them over to the Blades."

"We've already handed them over..."

"You know what I mean," she interrupted angrily, waving her hands, "if we go through with this, we're sentencing all these kids to something terrible."

"So what, Erin, what do you want to do? Break them all free, run back to the Evardene? Spend the rest of our lives running from the Blades and every government on the continent?" Holton fixed with a harsh glare, "Give up this future we've been working so hard to create?"

She was defiant, holding her chin up and meeting his gaze. He sighed and ran a hand through his hair, cursing under his breath. Finally he looked at her, trying his best to speak through the haze, "Don't worry Erin, if it comes to that, we'll figure something out. We always do."

She looked skeptical, but let the matter drop, and they sat drinking the rest of the bottle in silence as the ocean slipped by in the dead of night.

I t was still dark when Holton woke again. He saw that Erin was passed out on the floor, the bottle clutched close to her chest. He pulled a blanket off one of the hammocks and covered her up, careful not to wake her. Then he slipped out of the room, closing the door behind him. It was near pitch black in the bowels of the ship. He wandered along without a torch, letting his hand run along the walls to help guide him. Most of the crew was still fast asleep.

This steam powered boat did not require a massive number of rowers or men to man the sails at all hours, so only a skeleton crew stayed awake this late to keep it on track. The whirring of the propeller blades were a constant companion, always droning on in the background like a wind that never lessened or grew. It set his nerves on edge, no matter how much he tried to block it out. He passed no one else as he found his way along, until he finally descended the stairs into the ship's hold. There, he found himself amongst the rows and rows of cages.

The small shapes of children huddled in their rags and soiled clothes, whimpering or mumbling in their forced slumber. They seemed so small. He ambled along, watching them, trying to remember how many Carrigan had said there had been. It seemed like so many. It was disconcerting to see them all gathered around like this at once, like he had somehow been able to ignore the numbers until now. Most were in their early years, but a few were edging up towards adulthood. He saw one young boy who might have been the same age as he was when he and Erin had fled their family farm. The boy had a mop of brown hair that was too long, hanging over his eyes in an unkempt mess. He stared at the boy for a long time.

Then he heard a groan. One that was distinctly not childish. He stalked along the row, crouching slightly, searching for the source. Then he saw it. All the way at the back, pressed against the rear wall, was a cage significantly larger than the rest. Inside, Prince Cassius Roth was huddled in the corner, wrapped in a ragged blanket. He straightened and approached the cage, watching the young man. He had his head between his knees and was cradling his left arm. Holton stood there, staring at him for a while, before speaking.

"Hurts, does it?"

The Prince looked up suddenly, eyes darting wildly around. When he noticed Holton, the look turned from surprise to fierce rage. He glared through the bars like a man trying to burn holes in something with his eyes, "What are you doing here?"

Holton said nothing at first. He stood a few feet away, just out of arm's length. He watched the Prince with a sort of morbid fascination, wondering at the young man's constitution. It actually surprised him that the Prince was conscious at all.

"Did they give you anything for the pain?" He asked finally, nodding towards the Prince's stump.

"A bit of clove leaf to chew on and some willow tea. Not that it makes much difference." He held the stump up so Holton could see it. It was a mess of bandages and layers of cloth that reeked of herbal poultice. Blood had stopped leaking out and was now dried, leaving large stains on the bandages. The cut had been clean and, thankfully for the Prince, it would heal well given the right attention. The Prince tucked it back under his other arm.

"You're lucky," Holton said casually, leaning against a crate beside him, "I've seen an injury like that go untreated and get infected. One of the guys I used to run with lost his arm up the elbow that way."

Cassius cast him a withering look, "Is that what you came here to tell me?"

Holton grinned. He fiddled with the head of his hatchet, still strapped at his waist, "Better watch that tone with me, boy. Or I might just have to take that other hand too."

The Prince kept his defiant look, "Are your masters going to let you do that?"

In a flash, he felt the rage boil up inside him. But he dampened it down and forced a grin, "Didn't stop me from taking the first one, did they?"

The Prince said nothing. He just stared back, still seated and cradling stump. Holton waited for a moment, then went on, "You know, you killed a man I considered a brother yesterday. If you weren't the son of a Baron you'd be dead right now."

A twitch crossed his face, something between a grimace and a frown. Cassius struggled to his feet, wincing at the pain. He was heavily favoring his left leg. The right one was bandaged tightly around the thigh like the ruin of his left hand. His stare was full of a ferocious defiance that took Holton by surprise.

"There are no titles down here, brigand. Open that door, take your revenge...now's your chance."

Holton blinked. For a moment, he was struck dumb by the sheer brashness of the Prince's demeanor. Finally he shook his head, grinning. He stalked up to the cage and put his face as close to the bars as he could without touching. He could smell the stink of sweat and blood on the Prince mixing with his general unwashed filth. He was reminded of the distinct odors of combat and freshly butchered meat that he had become so familiar with over the years. He met the Prince's gaze with a steady, harsh gaze, unsympathetic to the man's obvious pain.

"You think I'd let you die a martyr's death? Spare yourself the shame of being the bargaining chip?" He gave the Prince the most withering look he could muster, "You're a fool, boy. You let your pride yank you around by the nose. You got your men killed. I'm not giving you the easy out. You're going to have to live with what you've done."

Cassius held his defiant stare for a moment longer. But he blinked and lowered his gaze, eyes falling to his bloodied stump. His shoulders slumped and his expression reminded Holton of the time he saw a man who had watched his ship sinking in the Blackwater Bay. For once, the Prince was lost at a loss for words. Satisfied, Holton started to turn to leave. But he was stopped by the sound of the Prince's voice, low and barely audible over the rhythmic beating of waves against the hull.

"What are you doing with the children, Holton?"

He turned back, surprised. Cassius was once again staring at him, eyes still haunted but hardened against the weight of his failure. He was again meeting Holton's eye, an expectant look which carried the uncanny command of nobility. Holton grinned and held his hands out.

"You've no sense at all of self preservation, do you boy?"

The Prince was undeterred, continuing as if he had not heard Holton's jeer.

"Tell me what they're going to do with these kids." He demanded, "Your masters, they have some great scheme, some plan. I know they do. But their intentions can't be benign. If they were, these children wouldn't be prisoners."

Holton felt his grin slip a bit, "You're in no position to be making demands, *my Lord*."

Cassius cocked his head, "Are you truly so wicked? That you'd be party to the pain of all these innocents?"

"Don't speak to me of wickedness," Holton snapped. He stalked forward until he was face to face with the Prince again, "were you not the one who was imprisoning children so far from the light? Did you not pursue me halfway across the continent to return those children to their fate?"

"Those children are practitioners of *witchcraft*. They are a danger to themselves and everyone around them." Cassius replied, his voice earnest. He shook his head and looked around the room, "These are innocent...can you not see plainly they've been stolen away from their homes?"

"Those children are no more a danger than any of these others." Holton growled through gritted teeth, surprising himself as he felt the heat rising in his chest, "But you and your kind would damn them to a lifetime in hell just to appease your precious sensibilities, wouldn't you?"

"My kind..." Cassius stared at him for a long moment.

"Nobles, Lords...North, South, you're all the same."

The Prince's eyes were shaded in the low light and Holton had a hard time reading his expression. He stood there for a long moment, waiting for the other man to respond. He was ready to take his leave when the Prince finally spoke up again.

"I don't imagine you would know much of the Covenant." His resolute tone bespoke no ill will. It was forthright, with a sense of passion that took Holton entirely by surprise, "We are a fellowship that is distinguished, not by blood, but by deeds and by oath. One cannot buy the titles of Dux, Valorus, Servitas nor Regalis. One cannot inherit it. It must be bestowed in recognition for great service and great strength of character."

Holton stared at the man on the other side of the cell bars. This speech had come on so suddenly, so unexpectedly, that he had not had the presence of mind to retort. He simply listened in surprise.

"We believe that there is a greater calling for men than that of rank or privilege, or personal gain or even the service to one's lord. That is why a brother of the Covenant may be risen from any class, not just from amongst the nobility. We serve a greater legacy than any one man, lord, or commoner. We believe that having the strength and means to protect the weak instills upon you the duty to do so."

For a long while, Holton could only stand as his mind attempted to make sense of the garble of self righteous idiocy the Prince had vomited upon him. Finally, he snorted. Then he shook his head, unbelieving.

"You nobles...you're all the same, aren't you? Do you really presume to lecture me about *duty*? About honor? *You*?"

In one quick motion, he pulled up his shirt and showed the Prince a particularly nasty scar on his right side. It was faded now, a spiderweb of white lines which had been reopened with new wounds and tattooed over in the lifetime that had followed its initial infliction upon his skin.

"Do you see this scar? This was the first time I was ever stabbed. I was twelve years old. Bandits had been raiding my village for months, killed people, stolen most we had that was of any value. We begged the Lord of the Steppes to send his men. But we were remote, too far and too small to be of any real concern. So we sent out messengers to everyone we could. We were desperate. We offered everything we had."

He was not trying to contain the rage in his voice anymore. He let his shirt fall. He spat his words, hands shaking as he fought the urge to reach through and slam the pompous Prince's face into the iron bars.

"Finally, someone came. Tell me, Prince, did you know of Dux Terrance DeVale?"

The Prince nodded silently.

"Yes, I thought you might. He was of your precious Covenant too. A great warrior, fought in many battles, or so we were told. He had been hunting bandits across the North and gotten word that those outlaws had settled near our village. We thought out prayers had been answered when he brought a contingent of warriors from the Wolfswood. But we were wrong. They were worse than the bandits. Far worse. They rode in and took over the town, took what they wanted and beat anyone who spoke out against them, or worse. They caught the bandits in a matter of days, strung them up outside of town and let their bodies feed the birds. But they never left. They said we owed them for their services."

Cassius' eyes had gone wide. He looked like he wanted to turn away, to stop listening. But Holton would not let him. He held the Prince's gaze in the witchlight.

"They planned to wait out the winter ice in our village. They threw families out of their own houses. Children were cast out into the snow. They ate through all our food stores and slaughtered most of our animals so they could feast every night. But the village girls got it the worst. We had to hide my sister in the barn to keep them unaware of her. After two weeks we had enough. The fight was bloody...and short. They killed everyone, burned the village to ashes and set out for the next town over."

Cassius swallowed, "That's not..."

Holton cut him off, "The great Dux Valorus gave me this wound himself. Lucky he was as sloppy as he was monstrous.

Left me with a ragged flesh wound, but nothing life threatening. I dragged my sister from the wreckage of our barn and into the woods while I was soaking the snow red. Took me the rest of the season to heal. Not to worry though, this story has a happy ending. I gutted Terrance in his own hall four years later. Cut him tail to tongue with all his retainers watching."

Cassius was staring at him, eyes wide with horror. He seemed to be trying to speak, but words refused to come out. Holton gave the Prince a last, vicious grin, enjoying the effect the story had on him, "He was the first of your kind I ever killed, but he won't be the last. How's that for a legacy?"

Then he spun and stalked away from the Prince, not waiting for a response. He passed through the rows of cages, ignoring the sleeping forms which lay within. The ship was still deathly silent as he climbed the stairs all the way back to the deck and burst out into the warm summer air. In the darkness, he saw the sea of stars stretching out above him in every direction. He leaned over the railing and saw them reflected in the black water, creating the illusion of an endless horizon as they met in the unseen distance. Holton turned towards the bow and looked out before them, letting the warm wind blow through his hair and cast it about his head in a wild mess of unkempt red locks. The *Sabre* cut through the ocean like a razor sharp blade through black velvet, dauntless as it hurtled with a remarkable speed towards the New World, leaving a trail of steam flowing through the sky behind it.

EPILOGUE

THE PROMISE

S am shook awake. Immediately, he could feel his body bobbing up and down in a semi consistent motion, like he was on the back of a horse. It was a strange thing, to wake up moving when one did not expect it, and it took him a moment to adjust to the sensation. He did not know how long he had been asleep, but somehow he was sure it had been a very long time. With some despair, the first thing he noticed was that he was still in his cage. He was not sure exactly how long this cage had been his home for, since time had seemed strange ever since he had been imprisoned. But just like his strange periods of sleep, he somehow knew it had been too long. He looked around the room and saw it was unfamiliar to him.

It was far larger than any he had found himself in before and it seemed strange somehow. The walls were gray and dark, but not like stone. They almost looked like they were made of metal, but surely that was impossible. To build something this large out of metal alone would surely be an impossible task. He was still surrounded by other cages and the small forms unconscious within. He recognized Evie still beside him, her curls hanging in a matted mess across her face. There was no sign of the boy Tomin, but Sam was sure he was somewhere nearby. He looked for something he could use to help them escape, anything that might give them some hope. That was when he saw the man.

He was separate from the rest of them, set off against a wall with no other cages placed within reaching distance. The man was huddled in the corner, head resting against the wall with his eyes closed. He had dark hair and a short beard, with tan skin like Sam's own. He looked filthy and disheveled, covered in dark stains and several bandages. Sam noticed with a start that one of those bandages was covering the stump of a missing hand. Despite his condition, the man looked strong and Sam decided to take a chance.

"Sir?" He called out in a low voice. His voice was hoarse from disuse and it hurt to speak. He wished desperately for a cup of water but there was none. When the man did not stir, he called out again, louder than before.

The man jolted as though he had been dozing. He blinked and shook himself a bit. He winced then, rubbing at his stump with his remaining hand as he looked around. When he saw Sam, he sighed and turned towards him, still sitting but leaning his back against the wall.

"So one of you has finally woken up, I guess that means the magician's spell isn't without its flaws after all." He said, voice impassive. Despite the clear pain he was in and his poor condition, his eyes were sharp, clear and focused on Sam with a clear intensity. He examined Sam with a critical eye for a bit before speaking again, "Where are you from, boy?"

"A small village, Reynoldstown, right on the border between the Dawn Plains and the Fiery Expanse." Sam cocked his head, "What about yourself, sir?"

"Me? I'm from the Horn, but I suppose it will be a long time before I see home again."

There was a note of bitterness in his voice that gave Sam pause. He asked his next question gently, hoping not to offend him.

"Sir, can you tell me where we are and where we're going? Do you know what these men intend to do with us?"

The man gave him a strange look, as though just realizing who he was talking to. Then he ran his hand through his hair and sighed, "I'll not lie to you boy; You're on a ship bound for the Lorrailia. I don't know what these people are planning, but I know they're dangerous and whatever it is can't be good."

Sam felt his breath catch in his chest, "The New World? But...I've never even left the Valley..."

He felt a sinking sensation in his stomach and most likely would have been sick if he had anything to vomit up. The cage suddenly felt even more confining and the waves of nausea hit him like the waves breaking against the hull of this ship. The sensation must have shown on his face as the man leaned forward with a look of concern.

"Hey, calm down. Take some deep breaths. You need to keep your wits about you. From what I can tell, you're one of the older ones among this lot. They're going to be frightened, and they're going to look to you for guidance. You need to be strong for them."

Sam sucked in air in ragged gasps, "B-but...I never...I can't..."

The man's voice held a sharp tone that cut through his panic like a razor, "You have to. What's your name?"

"Sam."

"Sam, my name is Cassius. My friends call me Cas." The man gave him a small grin that seemed meant to instill confidence, "We're going to get out of this, Sam."

"How could you possibly know that?" Sam asked, shaking his head. He glanced down at the man's bandaged stump and filthy clothes, "Are you going to free us?"

"I will be sure it is part of the negotiation when they trade for me, if I can." He answered, his tone earnest.

Something about the look in his eyes made Sam stop and wonder if this man truly could free them, "Who are you, sir?"

Cassius hesitated, but then responded, "I am Cassius Roth, Prince of the Barony of the Horn."

Sam felt a chill run through him. He had never even seen someone of nobility, having lived his entire life in his tiny, backwater village, much less had a conversation with them. He found it difficult to formulate the words to respond, "Y-you're a hero! Part of the Covenant!"

The man seemed to deflate somewhat at that. He looked down and did not speak for a long while. When he finally spoke, he sounded dejected, "Not much of one anymore, I'm afraid."

He held up his stump, as if showing all the proof one might need to verify his claim. Sam stared at it for a moment before continuing, "But...you *are* still part of the Covenant, are you not?"

"I...was stripped of my title."

"But that doesn't change anything, does it? You're still the same man I've heard all the stories about?" Sam insisted.

"Stories?" Cassius seemed puzzled by this comment.

"Yes!" He exclaimed, voice involuntarily rising an octave, "You're the daring Prince of the Horn, the man who killed the Pirate Lord Gant! You and your father hunted down those bandits, the Gray Brigade, that were terrorizing the villages near Hardtop, right?"

Cassius looked uncomfortable with the questions. He rubbed at his stump in a distracted way, not meeting Sam's eyes. Sam kept going, undeterred.

"You won the Sun's Summit tournament as a child! You fought the Northern Raiders! You're one of the youngest people to ever face the Crucible, to swear the Covenant!"

The Prince still would not meet his eyes. He stared at his stump as he mumbled in response, "That was a long time ago...I'm not the same man I was."

Sam faltered. The pain that was painted across the man's face was terrible to see. He saw shades of every type of regret there. He chewed his lip in frustration. This broken man was his only hope.

"Last cycle, during the harvest season," Sam said softly, looking out across the rows and rows of cages, "my father let me leave
the farm early to go to the festival. There was work to be done
still, but he must've seen how badly I wanted to go. I spent my
afternoon drinking amber ale, filling my gut and dancing with
the girls in the town square. It was a good day. I remember, there
was a minstrel from up north there that year. He played sweet
music and kept everyone on their feet most of the night. But
once the fires had died down and the dancing was done, he told
stories. He sang about the lords and ladies at court, about battles
long past and about the great warriors and their deeds."

Cassius still stared at the floor. The look on his face had not
changed. The ship pitched and rolled on the sea, causing Sam to
feel like his stomach was unsettled once again. He was not sure
if the Prince was listening, but kept going anyway.

"He told us about the ancient deeds of Rearden the Great,
Titus the Black and others. He of course mentioned Brutus the
Brave, they always do." Sam grinned a bit, remembering how he
had sat on the grass and was enthralled by the tales of these great
men who had helped shape their country, "But do you know
what tales we loved the most? What people wanted to hear over
and over again? The tales of the Covenant now. Your tales."

Cassius looked up at him. His eyes were cloudy, but he did
not attempt to wipe them clear. He looked at Sam with a pro-
found expression of helplessness.

"Your kind have always been our heroes." Sam said plainly,
"I'd always wished I could meet one of you in person, and here
you are."

There was a moment of silence which hung in the air between
them. They listened to the waves and the sounds of feet slapping
against the decks above them. Sam watched the Prince for what
seemed like an eternity, waiting for a reply.

"What would you have me do, Sam?" He finally said in a
quiet voice, barely more than a whisper.

"You must get us out of this." Sam said, leaning forward and grasping the bars with both hands. He put his face at the edge of the cage and no longer tried to suppress the desperation in his voice, "You're the only chance we have."

Cassius still looked as though the guilt was chewing a hole right through him, "I *tried*, Sam. I...failed. I got my men killed and myself maimed for my efforts."

"You have to try again!" Sam demanded, "You can't wait for someone to bargain for you. It's going to take too long. These people are never going to give us up. They went through too much effort to catch us all. You know it's true."

"They might not..." Cassius tried to deflect, but Sam was having none of it.

"They will!" He waved his hands around the room full of slumbering prisoners, "They kidnapped all of us and are shipping us to the New World. I don't know what their plan is but...I heard them talking. Heard him, the man in the red cloak. Whatever their plan is, it won't end with us walking away! We won't survive it!"

Sam watched as the Prince seemed to struggle with the massive weight of misgivings and self doubt. He held his breath and waited, silently praying to all the gods that this man was the courageous hero of the stories he had heard so many times over the years. Then there was a noise. Somewhere behind them, a door opened and slammed shut. He glanced around wildly, then groaned when he located the source of the noise.

The man in the red cloak had entered the room and was strolling along the isle, carefully avoiding touching any of the cages as he made his way towards Sam. He was as clean and unblemished as the day Sam had first seen him. His blonde hair was perfectly quaffed and his cloak had no sign of dust or damage on it all. Once he had reached his cage, he leaned down and gave him a small, infuriating smirk.

"Ah, it's you again." The man said, staring at him, "You are a troublesome one, aren't you?"

Sam reached out as fast as he could and tried to grasp the man by any scrap of cloth he could reach. But the man was bare inches outside of his grasp. He growled in frustration and pushed against the immovable bars of his cage even harder. He felt the bars dig into his chest and side of his face but he ignored it desperately grasping at the air. The blonde man only grinned even wider. He waited and watched until Sam tired himself out and gave up, sinking into a heap on the floor of his cage.

"Please..." Sam said in a small voice. He fought the tears that welled up unbidden in his eyes but he could do nothing to stop them, "Just let us go. We didn't do anything to you."

The man gave a laugh that held no joy at all. He motioned to the room full of cages around them, "You think I'm going to let you go, after all the work we've done to gather you all up?"

Sam hugged his knees and looked over at Evie, "Then just let them go. The younger ones. They shouldn't have to suffer this."

The blonde man clicked his tongue and shook his head. He reached into his pocket and pulled out a small, silver bell, "You're really in no position to bargain, lad."

He toned the silver bell three times and watched as Sam began to feel the tiredness creep up on him again. His mind became foggy and he could not focus on anything. Sam fought it with everything he had, but whatever spell the mage had laid on him was too much. He saw the man's grin one last time as he began to sink down to the ground, unable to sit up any longer.

"That should keep him out until we get to port." He heard the blonde man mutter.

He heard boot steps getting fainter and fainter until the door opened and then slammed shut, leaving the entire chamber in silence once again. He struggled against his eyes as they shut, fluttering closed. He heard a voice calling out, just audible through the rapidly growing fog in his brain.

"Sam," it was Cassius. The Prince had remained silent throughout the entire exchange and Sam had all but forgotten about him, "Sam, I don't know if you can hear me, but I'm going to do it. No matter what happens, I'm going to get you out of here. All of you. I don't know how, but I'm going to do it. I promise."

Sam tried to grunt in approval but his voice was no longer working. He saw the bars of his cage one last time before sinking back into the darkness of a dreamless slumber. But this time, as he lay there unconscious, a small smile spread across his lips as he felt a sense of hope for the first time since he had left his village and been lured into the woods what seemed like a lifetime ago.

The End

The Scion Conspiracy
Crucible of Legacy, Book I

DEAR READER

To all those readers who chose to give this book a chance, to pick it up off the shelf or download it on your device, I want to take a moment to say a heartfelt thank you. I have loved stories and storytelling since I was a child, and it has always been my dream to write novels of my very own. I have spent so much time and poured so much of myself into the process of making this series a reality. But in truth, writing the book is only half the battle. It is you, the readers, that make or break every book. You determine if a book will be a success, and your support and recommendations are what drive the career of every successful author. Without you, none of this would be possible. So again, I say thank you. Just by reading this book, you are helping me achieve a dream I have had since I was a kid.

Be assured, it is my intention to keep writing, to finish this series and see these character's stories through to their conclusions. I hope that you have enjoyed my work so far and will continue this journey with me. If so, I want ask you one more favor. Please consider rating and reviewing *The Coldwater Job* on Amazon and any other book related sites you might use. Ratings and reviews are the lifeblood that keep books relevant and help them stand out in a competitive and ever growing market. Your reviews directly support my work and might be the thing that convinces others to give this book a shot. Hopefully, with your support, I can keep growing this passion project of mine and get my work into the hands of many more readers just like you.

If you enjoyed this novella, check out *The Coldwater Job, A Crucible of Legacy Novella* available for free for those who subscribe to my newsletter on mikecahoon.com! Also available for purchase everywhere books are sold.

For those who have made it this far, thank you so much for your support, your time and your belief in me.

Sincerely,
Mike Cahoon

ABOUT THE AUTHOR

Mike Cahoon is an independent author with a deep love of stories across many genres and mediums, but he always holds a special place in his heart for his personal holy trinity of fantasy, science fiction and horror. Growing up, he was a terrible student despite his teacher's and parent's best attempts to get him to apply himself. Despite this, he had a passion for reading and writing which has stubbornly stuck with him throughout his entire life. Now he is finally embarking on his own literary journey and getting the stories out of his head that have been knocking around in there for decades.

Born and raised in Atlanta, Mike has spent most of his adult life as a firefighter in his community. He still resides in the metro area where he lives the suburban life with his wife, two daughters and their great, big dog. When he's not writing, he enjoys anything outside, cooking for his family, being exceedingly okay at jiu jitsu and drinking too much coffee.

If you would like to keep up with Mike and get updates on his various projects, sign up for his newsletter on mikecahoon.com and be sure to follow him on social media @mikecahoon_author.